MUMMY, NURSE… DUCHESS?

BY
KATE HARDY

FALLING FOR THE FOSTER MUM

BY
KARIN BAINE

MILLS
BOON

Paddington Children's Hospital

Caring for children—and captivating hearts!

The doctors and nurses of Paddington Children's Hospital are renowned for their expert care of their young patients, no matter the cost. And now, as they face both a heart-wrenching emergency and a dramatic fight to save their hospital, the stakes are higher than ever!

Devoted to their jobs, these talented professionals are about to discover that saving lives can often mean risking your heart…

Available now in the thrilling **Paddington Children's Hospital** miniseries:

Their One Night Baby by Carol Marinelli

Forbidden to the Playboy Surgeon by Fiona Lowe

Mummy, Nurse…Duchess? by Kate Hardy

Falling for the Foster Mum by Karin Baine

And coming soon…

Healing the Sheikh's Heart by Annie O'Neil

A Life-Saving Reunion by Alison Roberts

MUMMY, NURSE... DUCHESS?

BY
KATE HARDY

Published in Great Britain 2017
By Mills & Boon, an imprint of HarperCollins*Publishers*
1 London Bridge Street, London, SE1 9GF

© 2017 Harlequin Books S.A.

Special thanks and acknowledgement are given to Kate Hardy
for her contribution to the Paddington Children's Hospital series.

ISBN: 978-0-263-92644-6

Dear Reader,

I was thrilled when my editor asked me to be part of the Paddington Children's Hospital series. I love working with other authors to build a world, and I was even happier to find that part of my book was going to be set in Italy—which is one of my favourite parts of the world.

It was also great fun to write about small children again—I loved reliving the days when mine enjoyed going to the park and the aquarium. And one of my best friends had twins a couple of months after I had my eldest, so that brought back memories too.

But Leo and Rosie have a lot of obstacles to overcome from their pasts before they can find happiness—and they're surprised to discover that being with each other is just the way to do it. So when Leo sweeps Rosie off to a glamorous ball he discovers that the castle where he grew up is much better filled with the laughter of children—and Rosie discovers that… Well, you'll have to read the book to find out!

I'm always delighted to hear from readers, so do come and visit me at katehardy.com or chat to me on Facebook.

With love,

Kate Hardy

To my fellow PCH authors,
who made writing this such an enjoyable experience.

Kate Hardy has always loved books, and could read
before she went to school. She discovered Mills & Boon
books when she was twelve and decided this was what
she wanted to do. When she isn't writing Kate enjoys
reading, cinema, ballroom dancing and the gym. You
can contact her via her website: katehardy.com.

Books by Kate Hardy

Mills & Boon Medical Romance

Christmas Miracles in Maternity

The Midwife's Pregnancy Miracle

Her Playboy's Proposal
Capturing the Single Dad's Heart

Mills & Boon Cherish

Holiday with the Best Man
Falling for the Secret Millionaire
Her Festive Doorstep Baby

Visit the Author Profile page
at millsandboon.co.uk for more titles.

Praise for
Kate Hardy

'With great story build-up and engaging dialogue,
A Baby to Heal Their Hearts by Kate Hardy is a sure
winner!'

—*Harlequin Junkie*

CHAPTER ONE

Paddington Children's Hospital

THE REDBRICK BUILDING loomed before Leo in the street; the turret, with its green dome, reminded him so much of Florence that it was almost enough to make him miss Tuscany. Then again, London had felt more like home than Florence, ever since he'd first come to study medicine here as a teenager.

As the car pulled to a halt, Leo could see Robyn Kelly waiting outside the hospital gates for him, her curly blonde hair gleaming brightly in the sun. When the Head of Surgery had asked him to come to Paddington to help out in the aftermath of the fire that had ripped through a local children's school, of course he'd said yes. Robyn had taken him under her wing when he'd been on his first rotation and had been feeling just a little bit lost; back then, he'd appreciated her kindness. And he'd also appreciated the fact that she'd seen him as a doctor first and a duke second, treating him as part of the team rather than as a special case.

This was his chance to pay just a little of that back.

There was a small group of protestors standing outside the gate, holding placards: 'Save Our Hospital' and 'Kids' Health Not Wealth'.

Which was one of the reasons why his contract was temporary: Paddington Children's Hospital was under threat of closure, with a plan to merge the staff and patients with Riverside Hospital. Not because the one-hundred-and-fifty-year-old hospital wasn't needed any more—the fact that the place was full to overflowing after the recent fire at Westbourne Grove Primary School proved just how much the hospital was needed—but because the Board of Governors had had a lucrative offer for the site. So, instead of keeping the hospital as an important part of the community, they planned to sell it so it could be turned into a block of posh apartments. The Board of Governors had already run staff numbers down in anticipation of the merger, to the point where everyone was struggling to cope.

Leo's lip curled. He'd grown up in a world where money didn't just talk, it shouted, and that disgusted him. It was the main reason why he was drawn to philanthropic medicine now: so he could give some of that privilege back. So when Robyn had explained the situation at Paddington's to him and said they needed someone with a high profile to come and work with them and get the hospital's plight into international news, Leo had had no hesitation in agreeing. It was a chance to use the heritage he loathed for a good cause.

Even though he knew the waiting photographers weren't there to take pictures of the protestors, Leo intended to make quite sure that the protestors and the placards were in every single shot. The more publicity for this cause, the better. So, right at this moment, he was here in his role as the Duke of Calvanera rather than being plain

Dr Marchetti. And that was why he was meeting Robyn outside the hospital gates in the middle of the morning, instead of being two hours into his shift. This was all about getting maximum publicity.

He took a deep breath and opened the door of the sleek, black car.

'Your Highness!' one of the photographers called as Leo emerged from the car. 'Over here!'

Years of practice meant that it was easy enough for him to deflect the photographers with an awkward posture, until he reached Robyn and the protestors. Robyn had clearly primed the picket line, because they crowded behind him with their placards fully visible; there was no way that any photograph of his face wouldn't contain at least a word or two from a placard. And then he shook Robyn's hand, looked straight at the cameras and smiled as the bulbs flashed.

'Is it true you're coming to work here?' one of the journalists called.

'Yes,' he said.

'Why Paddington?' another called.

'Because it's important. The hospital has been here for a hundred and fifty years, looking after the children in the city. And it needs to stay here, instead of being merged with Riverside Hospital, outside the city,' he answered.

'Moving the patients to Riverside means the kids will have better facilities than at this old place,' one of the journalists pointed out.

'State of the art, you mean?' Leo asked. 'But when it comes to medicine, *time's* the most important thing. You can have the most cutting edge equipment in the world—but if your patient doesn't reach those facilities in time, all that fancy stuff isn't going to be able to save a life. It'll be too late.'

The journalist went red and shuffled his feet.

'You don't need flashy equipment and modern buildings to be a good hospital,' Leo said. 'You need to be *accessible*. What would've happened to the children of Westbourne Grove Primary School if Paddington had been closed? How many of them wouldn't have made it to those lovely new buildings and all the state-of-the-art equipment at Riverside in time to be treated?'

He was met with silence as the press clearly worked out the answer for themselves.

'Exactly. And I'm very happy for you all to quote me saying that,' he said softly. 'Talk to these guys.' He gestured to the protestors, knowing from Robyn that several of them had been treated here years ago and others had recently had their own children treated here. 'Find out their stories. They're much more interesting and much more important than I am.'

'I think you made your point,' Robyn said as they walked into the hospital together.

'Good,' Leo said as she led him in to the department where he was going to be working, ready to introduce him to everyone. 'Paddington's is an important facility. An outstanding facility. And I'll do everything I can to help you publicise that.'

Rosie Hobbes stifled a cynical snort as she overheard the Duke of Calvanera's comment. Who was he trying to kid? More like, he was trying to raise his own profile. Why would someone like him—a rich, powerful playboy— care about the fate of an old London hospital?

She knew he'd agreed to come and help at Paddington's because he'd trained with Robyn, years ago; but it was still pretty hard to believe that an actual duke would want to do a job like this. Who would want to work in a hospital that was currently full to the brim with patients but badly understaffed because the Board of Directors hadn't replaced anyone who'd left, in line with their plan to move everyone out and sell the place?

Especially a man who was so good-looking and seemed so charming.

Rosie knew all about how charm and good looks could hide a rotten heart. Been there, done that, and her three-year-old twins were the ones who'd nearly paid the price.

Thinking of the twins made her heart skip a beat, and she caught her breath. It had been just over a year now, and she still found panic coursing through her when she remembered that night. The threats. The dead look behind that man's eyes. The way he'd looked at her children as if they were merely a means to getting what he wanted instead of seeing them as the precious lives they were.

She dug her nails into her palms. Focus, Rosie, she told herself. Freddie and Lexi were absolutely fine. If there was any kind of problem with either of the twins, the hospital nursery school would've called her straight away. The place was completely secure; only the staff inside could open the door, and nobody could take a child without either being on the list as someone with permission to collect a child, or giving the emergency code word for any particular child. Michael was dead, so his associates couldn't threaten the twins—or Rosie—any more. And right now she had a job to do.

'Everything all right, Rosie?' Robyn asked.

'Sure,' Rosie said. Her past was *not* going to interfere with her new life here. She was a survivor, not a victim.

'I just wanted to introduce you to Leo,' Robyn continued. 'He'll be working with us for the next couple of months.'

Or until something even more high profile came along, Rosie thought. Maybe she was judging him unfairly but, in her experience, handsome playboys couldn't be trusted.

'Leo, this is Rosie Hobbes, one of our paediatric nurses. Rosie, this is Leo Marchetti,' Robyn said.

'Hello,' Rosie said, and gave him a cool nod.

He gave her the sexiest smile she'd ever seen, and his dark eyes glittered with interest. 'Delighted to meet you, *signora*,' he said.

Rosie would just bet he'd practised that smile in front of the mirror. And he'd hammed up that Italian accent to make himself sound super-sexy; she was sure he hadn't had an accent at all when he'd walked onto the ward with Robyn. She should just think herself lucky he hadn't bowed and kissed her hand. Or was that going to be next?

'Welcome to Paddington's, Your Highness,' she said.

He gave her another of those super-charming smiles. 'Here, I'm a doctor, not a duke. "Leo" will do just fine.'

'Dr Marchetti,' she said firmly, hoping she'd made it clear that she preferred to keep her work relationships very professional indeed. 'Excuse me—I really need to review these charts following the ward round. Enjoy your first day at the Castle.'

The Castle? Was she making a pointed comment about where he came from? Leo wondered. But women weren't usually sharp with him. They usually smiled back, responding to his warmth. He liked women—a lot—and they liked him. Why had Rosie Hobbes cut him dead? Had he done something to upset her?

But he definitely hadn't met her before. He would've remembered her—and not just because she was tall, curvy and pretty, with that striking copper hair in a tousled bob, and those vivid blue eyes. There was something challenging about Rosie. Something that made him want to get up close and personal with her and find out exactly what made her tick.

She hadn't been wearing a wedding ring. Not that that meant anything, nowadays. Was she single?

And why was he wondering that in any case? He was here to do a job. Relationships weren't on the agenda, especially with someone he worked with. He was supposed to be finding someone suited to his position: another European noble, or perhaps the heir to a business empire. And together they would continue the Marchetti dynasty by producing a son.

Right now, he still couldn't face that. He wasn't ready to trap someone else in the castle where he'd grown up, lonely and miserable and desperate for his father's approval—approval that his father had been quick to withhold if Leo did or said anything wrong. Though what was wrong one day was right on another. Leo had never been able to work out what his father actually wanted. All he'd known for sure was that he was a disappointment to the Duke.

He shook himself. Now wasn't the time to be thinking about that. 'Thank you,' he said, giving Rosie his warmest smile just for the hell of it, and followed Robyn to be introduced to the rest of the staff on the ward.

Once Rosie had finished reviewing the charts and typing notes into the computer, she headed on to the ward. Hopefully Dr Marchetti would be on the next ward by now, meeting and greeting, and she could just get on with her job.

Why had he rattled her so much? She wasn't one to be bowled over and breathless just because a man was good-looking. Not any more. Leo had classic movie-star looks: tall, with dark eyes and short, neat dark hair. He was also charming and confident, and Rosie had learned the hard way that charm couldn't be trusted. Her whirlwind marriage had turned into an emotional rollercoaster, and she'd promised herself never to make that mistake again. So, even if Leo Marchetti was good friends with their Head of Surgery, Rosie intended to keep him at a very professional distance.

She dropped into one of the bays to check on Penelope Craig. Penny was one of their long-term patients, and the little girl had been admitted to try and get her heart failure under control after an infection had caused her condition to worsen.

'How are you doing, Penny?' Rosie asked.

The little girl looked up from her drawing and gave her the sweetest, sweetest smile. 'Nurse Rosie! I'm fine, thank you.'

Rosie exchanged a glance with Julia, Penny's mother. They both knew it wasn't true, but Penny wasn't a whiner. She'd become a firm favourite on the ward, always drawing special pictures and chattering about kittens and ballet. 'That's good,' she said. 'I just need to do—'

'—my obs,' Penny finished. 'I know.'

Rosie checked Penny's pulse, temperature and oxygen sats. 'That's my girl. Oh, and I've got something for you.' She reached into her pocket and brought out a sheet of stickers.

'Kittens! I love kittens,' Penny said with a beaming smile. 'Thank you so much. Look, Mummy.'

'They're lovely,' Julia said, but Rosie could see the strain and weariness behind her smile. She understood only too well how it felt to worry about your children; being helpless to do anything to fix the problems must be sheer hell.

'Thank you, Rosie,' Julia added.

'Pleasure.' Rosie winked at Penny. 'Hopefully these new drugs will have you back on your feet soon.' The little girl was desperate to be a ballerina, and wore a pink tutu even when she was bed-bound. And Rosie really, really hoped that the little girl would have time for her dreams to come true. 'Call me if you need anything,' Rosie added to Julia.

'I will. Thanks.'

Rosie checked on the rest of the children in her bay, and was writing up the notes when her colleague Kathleen came over to the desk.

'So have you met the Duke, yet?' Kathleen fanned herself. 'Talk about film-star good looks.'

Rosie rolled her eyes. 'Handsome is as handsome does.' And never again would she let a handsome, charming man treat her as a second-class citizen.

'Give the guy a break,' Kathleen said. 'He seems a real sweetie. And his picture is already all over the Internet, with the "Save Our Hospital" placards in full view. I think Robyn's right and he's really going to help.'

Rosie forced herself to smile. 'Good.'

Kathleen gave her a curious look. 'Are you all right, Rosie?'

'Sure. I had a bit of a broken night,' Rosie fibbed. 'Lexi had a bad dream and it was a while before I got back to sleep again.'

'I really don't know how you do it,' Kathleen said. 'It's tough enough, being a single mum—but having twins must make it twice as hard.'

'I get double the joy and double the love,' Rosie said. 'I wouldn't miss a single minute. And my parents and my sister are great—I know I can call on them if I get stuck.'

'Even so. You must miss your husband so much.'

Rosie had found that it was much easier to let people think that she was a grieving widow than to tell them the truth—that she'd been planning to divorce Michael Duncan before his death, and after his death she'd reverted back to her maiden name, changing the children's names along with hers. 'Yes,' Rosie agreed. And it wasn't a total lie. She missed the man she'd thought she'd married—not the one behind the mask, the one who put money before his babies and his wife.

She was busy on the ward for the rest of the morning and didn't see Leo again until lunchtime.

'I believe we'll be working closely together,' the Duke said.

She rather hoped he was wrong.

'So I thought maybe we could have lunch together and get to know each other a bit better,' he added.

'Sorry,' Rosie said. 'I'm afraid I have a previous engagement.' Just as she did every Monday, Wednesday and Friday when Penny was in the hospital.

He looked as if he hoped she'd be polite and invite him to join her in whatever she was doing. Well, tough. This wasn't about him. It was about her patient. 'I'm sure Kathleen or one of the others would be very happy for you to join them in the canteen,' she said.

'Thank you. Then I'll go and find them,' he said, with that same charming smile.

And Rosie felt thoroughly in the wrong.

But Leo had already turned away and it was too late to call him back and explain.

Why was Rosie Hobbes so prickly with him? Leo wondered. Everyone else at Paddington Children's Hospital had seemed pleased that he'd joined the team and had welcomed him warmly. Everyone except Rosie.

Did she hate all men?

Possibly not, because earlier he'd seen her talking to Thomas Wolfe, the cardiology specialist, and she'd seemed perfectly relaxed.

And why was he so bothered when she was just one member of the team? Wherever you worked, there was always a spectrum: people you got on really well with, people you liked and people you had to grit your teeth and put up with. He was obviously one of the latter, where Rosie was concerned, even though today was the first time they'd met. He knew he ought to just treat her with the calm professionalism he reserved for people who rubbed him up the wrong way. But he couldn't help asking about her when he was sitting in the canteen with a couple of the junior doctors and two of the nurses.

'So Rosie doesn't usually join you?' he asked.

'Not when Penny's in,' Kathleen said.

'Penny?'

'You must've seen her when Robyn took you round,' Kathleen said. 'One of our patients. Six years old, brown hair in plaits and the most amazing eyes—grey, with this really distinctive rim?'

Leo shook his head. 'Sorry. It doesn't ring a bell.'

'Well, you'll definitely get to know her while you're here. She has heart failure, and she's been in and out of here for months,' Kathleen explained. 'She's a total sweetheart. Rosie's one of the nurses who always looks after her. When she's in on a Monday, Wednesday or Friday, Rosie spends her lunch break reading her ballet stories.'

'Because the little girl likes ballet, I presume?' Leo asked.

'Lives and breathes it. And also it gives her mum or dad a break, depending on who's taken the time off to be with her,' Kathleen explained.

'So Penny's special to Rosie?'

'She's special to all of us,' Kathleen said. 'If you've seen any drawings pinned up in the staff room or the office, nine times out of ten it'll be one of Penny's.'

'Right.' Leo wondered why Rosie hadn't told him that herself. Or maybe she'd thought he'd have a go at her for being unprofessional and showing too much favouritism to a patient.

He chatted easily with the others until the end of their lunch break, then headed back to the ward. The first person he saw was Rosie, who he guessed had just left her little patient.

'So did Penny enjoy her story?' he asked.

Colour flooded into her cheeks. 'How do you know about that?'

'Kathleen said you have a regular lunch date with her when you're in.'

'It gives Julia and Peter—her parents—a chance to get out of here for a few minutes to get some fresh air,' she said. 'And it isn't a problem with Robyn.'

So she *had* thought he'd disapprove of the way she spent her lunch break. 'It's very kind of you,' he said. Was it just because Penny was a favourite with the staff, or did Rosie maybe have a sister who'd gone through something similar? It was too intrusive to ask. He needed to tread carefully with Rosie or she'd back away from him again.

'She's a lovely girl.'

'Maybe you can tell me about her after work,' he said. 'I hear there's a nice pub across the road. The Frog and...?' He paused, not remembering the name.

'Peach,' she supplied. 'Sorry. I can't.'

Can't or won't? he wondered. 'Another previous engagement?'

'Actually, yes.'

Another patient? He didn't think she'd tell him. 'That's a shame. Some other time.'

But she didn't suggest a different day or time.

He really ought to just give up.

A couple of his new colleagues had already made it clear that they'd be happy to keep him company if he was lonely. It could be fun to take them up on their offers, as long as they understood that he didn't do permanent relationships.

Except there was something about Rosie Hobbes that drew him. It wasn't just that she was one of the few women who didn't respond to him; his ego could stand the odd rejection. But she intrigued him, and he couldn't work out why. Was it that she was so different from the

women he was used to, women who swooned over him
or flattered him because he was a duke? Or was it something deeper?

It had been a long time since someone had intrigued
him like this. Something more than just brief sexual attraction. And that in himself made him want to explore
it further—to understand what made Rosie tick, and also
why he felt this weird pull towards her.

Tomorrow, he thought. He'd try talking to her again
tomorrow.

Rosie was five minutes late from her shift, and the twins
were already waiting for her with their backpacks on.
They were singing something with Nina, one of the nursery school assistants, who was clearly teaching them actions to go with the song. Rosie felt a rush of love for
them. Her twins were so different: Lexi, bouncy and confident, with a mop of blonde curls that reminded Rosie a
little too much of Michael, and yet other than that she was
the double of Rosie at that age. And Freddie, quieter and
a little shy, with the same curls as his sister except mid-
brown instead of golden, and her own bright blue eyes;
thankfully he hadn't turned out to be Michael's double.
Rosie was determined that her children were going to
know nothing but love and happiness for the rest of their
lives—and she really hoped that they wouldn't remember what life had been like when their father was around.

'Mummy!' The second they saw her, Lexi and Freddie rushed over to her and flung their arms round her.

'My lovely Lexi and Freddie.' Rosie felt as if she could
breathe properly again, now she was back with her babies.
Even though she loved her job and she knew the twins
were well looked after in the nursery school attached to

the hospital, she was much happier with them than she was away from them.

'So what have you been doing today?' she asked, holding one hand each as they walked out of the hospital.

'We singed.' Lexi demonstrated the first verse of 'The Wheels on the Bus,' completely out of tune and at full volume.

'That's lovely, darling,' Rosie said.

'And we had Play-Doh,' Freddie added. 'I maked a doggie. A plurple one.'

Rosie hid a smile at his adorable mispronunciation. 'Beautiful,' she said. She knew how badly her son wanted a dog of their own, but it just wasn't possible with their current lifestyle. It wouldn't be fair to leave a dog alone all day; and she couldn't leave the twins alone while she took the dog for the kind of long walk it would need after being cooped up all day, and which the twins would be too tired to do after a day at nursery school.

'We had cookies,' Lexie said.

'Chocolate ones. Nina maked them. They were crum—crum—' Freddie added, frowning when he couldn't quite remember the new word.

Crumbly? Or maybe a longer word. 'Nina made them,' Rosie corrected gently, 'and they were scrumptious, yes?' she guessed.

'Crumshus!' Lexie crowed. 'That's right.'

The twins chattered all the way on the short Tube journey and then the ten-minute walk home. They were still chattering when Rosie cooked their tea, and gave them a bath. Although Freddie was a little on the shy side with strangers, he strove to match his more confident sister at home.

And Rosie was happy to let them chatter and laugh.

She'd worried every day for the last year that their experience with Michael's associate had scarred them; but hopefully they'd been too young to realise quite what was going on and how terrified their mother had been.

Once the twins were in bed, she curled up on the sofa with a cup of tea and a puzzle magazine. A year ago, she would never have believed she could be this relaxed again. Some things hadn't changed; she was still the one who did everything for the twins and did all the cooking and cleaning. But she no longer had to deal with Michael's mercurial mood swings, his scorn and his contempt, and that made all the difference. Being a single parent was hard, but she had the best family and good friends to support her. And she didn't have Michael to undermine her confidence all the time.

Various friends had hinted that she ought to start dating again. Part of Rosie missed the closeness of having a partner, someone to cuddle into at stupid o'clock in the morning when she woke from a bad dream. But she'd lost her trust in relationships. Good ones existed, she knew; she'd seen it with her parents and with friends. But Rosie herself had got it so badly wrong with Michael that she didn't trust her judgement any more. Trusting another man, after the mess of her marriage, would be hard. Too hard. Plus, she had the twins to consider. So she'd become good at turning the conversation to a different subject rather than disappointing her well-meaning friends and family, and any direct suggestions of a date were firmly met with 'Sorry, no.'

Just as she'd rebuffed Leo Marchetti this evening, when he'd suggested that they went for a drink in the pub over the road after work.

Had she been too hard on him?

OK, so the guy was a charmer, something that set all her inner alarm bells clanging. On the other hand, today had been Leo's first day at Paddington's. The only person he knew at the hospital was Robyn, so he was probably feeling a bit lost. Guilt nagged at her. She'd been pretty abrupt with him, and it wasn't his fault he'd been born with a Y chromosome and was full of charm. She needed to lighten up. Maybe she'd suggest having lunch with him tomorrow.

But she'd make it clear that lunch meant lunch only. She wasn't in a position to offer anything more. And, if she was honest with herself, it'd be a long time before she was ready to trust anyone with anything more. If ever.

CHAPTER TWO

'YOU'RE IN CLINIC with Rosie, this morning,' Kathleen said to Leo with a smile when he walked onto the ward. 'It's the allergy and immunology clinic.'

'Great. Just point me in the right direction,' he said, smiling back.

Hopefully Rosie would be less prickly with him today. And if they could establish a decent working relationship, then he might be able to work out why she drew him so much, and he could deal with it the way he always dealt with things. With a charming smile and a little extra distance.

He looked through the files while he waited for Rosie to turn up.

'Sorry, sorry,' she said, rushing in. 'I was held up this morning.'

'You're not late,' he pointed out, though he was pleased that she didn't seem quite so defensive with him today.

'No, but...' She flapped a dismissive hand. 'Has anyone told you about today's clinic?'

'Kathleen said it was the allergy and immunology clinic, so I'm assuming some of these patients have been coming here for a while.'

'They have,' she confirmed.

'Then at least they have some continuity with you,' he said with a smile. 'Are you happy to call our first patient in?'

Their first patient was an eighteen-month-old girl, Gemma Chandler. 'The doctor asked me last time to keep a food diary with a symptom chart,' her mother said.

'May I see them, please?' Leo asked.

She took it out of her bag and handed it to him; he read the document carefully. 'So she tends to get tummy pain, wind and diarrhoea, and sometimes her tummy feels bloated to you.'

Mrs Chandler nodded. 'And sometimes she's come out in a rash on her face and it's been itchy. It's really hard to stop her scratching it.'

'There are some lotions that help with the itch and last a bit longer than calamine lotion,' Leo said. 'I can write you a prescription for that. And you've done a really good job on the diary—I can see a very clear link between what she's eating and her symptoms.'

'It's dairy, isn't it?' Mrs Chandler bit her lip. 'I looked it up on the Internet.'

'The Internet's useful,' Leo said, 'but there are also a lot of scare stories out there and a lot of wrong information, so I'm glad you came to see us as well. Yes, I think it's an allergy to dairy—more specifically lactose intolerance. What that means is that Gemma's body doesn't have enough of the enzyme lactase to deal with any lactose in the body—that's the sugar in milk. What I think we need to do is try an exclusion diet for the next fortnight to confirm it. So that means I'd like you to check the labels for everything and make sure there's no milk in anything she eats or drinks. If you can keep doing the food diary and symptom chart, we can review everything in a fortnight.'

'We can give you some information leaflets about substitutes and vitamin supplements,' Rosie said. 'You can give Gemma rice milk instead of cow's milk, and sunflower margarine instead of butter.'

'Gemma's meant to be going to her cousin's birthday party, next week.' Mrs Chandler sighed. 'So that's going to be difficult—she won't be able to have any of the sandwiches or any of the cake, will she?'

'You could do a special packed lunch for her,' Rosie suggested. 'And I'm sure if you tell your family and friends, they'll help you work things out.' She handed Mrs Chandler a leaflet. 'Eating out with a toddler can be tricky enough, but having to take a food allergy into account can make it seem overwhelming.'

Was she talking from personal experience? Leo wondered. Or was it because she'd worked with so many patients in the allergy clinic? Not that he could ask without being intrusive, and he didn't want to give Rosie any excuse to back away from him.

'There are some good websites on the back of the leaflet for helping you to find places where they offer dairy-free options,' Rosie said.

'Thank you,' Mrs Chandler said.

'And we'll see you and Gemma again in a fortnight to see how things are. If her symptoms are better,' Leo said, 'I'll refer you to a dietitian so you can get proper support with a long-term exclusion diet. And in the meantime, if you have any questions or you're worried about anything, give us a call.'

Mrs Chandler nodded. 'Will she ever grow out of it? I've heard that some children do.'

'We really can't tell, right now,' Leo admitted. 'I think this is something we'll need to take one step at a time.'

Once the Chandlers had gone, while Leo was writing up the case notes, Rosie got out the next patient's notes. 'Sammy Kennedy. He's a sweetheart.'

'What's he seeing us about?' Leo asked.

'He has CAPS.'

Cryopyrin-Associate Periodic Syndrome. Leo knew it was an auto-inflammation disorder where the immune system was overactive and caused prolonged periods of inflammation, rather than the body producing antibodies against itself. 'That's rare,' he said. 'About one in a million. Actually, I've only seen one case before.'

'Sammy's my only case, too,' she said. 'Most patients with CAPS in the UK have Muckle-Wells Syndrome, and that's the variant Sammy has.'

'Tell me about him,' Leo invited. Sure, he could read the file, but this way he got the chance to interact with Rosie. And he liked how quick her mind was.

'He's eight years old and he's been coming here for nearly a year. He comes to clinic with his mum roughly every eight weeks. We check his knees and ankles and do bloods to measure the inflammation levels, and then we give him an injection of the drug that keeps his MWS under control,' she explained.

'That's the drug that blocks interleukin 1β, yes?' he checked.

'Yes,' she confirmed. 'The treatment's still new enough that we don't know the long-term effects, but we're hoping that it will stop more severe problems developing as he grows older.'

'Such as deafness?'

'Exactly,' she said. 'Are you ready to see him now?'

He nodded. 'Absolutely.'

Rosie went out into the reception area and came back with Sammy and his mother.

Leo smiled at them. 'Hello. I'm Dr Marchetti—you can call me Dr Leo, if you prefer. And you're Sammy?'

The little boy nodded.

'Tell me how you're doing, Sammy,' Leo invited.

'Sometimes I have good days, and sometimes I get bad days,' Sammy said, shrugging.

'OK. What happens when you have a bad day?'

'Mum says it's a flare-up. It affects my tummy, my knees and my head. I get a rash, and it's always at night.' Sammy grimaced. 'Show him, Mum.'

Mrs Kennedy took out her phone and showed them a picture of the nettle rash on Sammy's stomach.

'How often do you get flare-ups?' Leo asked.

'Every couple of weeks. But it's not been so bad, lately.'

'Are you happy for us to examine you?' Leo asked.

Sammy gave him a rueful smile. 'I know the drill. You ask me questions, look me over, take blood and then give me the injections.'

'That's a pretty good summary,' Leo said, smiling back.

'I don't like the injections,' Sammy said. 'They sting and they make my skin sore. But I guess it's better than the rash.'

'A lot of people don't like injections, so you're not alone there,' Leo said. 'Is there anything you'd like to add or ask, Mrs Kennedy?'

'We're getting to be old hands at this, now,' she said. 'It's fine.'

Between them, Rosie and Leo examined Sammy,

and she took a blood sample. Then Leo administered the drug.

Sammy flinched.

'I'm sorry it stings,' Leo said.

'It's all right,' Sammy said, clearly trying to be brave.

'I have something for you,' Rosie said. 'That is... Unless you're too old to have a lolly for being brave?'

Sammy grinned when he saw the red and white lolly. 'As if I'm going to turn down a lolly. Especially when it's in my team's colours!'

'You're a football fan?' Leo asked.

Sammy nodded. 'I'd like to be a footballer, but my CAPS is going to get in the way a bit, and I don't want to let my team down. But I guess I could be a scientist when I grow up and invent a needle that doesn't hurt when you give someone an injection.'

'That,' Leo said, 'is a brilliant idea, and I think it deserves something extra.' He produced another red and white lolly. 'Don't tell Rosie I raided her lolly jar,' he said in a stage whisper.

Sammy laughed. 'See you in a couple of months, Dr Leo.'

'See you,' Leo returned with a smile.

When the Kennedys had left, he looked at Rosie. 'Sammy's a nice kid.'

'He is,' she agreed. Then she paused. 'I was a bit abrupt with you yesterday. Sorry. So, um, I was wondering, would you like to have lunch with me today? Just as colleagues,' she added hastily.

Again he glanced at her left hand and saw no sign of a wedding ring. Did she really mean having lunch together just as colleagues, or did she feel the same pull of attraction towards him that he felt towards her?

It might explain why she'd been so prickly yesterday; she might be just as spooked by her reaction to him as he was by his reaction to her. Though quite where they went from here, he had no idea. What he'd seen of Rosie so far told him that she was very professional—straight-talking, yet deeply caring towards her patients. He liked that. A lot.

But he also had the strongest impression that Rosie Hobbes wasn't the sort to have a casual fling. Which meant she was off limits, because he wasn't looking for something serious and long-term.

'Just as colleagues,' he agreed.

Once they'd seen the last patient at the clinic, they headed for the canteen. Leo noted that she chose a healthy salad and a mug of green tea—not that his own sandwich and coffee were *that* unhealthy. But Rosie clearly looked after her health.

'So how are you settling in?' she asked when they'd found a table.

'To the hospital or to London?'

'Both, I guess.'

'Fine,' he said. 'The staff all seem really nice here, and I trained in London so I feel pretty much at home in the city.'

'That's good.'

There was a slightly awkward silence, as if she didn't really know what to say to him next. It might be easier to keep the conversation going, Leo thought, if he asked her to tell him more about Paddington Children's Hospital and its predicament.

'Obviously Robyn told me about the Board of Directors and their plans, when she asked me to come and work here,' he said, 'so I understand why we're so short-staffed at the moment. But I gather there was a fire at a local school which made things a bit trickier?'

She nodded. 'It was about a month ago. The fire started in the art department, apparently. I'm not sure if it was a broken heater or something that caused the initial fire, but some of the paper caught light.'

'And everything else in an art department tends to be on the flammable side,' he said.

'Exactly. It was pretty scary. The school did what they could to get the kids out, but we were overflowing with patients suffering from everything from smoke inhalation to burns. Simon Bennett had severe facial burns; he's due for some reconstruction surgery, so he's in and out for check-ups at the moment, poor lamb.' She winced. 'And then there's little Ryan.'

'Ryan?' he asked.

'Ryan Walker. He was one of the last to be rescued. The poor little lad was hiding in a cupboard. He heard the firemen when they'd put the fire out in his classroom and came out of the cupboard, but then a beam snapped and hit him on the head.'

'He's lucky to be alive, then,' Leo said.

She nodded. 'But the poor little mite was very badly hurt. He had a craniectomy the other day. Right now he's under sedation and has a helmet on to protect him until the surgical team can replace the skull flap.'

'Poor kid,' Leo said.

'I know. But just think—if we'd been moved to Riverside,' she said softly, 'he wouldn't have made it. And the same's true for Simon.'

'So you're fighting for the hospital to be saved.'

'Victoria's set up a committee—actually, Quinn, Simon's foster mum, is on the committee. We've got protestors outside the gates twenty-four-seven. Though you already know that,' she said. 'You were photographed with them yesterday.'

And the photographs had since been used all round the globe. 'Might as well make the press do something useful,' he said dryly.

'Do the press hound you all the time?' she asked.

'Off and on. It depends if it's a slow news day—but they're rather more interested in the Duke than in the doctor.' He paused. 'Is that why you said about a castle yesterday?'

'Castle?' She frowned for a moment, and then her expression cleared. 'It's what all the staff call the hospital, because of the turrets.'

'Oh.'

She stared at him, looking slightly shocked. 'Hang on. You thought I was having a dig about you being a duke?'

'We didn't exactly get off on the right foot together yesterday,' he pointed out.

'No—and I guess I was a bit rude to you. Sorry.'

He appreciated the apology, though he noticed she didn't give him any explanation about why she'd been so abrupt with him.

'For the record,' he said, 'I did grow up in a castle. And I can tell you it's not all it's cracked up to be. For starters, castles tend to be draughty and full of damp.'

'And full of suits of armour?'

He smiled. 'We do have an armoury, yes. And I have been thinking about opening the place to the public.' Which might give his mother something more immediate to concentrate on, instead of when her son was going to make a suitable marriage and produce an heir to the dukedom.

'But I really don't understand,' she said, 'why a duke would want to be a doctor. I mean, don't you have to do loads of stuff for the dukedom?'

'I delegate a fair bit of it,' he said, 'and I have good staff.'

'Which again makes you different from any other doctor I've met.'

He wondered: was that different good, or different bad?

'I don't know anyone who has staff,' she said. 'Anyone at all. In fact, I don't even know anyone who hires a cleaner.'

'Guilty there, too,' he said. 'Obviously I know how to use a vacuum cleaner, but there are a lot of other things I'd much rather do with my free time.'

She said nothing.

'I want to be a doctor,' he said softly, 'because I want to make a real difference in the world.'

'Can't you do that as a duke?'

'Not in the same way. I don't want to just throw money at things. It's not enough. I want to make the difference *myself.*'

'From the way you talk,' she said, 'anyone would think you don't actually like being a duke.'

He didn't.

'Let's just say it's not what everyone thinks it would be like—and plenty of people see the title first and not the man.'

She reached out and squeezed his hand in a gesture of sympathy. His hand tingled where her skin touched his, shocking him; he was used to being attracted to women, but he wasn't used to having such a strong reaction to someone and he wasn't quite sure how to deal with it.

She looked as shocked as he felt, as if she'd experienced the same unexpected pull. 'Sorry. I didn't...' Her words trailed off.

Didn't what? Didn't mean to touch him? Or didn't expect to feel that strong a physical reaction?

He had the feeling that she'd find an excuse to run if he called her on it. 'No need to apologise. It's nice that you understand,' he said. 'So have you been working at *this* castle very long?'

'For nearly a year,' she said.

'Where were you before?'

'The other side of London, where I trained.'

He noticed that she hadn't actually said where. Why was so she cagey about her past?

He'd back off, for now. Until he'd got his head round this weird reaction to her and had made sense of it. And then maybe he'd be able to work out what he wanted to do about it. About *her*.

On Wednesday lunchtime, Rosie disappeared, and Leo remembered what Kathleen had said to him: Rosie read to Penny every other day, when she was in. Not quite able to keep himself away, he found himself in the corridor outside Penny's room. Rosie's voice was clear and measured as she read the story, and every so often he could hear a soft giggle of delight from Penny.

'Rosie's so lovely with her,' a voice said beside him.

He looked round; the woman standing next to him looked so much like Penny that there was only one person she could be. 'You're Penny's mum, yes?'

'Julia.'

'Dr Marchetti,' he said, holding out his hand to shake hers. 'Although your daughter isn't one of my patients because I'm not a heart specialist, I work with Rosie, and Rosie told me all about Penny.'

'Rosie's such a lovely woman. So patient. And it's so kind of her to read to Penny in her lunch break.'

'I think you'd probably have a queue of staff there, if you asked,' Leo said. 'From what I hear, Penny's a firm favourite. And her kitten pictures are pinned up in the staff room—they're adorable.'

'Aren't they just?' But behind her smile Julia's eyes were sad. 'I'm sorry, I'm probably keeping you from a patient.'

'It's fine,' Leo reassured her. 'But if there's anything you need?'

'Rosie's there,' Julia said. 'But thank you.'

'I'll let you get on.' He smiled at her, and headed back to his office to prepare for his next clinic. But all the same he couldn't get Rosie out of his head.

Thomas propped himself against the desk where Rosie was sitting 'Obviously I've read the file, but you've seen Penny more than anyone else this week. How do you feel she's doing?'

Rosie grimaced. 'There doesn't seem to be any change in her condition this week, even though we've been juggling her meds as you asked us to do.'

'So it's not working. I'm beginning to think that the only way forward for her now is a transplant.' He sighed. 'Julia's in today, isn't she? I'll ask her to get Peter to come in as well, so I can talk to them together.'

It wasn't going to be an easy conversation, Rosie knew. 'Do you want me to be there when you talk to them?'

He shook his head. 'Thanks for the offer. I know you've been brilliant with them, but this is my responsibility. It's going to come as a shock to them.'

'You know where I am if you change your mind,' she said gently.

'Thanks, Rosie. I appreciate it.'

Thomas looked almost bruised by this, Rosie thought, but he clearly wasn't going to let anyone close enough to support him. She remembered how it had felt when things with Michael had gone so badly wrong, so she wasn't going to push him to confide in her. But it was always good to know that someone could be there for you if you needed that little bit of support. 'Thomas, I'm probably speaking out of turn, but are you OK?'

'Sure.' He gave her an over-bright smile which clearly underlined the fact that he wasn't OK, but he wanted her to back off.

'Uh-huh,' she said. She didn't quite have the nerve to suggest that maybe he could talk to her if he needed a friend. 'I guess I'll see you later, then.'

He nodded, and left the nurses' station.

Rosie hated this situation. Whatever way you looked at it, someone would lose. She really hoped that Penny would get the heart she needed; though that would also mean that a family would be bereaved, so it kind of felt wrong to wish for a heart. The best of all outcomes would've been if Penny had responded to the drug treatment, but it wasn't to be.

And poor Julia. Rosie could imagine how she'd feel if she was in Julia's place, worried sick about Freddie or Lexi and knowing that they might not be able to get the treatment they needed so badly. Despite the misery of her life with Michael, he had given her the sheer joy of the twins. She had a lot to be thankful for.

But now wasn't the time to dwell on that. She had a clinic to do.

* * *

Leo happened to be checking some files at the nurses' station when Rosie walked over. He could see that she looked upset, and the words were out of his mouth before he could stop them. 'Do you want to go for a drink after work and tell me about it?'

She shook her head.

'Don't tell me—a previous engagement?' he asked wryly.

'I'm afraid so.'

'A chat in the ward kitchen, then.'

'Thanks, but I have obs to do.'

'Thirty minutes,' he said, 'and you can take a five minute break—and I'm not pulling rank, before you start thinking that. You look upset and I'm trying to be supportive, just as I would with any other colleague who looked upset.'

She looked surprised, and then rueful. 'All right. Thirty minutes,' she said. 'Thank you.'

While she was doing her patients' observations, he finished his paperwork and then nipped out briefly to Tony's Trattoria, the place across the street that he'd been told sold decent coffee, to buy two cappuccinos.

He'd half expected Rosie to make some excuse not to see him, but she arrived in the staff kitchen at the same time as he did.

'Thank you.' She smiled as he handed her one of the distinctive paper cups. 'Someone told you about Tony's, then?'

'Decent Italian coffee? Of course—and it's much better than the coffee in the hospital.'

'We have instant cappuccino here in the ward kitchen,'

she reminded him, gesturing to the box of powdered sachets.

'That stuff isn't coffee, it's an abomination.' He smiled back at her. 'So are you going to tell me what's wrong?'

Her beautiful blue eyes filled with sadness. 'I was talking to Thomas earlier. It's Penny.'

He frowned. 'What about Penny?'

'We've been juggling her meds all week and it's just not working.' She shook her head in seeming frustration. 'Thomas says we're probably going to have to look at a transplant, so he's going to do an assessment. But even if she's on the list there's no guarantee she'll get a heart. It could be anything from days, to months, or even more than a year before a suitable heart is available, and it feels horrible to wish for a heart for her because it means that another family's lost someone they love.'

'But at least they have the comfort that their loved one has saved a life by donating their organs after death,' he said softly. 'And you're thinking a heart might not arrive in time?'

'You know that one in five cases don't. Those are really big odds, Leo. And she's such a lovely little girl.'

'Hey.' He gave her a hug. Then he wished he hadn't, because holding her made him want to do more than that. Right at that moment, he wanted to kiss her tears away—and then kiss her again and again, until he'd made her forget her worries.

When he pulled back slightly and looked her in the eye, her pupils were so huge that her vivid blue irises seemed more like a narrow rim. *So she felt it, too.* He looked at her mouth, and ached to find out for himself how soft and sweet it tasted. He shifted his gaze and caught her looking at his mouth, too. Could they? *Should* they?

He was about to give in to the impulse and dip his head to hers when she pulled away. 'Sorry. It's not appropriate to lean on you like that.'

Leo knew she was right. Except he was the one who'd behaved inappropriately. 'The fault's all mine,' he said. 'I guess it's being Italian that makes me—well…'

'Hug people?' she finished.

'Something like that.' But he wasn't ready to let things go. 'Are you sure I can't take you to dinner tonight?'

'I'm sure. Thank you for the offer, but no.'

And yet there was a hint of wistfulness in her face. He was sure he wasn't just being a delusional, self-absorbed male; but why did she keep turning him down whenever he asked her out? If she'd said that she was married, or in a relationship, fair enough. He'd back off straight away. But she hadn't said that, which made him think that it was some other reason why she kept saying no. But he could hardly ask anyone else on the ward without the risk of becoming the centre of hospital gossip, and he loathed gossip.

Maybe he'd just keep trying and eventually he'd manage to wear her down. Because he really liked what he'd seen so far of Rosie Hobbes, and he wanted to get to know her better. And he wanted to work out why she attracted him so strongly, what made her different from the usual women he dated.

'Thanks for the coffee and sympathy,' Rosie said. 'I'd better get on.'

'See you later,' he said.

The problem was, Rosie thought, Leo Marchetti was

actually *nice*. She'd been on ward rounds with him a couple of times now and she'd seen that he was lovely with both the kids and their parents. A couple of the mums had tried to flirt with him, but he'd stayed totally professional and focused on the children. And he'd been especially good with the more worried parents, explaining things in a way that stopped them panicking.

She was tempted to take him up on his offer of dinner out. Really tempted.

Except she wasn't in the market for a relationship, and it wouldn't be fair to date anyone until she was ready to trust her heart again. And nothing could really happen between her and Leo. He was a duke and moved in the kind of social circles that would never see her as his equal; and, after her experiences with Michael, she refused to put herself in a position where anyone would treat her as second class. It couldn't work, so there was no point in thinking about it. Besides, she already had the perfect life: two gorgeous children, a brilliantly supportive family and a job she adored. Wanting more—wanting a partner to share that with—was just being greedy.

Plus, her judgement was rubbish when it came to men. She'd fallen hook, line and sinker for every lie that Michael had told her.

So she needed to keep thinking of Leo as just another colleague. Yes, he was attractive; and she was beginning to like him a lot. But that was as far as it could go.

CHAPTER THREE

ON FRIDAY MORNING, Leo was talking to Rebecca Scott, the transplant surgeon, on the ward. 'Rosie tells me that Thomas is putting Penny on the transplant list.'

Was it his imagination, or did Rebecca freeze for a second when he mentioned Thomas's name? Rebecca and Thomas were always very professional with patients, but he'd noticed that they never shared a smile or any personal comments with each other, the way they did with other staff members. He had a feeling that something was definitely going on—or maybe something had happened in the past.

He knew all about complicated relationships. He was careful to keep his own as simple as possible, so the women he dated didn't have any expectations that he wouldn't be able to live up to. But, whatever the differences were between Rebecca and Thomas, it was none of his business. As long as everyone on the team was kept informed about any issues with their patients, nothing else mattered. He needed to keep out of this.

'Yes.' There was a flicker of sadness in her eyes, quickly masked. 'Are you settling in to the hospital OK?'

'Yes, thanks.' Clearly Rebecca wanted to change the subject. Well, that was fine by him. The last thing he wanted to do was accidentally trample over a sore spot. 'Everyone's been very welcoming and I haven't had to sit in a corner on my own at lunchtime.'

She smiled. 'That's good. Well, I'm due in Theatre, so I'll let you get on. But give me a yell if there's anything you need.'

'Thanks. I will.'

Rosie spent her usual Friday lunchtime reading to Penny and talking about kittens and ballet. She knew Thomas had talked to Peter and Julia about putting their daughter on the transplant list, and gave Julia an extra hug at the door. 'We're all rooting for her, you know. We're not supposed to have favourites but our Penny's special.'

A tear trickled down Julia's cheek and she clearly couldn't speak.

'It's OK,' Rosie said softly. 'I'm a mum, too, so I know exactly how I'd feel in your shoes.'

'We really appreciate you reading to her,' Julia said.

Rosie smiled back. 'No problem. My two are more into dinosaurs than anything else at the moment, but when Lexi's older I'm sure she'd enjoy the kind of stories I've been reading to Penny.'

In the middle of the afternoon, she was at the nurses' station, writing up notes, when Leo came over and handed her a paper cup of cappuccino. 'Good afternoon. I brought you something to help you write up your notes,' he said.

'That's really nice of you, Leo, and I love the coffee from Tony's,' she said, 'but that's the second time you've bought me coffee this week and now I feel in your debt. Which makes me feel uncomfortable.'

'There's no debt.' He paused. 'Or maybe you could

buy me a coffee after work, if that would make you feel better.'

Buying him a coffee to make them even would make her feel better, but she absolutely couldn't do anything after work. 'Sorry. I can't.'

'Or come out with me for a pizza at the weekend,' he suggested. 'We can go halves and you can buy me a coffee then.'

How easy it would be to agree to have dinner with him.

And it worried Rosie just how much she was starting to like Leo Marchetti. He was kind, he was great with patients and parents and staff alike, and he was beautiful to look at with those dark, expressive eyes and a mouth that promised sin.

It would be so, so easy to say yes.

But how did she know that she wasn't going to be repeating her past mistake and fall for someone who made her heart beat faster but would let her down when she needed him? Leo seemed a nice guy on the ward—but would he be different in a relationship that wasn't strictly professional? Would he turn out to have feet of clay?

There was one way to find out. She could agree to one date. Then, if Leo took one look at the twins and ran for the hills, she'd know she'd been right about him all along. And she was pretty sure that he would leave her alone once he knew she was a single mum of three-year-old twins.

'All right,' she said. 'But, as you've been buying me coffee, *I'll* take *you* out for a pizza.'

He blinked, looking slightly shocked that she'd actually said yes. 'When?'

'Tomorrow night.' Before her nerve broke.

'OK. That's good. I'll pick you up,' he said. 'What time?'

She frowned. 'Hang on. I thought I was taking you out for pizza? Shouldn't I be the one picking you up?'

'Change of plan. I'm taking you out for dinner,' he said.

So once she'd agreed to something, then he changed the goalposts? Well, Leo would find out the hard way that her goalposts weren't changeable. Her children came first. And that wasn't negotiable.

'Six o'clock, then,' she said, and wrote down her address for him.

'And your phone number? In case of emergencies and change of plans?'

She wrote that down, too.

'Thanks. I'll text you later so you have my number.'

'OK.'

'I'll let you get on,' he said. But before he walked away, he touched the back of his fingers briefly against her cheek—and every nerve-end sizzled at his touch. Just like Wednesday afternoon, when he'd hugged her and then he'd been at the point of actually kissing her. Worse still, she'd been thinking along the same lines.

This really wasn't good.

Rosie had to force herself to concentrate on the paperwork until the end of her shift, and then she headed down to the hospital nursery school to pick up the twins. Right at that moment, she wasn't sure if she'd just made a huge mistake in suggesting going out to dinner with Leo.

But it would settle things once and for all: she was pretty sure he'd look at the twins, make some charming excuse and scuttle off. And then he'd never ask her for another date. She'd be off the hook.

Leo could hardly believe that Rosie had actually agreed to a date.

Six o'clock seemed a little early for him to pick her up, but maybe they could go for a drink before they went out to dinner. He caught Robyn at the end of his shift. 'Just the person I wanted to see.'

'Something you need at work?' she asked.

He smiled. 'No—everything's fine and I'm really enjoying working here. This is personal. I was wondering if you could recommend a nice restaurant locally.'

'Oh, is your mother coming over to stay?'

He shook his head. 'Right now Mamma's a little frail, so I'd rather she stayed in Tuscany where she can be looked after properly.' He squished the faint feeling of guilt that really he ought to be the one keeping an eye on his mother, as her only child and a qualified doctor. But he specialised in paediatrics, not geriatrics, so she was getting better care than he could give her. And he called her every day when he wasn't in Tuscany; he wasn't neglecting her completely.

'So do you mean somewhere romantic?' Robyn teased.

He actually felt himself blush. 'Yes.'

She mentioned a couple of places and he made a note of them on his phone.

'Dare I ask who the lucky woman is?'

He smiled at her. 'Now, now. A gentleman doesn't tell tales.'

She laughed. 'Leo, you might be a gentleman, but you'll date her twice and be utterly charming, and then you'll end it before she has a chance to get close to you.'

'I date women more than twice,' he said. He knew she was teasing, but he also knew that she had a point. He never had let a woman close to him, since Emilia. Maybe he ought to leave Rosie well alone.

The problem was, he didn't want to. She drew him, with that odd mixture of warmth and wariness. He wanted to get to know her better and understand why she drew him like this. And, if he was honest with himself, she was the first woman since Emilia who'd made him feel this way. Which was another reason why he should just drop this: the last time he'd felt that incredible pull towards someone, it had gone badly wrong.

When he got home, he booked the table at one of the restaurants Robyn had suggested. But, the next day, he couldn't settle to much; he was too filled with anticipation. It made him feel a bit like a teenager again, though the teenage Leo Marchetti had ended up with a heart so broken that he'd had to escape from Rome to London before he could mend himself. He'd never want to go through his teens again, with all that uncertainty and that desperation to please someone who constantly changed the goalposts and made the young Leo feel that he'd never be able to match up to expectations. And he didn't have to ask anyone's permission to date someone.

He shook himself. His father was dead and Leo was comfortable in his own skin now. He knew who he was and what he was good at—and he didn't have to please anyone but himself.

Late that afternoon, he drove to Rosie's and parked his low-slung two-seater convertible on the road outside her house.

She answered the door wearing understated make-up and a little black dress: very different from how she usually was at work, with no make-up and a uniform.

'You look lovely,' he said, and then felt like a fool when she raised one eyebrow.

'Not that you don't usually look lovely,' he said, feeling even more gauche. Which was weird, because normally he was relaxed with women. He *liked* their company. Why was he so awkward with Rosie?

She smiled. 'Thank you for the compliment. Come in.'

He stopped dead in the doorway when she ushered him into the living room and he saw two small children playing with a train set on the floor. The brown-haired boy and golden-haired girl were clearly Rosie's children, as they had her bright blue eyes and her smile. And they looked to be around the same age, so he guessed that they were twins.

He couldn't see a babysitter anywhere, unless maybe someone was in the kitchen or something.

And the penny dropped when he looked at Rosie's face.

She'd invited him to pick her up here, expecting him to take one look at the children and make a run for it.

That really smarted. Had his reputation already spread through the hospital, if she thought he was that shallow?

Then again, maybe she'd been badly hurt by the twins' father. Until he knew the full story, he shouldn't judge her the way she'd obviously misjudged him.

'So that's dinner for four?' he asked.

She shrugged, and lowered her voice so the children couldn't hear. 'I come as a package, Leo.'

'It would've been useful to know that.'

'So you could back off earlier?'

She was really that sure he was so unreliable? Or had

someone made her believe that about all men? 'No,' he said. 'So I could've brought a four-seater car with me instead of a two-seater.'

Colour flooded into her face. 'Oh.'

'I would be delighted to take you all out,' he said, keeping his voice as low as hers, 'but either we need to use a taxi or—if you have appropriate seats—your car. Is there any particular place the children like eating out?'

Leo wasn't running away.

And he'd asked where the twins liked eating out, not where she liked eating out.

He was putting her children first.

Shame flooded through Rosie. She'd misjudged him. Badly so. Every single assumption she'd made about him had been based on Michael's behaviour, and that wasn't fair of her. OK, so the hospital grapevine said Leo dated a lot, but she hadn't heard anything about him leaving a trail of broken hearts behind him. It was possible to be good-looking and be a decent human being as well. She knew her experiences with Michael had made her unfairly judgemental, but it was so hard not to just leap in and make assumptions.

'Thank you,' she said, feeling like an ungrateful monster. 'Are you sure about this?'

'The children are obviously dressed up, ready to go out,' he said. 'I'm not going to disappoint them.'

'I said I'd take them out,' she admitted.

'So how were you going to explain me to them?'

'You're my colleague. You popped in to tell me something about the hospital, and you couldn't come for a pizza with us because you're already due somewhere else.'

He raised an eyebrow. 'So you really did think I'd take one look at the children and scuttle away.'

'Yes, and I apologise. I was wrong to judge you on someone else's behaviour.' She closed her eyes briefly. 'I'll explain later, but I'd prefer not to discuss it in front of the twins.'

'All right. So shall I cancel our table while you book us a table somewhere that the twins like?'

This was way, way more than she deserved. 'Thank you,' she said. She'd already booked the table; but, sure that he wouldn't join them, she'd booked it for three rather than for four. It wouldn't take much to change that. 'And I'm sorry.'

Leo said nothing, just gave her a grave little nod that made her feel about two inches tall.

Leo walked back into the hallway and called the restaurant to cancel his booking. Once he'd ended the connection, he waited for Rosie to finish her own call, then followed her into the living room and crouched down to the twins' level. 'Hello. I'm Leo.'

The little boy refused to look at him, but the girl smiled at him. 'I'm Lexi. My name starts with a *luh*, like yours.'

'Delighted to meet you, Lexi.' He shook her hand, then looked at the little boy. 'And you are...?'

The little boy dipped his head and looked up shyly.

He had Rosie's eyes, Leo thought, huge and piercing and beautiful.

'He's Freddie,' Lexi said.

Did he always let his sister do the talking for him? Leo wondered. 'Delighted to meet you, too, Freddie,' he said, and held out his hand.

But the little boy looked wary and refused to take his hand.

Was Freddie wary of all men, or just of him? Leo wondered. Given that there was no evidence of the twins' father, had there been some kind of super-bitter divorce? It would perhaps explain why Rosie had been so quick to judge him harshly—and maybe the twins' father was the person she'd referred to when she'd talked about judging Leo on someone else's behaviour.

'I work with your mummy at the hospital,' he said.

'We go to school at the hospital,' Lexi said.

'School?' They looked a bit young to be at school.

'Nursery school,' Rosie explained.

That made a lot of sense. Now he understood why she rushed off at the end of every shift and had consistently refused to meet him after work: she needed to pick up her children straight after work.

'How old are you, Freddie?' he asked.

The little boy said nothing, and Lexi—clearly the more confident of the two—nudged him, as if to say, *Answer the man.*

'Freddie's a little bit shy,' Rosie said.

'Mummy says don't talk to someone you don't know,' Lexi said.

'Quite right,' Leo said.

'But you know Mummy, so we can talk to you,' Lexi added.

'Three,' Freddie said reluctantly. 'I'm three.'

'I'm three and a little bit,' Lexi said. 'I was borned before Freddie.'

Leo had to hide a smile at both her charming grammatical mistake and the importance of her tone. 'So you're the older twin, Lexi.'

Freddie seemed to have a burst of confidence, be-cause he said, 'Mummy's taking us out. We're having pizza for tea.'

'And I'm going with you,' Leo told him.

'Why?' Lexi asked.

'Lexi, that's rude,' Rosie warned.

'It's fine,' Leo reassured her. 'I'm coming with you because your mummy's very kind. I haven't worked at the hospital for very long and I don't know many people, so she thought I might be lonely this evening and said I could maybe come for pizza with you. If that's all right with you both, Freddie and Lexi?'

The twins looked at each other.

'So Mummy's your friend?' Freddie asked.

'She is,' Leo confirmed, not quite daring to meet Rosie's eyes. Friendship definitely didn't describe their relationship. But it would do for now.

'Then you're our friend, too,' Lexi said. Her smile was so much like Rosie's that it made Leo's heart feel as if it had just flipped over. Given how wary Rosie had been with him, it wouldn't be surprising if her children were just as nervous with people. Yet Lexi had seemed to accept him almost instantly.

'Are you coming to the park with us?' Freddie asked.

'We're not going to the park tonight, Freddie,' Rosie said.

'Tomorrow?' Lexi asked hopefully.

'We'll see. But we need to go for pizza now, so we have to put the trains away.'

Freddie stuck out his lower lip. 'But we want to play trains when we get back.'

'We'll see,' Rosie said. 'For now, we need to put the

trains away before we go out. Shall we have a race and
see who can put the track away fastest?'

'Me!' Lexi said.

'Me!' Freddie echoed.

Between them, they dismantled the wooden track and
put it into a large plastic lidded box. Leo held back, watching them. Rosie was strict with her children rather than
spoiling them, insisting that they clear up and have good
manners. But he was also pretty sure that Rosie Hobbes
would never, ever starve her children of love. In her case,
firm went with fair, and he'd just bet that she told the
twins every day—several times—that she loved them.

How different his own childhood had been. His mother
had spoiled him but had never stood up for him, and his
father had been cold and manipulative, seeing Leo firstly
as the future Duke and only secondly as his child. The
child who constantly disappointed him.

He pushed the thoughts away. Now wasn't the time
to dwell on that.

'Do you mind me driving?' Rosie asked Leo when she'd
strapped the children into their car seats.

'No.'

She grimaced. 'Sorry. Judging again. I don't mean to.'

'Any man who has a problem with a woman driving,'
Leo said softly, 'needs to get a life.'

Which made her warm to him even more.

The children insisted on singing all the way to the
pizza place; Rosie knew she was being a coward by letting it give her the excuse not to make small-talk with
Leo, but right now she felt so wrong-footed.

She made each child hold her hand on the way in to
the restaurant; once they were seated, with Lexi next to

him and Freddie opposite, Leo asked the children, 'So is this your favourite place to eat?'

'Yes! We love pizza,' Lexi said.

'Me, too,' Leo said, 'because I was born in Italy, where pizza comes from.'

'Where's Italy?' Lexi asked.

Rosie was about to head her off, knowing that her daughter could ask a million questions and then a million more, but Leo took out his phone and pulled up a map. 'See that long, thin country there that looks a bit like a boot? That's Italy. And I come from here.' He pointed out a region to the north-west of the country.

Tuscany. The part of Italy Rosie had always wanted to visit. She and Michael had planned a tour of the area, stopping off at Florence and Siena and Pisa—but then he'd had to cancel their holiday because he was starting a new job. More like, she thought grimly, he'd gambled away the money he'd been supposed to use for their flights and hotels, and she'd been too naive to realise. She'd believed every word he'd said.

'Are the houses pretty?' Lexi asked.

'Very pretty.' Leo pulled up some pictures to show her. 'See?'

'That one looks a bit like the hospital,' Lexi said, ''cept it's yellow, not pink.'

'Are there castles in Italy?' Freddie piped up.

'There are castles,' Leo said, and found some more pictures. 'In Italy we call a castle a *palazzo*.'

'*Pal—*' Freddie began, and stopped.

'*Palazzo*. Like a palace,' Leo said. '*Pal-at-zo.*'

'Pal-as-o,' Freddie repeated, not quite getting it, but Rosie noticed that Leo didn't push him or mock him. Instead, he was actually encouraging the little boy to talk.

'Are there princesses in the castle?' Lexi asked.

'The waitress is here, Lexi. We need to tell her what we want to eat,' Rosie interrupted gently.

'Dough balls,' Lexi said promptly.

'Dough balls, what?' Rosie reminded her.

'Dough balls, please,' Lexi said.

'Me, too, please,' Freddie said.

'That's three for dough balls, please,' Leo said.

Rosie smiled. 'Four for dough balls, please, two small *margherita* pizzas for the children, a four cheeses thin crust for me and…' She paused and looked at Leo.

'A *quattro stagioni* thin crust for me, please,' Leo said.

Lexi's eyes went round. 'What's a cat—?' She stopped, looking puzzled.

'*Quattro stagioni,*' Leo said. 'It means "four seasons" in Italian, and each quarter of the pizza has a topping of food you find in each season. Do you know what the seasons are?'

'Like spring,' Rosie prompted when Lexi was uncharacteristically quiet.

Lexi shook her head.

'That's OK,' Leo said. 'Spring's when the daffodils and bluebells come out, summer's when it's hot, autumn's when all the leaves turn gold and fall off the trees, and winter's when it's cold and snowy.'

Of course Leo was good with kids, Rosie thought. He was a paediatrician and spent every working day treating children. It stood to reason that he'd be good with children outside work, too. But she appreciated the way he'd explained the concept simply and without fuss, rather than dismissing Lexi's question or ignoring her.

Lexi continued quizzing Leo about Italy while they were waiting for their meal, and even Freddie started to come out of his shell when Leo started asking him about his favourite trains. He also helped Freddie cut up his pizza without making a big deal of it, and Rosie felt the barrier round her heart start to crack.

This was what she'd always thought having a family would be like.

Except Michael hadn't wanted that. She and the children simply hadn't been enough for him. And OK, she could deal with the fact that maybe he'd made a mistake in choosing her as his life partner; but how could he have turned his back on his children? All this time later, it still hurt.

Leo was used to dealing with children at work, but very few outside. And he was surprised to discover how at ease he felt with chatterbox Lexi and shy Freddie.

Every so often, he glanced across at Rosie, to check that she was comfortable about the way he was chatting with her twins, and he was amazed to see that she actually looked relaxed—something he most definitely wasn't used to seeing from her at work.

Leo didn't do relationships; Robyn's teasing assessment had been very close to the mark. Yet he found himself drawn to this little family. And he was actually enjoying himself, answering Lexi's barrage of questions and trying to tempt Freddie out of his shell.

This was the kind of childhood he wished he'd had. Where his father might have cut up his meals for him without making a big deal about it, rather than making him eat his meals on his own in the nursery until he was old enough to know which knife and fork to use, and use them without spilling anything. Where his mother would have helped him decorate his whipped ice-cream sundae with sprinkles and jelly beans, not minding if anything spilled on the table or on her clothes. Though he had a feeling that she'd been acting on his father's decisions rather than her own; if you were fragile and you were married to a bully, it would be easier to agree with him than to risk a fight.

You couldn't change the past.

But maybe, he thought, his future could be different.

And maybe it didn't mean having to find himself a 'suitable' noble bride and producing an heir to the dukedom. Maybe it was about finding the life and the family that he wanted.

Maybe.

CHAPTER FOUR

AFTER THE MEAL, Rosie drove them back to her house.

It would be rude not to invite Leo in for coffee; but she was pretty sure that he'd make an excuse not to come in. Although he'd been lovely with the children, tonight hadn't been the romantic date for two he'd been expecting, and she wouldn't blame him for feeling just a bit disgruntled with her. When she'd planned this evening, she'd thought it was the best way of making him understand she wasn't interested in a date; but now she could see how stupid and selfish she'd been. She should've just told him straight.

Except a little part of her *had* wanted to date him.

And Leo Marchetti made her feel seriously flustered.

'You're welcome to come in for coffee,' she said, 'but I quite understand if you need to get going.'

His dark eyes were unreadable. 'Coffee would be lovely, thank you.'

Oh, help. He wasn't rushing away as fast as he possibly could. This felt as if she'd leaped out of the frying pan and into the fire.

'I'll put the kettle on, if you don't mind waiting while I put the children to bed?' she asked as she closed the front door behind them.

'I don't want to go to bed,' Lexi said.

'It's bedtime now, Lexi,' Rosie said firmly. 'And if you want to go to the park tomorrow, you need to get enough sleep tonight. I'll read you a story.'

'I want Leo to read me a story,' Freddie said. 'He's my friend.'

'Leo...' She paused, trying to think up a reasonable excuse.

'—would be delighted to read you a story,' Leo cut in gently. 'Do you have a favourite story, Freddie?'

'Dinosaurs!' Freddie said, and charged up the stairs.

'Thank you,' Rosie mouthed to him.

Once Rosie had brushed the children's teeth and Lexi and Freddie were in their pyjamas, cuddled beneath their duvets, Leo sat on the panda-shaped rug on the floor between their beds, holding the book that Freddie had picked out.

'*One* story,' Rosie said, and kissed them both. 'I'm going to put the kettle on for Leo and me to have coffee. Night-night. I love you, Freddie. I love you, Lexi.'

'Love you, Mummy,' they chorused. 'Night-night.'

In her small galley kitchen, Rosie could hear Leo reading the story. She loved the fact that he actually put on different voices for different dinosaurs; but part of her wanted to cry. This was something the children had really missed out on; although their grandfather often read to them, it wasn't quite the same as having their father read them a bedtime story every night.

Being a parent sometimes felt like the hardest, loneliest job in the world; although her parents and her sister were brilliantly supportive, it wasn't the same as having someone with her all the time. Someone to help make the decisions.

Once Leo finished the story, he sang a lullaby to them. Rosie didn't recognise the words and was pretty sure that he was singing in Italian, but he had a gorgeous voice. It was something that Michael had never bothered doing, and he'd actually smashed the CD of children's songs she'd bought for the car because he said it annoyed him and he couldn't put up with the twins caterwauling the same song over and over again.

Michael.

She was going to have to tell Leo about Michael. She'd promised him an explanation and she wasn't going to back out; but it wasn't a pretty story and even now she felt sick about how poor her judgement had been.

She busied herself making the coffee until she heard Leo come down the stairs. 'Thank you for reading to them—and for singing a lullaby. That was really kind of you.'

'No problem,' he said. 'They're nice kids.'

'Thank you.' She added milk to her own mug, then handed him the other. 'It's instant,' she warned, 'but it's decent instant coffee.'

'"Decent" instant coffee? I'm not entirely sure there is such a thing,' Leo said with a smile, 'but thank you.' He glanced at the drawings held to the outside of the fridge with magnets. 'I like the pictures.'

'The pink one is Lexi's and the yellow one is Freddie's. They feel about dogs the way that Penny at the hospital feels about kittens,' Rosie said ruefully. 'Nearly all their pictures are of puppies.'

'But you don't have one?'

She shrugged. 'I'd love one. But it wouldn't be fair to leave a dog on its own all day.'

Which was why he didn't have a dog, either. He took a sip of the coffee.

'Is it as bad as you thought it would be?' she asked, looking slightly worried.

Yes. Not that he was going to tell her that. 'It's drinkable.'

'But you'd prefer proper coffee?'

He shrugged and smiled. 'I'm from Tuscany. We Italians take our coffee seriously.'

'I guess.' She looked awkward. 'Well, come through.'

He followed her into the living room. Like her kitchen, it was tiny; yet it was also cosy, and there were photographs of the children on the walls, from what was clearly their very first picture in hospital through to a more recent-looking one that he assumed had been taken at the hospital nursery school.

And there were lumps of clay on the mantelpiece that were clearly meant to be dogs. Leo couldn't remember his parents ever displaying his artwork. Then again, maybe dukes and duchesses weren't supposed to put their young children's very first clay models among the Meissen and Sèvres porcelain.

'I enjoyed tonight,' he said. And he was surprised by how much he had relished the feeling of being part of a normal family.

'I'm afraid the twins can be a bit full-on,' she admitted, 'especially when Lexi starts chattering away. She really could talk the proverbial hind leg off a donkey.'

'She's lovely,' he said, 'and it's good that she's confident.'

'Probably because she's the elder twin—well, by all of fifteen minutes—and girls' language seems to develop faster than that of boys. Though I worry about Freddie,' she said. 'He's so shy.'

'Lots of young children go through a shy phase.' They could pussyfoot around the subject for ever, or he could push her just a little bit to find out why she'd been so sure he would walk away as soon as he saw the twins. 'Until tonight, I had no idea you had children.'

'Or you would never have asked me out?'

'That isn't what I said.'

'No. Sorry.' She sighed. 'And I'm really sorry I misjudged you. And I misled you. It was wrong of me.'

He might as well ask her outright. 'Who hurt you so badly, Rosie? Who broke your trust?'

She grimaced. 'Michael. My ex.'

'Freddie and Lexi's father?'

She nodded. 'I owe you the truth. But not everyone at work knows the whole story and I'd prefer to keep it that way.'

He could understand that. He didn't exactly tell many people about his own past. 'I won't betray your confidence.'

She looked at him, her eyes a piercing blue; and then she seemed to make the decision to trust him. 'I met Michael at a party when I was twenty-two, a year after I'd finished my nursing training. He was a friend of a friend. I thought he was charming and fun when I met him, and he was the most good-looking man I'd ever met. I couldn't believe it when he actually asked me out. And dating him was like nothing I'd ever experienced before. We went to the most amazing places—Michelin-starred restaurants, VIP seats at concerts for really big-name bands, and he whisked me away to the poshest hotel in Paris for my birthday. He completely swept me off my feet.'

She looked away. 'We'd been together for three months when he asked me to marry him. Of course I said yes. I'd fallen in love with the sweetest, most charming man and I could hardly believe that he felt the same way about me. He made me feel so special.'

But obviously things had gone sour.

'And then it wasn't fun any more?' he asked gently.

'He changed,' she said, 'when I fell pregnant—it happened pretty quickly and, although he told me he was thrilled to be a dad, it didn't feel like it. He changed jobs a lot. I thought it was because he was ambitious and wanted to make a good life for our children.'

Leo didn't need to ask for the 'but'.

'He started coming home later and later,' Rosie said. 'And then the bailiffs came round. Michael told me that he was taking care of the bills and the money, and it was my job to take care of the children.' She looked away. 'Except he wasn't actually taking care of the money. I had no idea at the time, but he had a gambling problem. When I finally saw our bank statement, I realised that we were in debt up to our eyeballs.' She took a deep breath. 'Gambling's an illness. I know that. And I believed in my marriage vows, being with him in sickness and in health, so I tried to support him. I found him a group that would help him beat the addiction, and a good counsellor. He promised me he'd go. That he'd stop gambling. For our children's sake.'

And it was very clear to Leo that Michael had broken that promise.

'The next time someone came round demanding money,' Rosie said softly, 'it wasn't a bailiff. Michael was in debt to—I don't know any names, but they definitely weren't the kind of people you'd want to cross. All the time I thought he was going to counselling and the support group, it turned out he was still gambling and getting into more and more debt. He'd bailed out of the support group and the counselling after the very first session. And this man...' She shuddered. 'He threatened the children. His eyes looked dead, Leo. He meant it. If Michael didn't pay the money he owed, something would happen to the children. That man looked at them as if they were just leverage, not precious little lives. There was no pity, no compassion. I've never been so scared in my life.'

'Couldn't the police protect you and the children?'

She shook her head. 'This guy didn't act as if he was afraid of the law. I threatened to call the police. He just looked at me, and he didn't need to say a word: I knew that if I reached for the phone he'd break every bone in my hands to stop me. And then probably a few more to teach me a lesson.' She grimaced. 'He said Michael had three days to pay up, or else.'

'And you didn't go to the police?'

'I did, the very second he left, but I had no evidence. I couldn't describe the man in detail, I didn't know any names, and Michael wasn't talking. And I was so scared, Leo. Not for me, but for my babies. They were only two years old, still toddlers. I couldn't risk anything happening to them.' She closed her eyes. 'I could have forgiven Michael for lying to me—but I couldn't forgive him for putting our babies in danger. I asked him why he didn't go to the support group or to counselling. He said he didn't want to. And you can't change someone, Leo. If they don't want to change, you can nag and nag and nag until you're blue in the face—and all you'll do is give yourself a headache because they won't listen or do anything different. I told him I was leaving with the children, and as he'd clearly chosen gambling over us I was going to divorce him so I could keep them safe. My parents were brilliant. They took us in until I found my job at the Castle and this flat, and could get back on my own two feet.'

'And you divorced Michael and the thugs never came back?'

She blew out a breath. 'That's the bit I regret. The bit where I think maybe I should've done more. Because he died before I could even get an appointment with the solicitor,' she said. 'He was in a car accident.'

Something in her expression told him that there was more to it than that. 'But you don't think it was an accident?'

'I don't know. He was the only one involved. Michael, a tree and a soft-top car that I found out later was about to get repossessed because he hadn't kept up the payments.' She bit her lip. 'That man said he had three days to pay up. And the accident happened the day after the deadline.'

'So you think the bad guys had something to do with it?'

'I don't have any proof. I don't know if the people he owed money to decided to make an example of him for anyone else who thought about not paying them back, or whether Michael knew he'd run out of options and he drove straight into the tree because he couldn't see any other way out of the mess he'd made. Either way, I know I should've done more to help him. The crash was on a little country road and it was hours before anyone found him.' She looked haunted. 'His legs were shattered in the crash, and he bled out. He died all on his own, Leo, thinking everything was hopeless.'

'It wasn't your fault that he died, Rosie,' Leo said. 'You tried to get him to go to counselling. You found him a support group. He chose not to go. He lied to you about it, he got into even more debt with the wrong kind of people and he put the children at risk. You can't be responsible for someone else's choices.'

'What he did was wrong, but he didn't deserve to die for it.' She dragged a hand through her hair, looking weary. 'I told the police everything I knew, but there wasn't any evidence to back it up. And the people he owed money to haven't come after me, so I guess they must have decided that his death cleared his debt.'

'Do you see anything of Michael's family?'

She shook her head. 'He fell out with them before he met me. They didn't come to the wedding, even though we invited them. They've never even seen the twins.' She swallowed hard. 'And they didn't come to Michael's funeral.'

'It must've been a really bad row.' Despite his differences with his own father, Leo had attended the funeral. He'd even sat by his father's hospital bed for twenty-four hours straight after the first stroke, hoping that they might have some kind of reconciliation and he could help his father towards recovery. But the elder Leo had been intractable, and they hadn't reconciled properly before the second—fatal—stroke.

He still felt guilty, as if he could've done more. So he understood exactly where Rosie was coming from. And he wasn't sure if it was more a need to give or receive comfort that made him put his arms round her.

That first touch undid him even more than the first time when he'd hugged her and almost kissed her. This time, the impulse was way too strong to resist.

He could feel the warmth of her body through the material of her dress and his shirt, and it made him want more. He knew he shouldn't be doing this, but he couldn't help dipping his head and brushing his lips against hers. His mouth tingled where it touched hers, and warmth slid all the way down his spine.

Rosie was still for a moment, as if shocked that he'd made such a bold move—but then, just when he was about to pull away and apologise, she slid her hand round his neck and kissed him back. It felt as if fireworks were going off inside his head.

When he finally broke the kiss, her cheeks were flushed and her mouth was reddened and full. He had a feeling that he looked in the same kind of state.

'Sorry,' he said. 'I shouldn't have done that.'

She stroked his face. 'It wasn't just you,' she said wryly.

'So what are we going to do about this?' he asked. 'I like you, Rosie.'

'I like you, too,' she admitted.

There was a 'but'. He could see it in her expression.

'But we can't do this,' she said softly. 'Right now I'm focused on my children and my career.'

'That's totally understandable,' he said. She was a single mum. Of course her children had to come first.

'And you're only here on a temporary contract. I guess you'll be going back to Italy when it's over.'

'Maybe, maybe not.' He shrugged. 'My plans are quite fluid at the moment.'

She frowned. 'But you have commitments in Italy. You're a duke.'

'And, as I told you the other day, I delegate a lot of the work. I have excellent staff.'

'But at the end of the day you're still the Duke, and you have responsibilities,' she said. 'I imagine you'll have to marry some European princess.'

'Not necessarily a princess,' he said.

'But not a commoner.'

'That was a sticking point for my father,' he said—and then was horrified to realise what he'd just blurted out.

This dismay must've shown on his face, because she took his hand and squeezed it. 'Don't worry. I'm not going to spread that round the hospital or rush out to spill the beans to the first paparazzo I can find.'

'Thank you.' And he believed she'd keep his confidence, the way he'd keep hers.

'Considering what I just told you,' she said, 'if you ever want to talk…'

'Thank you.' Though he had no intention of telling her about his past. About Emilia, the girl he'd fallen in love with in his first week at university—and how his father had disapproved of Emilia's much poorer background. Leo hadn't realised it at the time, but his father had made life hard for her behind the scenes; his father had pulled strings and made it clear that he'd ruin her life if she didn't stop seeing Leo. Emilia had resisted for a while, but in the end she'd broken up with Leo. And she'd left university, too; he hadn't been able to track her down.

He'd learned the hard way that 'love conquers all' wasn't true. He'd loved Emilia and she'd loved him, but it hadn't been enough to overcome his father's opposition. And Leo hadn't been prepared to settle for an arranged marriage without love, or to bring a child into the dysfunctional world he'd grown up in. He wanted to change things. To make a difference to the world. To do *good*. And so he, too, had left the university at Rome, and applied to read medicine in London. His father had threatened to disown him, and by that point Leo had stopped caring about trying to please someone who could never, ever be pleased. He'd simply smiled and said, 'Do it.'

His father hadn't disowned him.

And Leo had still been stuck with the dukedom.

'Tell me,' she said softly.

He shook his head. 'Old news. And you can't change the past. I've come to terms with it.'

'Have you?'

'Probably not.' He couldn't stop himself running the pad of his thumb along her lower lip, and his whole body tightened when her beautiful blue eyes went dark with the same desire that flooded through him. 'What are we going to do about this thing between us?'

'I don't know. Pretend it isn't happening, I guess,' she said. 'I have to put the children first.'

'Agreed.'

'And you're probably not going to be around for long. I can't bring you into their lives, only for you to leave as soon as they get attached to you. I won't do that to them.'

It was so easy to break a child's heart. He knew that one first-hand and still had the scars from it. 'So see me when they're not around.'

'I'm a single mum, Leo. When I'm not at work, I'm with them all the time.'

'And at work we're both busy. I won't ask you to give up your lunchtimes reading to Penny. That wouldn't be fair to anyone.'

'So we're colleagues.' She paused. 'Maybe friends.'

That wasn't enough. 'I want to see you, Rosie,' he said softly. 'There has to be a way. Tell the children what you told them today—that I'm new at work and don't know many people at the hospital. That's true.'

She was silent for so long that he thought she was going to say no. Then she grimaced. 'Leo, I'm not very good at relationships.'

Neither was he.

'I find it hard to trust,' she admitted.

Given what she'd told him about her ex, that was understandable. 'I don't have any easy answers,' he said, not wanting to brush her feelings aside and make her feel that she was making a fuss over nothing. But he didn't want to make some glib, smooth reply, either. 'I have no idea where this is going. But I like you, Rosie, and I think you might like me. So isn't it worth a try?'

Again, she was silent while she thought about it. Finally, she nodded. 'As far as the children are concerned, you're *just* my friend from work. My friend who isn't going to be around for very long.'

'That's fair.' He paused. 'And when they're asleep… Then I get to hold your hand. To talk to you. To kiss you.'

She went very pink, and Leo couldn't resist stealing another kiss. Rosie Hobbes, now she was letting him a little closer, was utterly adorable.

'It's Sunday tomorrow,' she said, and Leo loved the fact that her voice had gone all breathy.

'So we can do something together, the four of us?'

'The park, maybe,' she suggested.

'That sounds good. Shall I pick you up or meet you there?'

'Meet us there,' she said. 'Half-past ten. I'll text you the postcode so you can find it on your satnav.'

'OK.' He stole another kiss. 'I'm going now. While I can still be on my best behaviour.'

The colour in her face deepened, and he guessed that she was wondering what it would be like if he wasn't on his best behaviour; even the thought of it made him feel hot and bothered.

'Tomorrow,' he said.

But on Sunday morning, when Leo was showering after his usual early-morning run, he realised how selfish he was being.

He'd let his attraction to Rosie get in the way of his common sense.

She was absolutely right. They shouldn't do this. She needed to put her children first. It wasn't fair for him to let her and the children get close to him, then walk away. She needed more than he could offer her—more than a fling. What did he know about a normal family life? This wasn't fair to any of them. He needed to do the right thing and call a halt.

As soon as he was dressed and his coffee was brewing, he texted her.

Sorry. Can't make it.

And hopefully by the time he saw her at work tomorrow he'd have a reasonable excuse lined up.

Sorry. Can't make it.

Rosie stared at the message on her phone.

So Leo had changed his mind about going to the park with her and the children. He hadn't even given a polite excuse, saying that he was needed at work or there was a family thing he had to sort out; he'd sent just a plain and simple statement that he wasn't coming.

So she'd been right to be wary of trusting him. OK, he hadn't bolted on seeing the twins and he'd even been really sweet with them, reading them a bedtime story and singing them a lullaby. But now he'd had time to think about it and clearly he'd realised that she wasn't what he wanted. She wasn't able to give him a simple, uncomplicated relationship; she came with baggage and a heap of mistrust. Plus, they came from such different worlds: he was the heir to a dukedom and she was a single mum of two. With all that, how could it possibly work?

She shouldn't have let down her guard last night. But instead she'd told him everything about Michael—and she'd let him kiss her.

What a fool she'd been.

Well, she'd still take the children to the park. They weren't going to miss out on a treat just because she'd been so foolish.

Tomorrow, when she had to face Leo at work, she'd act as if nothing had happened. And she'd keep him at a distance for the rest of his time at Paddington Children's Hospital.

CHAPTER FIVE

On Monday morning, Rosie kissed Freddie and Lexi goodbye at the hospital nursery school. 'See you after work,' she said with a smile.

'Are we going to have pizza with Leo tonight?' Freddie asked.

'No.'

Nina, the children's favourite classroom assistant, raised an eyebrow. 'Who's Leo?'

Oh, help, Rosie thought. Still, at least she was here when the subject was raised—and now she could make it very clear that the man the twins had adored when he'd met them on Saturday was absolutely not going to be a fixture in their lives. 'He's a new colleague,' Rosie said. 'You know what it's like when you start a new job and you don't know anyone. There's nothing worse than being all alone on a Saturday night, so I invited him to join us for pizza.'

'Uh-huh.' Nina didn't look the slightest bit convinced.

Rosie definitely didn't want this turning into hospital gossip. 'I think he has a soft spot for one of the nurses in the Emergency Department,' she said. It wasn't true, but she hadn't been specific so it wasn't *quite* the same as spreading a rumour. She was just deflecting the attention from herself. 'So now—thanks to the twins—he knows a nice pizza place to take someone to.'

'Right,' Nina said, still not looking completely convinced.

'My shift starts in five minutes. I need to go,' Rosie said, kissed the twins goodbye again and left before Nina could quiz her any further.

And of course the first person she saw when she walked onto the ward *would* have to be Leo Marchetti.

The man she'd thought would run a mile, but had surprised her.

The man who'd sung a lullaby to her children, then kissed her until her knees had gone weak.

The man who'd then changed his mind and lived all the way down to her original expectations.

'Dr Marchetti,' she said, and gave him a cool nod.

'Ros—' he began but, at her even cooler stare, he amended his words to, 'Nurse Hobbes.'

Worse still, she discovered that she was working in the allergy clinic with him all day.

Well, she could be professional. She could work with the man and make sure that their patients had the best possible care. And she'd make quite sure that all their conversations revolved around their patients.

'Our first patient is Madison Turner,' she said. 'She's six, had anaphylactic shock after being stung by a wasp, and this is her second appointment for venom immunotherapy. Two weeks ago, she had six injections over the course of a day and she responded well.'

'Good. So today she's due for three injections,' Leo said. 'Would you like to bring her in?'

'Of course, Dr Marchetti.' By the end of today, Rosie was sure she'd be sick to the back teeth of being polite and professional, but she'd do it for the sake of their patients. And she'd be very glad when her shift was over.

When she brought Madison and her mother in, Leo smiled at them and introduced himself. 'Good morning. You already know Nurse Hobbes. I'm Dr Marchetti—Dr Leo, if you prefer.'

'Good morning,' Mrs Turner said.

'Hello, Dr Leo,' Madison said shyly.

'Before we start, can I just check that you have your emergency kit with you,' Rosie asked, 'and that Madison had her antihistamines last night?'

'We did everything you said in your letter,' Mrs Turner confirmed.

'That's great. So how have you been doing since you came in last?' Leo asked Madison.

The little girl looked at her mum, who smiled and said, 'She's been fine. No problems. Her hay fever flared up a bit on the day we came here last, but Rosie had already told us to expect it and everything was fine after that.'

'Good. Today's going to be very similar to last time, except Madison will only have three injections instead of six,' Leo explained. 'We'll space them an hour apart, but we'd like you to stay in the department for an hour or so after she has the last one, so we can keep an eye on her in case of any allergic reactions.'

Mrs Turner patted her bag. 'We have books and a games console,' she said, 'plus drinks and snacks—nothing with nuts, in case someone else is allergic to them.'

'That's perfect,' Rosie said with a smile. 'If everything's OK today, we'll see you for a single injection next month, and then a monthly maintenance dose. Madison, Dr Leo needs to have a quick look at you and I need to take a few measurements and get you to blow into a tube for me—that's to check how your breathing is, so we're happy you're fine to have your next treatment. Is that OK?'

The little girl nodded, and between them Leo examined her and Rosie took all the obs and did a lung function test. 'Everything's fine,' she confirmed to Leo.

'Nurse Hobbes has some special cream so the injection won't be so sore,' Leo said, and Rosie used the anaesthetic cream to numb the injection site on Madison's skin.

'Mrs Turner, if Madison has any kind of allergy symptoms between now and the next injection, we'd like you to tell us straight away,' Leo said. 'I realise you probably already know them, but I like to be clear so I'll repeat them, if you don't mind. If Madison has a rash or any itching, if she feels dizzy or light-headed or generally not very well, if there's any swelling of her face, lips or tongue, if it's hard for her to breathe or if her heartbeat's too fast, then we need to know right away.'

'Got it,' Mrs Turner said.

'Madison, can you look at the butterfly on the ceiling and count the spots for me?' Leo asked, and swiftly administered the injection before she'd finished counting.

'Seven,' Madison said.

He smiled at her. 'Good girl. Thank you. We'll see you in an hour.'

Rosie followed the Turners out to the waiting room. 'Let us know if you're worried about anything,' she said. 'And you might find that, just like last time, Madison's hay fever is a little bit worse tonight, but an antihistamine will help.'

'We're prepared for that, thanks to you,' Mrs Turner

said. 'No hot baths tonight, either, and we need to just have a very quiet and lazy evening, right?'

'Right,' Rosie confirmed with a smile.

Leo noticed that Rosie was being super-professional with him. She only spoke to him when necessary between patients, and kept popping out to check on the children who, like Madison, were waiting between immunotherapy treatments. It felt as if she was avoiding him as much as she could.

He could understand why. After all, he'd been the one to back off on Sunday morning. He hadn't even given her a proper explanation, because he couldn't find the right words and he'd been selfish enough to take the easy option of saying nothing. To back away, just as he always did.

He sighed inwardly. He hadn't been fair to Rosie. He knew he ought to let her go, because he couldn't offer her a future; yet, at the same time, he was drawn to her and to the way that he'd felt as if he were part of a family on Saturday night. The whole thing threw him. He wasn't used to feeling confused and torn like this—torn between doing what he knew was the right thing and doing what he really wanted to do.

Rosie Hobbes was special. Walking away from her might be the stupidest thing he'd ever done. Yet at the same time he knew she was vulnerable; it wouldn't be fair of him to get involved with her and then walk away when his temporary contract came to an end.

The more he worked with her and saw the calm, kind way she dealt with even the most difficult and frightened of their little patients, the more he wanted her in his life.

Should he follow his heart or his head?

He still didn't have an answer by the end of the morning's clinic, but he needed to talk to her. The least she deserved was for him to apologise for backing off on Sunday and to explain why he'd acted so hurtfully.

'Ros—Nurse Hobbes,' he corrected himself. 'Can I talk to you over lunch?'

She shook her head. 'I'm reading to Penny.'

Of course. It was Monday. How could he have forgotten? 'After work?'

Again, she refused. 'I need to pick up the children.'

'Then during your break, this afternoon,' he said. 'I really think we need to talk.'

'There's absolutely nothing to say. We work together.' But her gaze had lingered just a little too long on his mouth. He had a feeling that she was remembering that kiss on Saturday and it was confusing her as much as it was confusing him. Or was he deluding himself?

'Please,' he said softly. 'Give me a chance to explain.'

She was silent for so long that he thought she was going to say no. Finally, she nodded. 'All right.'

'Coffee at Tony's?' he suggested, thinking there might be a tiny bit more privacy there than in the hospital canteen.

'There isn't really enough time. I'll meet you in the ward kitchen,' she countered.

He could put up with the vile instant coffee; what bothered him more was that it was usually busy in the ward kitchen. 'I'd rather talk somewhere a little quieter,' he said.

She was implacable. 'That's as quiet as you're going to get.'

'Fair enough.'

To his relief, the kitchen was empty when he got there

at the beginning of their afternoon break. He filled the kettle and switched it on, and had just made the coffee when she walked in.

'Thank you,' she said as he handed her the mug.

'No problem, Rosie.' Again, she skewered him with a look for using her first name. He sighed. 'If you would prefer me to call you "Nurse Hobbes", fine—but it's a bit formal for someone who kissed me back on Saturday night.'

'We all make mistakes.'

'Yes, and I made rather more of them than you did, this weekend,' he said wryly. 'Rosie.' This time, to his relief, she didn't correct him. 'I want to spend time with you,' he said. 'You *and* the twins.'

'Which is why you promised them you'd go to the park with us on Sunday, but you called it off at the last minute and didn't even give a reason?' she asked.

He raked a hand through his hair, knowing she was right to be upset with him about it. 'I wanted to go. But the three of you are vulnerable, and I don't want to lead you on.'

'It's not fair to Lexi and Freddie to let you into their lives, only for you to disappear again,' she said. 'Do you even know how long you're going to be in London? You're on a temporary contract, after all.'

'It's for a couple of months, but we might be able to extend it. If not, there are other hospitals in London.'

She frowned. 'So now you tell me that you're planning to stay in London?'

He couldn't answer that properly. 'It's possible.'

'Even so, you're a duke and I don't have even a drop of blue blood. I'm a single mum of two, and I'm just about the most unsuitable person you could get involved with.'

'You're kind, you're straight-talking and you're sweet,' he corrected, 'and I don't care about blue blood or difficult pasts.'

'You might not,' she said dryly, 'but your family might.'

'The one person who might've protested—no, I'll be honest with you,' he corrected himself, '*would* have protested, is dead.'

She looked completely confused.

He sighed. 'I trust you to keep my confidence, the way I'm keeping yours about Michael.'

She flinched, then nodded. 'Of course.'

'I didn't have the greatest time growing up.' It was the first time he'd really talked about it to anyone, and it made him uncomfortable. Like rubbing on a bruise so deep it hadn't even started colouring his skin yet. 'My father had pretty set views on life. I knew I was supposed to study for some kind of business degree to prepare me for taking over my father's duties on the estate and eventually inheriting the dukedom, and I guess I rebelled by going to university in Rome rather than nearby in Florence. I thought I'd get a bit more freedom there.'

'But you didn't?'

He shrugged. 'At first, I really thought I had. I fell in love with a girl I met in my first week there—Emilia. I thought she loved me, too. She was sweet and kind and clever, and I was so sure my parents would love her as much as I did.' He paused. 'And then I made the mistake of taking her back to Tuscany for the weekend.'

'Your parents didn't like her?'

'My mother did. My father decided that she wasn't good enough for me. So he warned her off.'

Rosie looked shocked. 'And she accepted that?'

'I didn't realise at the time how much he leaned on her. She must have resisted him at first, but then suddenly there were all these little administrative mistakes that made her life difficult—her finances were late, or her rent showed up as unpaid, even though she'd paid it and had a receipt. Her marks started dropping and her future at the university was under threat. Her part-time employer suddenly changed his mind about her working for him, and she didn't even get an interview for everything else she applied for. I didn't connect it at the time, but my father was behind it all. The longer Emilia dated me, the harder it got for her, until she did what he wanted and broke up with me. Then she left the university,' he said quietly.

'That's awful,' Rosie said.

'I tried very hard to find her—I even used a private investigator—but she went completely to ground. I had a feeling my father was behind her disappearance, so I confronted him about it.' It had been the worst row they'd ever had. The first time Leo had really stood up for himself. His father had taken it extremely badly. 'Let's just say my father epitomised everything I don't stand for. And that's when I realised that he was never going to change. He'd manipulated her and he was always going to try and manipulate me because that was who he was. I could either let him do it, or I could stop trying to please a man who'd never be pleased, no matter what I did. I might have to inherit the dukedom, but I decided I'd do it my way. I left Rome and I applied to read medicine in London—so I'd have a career where I could give back some of my privileges, instead of trying to take more.'

She reached out and took his hand. 'I'm sorry you didn't have the right support when you were younger.'

'Plenty of people have had it much worse than me. I shouldn't complain.'

'What about your mum? Didn't she try to talk your dad round?'

'My father was quite forceful in his views,' he said. 'It was easier for her to agree with him.'

'That's something I don't understand,' she said softly. 'Because I'd never let anyone hurt my children. Including their father. That's why I left Michael, and why I changed the children's names along with mine.'

'You're a strong woman,' he said. 'Not everyone is like that.' His mother probably would've liked to be, but Leo came from a line of old-fashioned men who believed that a woman's place was to shut up and agree with her husband, and a child's place was to ask 'how high?' when his father said 'jump'. And his mother's family was the same. Even the kindest heart could get beaten into submission. And sometimes words left more scars than physical blows. He could understand now why Beatrice hadn't tried to stand up to her husband.

'Not everyone has the support behind them to help,' Rosie said, going straight to the core of things. 'My family was brilliant. They backed me.'

'You're one of the lucky ones,' he said.

'Did you try looking for Emilia again when you came to London?'

'I found her before that,' he said.

The bleakness in Leo's eyes told Rosie this wasn't a story with a happy ending. 'What happened to her?' she asked gently.

'After Emilia left Italy, she did charity work in Africa. While she was out there, she caught a virus.' He looked away. 'She was too far from the medical care she needed. She never made it home.'

Rosie winced. 'That's so sad. Is that why you chose to study medicine?'

'It's one of the reasons, yes,' he said. 'Plus, everyone's equal in medicine. And it means I can give something back.'

Leo Marchetti was a good deal more complicated than she'd thought he was, Rosie realised. Despite all that privileged upbringing, he'd had his heart well and truly broken. Not just because he'd lost the woman he'd fallen in love with, but because his father sounded like a complete control freak. If he'd been so desperate to control Leo that he'd bullied Emilia into leaving, what else had he done? It sounded as if Leo's mother hadn't been able to stand up to her husband, either.

No wonder Leo was wary about families, after such a miserable childhood. No wonder he hadn't wanted any relationship to get serious. But she came with a family: how could it work out between them?

'So where do we go from here?' she asked.

'If I'm honest, I don't know,' he said. 'I understand why you don't want to get involved. I'm not exactly looking for a relationship, either.'

At least he was up front about it. 'The papers all say you're a playboy.'

He grimaced. 'The press will say anything to sell copies. Yes, I've dated a lot in the past, but I don't make promises I can't keep and I don't lie my way into someone's bed. I offer my girlfriends a good time, yes, but I make it clear that it's fun for now and not for always.'

'I have the twins to think of,' she said. 'I can't just have a fling with you because it's not fair to them. And you can't offer me more than a fling, so...' She spread her hands. 'Maybe we should just call it a day. Maybe we can be friends.'

'I don't want to be just your friend,' he said.

'So what do you want?' she asked.

'That's the thing, Rosie,' he said. 'I want you.'

His dark eyes were soulful and full of sincerity. And even though Rosie found it hard to believe anything a man told her—she'd heard too many lies to take things at face value any more—Leo had shown her that he trusted her. He'd told her things that the gossip magazines would no doubt love to know—and he was trusting her not to break the story to the press. So maybe, just maybe, she could trust him.

'My head's telling me I should back away now —that it's going to cause no end of complications if I do what my heart's telling me to do,' he said.

'What's your heart telling you to do?' she asked.

'Something different. To take a risk,' he said. 'I like you and I think you like me.'

His admission made her feel as if all the air had just been sucked out of her lungs. Yes. She did like Leo. She thought she could like him a lot. But seeing him... Would that be a huge mistake? 'So what are you suggesting?' she asked.

'That we see where this takes us.'

'We've already discussed this. I come as a package, Leo. I have two three-year-olds,' she reminded him.

'I appreciate that, and I'm including them in this whole thing. We've already told them that I'm your friend from work. Right now, they don't need to know anything more complicated than that. As far as they're concerned, you're being kind to me because I don't know many people. And, actually, that's a really good example to set them.'

Rosie thought about it. Maybe this was a way to have it all—to see Leo on more than just a friendship basis, but for the twins to think that he was just her friend.

But what if she got it wrong? What effect would it have on Lexi and Freddie if they got close to him and then he disappeared out of their lives?

On the other hand, she knew it would be good for Freddie to have another male role model in his life, even if it was only for a little while. And the Leo Marchetti she was beginning to know was a decent man. He'd be a good role model.

'No strings,' she said. 'And the children don't get hurt. They come first.'

'Absolutely,' he said.

Excitement fluttered low down in her belly. This was the first time in nearly five years that she'd agreed to date someone. And Leo Marchetti wasn't just someone: he was the most attractive man she'd met in a very long time.

'So what happens now?' she asked. 'I'm a bit rusty when it comes to dating.'

He smiled. 'It's not exactly the thing I'm best at, either. Which is how come I've got this stupid reputation as a playboy. Even though I'm not one really.' He swallowed hard. 'Since Emilia, I haven't met anyone I've wanted to get close to. Until now. Until *you*.'

Which was honest. And he'd gone a step further with her, admitting that he didn't have a clue where this was going to take them. 'Thank you for being honest,' she said. And she needed to be equally as straight with him: they didn't have a future. How could they, when their worlds were so different? 'Just so it's clear, I'm not looking for a stepfather for Freddie and Lexi.'

'So is this going to make us friends with benefits?' he asked.

'I don't know—but I think we've all been hurt enough. Just as long as we don't expect too much from each other, I guess.'

'We'll play it by ear, then, and muddle through together,' he suggested.

'OK.'

'When are you free this week?' he asked.

'I was going to take the children to the park on Wednesday, on the way home from here. You could come with us, if you like, and then have dinner with us at home afterwards?'

He smiled. 'Thank you. I'd like that very much.'

Rosie wasn't sure if she was doing the right thing or not, but maybe her sister and her parents and her closest friends were right and it was time to try again, put the past behind her. Leo had been damaged, too, and she realised now that he'd backed away on Sunday more from a fear of hurting anyone than from seeing the children as a burden. Maybe a few dates with no strings would do them both good. 'Wednesday, then. And we're both due back in clinic.'

'Indeed. And thank you, Rosie. For giving us a chance.' He leaned forward and kissed her on the cheek. It was the lightest contact, but it made her skin tingle. And she remembered how it had felt when he'd kissed her properly on Saturday.

A new beginning.

Maybe it wouldn't work out.

But they were both adults. They'd make sure that Freddie and Lexi weren't hurt; and they could try to enjoy this thing between them while it lasted.

CHAPTER SIX

On Wednesday afternoon, Leo collected something he'd stowed in his locker, then waited for Rosie outside the hospital while she collected the twins from the hospital nursery school.

Lexi gave him an accusing look when they stopped in front of him. 'You didn't come to the park with us. You said you would.'

'I know, and I'm sorry I let you down. But your *mamma* says we can go today on the way home,' Leo said.

'Are you coming with us?' Freddie asked, looking faintly suspicious.

'I am, if you don't mind,' Leo said solemnly. He held out the bag he was carrying. 'I thought maybe we could play ball. If you like playing ball?'

'I want to go on the swings,' Lexi said.

'And I want to go on the slide,' Freddie said.

'How about,' Rosie suggested, 'we do all three?'

The twins looked at each other, then at her, and nodded.

As they walked to the park, Leo was surprised and touched that Freddie wanted to hold his hand on the way. It gave him an odd feeling. He couldn't really remember going to a park when he was small, even with his nanny;

whereas clearly this was something that Rosie did regularly with her children and they all looked forward to it.

Once they were at the small enclosed playground, Leo pushed Lexi on the swings while Rosie pushed Freddie.

This was all very, very domestic and so far out of Leo's experience that it scared him stupid. Though he knew that if he backed away from Rosie again, she wouldn't give him another chance. He had to damp down the fear of the unknown and the fear of getting too involved.

They headed for the slide next. It was high, and wide enough for about four people to go down at a time; Leo was slightly surprised that Rosie, who was a bit on the over-protective side where the twins were concerned, was actually letting them go on it.

'Will you slide down with me, Leo?' Freddie asked.

'What's the missing word, Freddie?' Rosie asked quietly.

'Please,' Freddie added swiftly, and Rosie gave him a thumbs-up.

'Sure,' Leo said. He helped the little boy climb up to the top of the slide and sat down next to him on the platform.

'I have to hold your hand or we can't go down,' Freddie informed him.

Leo wasn't sure whether that was Freddie's way of saying that he was a bit scared, or whether it was one of Rosie's rules to keep her children safe on the slide. Either way, he wasn't going to make a fuss about it. 'Sure,' he said, and held Freddie's hand. 'Ready?'

'Ready,' the little boy confirmed.

'After three. One, two, three—go!'

Rosie took her phone out of her bag and snapped a

photograph of them on the way down, then smiled at him as they reached the bottom.

The sudden rush of adrenaline through Leo's blood had nothing to do with the slide and everything to do with that smile.

Lexi and Rosie went next, and Leo took a picture of them on his phone.

'You go down with Mummy, next,' Lexi said when they walked over to Leo and Freddie.

What could he do but agree?

At the top, Freddie called, 'Mummy, take a picture!'

'Do you mind?' Rosie asked.

He knew she wouldn't pass it to the press or make life difficult for him. 'Sure.'

Once Rosie had taken the photo and tucked her phone back into the pocket of her jeans, Lexi called, 'You have to hold hands!'

If he refused, then he'd be undermining Rosie's rule for the children—which wouldn't be fair. If he held her hand, he'd be undermining his own resolve not to get too close. Either way, this was going to be tricky.

'Ready?' Rosie asked softly.

'Yes,' he lied.

She took his hand. His skin tingled where it touched hers and he suddenly really wanted to kiss her, but he managed to hold himself in check. That was absolutely not going to happen in front of the children.

Sliding down towards the children, seeing them clap their hands with glee, made something around the region of his heart feel as if it had just cracked. And then going down the slide again with Lexi, and finally the four of them together, all holding hands and whooping at the

same time... It was something he'd never done before.
Something that felt really, really good.

They played ball and had another last go on the swings
before Rosie called a halt. 'Time for tea,' she said.

'We're having macanoni, 'cause it's Wednesday,' Freddie told him seriously as Rosie unlocked her front door.

Leo hid a smile at the little boy's charming mispronunciation. 'I love macaroni,' he said.

'Good, because I feel a bit bad cooking pasta for an
Italian,' Rosie said.

Leo laughed. 'Macaroni cheese isn't actually Italian.
It was invented in England.'

'Seriously?'

'Seriously—obviously there have been pasta and
cheese dishes in Italy for centuries,' he said, 'and some
were even recorded in a fourteenth-century Italian cook-
book called *Liber de Coquina*. There's a version in an
English cookery book around the same kind of date, but
the first modern recipe for macaroni cheese is actually
in an English book from the middle of the eighteenth
century.'

Rosie looked even more surprised. 'How do you know
this? Did you study cookery or something before you
studied medicine?'

'I found out in the general knowledge round at a pub
quiz,' he admitted. 'Anyway, I really don't care who invented it. I like it.' He paused. 'Anything I can do to
help?'

'Sure. You can help lay the table with Freddie and
Lexi, and help them with the drinks,' she said. 'And if
you want some wine, there's a bottle in the rack.'

'I'll have whatever you're having,' he said.

She smiled, and his heart felt as if it had done a backflip. 'I like red or white, so pick what you prefer. Oh, and we have strawberries for pudding.'

While the macaroni cheese—which she'd clearly made the previous night—was heating through in the oven, Rosie started chopping salad, and he helped the twins lay the table and put beakers out for water.

'Mummy says we're not big enough to carry a jug yet,' Lexi confided, looking slightly forlorn.

'You will be, soon,' he said, and filled the jug with water before taking it to the table and opening a bottle of red wine for himself and Rosie.

He chatted to the twins while Rosie finished up in the kitchen, enjoying the way they opened up to him and told him all about their day, what they'd drawn and sung and glued. And it somehow felt natural to let them curl up each side of him on the sofa and teach him one of their nursery songs.

Rosie lingered in the doorway, watching Leo with her two very earnest children. Of course he was good with kids; it was his day job, after all. But she liked the way he behaved with them, persuading them to take turns and giving shy Freddie that little bit of extra encouragement so his confidence started to grow to match his sister's.

Was Leo Marchetti the one who could change her life for the better?

Or would he back away again when he realised that treating children in a hospital was very different from living with them every day?

At least they'd agreed that he wouldn't let the children get too attached to him: that as far as the twins were concerned Leo was simply her colleague and a friend, and not a potential replacement father.

She brought in the dish of macaroni cheese and served up, encouraging the twins to add salad to their plates.

'This is very nice. Thank you,' Leo said after his first forkful.

Was he just being polite? Rosie wondered. This was a far cry from his normal life. Although she was a reasonable cook, she didn't kid herself that she made anything exceptional. This was all just ordinary stuff. Very domestic. A world away from how the Duke of Calvanera lived.

Once they'd finished their pasta and demolished a large bowl of strawberries between them, Rosie announced that it was time for bath and bed.

'But we want to stay up with Leo!' Lexi protested.

'Bath and bed now,' Rosie said firmly. 'Otherwise you'll be too tired to do anything at nursery school tomorrow morning. And I happen to know you're doing splatter painting tomorrow.'

'Yay! My favourite,' Freddie said. 'Lexi, we have to have our bath now.'

'I'll do the washing up,' Leo offered.

Rosie shook her head. 'It's fine. I understand if you need to get on.'

'No. You cooked. Washing up is the least I can do,' Leo said.

'Will you read us another bedtime story?' Lexi asked.

'Please?' Freddie added.

'That's up to your mum,' Leo said.

How could she refuse? 'If you don't mind, Leo, that would be lovely.'

He came upstairs when she'd got the twins bathed and in their pyjamas. 'So what story would you like tonight?'

'The dinosaur story, please!' they chorused.

Rosie leaned against the door jamb and watched him

read to the children. He seemed to be enjoying himself, and the children enjoyed it enough to cajole him into reading a second story to them.

'Time to say goodnight,' she said gently when he'd finished, knowing that they could badger him into half a dozen more stories.

Lexi held her arms up towards him. 'Kiss goodnight,' she said sleepily.

'Me, too,' Freddie said, doing the same.

Leo glanced at Rosie for permission. Part of her felt she ought to say no—she didn't want Leo getting close to the children and then leaving. Yet how could she deprive them of that warmth—a simple, sweet kiss goodnight? She gave a tiny nod.

'Goodnight. Sleep tight,' he whispered, kissing each of them on the forehead in turn, and being hugged tightly by both twins.

'Thank you,' she said quietly when they were downstairs again. 'I appreciate you being kind to them.'

'They're lovely children,' Leo said.

Was that a hint of wistfulness she saw in his face? she wondered.

'And I enjoyed this evening. I can't remember the last time I went down a slide.'

Definitely wistfulness, Rosie thought. Leo clearly hadn't had much of a chance to visit a playground when he was young. Poor little rich boy, probably having everything his parents could buy him and yet not having a normal childhood where he was free to run and laugh and play.

'I'm glad you came with us.' She paused. 'Would you like another glass of wine?'

He shook his head. 'I left my car at the hospital.'

Which was his cue to leave. And probably the best thing, she thought.

'But I'd like to stay for a little longer, if that's OK with you,' he said.

He rested his palm against her cheek, and her mouth went dry.

It went drier still when he rubbed the pad of his thumb against her lower lip.

And then he bent his head and brushed his mouth against hers. What else could she do but slide her hands round his neck and lean against him, letting him deepen the kiss?

She was dizzy by the time he broke the kiss.

'My beautiful Rosie,' he whispered. 'Right now I just want to hold you.'

Unable to form any kind of coherent sentence, she simply nodded.

She hadn't expected him to scoop her up and carry her to the sofa, and it made her knees go weak. 'That's...' All the rest of the words went out of her head when he sat down and settled her on his lap.

'A bit caveman-like,' he finished wryly. 'But you're irresistible. You remind me of Titian's *Flora*.'

'Flora?'

He took his phone from his pocket, looked up the portrait on the Internet and handed the phone to her. 'Obviously your hair's shorter—but you're beautiful, like her.'

All curves, Rosie thought as she looked at the portrait. Michael had liked her curves until she was pregnant; then he'd considered her to be fat and unattractive.

She pushed the thought away and handed the phone back to Leo. 'Thank you for the compliment. Sorry. I don't know a lot about art.'

'I spent a lot of time in the Uffizi in my teens,' he said. 'This was always one of my favourites.' He stole another kiss. 'Tell me about your teens.'

'There isn't really that much to tell. I spent my time with my sister and friends, doing the kind of things teenage girls do,' she said. 'Trying out different make-up, doing each other's hair, talking and listening to music.' She smiled. 'And films. Monday night was cheap night when I was a student nurse, so a group of us used to go out every Monday when we weren't on placement or doing a late shift.'

'Any particular favourites?' he asked.

'We'd see anything and everything,' she said. 'Freddie and Lexi like the cinema, too. I try to take them to see all the animated films, because they're so magical on a big screen. One or other of them always needs the loo halfway through, but they love going to see a film.'

Again, he looked wistful. Clearly his parents hadn't done that sort of thing with him when he was young. 'Maybe we could do something like that at the weekend.'

'Maybe,' she said. 'So your teens were spent mooching about museums?'

'And studying. And trying to wriggle out of deadly dull functions.'

Where his father had shown him off as the heir? She sensed it was a sore spot, but she didn't know what to say. The only thing she could think of to do was to kiss him. Judging by how dark his eyes were when she finally broke the kiss, it had been the right thing to do.

She stayed curled on his lap with her arms round him, just chatting idly. Finally, he stole a last kiss. 'I'd better let you get some sleep.'

'Are you OK to get back to your car from here?'

He smiled. 'Yes, but thanks for asking.'

She had the strongest feeling that people didn't tend to try to look after Leo Marchetti very much. Maybe it was because he was so capable and efficient at work; or maybe it was because everyone assumed that the Duke's personal staff kept his life completely in order. But did anyone really see the man behind the doctor and the dukedom? 'I'll see you at work tomorrow, then.'

'Yes. Goodnight.'

Rosie was still smiling when she'd finished brushing her teeth and was curled up in bed. Just spending time with Leo had felt so good. Her children liked him, too. So did she dare to keep dreaming that this might actually work out?

On Thursday, Leo was working in clinic while Rosie was working on the ward, but he caught up with her at lunchtime.

'Had a good morning?' he asked.

'Yes and no.' She sighed. 'I was looking after young Ryan today.'

'How's he doing?'

'He's showing small signs of improvement, but he's still unconscious.' She bit her lip. 'It's really tough on his parents.'

'Do you think he's going to recover?' Leo asked.

'I really don't know. In some respects, it's kind of early days; in others, it...' She shook her head and grimaced. 'And then there's Penny.'

The young patient who was a favourite with everyone who met her. 'She's on the transplant list now?'

'Yes. And now it's a waiting game.' Rosie stared into her coffee. 'They're both so young. And, despite all the advances in medicine and the different treatments, are we really going to make the right difference to either of them?'

'Yes. Years ago, they wouldn't even have come this far,' Leo reminded her. 'But you're right. It's hard on the parents.'

'I was just thinking. If the worst happens—and I really hope it doesn't, for his family's sake—then it would be good if Ryan turned out to be a match for Penny,' Rosie said softly.

'So at least one of them would be saved?'

She nodded, and he reached across the table to squeeze her hand briefly.

'Sometimes this job is tough,' he said.

'You're telling me.' She blew out a breath. 'Sometimes I look at Penny and Ryan and Simon, and it makes me want to run down to the hospital nursery school so I can hug Freddie and Lexi really, really tightly.'

'Of course it does. You're a mum, so you have a pretty good idea of what your patients' parents are feeling.'

'I just wish I had a magic wand.'

'Me, too,' he agreed softly. 'But we're doing the best we can.' Even if it sometimes felt as though it wasn't enough.

On Friday night, Leo texted Rosie.

Do you want to go to the cinema tomorrow? Have looked at schedules.

Nothing really suitable, was the reply.
Was she backing away from him?
His phone beeped again.

How about the aquarium?

Fine. Meet you when and where?

Tube station at ten? she suggested.

I'll be there.

She was already there when he walked to meet her.
The twins jumped about in excitement when he walked
up to them, and hugged him round his knees—something he hadn't expected, and another little shard of ice
around his heart melted.

'We're going to see the sharks!' Freddie said.

'And the starfishies,' Lexi added. 'I love starfishies.'

Clearly this was something they were really looking
forward to. It was another thing way outside his experience, but Leo found himself thoroughly enjoying the
visit, and the twins' excitement was definitely infectious.
He lifted one or the other up every so often so they could
have a closer look at the occupants of a tank; and he noticed that Rosie got them to count the fish and name colours and shapes.

'How many arms does your starfish have?' he asked
Lexi.

She counted them, then beamed at him. 'Five!'

'Well done.' He smiled back at her.

There was a play area in the central hall where the
youngest children could do colouring and older ones
could answer quizzes. On impulse, when Lexi and Freddie sat down, he crouched beside them. 'Shall I draw
something for you to colour?'

'Yes, please!' they chorused.

'A shark for you, Lexi, and a starfish for you, Freddie?' he asked, teasing them.

'No, that's silly—it's the other way round!' Lexi said.

Freddie just clapped his hands with glee as he watched Leo draw.

He glanced up at Rosie. Were those tears he saw in her eyes? But why? What had he done wrong?

Once they'd finished laboriously colouring in the shapes, they looked at Rosie. 'Can you write our names, please, Mummy?' Lexi asked.

'Sure. Can you spell them for me?' Rosie asked. Leo watched as both children looked very earnest and spelled out their names phonetically; Rosie wrote down what they said.

'Thank you, Mummy,' Freddie said, then turned to Leo and gave him the shark picture. 'This is for you.'

'So's this,' Lexi added, not to be outdone and thrusting her starfish picture at him.

'Thank you, both of you,' Leo said. 'I'll put the pictures up when I get home.'

'On your fridge, like Mummy does?' Lexi wanted to know.

'Absolutely like Mummy does,' he said with a smile.

When they walked through the shark tunnel, the twins were both shrieking with joy and pointing out the sharks swimming overhead. Rosie was smiling, but she took their hands and crouched down beside them for a moment. 'I know you're excited, but you'll scare the sharks if you keep screaming. Can we pretend to be mice?'

'But mice don't live in the sea,' Freddie said. 'They live in houses.'

'You could be a new species,' Leo said. 'Sea mice.'

The twins thought about it, then nodded and were

much quieter—still pointing out the sharks but careful to whisper.

Rosie caught Leo's eye. 'Thank you,' she mouthed.

Once they were through the tunnel and Rosie had bought a new storybook about Sammy the Shy Shark, they headed out to the South Bank. They all enjoyed hot dogs from one of the street food vendors, then sat down on a bench to eat *churros* with chocolate sauce while they watched some of the street entertainers, a juggler and a woman making balloon dogs. Both children ended up with their faces covered with chocolate, and Leo made the mistake of buying them each a balloon dog before Rosie had wiped their hands and faces clear—they insisted on kissing him thank you, smearing his cheeks with chocolate.

Rosie laughed and took a photograph of them all posing with chocolaty faces before giving him a wipe from her handbag and cleaning the twins up.

By the time they were back at Rosie's, the children were worn out. They managed half a sandwich before they nearly fell asleep at the table.

'No bath tonight, I think,' she said with a smile. 'Straight to bed with a story.'

Leo helped her get the children into their pyjamas and tucked them in; again, the domestic nature and the closeness made him feel as if something was cracking around his heart.

'I didn't think about dinner tonight. The best I can offer is a takeaway,' she said.

'Which would be lovely. And I'll pay, because you fed me on Wednesday,' he said.

They shared a Chinese meal, then curled up on the

sofa. 'I meant to ask you earlier,' he said. 'What did I do to upset you?'

'Upset me?' She looked confused.

'In the aquarium. You looked as if you were blinking back tears.'

'Ah. That.' Her face cleared. 'You drew them a picture of their favourite sea creatures so they could colour them in.'

She didn't say it, but he had the strongest feeling that Michael had never done anything like that. 'I didn't mean to make you cry.'

'They were happy tears,' she said softly.

'Even so, I can still kiss you better.' And how right it felt, to hold her close and kiss her until they were both dizzy.

Leo was beginning to think that this might be what he actually wanted his life to be like—a job he adored at the hospital, and the warmth and domesticity of Rosie and the twins. He just needed to find a way to square it with his duties in Tuscany. Though he knew it was way too early to be thinking about that. For now, he'd just enjoy spending time with her.

At the end of the evening, he kissed her goodnight. 'See you at work on Monday.'

'See you Monday,' she agreed. 'And thank you for today. I had a fabulous time and so did the twins.'

'Me, too,' he said.

'Oh, before I forget.' She rummaged in her handbag and brought out a tiny paper bag with the logo of the aquarium on it.

'What's this?' he asked.

'Just a little something.'

He opened the bag to find two magnets: one shaped like a shark and one like a pink starfish.

'You told the twins you were going to put their pictures on your fridge. I'm guessing that you might be a bit short on magnets,' she explained.

'I am,' he agreed. His flat was pristine, like a show house, with no little decorative touches whatsoever. The magnets and the pictures might just be the first step to turning it into a home. 'Thank you.' He kissed her again, more lingeringly this time. 'Monday.'

'Monday,' she said.

And for the first time in a very long time, Monday morning felt like a promise.

CHAPTER SEVEN

'ARE YOU BUSY at the weekend?' Leo asked Rosie on Monday evening.

'Why?'

He stole a kiss. 'It's rude to answer a question with a question.'

'I don't have anything planned,' she said.

'Good.' He paused. 'Do the children have passports?'

'Yes, though they haven't actually been abroad. Why?'

'I was just wondering—would you like to come to Tuscany for the weekend?'

She blinked. 'Tuscany? Are you…' It was suddenly hard to breathe. 'Leo, are you asking me to meet your family?'

'Yes and no,' Leo hedged.

'Which doesn't exactly tell me anything,' she pointed out.

'There aren't any strings. I need to be in Tuscany for the weekend, and I thought you and the children might like to enjoy a bit of summer sun. Plus, I've been telling Lexi that the best ice cream ever comes from Italy, and it's about time I proved it.'

'So would we be staying at your family home?'

'The Palazzo di Calvanera. Yes.' He smiled at her.

'Mamma's a little frail. Although I speak to her every day, and I know her companion will tell me if she's in the slightest bit worried about my mother's health, I like to keep an eye on her myself as well. Going to see her at the weekend will put my mind at rest.'

Of course Leo would be a dutiful son.

But Rosie also remembered what he'd told her about Emilia, the girl he'd fallen in love with at university. The girl his family hadn't considered good enough for him. Would Leo's mother decide that, as a single mum of two, Rosie was also completely the wrong sort of person for her son?

'Maybe your mother would prefer you to visit on your own,' she suggested warily.

'I'm sure she'd enjoy meeting you and the children.'

How could she explain her worries? That this was suddenly sounding really serious—as if he was starting to expect things of their relationship? Things that she might not be able to deliver? 'You and me... It's still very early days,' she said.

'True.' He drew her hand up to his mouth and kissed the backs of her fingers.

'I don't want to give your mother the wrong impression.'

'There's no pressure,' he reassured her. 'I just thought you might like to see the *palazzo*. It has an amazing rose garden. And a lake. The children will love running around the place.'

A lake. Which might not be fenced off. Which would be dangerous for the children. She pushed the thoughts away. She could run faster than they could, and she could swim. There was a more immediate danger than the one she was imagining. 'Meeting your mother—does that mean you expect to meet my family?'

'I've already met the twins,' he pointed out.

'That isn't what I mean, and you know it. This thing between us... We agreed we'd take things slowly and see what happened.'

'Which is exactly what we're doing.'

What, when he was asking them to visit his family home and to meet his mother?

Her doubts must have shown on her face, because he said again, 'Rosie, there's no pressure. Tuscany will just be a little break for us, that's all. A chance to have some fun. And I can show Freddie the suits of armour and Lexi all the portraits of the Duchesses.'

He wasn't playing fair. He knew she'd find it hard to say no where her children were concerned. 'Supposing your mother doesn't like me?'

'My mother,' he said softly, 'will like you very much. You're honest, you're open and you're caring. And she's not bothered about blue blood.'

But his father had been very bothered indeed.

Again, her feelings must have shown on her face, because he added, 'My father would have thought you way too uppity. You wouldn't have liked him very much, either. But Mamma's different. She doesn't share his views. You'll like each other.'

'I don't know,' she said.

'If you're worried about the travelling, I'm using a friend's plane. There won't be lots of queuing at the airport or anything.'

She blinked. 'Hang on. You're using a private plane?'

'It's not as fancy as it sounds. It's quite small,' Leo said.

'My friends own *cars*, not planes.' She couldn't quite

get her head round this. 'Leo, I think your world is very, very different from mine.'

'Not at heart, it isn't. And actually I was going to ask you a favour over the weekend.'

'So there are strings attached?'

'No. Of course not.' He frowned. 'You can say no. But part of my duties… The main reason I'm going back is because there's a charity ball in aid of a clinic I support, and I need to be there.'

'What kind of clinic?'

'Paediatric medicine. For children whose families can't afford to pay for treatment,' he explained.

She frowned. 'So healthcare in Italy isn't like it is in England?'

'It's actually very similar, a mix of public and private healthcare,' he said. 'Family doctors are paid for by the Ministry of Health, like they are here in England, and emergency care and surgery are both free. You pay some money towards medication, depending on your income; and if your family doctor refers you to a specialist or for diagnostic tests, you only have to pay a little bit towards it. But waiting times can be quite long, so there are private hospitals where you can pay a bit more money to see the specialist or have treatment a bit sooner.'

'And that's what this clinic is? A private hospital, except patients don't pay?'

He nodded. 'I also work there when I'm in Italy.'

He'd said that he had an interest in philanthropic medicine. Obviously supporting this clinic was part of that, Rosie thought.

'So I was wondering if you might accompany me to the ball.'

'What about the children?' Rosie asked. They could

hardly go to a glitzy ball. Apart from the fact that they were too young to attend in the first place, the ball probably wouldn't start until way past their bedtime.

'I can arrange a babysitter for them,' he said.

'No.'

He frowned. 'What do you mean, no?'

'Leo, do you really expect me to leave my children in a strange place with someone I don't know?'

'It's my home, and I know the babysitter,' he pointed out. 'I think I already told you that my mother has a companion, Violetta. Her daughter Lisetta lives nearby and I'm sure she'd be very happy to babysit.'

So he hadn't even asked the babysitter yet? Then again, that was fair—he hadn't known if Rosie would say yes or no to his invitation. Even so, the whole idea freaked her. 'Leo, the point is that *I* don't know her,' she countered. 'Yes, I know it's your home, but do you seriously think I'd be happy to leave my children in a country where they don't speak the language—where *I* don't speak the language, for that matter—with someone they don't know and I don't know?' She took a deep breath. 'Look, I know I'm overprotective, but no mother on earth would agree to anything like that.'

He looked at her. 'But *I* know Lisetta. I've known her for years. Isn't that good enough?'

'How can you not see that it isn't?' Rosie asked.

Leo thought about it. Part of him thought that Rosie was being unreasonable; it wasn't as if he was asking her to leave the children with someone who was a complete stranger. He'd known Lisetta since she was small, and he knew she was kind and she was good with children. Then again, a year ago, Rosie's husband's associate had threatened to hurt the children. Of course she'd be more protective than the average parent.

'I've known Lisetta for years and I trust her,' he said. 'Of course I understand that you're worried. It's natural. But I trust Lisetta, and I hope you know me well enough to realise that I'd be careful with your children and I wouldn't expect you to leave them with just anybody. I also have a security team at the *palazzo*, so no stranger will ever get anywhere near the children. They'll be perfectly safe. I guarantee that.'

She blew out a breath. 'OK. Let's put it another way. Your mum's not in the best of health. Would you bring her over to London and then leave her on her own for the evening with someone she didn't know—someone who didn't speak the same language as her—while you went out partying?'

'It isn't partying. It's a charity ball and attending it is part of my duties to the clinic—to the estate, actually, because some of the funds for the clinic come from the estate. Anyway, my mother speaks good English, and so does Lisetta. There won't be a language barrier for the children.'

Rosie put her hands over her face and groaned in apparent frustration. 'You're really not listening to me. Would you leave your mother with someone she didn't know and you didn't know, either—say, my neighbour?'

'If you vouched for your neighbour, then yes. Your word is good enough for me.'

'And I guess in that situation your mother could call you if there was a problem. But it's not the same thing for the children. The twins won't be able to call me if they're worried. They're only three.' She shook her head. 'It's lovely of you to ask me, Leo, but I really can't leave them with a stranger, even though she's somebody you know. I just can't do it.'

'What if,' Leo said, 'we took a babysitter with us—someone you know?'

'How do you mean?'

'The twins talk a lot about Nina from the nursery school. I'd be happy to pay her to come with us for the weekend, if she's free. Obviously I'll organise things so she flies with us and she'll stay with us at the *palazzo*. Would that make you able to come to the ball with me?'

'I…' She looked torn.

'Rosie. Of course the children come first. Always,' he emphasised. 'But you also need some time for you. You're their mum, yes, and that's important; but that's not all of who you are. You're also a person in your own right. Come and have some fun with me. Just for a few hours. Dinner, a little dancing. I promise you'll be home by midnight.'

'I don't speak any Italian.'

That was a much easier problem to overcome. 'I can teach you a couple of phrases and translate for you if you need me to, and anyway, a lot of people at the ball will speak English.'

She bit her lip. 'Leo, I'm sorry, but this is a big deal. I really need to think about it.'

At least it wasn't a flat no. 'All right.' He paused. 'If you do say yes, then I'd like to buy you a dress for the occasion.'

'I'm perfectly capable of buying my own…' Her voice tailed off as she clearly realised what the ball entailed. 'It's a formal ball. That means black tie and haute couture, doesn't it?'

'White tie,' he said.

'Which is even more posh!'

'It's not that different. A white bow tie and waistcoat instead of a black bow tie.'

'But it's a proper tailcoat, not a dinner jacket.'

'Yes.'

She grimaced. 'If I go—and I do mean *if*—then maybe I can hire a dress from one of those agencies that specialise in posh clothes.'

'Or alternatively you could let me buy you a dress. Not because I'm trying to control you,' he said carefully—he definitely wasn't walking in his father's shoes, 'but because you'd be doing me a huge favour and you shouldn't be out of pocket for being kind.'

'I'll think about it.' She took a deep breath. 'You said about going this weekend. That's not when the ball is, though, is it?'

'Um, actually—yes.'

She blinked. 'That's not a lot of notice, Leo.'

'I know.' He stole a kiss. 'Obviously I've known about the ball for a while. But when I originally arranged to attend it I didn't know I was going to work in London, or that I was going to meet you.'

She bit her lip. 'I'm really not sure about this.'

'Talk it over with someone you trust,' he said. 'If you decide to come with me, then maybe we can go shopping for a dress on Thursday night. Babysitter permitting, of course.'

'All right.'

'Tell me your decision on Wednesday,' he said. 'Will that give you enough time to think about it?'

'I guess so.' Though she didn't sound sure. Clearly he'd pushed her too far, too fast.

'No strings,' he said again. 'If you say no, I won't be offended. But I'd like to spend some time with you and the children.'

That evening, after Leo had gone, Rosie texted her sister.

Need some advice. Are you free tomorrow night?

Daisy rang her straight away. 'I can talk now.'

Oh, help. That didn't give her any time to think about what she was going to say. 'Uh-huh.'

'Rosie? What's wrong?'

'Not wrong, exactly' She sighed. 'I've been, um, see-ing someone.'

'Seriously? That's great! So come on—tell me every-thing. What's his name, how did you meet him, what's he like?'

She should've known that her sister would give her a burrage of questions. She answered them in order. 'Leo, at work, and he's nice.'

'So why do you need advice?'

This was complicated. 'Daze—I need this to be con-fidential, OK?'

'Now you're worrying me. Please tell me you haven't met another Michael.'

'He's about as opposite from Michael as you can get,' Rosie reassured her.

'So what's the problem?'

'He's working here on a temporary contract. He's from Italy. And he wants the children and me to go to Italy with him at the weekend.'

'This weekend? To meet his family?'

'Yes. And to go to a charity ball.'

'A charity ball.' Daisy sounded concerned. 'That's a bit flashy. Actually, Ro, that sounds like Michael.'

'It's not quite the same. The ball's in aid of a paediatric clinic that Leo supports. They treat children from families who can't afford to pay,' Rosie explained.

'Whereas Michael would've been all about the glitz and the glamour and it wouldn't actually matter what the charity was,' Daisy said dryly. 'OK.'

'I, um, neglected to tell you that he's also a duke.'

'A duke? What? So how come he's a doctor if he's a duke?'

'It's complicated. But he's a good man, Daze. The children like him.'

'Hang on. He's met the children, and you hardly know him?' Daisy sounded even more shocked.

Rosie squirmed. 'I didn't behave very well. He kept asking me out and he wouldn't take no for an answer. I said yes and met him with the twins. I, um, assumed he'd take one look at the twins and bolt. But he was good with them, Daze. Really sweet.'

'I'm trying to work this out. You've only known him a little while?'

'A couple of weeks,' Rosie confirmed.

'I'm still trying to get my head round the fact that you've let him anywhere near the children.'

'Because he'd need ten people to vouch for him in writing, and sign it in blood?' Rosie asked wryly. 'I'm not that bad, Daze.'

Her sister's silence said otherwise.

Rosie sighed. 'They think he's Mummy's friend who just started at the hospital and doesn't know many people yet, so they're being kind and being his new friends, too.'

'And Freddie actually talks to him?'

'Freddie's really come out of his shell with him,' Rosie said. 'Lexi likes him, too.' She bit her lip. 'But it's going too far, too fast.'

'Maybe not. If Freddie's talking to him that tells me the guy has to be something special,' Daisy said. 'So what's the problem with Italy and the ball? Apart from the fact that it sounds as if he only just asked you and that's not a lot of notice, I mean.'

'He wants someone he knows to look after the twins.'

'Someone you don't know. And you said no.' Daisy paused. 'Does he know about Michael and that debt-collector?'

'Yes. I'm not being overprotective of the children, am I?'

'You're pretty much a helicopter mum,' Daisy said, 'but in the circumstances it's understandable.'

'Then he suggested we could ask Nina from the nursery school to go with us, to look after the children—he's going to pay her if she can do it,' Rosie took a deep breath. 'He said he thinks we all need a bit of fun.'

'He's got a very good point,' Daisy said. 'It's way past time you had some fun in your life. You've been a single parent for a year; and Michael left you to do everything for the twins, so you were practically a single parent before that, too. The only thing you've gone to without them was your ward's Christmas meal last year, and I had to nag you into that. Go and enjoy it, Ro.'

'Really?'

'Really,' Daisy said. 'What are you going to wear?'

'It's a posh do. He, um, offered to buy me a dress.' There had been a time when she'd had several suitable dresses. She'd sold them all to help pay off the debts Michael had left her with. Nowadays, she lived in either

her nurse's uniform or casual clothes, neither of which would be remotely suitable. 'That's not because he's being flashy, but because he says I shouldn't be out of pocket for doing him a favour.'

'Actually, he sounds really thoughtful. *Nice*,' Daisy said. 'When are you going shopping?'

'If I say yes, it'll be Thursday night.' She paused. 'Daze, I know it's short notice, but could you—?'

'Of course I'll babysit,' Daisy interrupted. 'And then I get to meet him when you bring him home. If I think he's a Michael in disguise, I'll tell you and you can back out. If he's not, then you can go to Italy and have some fun with him. When's the last time you went out dancing?'

'Before the twins were born,' Rosie admitted.

'So that's well over three years. Go,' Daisy said. 'And if Nina can't come with you at the weekend, I will.'

'Daze, that's…' Rosie felt her eyes film with tears.

'That's what sisters are for. You'd do it for me if I was in your shoes,' Daisy said.

'Thank you.'

'So I'll pick the children up from the nursery school at five on Thursday.'

Daisy was on the very short list of people who were authorised to pick the twins up in Rosie's absence; in accordance with the nursery school rules, Rosie had supplied photographs and code words, so she knew that it wouldn't be a problem.

'Thanks, Daze. I owe you one.'

'Just make sure you've got pizza, dough balls and strawberries in your fridge on Thursday, and we're quits,' her sister said, laughing. 'I love you, Ro. And it'll be so nice to see you having a bit of fun, for once.'

* * *

It turned out that Nina was free at the weekend and was more than happy to come to Italy with them. So on Thursday evening Rosie went shopping with Leo.

She stared at him in dismay as they reached the doors of a very posh department store. 'Leo, this place is really pricey.'

He shrugged. 'I hear their dresses are nice.'

'But—'

'But nothing,' he said gently. 'You need a dress for the ball.'

'It makes me feel a bit like Cinderella,' she muttered.

'Firstly,' he said, 'I'm not Prince Charming. Secondly, you're a first-class nurse, not a kid whose family treats her badly and turns her into a skivvy. And, thirdly, is it so bad to enjoy a little bit of glitz and glamour just for one evening?'

When the price was as high as she'd paid with Michael, yes.

'I said there were no strings,' he said. 'And I meant it.'

And she was behaving like a whiny, attention-seeking brat. He was trying to do something nice for her, and she was practically throwing it back in his face.

'Thank you,' she said, determined to make the effort so he felt appreciated.

Once she'd pushed Michael to the back of her mind, she actually found herself enjoying the evening, trying on different dresses.

'Might I make a suggestion?' the assistant asked.

'Sure,' Rosie said.

'With your hair, this one will look stunning,' the assistant said, and brought out a turquoise floor-length chiffon gown. The dress had a sweetheart neckline, and white lace and sparkling crystals adorned the straps.

'Your hair and the dress are the opposites on the colour wheel,' the assistant said. 'And I know the perfect shoes for this, too. What size are you?'

'Five and a half,' Rosie said. 'Standard width.'

'Wonderful. Leave this to me.'

By the time Rosie had changed into the dress, the assistant had brought over a pair of copper-coloured strappy high heels. They fitted perfectly.

'Would you like to show your boyfriend?' the assistant asked.

Leo wasn't exactly her boyfriend... 'OK,' she said.

The look on his face when she walked out of the changing room told her everything. And warmth spread through her when he opened his mouth and no words came out. Could she really make this clever, gorgeous man speechless?

'You look amazing,' he said finally. 'Well, you look amazing in jeans as well. But that dress is perfect.'

'Thank you.'

'But you need an evening bag as well.'

'Why?' she asked.

'For your phone,' he said. 'Because I presume you're going to call Nina on the hour to check on the twins.'

She winced; she'd sent Daisy three texts already this evening. 'Am I being overprotective?'

'A little,' he said. 'But I understand why.'

'Thank you. And I do appreciate...' She gestured to the dress.

'My pleasure. You look amazing,' Leo said again.

'Thank you. But I feel guilty about you spending so much money on me.'

'You're doing me a favour,' he reminded her. 'As I said, you shouldn't be out of pocket for that.'

Once she'd changed back into her everyday clothes, the assistant had found the perfect sequin bag to match the shoes and Leo had paid for her outfit, he took the bags, slid his free arm round her shoulders and shepherded her out of the shop. 'Dinner?' he asked. 'And I'm pretty sure you texted your sister at least twice to check on the twins, so if there was a problem we'd have been on our way back to yours an hour ago.'

'Busted,' she admitted. 'And I sent her a picture of me in the dress.'

'And she approved?'

'Very much so.' She felt the colour flicker into her face. 'She said not to rush back.'

'Dinner, then,' he said.

He found a small restaurant, and she smiled as she glanced through the menu. 'This would definitely be too fancy for the twins. I can't remember the last time I ate out at a restaurant where I didn't check the menu out beforehand to make sure it was child-friendly.'

'Enjoy,' he said. 'And this is my treat. No arguments.'

'Thank you,' she said.

The food was amazing: crab with avocado and grapefruit, followed by pan-fried halibut on a bed of seaweed with morels and Jersey royals. She had just enough room left afterwards to share a passion fruit *crème brûlée* with him; and it was oddly intimate, sharing a dessert so that every so often their fingers brushed together.

This felt like a proper date.

The first she'd been on for years and years.

It made her feel unexpectedly shy.

'Everything OK?' he asked.

She nodded. 'You and me, on our own.'

'I enjoy being with the children,' he said. 'But it's also nice to be with you on our own, too.'

She liked the fact that he was still putting the twins first—the way their own father hadn't.

And holding hands with him across the table while they had coffee and *petits fours* felt incredibly romantic. He clearly felt the same, because he held her hand all the way home.

She paused on the doorstep. 'Given that I'll be meeting your family this weekend, would you like to meet my sister this evening?' Or was this rushing things too much?

'I'd love to meet her,' he said.

'Come in,' she said, and opened the front door.

The woman who emerged from the living room looked very like Rosie, Leo thought, with the same copper-coloured hair and bright blue eyes. Rosie didn't even need to introduce them because it was so obvious that the other woman was her sister.

'Ro, the twins are both asleep—and, no, you don't have to rush up to check on them, because you know I won't let anything happen to them.' She smiled at him. 'I'm Daisy, Rosie's big sister. You must be Leo.'

Direct and to the point. He liked that. He shook her hand. 'I'm very pleased to meet you.'

'I hear you're taking my sister to Italy for the weekend.'

'No strings, no pressure, and the children come first,' he said immediately.

'I'm glad to hear it.' She smiled again. 'Come and help me make coffee while my little sister completely ignores what I said and rushes upstairs to check on her babies. And considering she's had several text updates from me...'

'Sorry,' Rosie mouthed, and fled upstairs.

'What you're doing for her—it's nice,' Daisy said.

'But she's already been hurt by a man who swept her off her feet, offered her the good life and let her down. I think the English saying is "handsome is as handsome does",' Leo said.

Daisy nodded. 'I realise you don't plan to do that to her, or you wouldn't even be discussing it with me.'

'Life is complicated,' Leo said. 'And sometimes I think you need to grab happiness with both hands, even if you find it in a place where you didn't expect it.'

'True,' Daisy said.

'I'll be careful with them,' Leo said softly. 'All of them.'

'Good.' Daisy took the coffee from the fridge. 'That's all I ask.'

'And it's nice that she has family to look out for her.'

'You don't?'

He coughed. 'I imagine that Rosie's already told you who I am and you've checked me out online.'

'Isn't that what you'd do if you had a little sister?' Daisy countered.

'Absolutely.'

'The gossip columns say you stop at three dates,' Daisy said.

That stupid reputation. He loathed it. 'I always make that clear up front.'

'Is that your deal with Ro?'

'No,' he admitted. 'I don't think either of us expected this and, if you want me to be honest with you, we don't have a clue where this is going. We're taking it step by step. But I would never deliberately hurt her or the children. As far as the twins are concerned, Rosie's being kind and befriending me because I don't know many people in London.'

'Fair enough,' Daisy said.

'You won't have to pick up the pieces,' he assured her solemnly.

'Daze, are you grilling him?' Rosie asked, appearing in the doorway.

'Big sister's privilege.' Daisy sounded completely unrepentant.

'I'd be more worried if she didn't,' Leo said. 'It's fine. I think Daisy and I understand each other.'

'We do,' Daisy agreed. 'And I want to see this dress properly. That selfie you sent me from the changing rooms was hardly visible.'

'Bossy,' Rosie grumbled, but went to change into her new finery.

Daisy was duly impressed. 'Stunning. You know Lexi's going to say you need a crown because you look like a princess. I can't remember which one has the blue dress?'

Rosie groaned. 'Cinderella.'

'We've already established that I'm not Prince Charming and my car's not going to turn into a pumpkin at midnight,' Leo said. 'Plus you love her, Daisy, and you don't make her be a skivvy.'

Daisy grinned. 'But you have dark hair, like the original Prince Charming, and you're taking my sister to a ball. Are you going to have to wear a royal outfit with a sash and gold epaulettes?'

He groaned. 'No. I'm just a duke. It's standard white tie.'

'White tie's super-posh. Does that mean you wear a top hat? Or an opera cloak?' Daisy asked.

He laughed. 'Now you're making me sound like a pantomime villain. No. And there's no monocle, either.'

'Pity. Because I think Freddie would love to try on your top hat.'

'Freddie,' he countered, 'would much rather have a dinosaur outfit.'

Daisy smiled. 'That's true. Right. Enough grilling from me. Let's go and drink our coffee.'

Rosie seemed more relaxed around her sister, Leo noticed. And he liked this fun, teasing side of her. He rather thought that she brought out the best in him, too. So maybe this would work out, after all. And if his mother got on as well with Rosie as he thought she might, this weekend could be the start of their future.

CHAPTER EIGHT

ON SATURDAY MORNING, Leo drove over to Rosie's house. They fixed the children's car seats in the back of his car, then stowed their luggage in the boot and picked up Nina.

'We're going to Italy to eat ice cream,' Lexi informed Nina, bouncing in her seat.

'And we're going to see knights in armour, with swords,' Freddie said. 'We're staying in a real castle!'

Nina laughed. 'I can see just how much you two are looking forward to it. I'm looking after you tonight while Mummy and Leo go to the charity ball.'

'Mummy looks like a princess in her dress,' Lexi said. 'It's so pretty.'

'You can tell me all about princesses and knights on the way,' Nina said, 'and we can colour in some pictures.'

'Yay!' the children chorused.

Michael had always upgraded their seats when they travelled, Rosie remembered; luxurious as it had felt at the time, it wasn't the same league as travelling with the Duke of Calvanera. Just as Leo had promised, there was no waiting around at the airport. And the plane, although small, was beautifully appointed, with deep, comfortable seats and lots of leg room.

'I still can't quite get my head around the fact that your friend owns a plane,' she said to Leo.

The children were enthralled by their first flight, especially when the pilot told them over the intercom that they could take their seat belts off. Leo took the children to the window and lifted them up so they could both see the land below.

'All the houses are tiny!' Lexi said in awe.

'And the clouds are all big and fluffy,' Freddie said.

They were overawed by seeing the mountains, too. And then finally Leo strapped them back into their seats for the descent so they could land at Florence.

Again, there wasn't a lot of waiting around. There was a limousine waiting for them at the airport, with car seats already fitted for the children. Rosie noticed that the driver was wearing a peaked cap and livery; she wondered if he was one of Leo's staff, or whether he'd just hired a car and driver for the journey.

As they headed into the hills outside Florence, Leo told the twins all about what they were seeing, and answered all their excited questions. Rosie was glad that she didn't have to make conversation, because adrenaline was pumping round her system. Supposing Leo's mother didn't like her? Would it be a problem that Rosie already had children? What if she did or said something wrong at the ball tonight and caused some kind of diplomatic embarrassment?

The nearer they got to the *palazzo*, the more her nerves grew.

And she was near to hyperventilating when the car stopped in front of a wrought-iron security gate set into a large stone wall.

'Here we are,' Leo said cheerfully. He climbed out of

the car and tapped a code into the keypad set into the wall, and the iron gates swung open.

There was a long drive flanked with tall cypress trees, and then the vista opened up to show the castle itself. It was a huge three-storey building made of honey-coloured stone with a tower at one corner. The tall, narrow windows with their pointed arches were spaced evenly among the facade, and there were colonnaded arches along the ground floor. The perfect fairy-tale castle, Rosie thought.

'Is that the princess's tower?' Lexi asked, pointing to the tower.

'No, it's my tower,' Leo said. 'My study is on the very top floor and the views are amazing. I have a bedroom and bathroom on the floor below it, and a sitting room on the floor below that.'

'So are you a prince?' Lexi asked.

He smiled. 'No. You know I'm a doctor because I work with your *mamma* at the hospital.'

'But you live in a castle. You must be a prince,' Lexi said.

'I'm a duke,' he said gently.

'What's a duke?' Freddie wanted to know.

'It's a bit like a prince,' Rosie said.

'I just don't wear a crown or robes or anything,' Leo said.

'But can you make people into knights?' Freddie asked.

'No.' Leo smiled at him. 'But I can show you some knights' armour, when we go inside.'

The front door opened as they got out of the car, and an older man with grey hair and wearing a top hat and tails came to meet them.

Leo made formal introductions. 'This is Carlo, who manages the house for me,' he said to Rosie, Nina and the children.

'*Buongiorno*. Welcome to the Palazzo di Calvanera,' Carlo said, removing his hat, and bowed stiffly. 'If there's anything you require, *signora*, *signorina*, please just ask.' He looked at Leo. 'Is your luggage in the car, Duca?'

Leo rolled his eyes. 'Carlo, you've called me Leo for the last thirty-odd years. That doesn't change just because we have guests—and did you borrow that outrageous outfit from your son's theatre company?'

'I might have done.' Carlo laughed. 'Leo, you're the Duca di Calvanera. Your butler is supposed to dress accordingly.'

Leo laughed back. 'And this is the twenty-first century, so dress codes are a thing of the past. I guess I should consider myself lucky that you didn't find some outlandish livery.'

'Gio had a great costume from *Twelfth Night*. I was tempted to borrow it,' Carlo admitted. 'Except his Malvolio is much thinner than I am. I couldn't even get the jacket on, let alone done up.' He bowed to Rosie again. 'My son Gio has a theatre company in Florence. Leo helped him start the business.'

Seeing the warmth between Leo and the older man, Rosie wasn't surprised that Leo had helped Carlo's son.

'Your *mamma* is in her usual sitting room with Violetta,' Carlo said to Leo. 'I'll bring the luggage in and ask Maria to arrange refreshments.'

'Thank you.'

'Welcome home, Leo. It's good to see you.' Carlo hugged him impulsively. 'It doesn't seem five minutes since you were the same height as this little *bambino* here.' He ruffled Freddie's hair.

Freddie immediately clung to Leo's leg and stared up at Carlo, wide-eyed.

'Sorry. He's a little shy,' Rosie said.

'No matter.' Carlo bent down so he was nearer to the children's height. 'What would you like to drink? Milk? Juice? Lemonade?'

'Milk, please,' Lexi said.

'Me, too,' Freddie whispered. 'Please.'

'Welcome to the *palazzo*,' Carlo said again, and ushered them inside.

The inside of the castle was equally grand. The entrance hall had marble columns and a marble chequered floor; the walls were dark red and hung with gold-framed pictures, while the ceiling had ornate plasterwork around the cornices and a painting in the centre. Rosie glanced around to see Venetian glass chandeliers, a suit of armour holding a massive pole-axe, a marble-topped gilt table bearing a huge arrangement of roses and an enormous grandfather clock.

Lexi looked delighted. 'It's just like the prince's castle in *Beauty and the Beast*.'

'You like *Beauty and the Beast*?' Leo asked.

Lexi nodded. 'And it's Mummy's favourite because Belle teaches the prince to be kind.'

'It's important to be kind,' Leo agreed.

Was he just being kind to her and the children? Rosie wondered. Or was there more to it than that?

At one end of the hall was a massive sweeping staircase with gilded railings and balusters. Rosie could imagine the Duchesses walking down the stairs, hundreds of years ago, wearing long swishy dresses with wide skirts.

Right at that moment, she felt slightly intimidated. Even though Carlo had been very welcoming, this was way outside her normal life. She'd visited stately homes in the past, enjoying the glimpse into a world so different from her own, but now she was staying in an actual castle as a guest. A castle whose owner had kissed her until she was dizzy.

'Carlo said Mamma is in her sitting room,' Leo said. 'Come and meet her.'

Rosie took Freddie's hand and Nina took Lexi's hand, and they followed him through the corridor into the sitting room where his mother was waiting. The room had an ornate plasterwork ceiling, but the walls were an unexpectedly bright turquoise. The huge windows let in lots of light and gave a view over the formal garden at the back of the *palazzo*; the marble floor was covered with silk rugs, but what worried Rosie was the furniture. The upholstery was either old-gold velvet or regency gold and cream stripes; the material wouldn't take kindly to small sticky hands.

'Don't touch anything,' she whispered to Freddie and Lexi.

The twins looked almost as intimidated as she felt.

'Allow me to introduce you,' Leo said. 'Mamma, Violetta, don't get up.'

Rosie noticed the stick propped against the sofa next to Leo's mother, and could guess why Leo had just said that.

'This is Rosie, her friend Nina from the hospital nursery school, and Rosie's children Freddie and Lexi. Rosie, Nina, Freddie and Lexi—this is my mother, the Duchess of Calvanera, and her friend Violetta,' Leo finished.

'*Buongiorno, Duchessa. Buongiorno,* Signora Violetta.' Rosie made a deep curtsey, and Nina followed suit.

'*Bwun-gy-or-no,*' Freddie and Lexi said, with Freddie bowing and Lexi curtseying and nearly falling over when she lost her balance.

'My dears, it's so nice to meet you. And we don't stand on ceremony at the *palazzo*. Please, call me Beatrice, and you really don't have to curtsey to me,' Leo's mother said, to Rosie's immense surprise. Hadn't Leo said that when he'd brought previous girlfriends here, his parents had reacted badly? Then again, he'd also said that his father had been difficult but his mother was sweet.

'And please call me Violetta,' Violetta added with a smile.

'Thank you for having us to stay, Beatrice,' Rosie said.

'Yes, thank you,' Nina added.

'You are all most welcome. Refreshments, I think, Leo. Go to the kitchen and ask Maria to arrange it.'

'Carlo is arranging everything,' Leo said.

'I think you should go yourself, Leo,' Beatrice said, looking pointedly at the doorway.

Leo was a little wary of leaving Rosie alone with his mother and Violetta. Then again, his mother hadn't been the problem with Emilia, and the *palazzo* definitely wasn't the same place without his father's iron fist. His father certainly wouldn't have been happy about the changes to the sitting room from the original moody dark green to the much brighter, warmer turquoise. Or the fact that his wife spoke her mind nowadays. '*Sì*, Mamma,' he said, and left for the kitchen.

As he'd half expected, Maria greeted him as warmly as Carlo had, fussing over him. 'It's good to have you back, Leo,' she said. 'The *palazzo* needs you.' She gave him a pointed look. 'And children. This place needs the laughter of children.'

Carlo had obviously told his wife just who had arrived with Leo. 'Which is what it will have, this weekend.' And maybe Rosie's children would help to banish some of the ghosts here. He hoped.

Leo returned to his mother's sitting room, carrying a massive silver tray of tea, cake and small glasses of milk for the children, and discovered that Lexi was sitting on his mother's lap, talking animatedly about princesses and crowns. He had to hide a smile; he should have guessed that the little girl would be the one to break the ice, and that it would take about ten seconds for her shyness to dissolve into her usual confidence. Freddie, the shyer twin, was sitting next to his mother on the sofa and holding her hand very tightly.

'Carlo's taken the luggage upstairs,' he said, and deftly poured the tea.

He could see Rosie eyeing the glasses warily. No doubt she was panicking that the twins would either spill the milk everywhere or break the glasses. 'The glasses are sturdy,' he said quietly to her, 'and spills are easily mopped up. Stop worrying.'

'Freddie, Lexi, you need to sit really still while you drink your milk,' Rosie said, not looking in the slightest bit less worried.

He handed the children a glass each.

'Maria has made us some of her special *schiacciata alla Fiorentina*,' he said, gesturing to the cake. 'It's an orange sponge cake with powdered sugar on top.'

Rosie looked aghast, clearly worrying about sticky fingers.

'Leonardo spilled more crumbs over the furniture

when he was little than I care to remember,' Beatrice said, 'so please don't worry about Lexi and Freddie spilling a few crumbs.'

'My daughter Lisetta, too,' Violetta said. 'She spilled blackcurrant all over that sofa over there.' She pointed to one of the regency striped sofas. 'They survive. Things clean up. Don't worry about sticky hands and spilled drinks.'

Rosie gave them both a grateful look.

The cake was still slightly warm and utterly delicious, and both children were scrupulously polite and careful, he noticed.

'Leo, why don't you show Rosie, Nina and the children round the *palazzo* while Violetta and I have another cup of tea? I'm sure Freddie will like to see our knights in armour.' Beatrice smiled at Rosie. 'I know it is the custom in Italy to drink coffee all day, but Leonardo introduced us to English tea some years ago and it's so refreshing in summer.'

'Thank you,' Rosie said.

'Knights and princesses!' Lexi said, and wriggled off Beatrice's lap, almost spilling the old lady's tea in the process.

'Lexi. Slow and calm, please,' Rosie said quietly. 'You nearly spilled Beatrice's tea just then.'

Lexi put a hand to her mouth in horror. 'Sorry,' she said.

'It's all right. Everything's exciting when you're little,' Beatrice said, ruffling her curls. 'And I think children should be heard as well as seen.'

Since when? Leo thought. When he'd grown up, the 'children should be seen and not heard' rule had been very much in evidence. The only real affection he'd been shown had been from his nanny, from Carlo—a much more junior servant in those days—and from Maria if he sneaked into the kitchens.

Then again, maybe that had been more his father's rule, and Beatrice had been as scared of her husband's mercurial temper as Leo had been. Certainly his mother seemed to have blossomed in widowhood. She was physically more frail, with her arthritis forcing her to use a stick, but mentally she seemed much stronger. Maybe his father had played the same nasty little games with her that he had with Leo, dangling the promise of love and then making it impossible to reach.

'Come with me,' Leo said, and showed Rosie and the children the other formal rooms. The dining room, with its polished table big enough to seat twenty; another sitting room; a ballroom with a slew of floor-to-ceiling windows and mirrors to double the light in the room; the room his staff used as the estate office during the week, the heavy old furniture teamed with very modern state-of-the-art computer equipment; the library, with its floor-to-ceiling shelves that Lexi announced was just like the one in *Beauty and the Beast*; the music room, with its spinet and harpsichord and baby grand piano.

Freddie gasped as Leo led them into the final room: the armoury. Suits of armour from various ages of the *palazzo* stood in a line, and instead of paintings on the walls there was a display of shields and swords.

'But that one's a *little* suit of armour,' Freddie said in awe, pointing to the child-sized suit of armour.

At the same age, Leo had been fascinated by the miniature suit of armour. His father had forbidden him to touch it, but the lure had been too great. The time Leo had been caught trying on the helmet, he'd been put on bread and water for three days for daring to disobey his father.

Well, he wasn't his father.

Deliberately, he walked towards the little suit and removed the helmet. 'This is ceremonial armour,' he explained. 'It was made for the son of one of the Dukes of Calvanera, a couple of hundred years ago. Do you want to try on the helmet?'

Freddie's eyes grew round. 'Can I? Please?'

'Sure.' Leo helped him put it on, then knelt down beside him. 'Time for a selfie, I think.'

'Me, too!' Lexi demanded.

Leo hid a grin when she swiftly added, 'Please.' No doubt Rosie had just reminded her about manners. 'Your turn, next,' he promised; and when she was wearing the helmet with the visor up he took a selfie of the two of them together.

Freddie was galloping on the spot, clearly pretending that he was a knight on a horse. Leo smiled and ruffled his hair before returning the helmet to the tiny suit of armour.

'Come and see upstairs,' he said, leading them back into the hall and up the wide sweeping staircase.

Portraits in heavy gilt frames hung on the walls of the staircase; clearly they were portraits of previous Dukes, because Rosie noticed that the fashions seemed to change and grow older, the higher they climbed. Which meant that the forbidding man in the very first portrait must've been Leo's father. Part of her wondered why he hadn't said as much; then again, the little he had told her about his father made her realise why they hadn't been close. Though she noticed that he didn't mention the next portrait up, either, which was presumably his grandfather; like Leo's father, the Duke looked stern and forbidding. Had all the Dukes of Calvanera been like that? In which case the *palazzo* must have felt more like a prison for a small child. She'd seen the expression on his face when his mother had talked about children being heard as well as seen; clearly his childhood hadn't been much fun.

The first-floor hall had a marble floor and another of the ornate painted ceilings, Rosie noticed. But the guest rooms turned out to be much simpler than the downstairs rooms; they had wooden floors and the walls were painted lemon or duck-egg-blue or eau-de-nil on the top half and white beneath the dado rail. The paintings still had heavy gilt frames, but they were of landscapes rather than people. French doors let light into the rooms, fluttering through white voile curtains.

'This is where you'll be sleeping tonight, Freddie and Lexi,' Leo said, showing them into a room with twin four-poster single beds.

'Oh, look, a princess bed!' Lexi said in delight, seeing the gauzy fabric draped at the head of one bed.

'And a prince bed,' he said with a smile, gesturing to the other one. 'Nina, I assumed you'd like to be next door, but if you don't like the room just let me know and we can move you to one you prefer.'

'It'll be just fine, thanks,' Nina said.

'The bedrooms all have their own bathrooms,' Leo said, and Rosie peeked in to see yet more marble on the floor, but the suite was plain white enamel and the gilt towel stand was relatively simple.

The next room was clearly Rosie's, because her dress was hanging up to let the packing creases fall out.

'Again, if you'd rather have a different room, just say,' Leo said.

'No. It's beautiful,' she said, meaning it.

'Can we see the tower?' Lexi asked.

'Sure.'

Leo's rooms were very different from the rest of the house, Rosie thought. He didn't show them his bedroom, but the walls of his sitting room were white and the furniture was much more modern than in the rest of the house, and the artwork was watercolours of the sky and the sea. The room at the top was his study; the walls were lined with books, but the desk was the same kind of light modern furniture they'd seen in his sitting room, and there was a state-of-the-art computer on his desk.

'And you need to see out of the window,' he said, lifting both twins up so they could see.

'You can see nearly to the edge of the world,' Freddie said in awe.

'Well, to the hills in Tuscany,' Leo corrected with a smile.

A tour of the gardens was next.

'We've finished our tea, now,' Beatrice said, 'so we'll join you.' She struggled to her feet, waving away Leo's offer of assistance, and steadied herself with her stick. 'I'm a little slower than I'd like to be, so I'll only walk with you as far as the roses,' she said.

'Thank you, Mamma,' Leo said.

Violetta took Beatrice's other arm, and the two older ladies led the way.

As soon as they were outside, Leo crouched down to Lexi and Freddie's level. 'You know Mummy has rules at the playground? I have rules here. You can run around as much as you like on the grass, but you don't go anywhere near the lake without Mummy, Nina or me holding your hand, OK?'

'OK,' the twins chorused solemnly.

'And the same goes for the fountain in the middle of the garden. You need to stay three big jumps away from it, unless one of us is holding your hand.'

Rosie loved the fact that he'd put the children's safety first, and explained it to them in a way they could understand.

As they walked along, her hand brushed against his. The light contact made all her nerve-endings zing. It would be so easy just to let his fingers curl round hers, but that wasn't appropriate right now—not in front of her children, his mother, Violetta and Nina. She glanced at him and he was clearly thinking the same, because he mouthed, 'Later.'

Later they would be dancing cheek-to-cheek at the ball. Desire sizzled at the base of her spine at the thought of it. She could imagine walking here through this garden with him when they got home, the warm night air scented with roses. And he'd kiss her with every step...

She shook herself, realising that Beatrice was telling them about the flowers and the fountain in the centre of the rose garden.

'This is so lovely,' she said. 'Do you ever open the gardens to the public?'

Beatrice shook her head.

'Maybe you should,' Violetta said. 'It would be good for the house to have visitors. You could have a little *caffè*, too.'

'It would be an excellent idea, Mamma,' Leo agreed.

'Perhaps. We'll wait here for you,' Beatrice said, and sat down on one of the stone benches by the fountain.

Leo took them to see the lake; once they'd finished their tour of the garden, they collected Beatrice and Violetta, then sat on the terrace at the back of the house in the shade, and Carlo brought them a tray of cold drinks.

'Can we play ball?' Lexi asked.

'Sure,' Leo said, and took the children into the middle of the lawn.

'Thank you,' Beatrice said to Rosie. 'It's so good to see my son looking relaxed and happy—and I know it's down to you.'

How much did she know? Flustered, and not wanting to make things difficult for Leo, Rosie said, 'We're just friends.'

'That's not the way you look at each other, child,' Beatrice said.

Rosie bit her lip. 'I wasn't sure you'd approve of me being Leo's girlfriend. I'm not from a noble family, and I already have two children.'

'That doesn't matter—and it's a pleasure to hear children laughing here.' Beatrice looked sad. 'It didn't happen as often as it should have when Leonardo was growing up.'

Leo had said his father was difficult, Rosie remembered.

Beatrice took her hand and squeezed it. 'As a *mamma*, all you want is to see your child happy, yes?'

'And you worry about them all the time,' Rosie agreed.

'I think we understand each other,' Beatrice said softly. 'And I'm glad he brought you here.'

So maybe, if this thing between her and Leo worked out the way Rosie was starting to hope it might, his family wouldn't object...

After Leo had tired the children out playing ball, they came back to sit in the shade.

'Why don't you have a dog?' Lexi asked.

'Lexi   that's rude,' Rosie said gently.

'No, it's fine. I don't have a dog because I'm too old,' Beatrice said. 'You can't take a dog for a proper walk when you have to walk with a stick. Not even a little dog.'

'We don't have a dog because Mummy works,' Freddie said dolefully.

'Let's do some colouring,' Rosie said, hoping to head them off.

Nina took pads of drawing paper and crayons from her bag. 'You can do a nice picture of the castle,' she said

But, as Rosie half expected, both children drew their favourite picture: a dog.

'This is for you,' Lexi said, giving her picture to Beatrice. 'It's a dog but you don't have to take it for walks.'

'And I drawed you one, too, so you have two and they won't be lonely,' Freddie said, not to be outdone.

Beatrice was close to tears as she hugged them. 'Thank you, both of you.'

'Maybe you can sing a song for Beatrice and Violetta,' Nina suggested. 'Like you do at nursery school.'

When the twins had finished their song, Beatrice smiled. 'This reminds me of my Leonardo singing songs, when he was little.'

'He singed to us last week,' Lexi confided.

'He sings a lot,' Freddie added.

'Maybe you should indulge your *mamma* and the children, Leo, and sing to us now,' Violetta suggested with a smile.

He groaned. 'I don't have any choice, do I?' But he

gave in with good grace and sang some traditional Italian songs.

This felt magical, Rosie thought, but she was still aware that this opulent, privileged world was nothing like her everyday existence. So she would let herself enjoy every second of the weekend, but she would keep in the back of her mind that this was just a holiday and she shouldn't get used to it. She and the children belonged in their tiny little terrace in London, not a duke's castle in Tuscany.

'So what is the children's routine?' Beatrice asked later.

'They usually eat at half-past five or so, and then have a bath before bed,' Rosie said.

'The ball starts at eight,' Leo said, 'and it will take us about half an hour to get there.'

'It won't take me long to get ready,' Rosie reassured him.

'I'm here to take care of the children,' Nina reminded them.

'And perhaps I can read a bedtime story,' Beatrice said. 'It's been a long time since I've read a goodnight story. Too long. I miss that.'

Was that his mother's subtle way of reminding him that he was supposed to get married and have an heir? Leo wondered. Then again, maybe she was just lonely and enjoying the chance to have some temporary grandchildren. She certainly seemed to have taken the twins to her heart, which gave him hope.

'Nina, I hope you will eat with Violetta and me tonight,' Beatrice said. 'Maria has planned something special for tonight.'

Nina went pink with pleasure. 'Thank you.'

Again, it showed Leo how different the *palazzo* was now. Under his father's rule, Nina would've been banished to the nursery with the children and treated as a servant.

Maria had made garlic bread shaped like teddy bears for the children, served with pasta and followed by ice cream. And she insisted that Rosie and Leo should have some *piadinas*, toasted flatbreads filled with cheese and ham. 'You can't dance all night on an empty stomach.' She waved her hand in disgust. 'The food's always terrible at a ball, all soggy canapés and crumbly things you can't eat without ruining your clothes. You need to eat something now.'

'Thank you, Maria,' Leo said, giving her a hug.

When they'd finished eating, Nina waved Rosie away. 'I'll do bathtime. Go and get ready—the children will want to see you all dressed up, and so do I.'

Rosie knew it would be pointless arguing, so she did as she was told and then headed for the children's bedroom.

'Look! Mummy's just like a princess,' Lexi said in delight.

'A special princess,' Freddie added.

Rosie smiled. 'Thank you.'

'But there's something missing,' Beatrice said thoughtfully. 'Violetta, I wonder, can you help me?'

The two older women left the room, and returned carrying some small leather and gilt boxes.

Rosie gasped when Beatrice opened the boxes to reveal a diamond choker, earrings and bracelet.

'These will be perfect with that dress. Try them on,' Beatrice said.

'But—but—these are *real* diamonds.' Put together,

they were probably worth more than she'd ever earn over the course of her entire lifetime, Rosie thought.

'Diamonds are meant to be worn, not stuck in a safe. I'm too old to go to a ball and I can't dance any more, not with my stick,' Beatrice said. 'So perhaps you can wear these for me, tonight.'

Warily, Rosie tried them on.

The jewels flashed fire at her reflection and made her feel like a million dollars.

'But what if I lose them?' she asked.

'They're insured,' Beatrice said. 'But you won't lose them—will she, Leo?'

'Of course she won't,' Leo said, entering the twins' room, and Rosie caught her breath. He looked amazing in a tailcoat, formal trousers and white tie, shirt and waistcoat.

'You have to take selfies,' Lexi said.

'I agree,' Beatrice said, and produced a state-of-the-art mobile phone. 'Use this. I will send you the pictures later.'

What could Rosie do but agree?

'Put your arm round Rosie's shoulder, Leo,' Violetta directed.

The touch of Leo's hand against her bare shoulder made desire shimmer through Rosie.

'*Bellissima.*' Beatrice smiled and took the photograph. 'Now off you go to the ball, and have a wonderful time.'

CHAPTER NINE

LEO DROVE THEM in to Florence in a sleek, low-slung black car—the kind of car Rosie had only ever really seen in magazines.

When she said as much, he gave her a rueful smile. 'I know I see myself more as a doctor than as a duke, but I have to admit that cars like this are my weakness. And it's the privileged bit of my life that pays for this.'

'But you don't spend all the money on yourself. We're going to a charity ball tonight,' she reminded him, 'in aid of a clinic you support financially. And Carlo said you supported his son's theatre company.'

'It's important to give something back.'

Rosie had a feeling that his mother might agree with him, but his father definitely hadn't. Though now wasn't the time to bring up the subject. Instead, she said, 'Right now I really feel like Cinderella. Is this car going to turn into a pumpkin at midnight?'

Leo laughed. 'No, but you look beautiful and this is going to be fun.'

And it was going to be just the two of them.

Well, and a lot of people that Leo knew either professionally or in his capacity as the Duke of Calvanera.

But tonight she'd get to dance with him; and for those

few moments it would be just them and the night and the music.

While Leo parked the car, Rosie called Nina to check that everything was OK. Reassured, she went into the ball, holding Leo's arm.

The hotel was one of the swishest in Florence, overlooking the River Arno. Like the *palazzo* in the mountains, the building was very old, but had been brought up to date. The ballroom was even more luxurious than the one at Calvanera, as well as being much larger; it had a high ceiling with ornate mouldings, painted in golds and creams. The floor-to-ceiling windows had voile curtains and heavy green velvet drapes; mirrors between the windows reflected even more light from the glass and gold chandeliers hanging from the ceiling and the matching sconces on the walls.

'This room's amazing,' she said.

'Isn't it just?' Leo agreed.

And everyone was dressed appropriately, the men in white tie and the women in an array of gorgeous dresses. Rosie had never seen anything so glamorous in her entire life.

A jazz trio was playing quietly on the dais at one end of the room.

'Dance with me,' Leo said, 'and then I'll introduce you to everyone.'

It had been quite a while since Rosie had been dancing, and Leo was a spectacular dancer; as he waltzed her round the room, it felt as if she were floating on air. And being in his arms felt perfect. Like coming home.

He introduced her to a stream of people, explaining that she was on the team with him at Paddington Children's Hospital in London; just as he'd reassured her earlier in the week, everyone spoke perfect English, and Rosie felt slightly guilty that all she really knew in Italian was *please*, *thank you*, *hello* and *goodbye*. Nobody seemed to mind; and, although she ended up talking mostly about medicine, she didn't feel as out of place as she'd half expected to be.

'Leo, can you excuse me for a second?' she asked after a quick glance at her watch.

'I know. You need to check on the children.' Though he wasn't mocking her; she knew he understood why she was antsy.

She went out to the terrace, where it was a little quieter, to make the call. Nina confirmed that everything at the *palazzo* was just fine—there hadn't been a peep out of either twin.

Rosie had just ended the call, slipped her phone back into her evening bag and was about to head back into the ballroom to find Leo when a man standing near to her on the terrace fell to the floor in a crumpled heap.

A woman screamed and knelt down beside the man—presumably his wife and Rosie said to her, 'I'm a nurse—can I help?'

'Mi scusi?'

Oh, no. Just when she really needed not to have a language barrier, she'd found one of the few people here who didn't speak English.

She gestured to the man, then clutched a fist to her heart, miming squeezing, and hoped that either he or the woman would realise that she was asking if he thought he'd had a heart attack.

'Mi ha punto una vespa.' He pointed to his hand.

Vespa? Wasn't that a motorcycle? She didn't have a clue what he'd just said.

'Una vespa.' His wife mimed flapping wings.

He seemed to be having problems breathing and was wheezing; and then Rosie's nursing training kicked in as she noticed the reddened area on his hand. He'd clearly been stung, or bitten by an insect, and was having a severe allergic reaction.

'Do you have adrenaline?' she asked, hoping that the Italian word was similar to the English one.

'Adrenaline?' The woman frowned and shook her head.

Rosie grabbed her phone and called Leo, who answered within two rings. 'Rosie? Is something wrong with the children?'

'No. I'm on the terrace with a man I think is having a severe allergic reaction to a sting. He and his wife don't speak English but between us we worked out they don't have adrenaline. I need you to talk to them for me to find out his medical history, for someone to ring an ambulance and for someone to put a call out to everyone at the ball in case someone else has an adrenaline pen we can borrow.' She handed the phone to the woman. 'Speak to Leo, *per favore*?'

There were glasses on a nearby table containing ice as well as the drinks; she grabbed a tissue from her bag and gestured to the ice. *'Per favore?'* she asked the people standing round the table. At the assorted nods, she grabbed the ice, put it in the tissue and put the makeshift ice pack on the man's hand. Gently, she got him to lie back on the terrace, and talked to him to keep him calm. 'It's going to be all right,' she said, knowing that he wouldn't understand what she was saying, but hoping he could pick up on her tone.

The man's wife finished talking to Leo and handed the phone back to Rosie.

'*Grazie,*' Rosie said. 'Leo?'

'His name's Alessandro and hers is Caterina. He's been stung before and the swelling was bad but he didn't think to talk to his doctor about it. The last time must have sensitised him, because he's never had an anaphylactic reaction before,' Leo explained. 'I've got an ambulance on its way and I've got a call out in the ballroom for an adrenaline pen.'

'Great. Thank you. How do I say "Everything will be OK"?'

'*Andrà tutto bene,*' he said. 'I'll be there as soon as I've found an adrenaline pen.'

'Thanks.' She hung up and squeezed Alessandro's hand and Caterina's in turn. 'Alessandro, Caterina, *andrà tutto bene,*' she said. 'Everything will be fine. An ambulance is coming.'

'*Grazie,*' Caterina said, looking close to tears. She, too, talked to Alessandro; Rosie didn't have a clue what she was saying, but Caterina's tone was reassuring and she was clearly trying to be brave and calm for her husband's sake.

To Rosie's relief, Leo arrived a couple of minutes later with an adrenaline pen. While he explained to Caterina and Alessandro why Rosie had laid him flat and put an ice pack over the sting, and what was going to happen next, Rosie glanced at her watch and then administered the adrenaline.

She really wasn't happy with Alessandro's breathing, and when he was still struggling five minutes after she'd given the first injection, she gave him a second shot.

Finally, the ambulance arrived. Leo spoke to the para-

medics to fill them in on what had happened; then they
carried Alessandro off on a stretcher with Caterina ac-
companying him.

'You saved his life,' Leo said.

'Not just me. You talked to Caterina, you got someone
to call the ambulance and you got the adrenaline pen.'

'But you saw what the problem was. Without you
working that out, it might have been too late by the time
the ambulance got here,' Leo said. He held her close.
'You, Rosie Hobbes, are officially a superstar.'

She shook her head. 'I'm just an ordinary nurse.'

'Ordinary is definitely not how I'd describe you,' Leo
said. 'Caterina's going to ring me from the hospital and
let me know how Alessandro gets on.'

'That's good.' She bit her lip. 'Talking of calling...'

'Of course. You need to check on the children.' He
stroked her face. 'Come and find me when you're done.'

'Thank you.' She called Nina. 'Is everything OK?'

'It's fine,' Nina said. 'Honestly, Rosie, you don't need to
worry. You know I'll call you if there's a problem. I have
Leo's number as well as yours and that of the hotel reception, and I'm sleeping right next door to the children—
so if one of them wakes up I'll hear them straight away.'

'Sorry. I do trust you. I'm just one of these really terrible overprotective mums,' Rosie said.

'Just a bit,' Nina said, though her tone was gentle. 'I
hope you don't mind, but I'm not planning to stay up until
you get back. Violetta has gone home and Beatrice has
gone to bed, and I'm going to read in my room for a bit.
So just try to relax and enjoy the ball, OK?'

'OK,' Rosie said. 'And thank you.'

She went to find Leo and relayed the conversation
to him.

'She has a point,' he said with a smile. 'You need to relax and enjoy this. Come and dance with me.'

Just having him there with her made her feel better, and Rosie finally managed to relax in his arms.

As she'd promised, Caterina rang from the hospital to tell Leo that Alessandro was recovering and would be sent home in the morning, along with an adrenaline pen that he'd make sure was with him at all times.

When the music slowed and the lights dimmed, Leo held Rosie close. And there in the ballroom, swaying to the music, it felt as if nobody else was there: just the two of them.

At the end of the evening, Leo drove them back to the *palazzo*. Although someone—presumably Carlo—had left the light on by the front door and in the hallway, Rosie was pretty sure that everyone in the *palazzo* was asleep.

'There's a full moon,' Leo said quietly, gesturing to the sky. 'And I'm not ready to go to bed yet. Come and walk with me for a while in the gardens.'

'Do you mind if I take my shoes off?' Rosie asked when he led her onto the lawn. 'I'm not used to wearing heels this high.'

'Sure,' he said, and let her lean on him while she removed the strappy high heels and placed them on one of the stone benches.

Every single one of Rosie's senses felt magnified as they walked hand in hand through the gardens. In the moonlight, the garden looked magical; beneath her feet, the lawn felt like velvet. She could smell the sweet, drowsy scent of the roses, and in the distance she could hear a bird singing.

'Is that a nightingale?' she asked.

'I think so.' He stopped and spun her into his arms. 'Dance with me, Rosie,' he whispered.

Instead of the jazz band, they had the nightingale; instead of the chandeliers, they had the moon and the stars; and there was nobody to disturb them in their makeshift ballroom.

She closed her eyes as Leo held her close and dipped his head so he could brush his mouth against hers. Every nerve-end was begging for more, and she let him deepen the kiss; his mouth was teasing and inciting rather than demanding, and she found herself wanting more and more.

'Rosie,' he whispered when he finally broke the kiss. 'I want you.'

'I want you, too,' she admitted.

'Come to the tower with me?' he asked.

'I need to check on the children first.'

'What if you wake them? Or Nina?' he asked.

'I won't.' But she needed to see them.

'OK. Let's do this,' he said softly. He scooped her up, stopping only at the stone bench to pick up her shoes, and carried her back to the *palazzo*.

He set her on her feet again and kissed her before unlocking the door and dealing with the alarm system. And then he reset it and led her to the children's room.

The night-light was faint but enough to show her that they were both curled up under their duvets. She smiled and bent down to them in turn, breathing in the scent of their hair and kissing their foreheads lightly, so as not to wake them.

Just seeing them safe made her feel grounded again.

'I'm sorry,' she whispered when they'd left the children and were heading for the tower. 'I know they're perfectly safe here and I'm being ridiculous.'

'But Michael's associate really frightened you.'

She nodded. 'It's so hard to get past that.'

'It's OK. I understand.' He scooped her up again. 'But now it's you and me. Just for a little while.'

Could she do this?

Could she put herself first—just for a little while?

When he kissed her again, she said, 'Yes.'

Leo's bedroom in the tower was so high up that he knew nobody would be able to see into the room. Moonlight filtered in through the soft voile curtains at the windows; he led Rosie over to the window, leaving the heavy drapes where they were, and pushed the voile aside for a moment. 'You, me and the moonlight,' he said, and kissed her bare shoulder.

She shivered, and slowly he lowered the zip of her dress. Her skin was so soft, so creamy in the moonlight. He turned her to face him, cupped her face in his hands and dipped his head so he could brush his mouth against hers, then pulled back so he could look into her eyes. Her pupils were huge, making her eyes look almost black.

'I want you,' he whispered. So badly that it was a physical ache.

'I want you too,' she answered, her voice slightly hoarse.

He slid the straps of her dress down and kissed her bare shoulders. When he felt her shiver, he paused. 'OK?'

'Very OK. Don't stop.'

He drew the gauzy material down further, then

dropped to his knees and kissed her bare midriff. She slid her fingers into his hair. 'Leo.'

He wanted everything. Now. And yet the anticipation was just as exciting. He helped her step out of the dress, then hung the garment over the back of a chair.

She stood there before him wearing only a strapless lacy bra, matching knickers, and diamonds.

He sucked in a breath. 'Do you have any idea how sexy you look right now?'

'I just feel underdressed,' she confessed, a blush stealing through her cheeks.

He spread his hands. 'Then do something about it, *bellezza*.'

'*Bellezza?*'

'In my language it means "beautiful",' he explained.

'Oh.' Her blush deepened; and then she gave him a smile so sexy that it almost drove him to his knees. 'You're beautiful, too,' she whispered. 'And I want to see you.'

'Do it,' he said, his voice cracking with need and desire.

Slowly, so slowly, she removed his jacket and hung it over the top of her dress. Then she undid his waistcoat, slid it from his shoulders and draped it over the top of his jacket.

Leo was dying to feel her hands against his bare skin; but at the same time he was enjoying the anticipation and he didn't want to rush her. The tip of her tongue caught between her teeth as she concentrated on undoing his bow tie, then unbuttoned his shirt. He could feel the warmth of her hands through the soft cotton, and it made him want more. He couldn't resist stealing a kiss as she pushed the material off his shoulders and let the shirt fall to the floor.

Then he caught his breath as finally he felt her fingertips against his skin.

'Nice pecs, Dr Marchetti,' she murmured. She let her hands drift lower. 'Nice abs, too.' She gave him a teasing smile, and excitement hummed through him. Where would she touch him next? How?

And he wanted to touch her. So much that he couldn't hold himself back; he traced the lacy edge of her bra with his fingertips. 'Nice curves,' he said huskily, and was rewarded with a sharp intake of breath from her.

Her hands were shaking slightly as she undid the buckle of his belt, then the button of his trousers.

'OK?' he asked.

'It's been a while,' she admitted. 'I guess a part of me's a bit scared I'll—well—disappoint you.'

How could she possibly be worried about that? 'You're not going to disappoint me,' he reassured her. 'And I didn't plan this. Tonight really was all about just dancing with you and having fun.'

'I wasn't planning this to happen, either.' Her eyes widened. 'I don't have any protection. I'm not on the Pill.'

'I have protection,' he said. 'But I don't want you to think I'm taking you for granted.'

In answer she kissed him, and he felt his control snap.

He wasn't sure which of them finished undressing each other, but the next thing he knew he'd dropped the diamonds on his dressing table and had carried her to his bed, and she was lying with her head tipped back into his pillows, smiling up at him.

'I've wanted you since the moment I first saw you,' he whispered.

'Even though I was horrible to you?'

'Even though.' He stole a kiss. 'I don't know what it was. Your gorgeous eyes. Your mouth. Your hair. But something about you drew me and I want you. Very, very badly.'

'I want you, too,' she confessed.

She reached up and kissed him back. When he broke the kiss, he could see that her mouth was slightly swollen and reddened from kissing him, and her eyes glittered with pure desire. It was good to know she was with him all the way.

He kissed the hollows of her collarbones, then let his mouth slide lower. She gasped when he took one nipple into his mouth; he teased it with the tip of his tongue until her breathing had grown deeper and less even. Then he stroked her midriff and moved lower, kissing his way down her body and circling her navel with his tongue. He loved the feel of her curves, so soft against his skin.

'Bellezza,' he whispered. 'You're so beautiful, Rosie.'

'So are you,' she said shyly, sliding her hands along his shoulders.

He kneeled back so he could look at her, sprawled on his bed. His English rose. And now he wanted to see her lose that calmness and unflappability he was used to at work. He wanted to see passion flare in her.

Keeping his gaze fixed on hers, he let his fingertips skate upwards from her knees. She caught her breath and parted her thighs, letting him touch her more intimately.

'Yes, Leo,' she whispered. 'Now.'

He reached over to the drawers next to his bed, took a condom from the top drawer, undid the foil packet and slid the condom on.

Then he kissed her again and whispered, 'Open your eyes, Rosie.'

When she did so, he eased his body into hers, watching the way the colour of her eyes changed.

She gasped, and wrapped her legs round him so he could push deeper.

He could feel the softness of her breasts against his chest, the hardness of her nipples.

'You feel like paradise,' he whispered.

'So do you.' Colour bloomed in her cheeks.

He held her closer, and began to move. His blood felt as if it were singing through his veins.

'Leo.' He felt her tighten round him as her climax hit, and it pushed him into his own climax.

Regretfully, he withdrew. 'Please don't go just yet,' he said. 'I need to deal with everything in the bathroom— but I'm not ready for you to leave just yet.'

'I'll stay,' she promised.

When Leo came back from the bathroom, Rosie was still curled in his bed, though she'd pulled the sheet over herself and she blushed when she saw that he was still completely naked.

He climbed into bed beside her and pulled her into his arms. 'Stay a little longer?'

He liked just lying there, holding her, with her head resting on his shoulder and his arm wrapped round her waist. There wasn't any need to make small talk; he just felt completely in tune with her. He couldn't remember ever feeling this happy before at the *palazzo*.

Rosie and the children really fitted in, here. He'd resisted the idea of having a family in Tuscany, not wanting to subject a child to the kind of misery he'd known here. But he wasn't his father; so maybe this place could actually house a happy family.

His last thought before he drifted into sleep was that maybe he, Rosie and the twins could be a family here…

———————

CHAPTER TEN

NEXT MORNING ROSIE WOKE, warm and comfortable and with a body spooned against hers. When she realised that she was still in Leo's bed, she was horrified. She'd only meant to stay for a little while—not for the whole night. Supposing the children had woken from a bad dream, needed her and found her missing?

'Leo. *Leo*,' she whispered urgently. 'I need to go back to my room before the children wake up.'

And she hadn't even bothered taking off her make-up last night. She probably looked like a panda this morning—a panda with a bad case of bed-head.

'With a combination of lots of fresh air and all that running around yesterday, they're probably still asleep,' he pointed out, and kissed her. 'Good morning, *bellezza*.'

Oh, help.

When he spoke in his own language to her, it made her knees go weak. And that sensual look in his eyes... Panicking, she began, 'Leo, I don't normally—'

He cut her off by pressing a finger gently to her lips. 'No apologies. Last night was last night. We didn't plan it.' He held her gaze. 'But I don't have any regrets.'

She could see by his face that he meant it.

Did she have regrets?

Yes and no.

She didn't regret making love with him. He'd made her feel wonderful. But it was way too tempting to let herself believe that this thing between them could turn from a fairy tale to real life. And she knew that couldn't happen. He needed to marry someone from his world and produce an heir to the dukedom.

'Thank you,' she said. 'But I really do have to go now.' She bit her lip. 'If you don't mind, I could do with a hand zipping up my dress.'

'I've got a better idea. I'll lend you a bathrobe,' he said. 'It'll be quicker. And I'll see you back to your room and carry your dress.'

'What if people see us?' she asked, worrying. She wasn't ashamed of what they'd done; but she didn't want people knowing about it. This was just between them. *Private.* And she needed some time to process it. To think about where they could possibly go from here. She couldn't do that if everyone knew about it.

'They won't,' he said, 'but if anyone sees me on the way back from your room I'll tell them I went outside for some fresh air before my shower.' He stroked her face. 'The *palazzo* is a little bit like a warren, and the least I can do is see you safely back to your room.'

It made sense. Otherwise she was at risk of going into the wrong room and embarrassing herself even further.

She shrugged on the fluffy white bathrobe he held out for her. It was way too big for her, but she tied the belt tightly.

He wrapped a towel round his waist, sarong-style; it looked incredibly sexy, and she had a hard job reminding herself that they were supposed to be just colleagues.

Except last night they'd been lovers.

'You need these, too.' Leo handed her the diamonds and she put them carefully in the deep pockets of his robe.

He carried her dress and shoes, and thankfully they didn't bump into anyone on the way back to her room. She put the jewels on the dressing table, then gave the bathrobe back to him.

Leo smiled and stole a kiss. 'I'll see you at breakfast, then. Do you know how to get to the breakfast room?'

'Down the stairs and then turn right?' she guessed.

He nodded. 'See you in a bit.'

Rosie hung up her dress, showered and dressed swiftly, then went into the children's room. They were just waking up and gave her the sweetest smiles.

'Mummy!' Freddie exclaimed. 'We missed you.'

'I missed you, too. I love you,' she told them both, and hugged them fiercely.

'Were there any princes and princesses at the ball?' Lexi wanted to know.

'No, but there were some very pretty dresses.'

'Did you take selfies?' Lexi asked.

'No.' She ruffled her daughter's hair. 'I need to get you both up now. We have to go down to breakfast.'

Rosie had just finished helping them get dressed when Nina came in. 'Sorry. I wasn't sure if they'd be awake yet.'

'It's fine. You're not supposed to be on duty twenty-four-seven,' Rosie said with a smile. 'I'll read them a story while you get ready, and we can all go down together.'

'That sounds good. Did you have fun last night?' Nina asked.

'Yes. The ball was great. And it really helped knowing that you were here with the children. Thanks so much for that.'

'No problem. They were angels.'

Once Nina was ready, they made their way to the breakfast room: a sunny room overlooking the terrace. Beatrice and Leo were already there.

'Good morning,' Beatrice said. 'Did you sleep well?'

Rosie didn't dare meet Leo's gaze. 'Very well, thank you.'

'Coffee, *signor, signorina*?' Carlo asked. 'And hot chocolate for the children?'

'That would be lovely, thanks,' Rosie said.

'Help yourself to pastries and *biscotti*,' Leo said.

'We tend to have a very light breakfast in Italy,' Beatrice said, 'but Maria can make you bacon and egg, if you prefer.'

'This is all perfect,' Rosie said with a smile. 'And thank you for the loan of your diamonds.' She returned the boxes to Beatrice.

'My pleasure, my dear,' Beatrice said. 'Now, tell me all about the ball.'

Rosie focused on the dancing and the dresses—but Leo had his own story to tell.

'She saved a man's life last night, Mamma,' he said. 'He was stung by a wasp and had a very bad allergic reaction. Thanks to Rosie, he made it to hospital and he'll make a full recovery.'

'It wasn't just me,' Rosie said, squirming. 'I couldn't have done it without you translating for me, and getting the ambulance and the adrenaline.'

'But if you hadn't noticed what the problem was,' he said gently, 'Alessandro might have died.' He smiled at Freddie and Lexi. 'Your mummy is amazing.'

'That's what Aunty Daze says,' Lexi confided.

Violetta arrived after breakfast; they spent the rest of

the morning in the gardens, with the children running round and playing ball with Leo. A couple of times, she caught his eye and wondered if he was remembering last night, when the two of them had danced barefoot in the moonlight among the roses.

On the way back to the airport, Leo switched on his phone and a slew of messages flooded in.

He grimaced and handed his phone to her.

The *Celebrity Life!* magazine website had run a report on the charity ball last night, asking who the beautiful woman was with the Duke of Calvanera—especially as she was wearing the Calvanera diamonds. Had someone finally caught the reluctant Duke?

There was a newer story attached to it: *Angel in Diamonds.* All about how she'd been a ministering angel to a man suffering from a near-fatal allergy to wasps, and saved his life.

Oh, no.

She grimaced and mouthed, 'Sorry.'

'It gets worse,' he mouthed back, and her dismay grew when he leaned over and flicked into a second website.

The journalists had dug up her past.

Rosie Hobbes, a twenty-five year old mother of twins, is a nurse at the beleaguered Paddington Children's Hospital. She was previously married to Michael Duncan, who died after his car collided with a tree, leaving a mountain of gambling debts.

Rosie stared at the screen, horrified, and totally shocked that her private life had been spilled over the press so quickly.

And then the fear seeped in.

What if Michael's former associates saw all this and decided that Leo, as the Duke of Calvanera, had plenty of money? Supposing they came after him, or threatened the children again? And Leo's mother was vulnerable at the *palazzo*, being elderly and frail. Although Violetta, Carlo and Maria would be with her, Rosie knew, would they be enough to keep her safe?

She didn't even know where to start asking questions, but looked helplessly at Leo.

'My PR team is doing damage limitation,' he said grimly.

'What's wrong?' Nina asked.

'Nothing,' Rosie fibbed—then grabbed her own phone from her bag and texted Nina.

Press gossip about me, things I don't want the children to hear but you probably need to know. Am sorry I didn't say anything before.

She sent Nina the link to the two articles.

'That'll probably be a text from my mum asking if I'm going to be home for tea tonight,' Nina said when her phone beeped.

Thankfully the children were too young to read many of the words, Rosie thought.

A few minutes later, Nina texted her back.

Poor you. Not fair of them to drag it all up. You OK?

Rosie sagged with relief; at least this wasn't going to be a problem at the hospital nursery school. She also knew that Nina wasn't a gossip.

I'm fine, she fibbed. Thanks for keeping it to yourself.

Try not to worry, Nina responded. Let me know if there's anything I can do. Thanks.

Leo was busy on his phone—Rosie assumed he was dealing with his PR team—but he reached over to squeeze her hand, as if telling her that everything was going to be all right.

But the more she thought about it, the more she realised that it wasn't going to be all right. She was completely unsuitable for him. The press would bring up her past over and over and over again, and he'd be tainted by association. Beatrice had been so kind and welcoming this weekend; but right now Rosie felt as if she'd thrown all that back in Beatrice's face.

Nina kept the children occupied with stories and singing and colouring all the way back to England, so they weren't aware that anything was wrong. And thankfully they fell asleep in the car so there weren't any awkward questions.

Leo dropped Nina home first but, when he was about to turn into Rosie's road, they could see a group of people waiting at the front of Rosie's house.

'The paparazzi,' he said with a sigh.

'But how do they even know where I live?' Rosie asked, shocked.

He groaned. 'Sorry. They can dig up practically anything. I should have thought about this earlier.' He drove past her road. 'You'd better stay at mine.'

'They're probably camped out there, too,' she said. 'Maybe you'd better drop us on the next road. We can cut through the back.'

'I can't just abandon you.'

'You're not abandoning me. You're dropping us off at a place where we can walk through to the back of my house unseen.'

'I don't like this,' Leo said.

'It's the only option,' she said firmly.

'One condition, then,' he said. 'You let me know you're home safely, and you call me if there's any kind of problem at all.'

'OK,' she promised.

She woke the children. 'We're going to play a game, now,' she said. 'We're going to pretend to be invisible, so we have to tiptoe home.'

'Yay!' Lexi said, then screwed up her face and whispered, 'Yay.'

Rosie couldn't help smiling. 'Say goodbye and thank you to Leo.'

'Bye-bye and thank you,' the twins chorused.

Thankfully they managed to get in the back door without incident, and Rosie shepherded the children upstairs. At least one of the waiting press must've seen a movement through the frosted glass panel of the front door, because the doorbell went, but Rosie ignored it.

Safely indoors, she texted Leo.

Going to put the children to bed.

Call me later, he texted back immediately.

Rosie continued to ignore the doorbell and ran a bath for the children.

'Mummy, it's the doorbell,' Freddie said. 'It might be the postman.'

'Not on a Sunday. Whoever it is can come back later,' Rosie said firmly, 'because I'm busy right now.'

The phone shrilled, and she ignored that, too—until the answering machine kicked in and a gravelly voice said, 'Mrs Duncan, you really need to answer your phone. We wouldn't want another accident, would we?'

She went cold.

Michael's associates. Nobody else would call her Mrs Duncan. But how had they got hold of her number? She'd moved from the place she'd shared with Michael, and her new number was ex-directory.

'As a children's nurse, you know how easily bones break.'

She had to suppress a whimper. That was a definite threat. They were going to hurt the children if she didn't do what they wanted.

'Mummy? Mummy, what's the matter?' Lexi asked.

'Nothing,' Rosie lied. 'I left the radio on in my bedroom.' She turned off the taps. 'Go and play in your bedroom for five minutes while I sort it out.'

She grabbed the phone and headed downstairs so the children wouldn't hear her. 'What do you want?' she whispered fiercely.

'About time you answered us, Mrs Duncan,' the gravelly voiced man said. 'You know what we want. What Michael owed us.'

'Michael's dead, and I don't have any money.'

'But your new boyfriend does. The Duke of Calvanera.'

'He's not my boyfriend,' Rosie said desperately.

'The papers are all saying he is.'

'The papers are just trying to sell copies. He isn't my boyfriend.'

'No? I believe the Duchess of Calvanera is quite frail. Imagine a fall and a broken hip at that age,' the man continued.

They were threatening Leo's mum as well as the children?

Fear made her feel queasy. But then she remembered her promise to herself after Michael's death: that nobody would ever make her feel a second-class citizen again. These people weren't going to bully her, either. 'I'm calling the police,' Rosie said.

There was a laugh from the other end of the line. 'You think they'll be able to do anything?'

'You threatened me. I'm recording every single word you say on my mobile phone,' Rosie lied.

'A recording proves nothing. But we know where you are. I'd advise you to talk to your boyfriend and get him to pay Michael's debts.'

The line went dead.

Oh, dear God. The nightmare that she'd thought was over had come back again. Except this time they'd been more explicit. They wanted money, or they'd hurt the children and Leo's mum.

She couldn't take that risk—but she also couldn't ask Leo to pay Michael's debts. And supposing the thugs decided they wanted interest as well? The only way she could think of to keep everyone safe was to end her relationship with Leo—and talk to the police. And even that might not be enough.

Florence had been perfect. Too perfect, maybe, because it had shown her the life she wanted. The future that maybe she could have with Leo. But the price was too high: she couldn't risk the safety of her children, Leo or Leo's mother.

She went back upstairs and chivvied the twins into the bathroom. They chattered away about the *palazzo* and the suit of armour, and Lexi was still clearly convinced that

Leo was really a prince. It took three bedtime stories to calm them down. But finally the children fell asleep, and Rosie went into her own room, shutting the curtains in case the paparazzi tried to get some kind of blurry shot of her through the window.

And now she needed to talk to Leo.

It was a call she didn't want to make—a call that would break her dreams and trample her heart—but she couldn't see any other solution.

Leo answered straight away. 'Are you OK?'

No. Far from it. 'Yes.' She took a deep breath. 'Leo— we can't do this any more.' And these were the hardest words she was ever going to have to say. They actually stuck in her throat to the point where she thought she was going to choke, but finally she managed to compose herself. 'We have to end it.' Which would wipe out the threat to the children and his mother, and by extension to Leo himself. But she also knew she needed to give him an excuse that he'd accept instead of trying to solve. 'The press are going to make life too difficult. So I'd rather you didn't see me or the twins any more.'

'Rosie, this will blow over and people will have forgotten about it by the middle of the week. It's probably a slow news day.'

That was true. But she had to convince him. Tell him she didn't want the kind of life he could offer her—even though she did. 'There are photographers camped outside my house.'

'They'll get bored and go away.'

That was true, too. Digging her nails into her palm and reminding herself that she had to do this for everyone's safety, she demanded, 'When? I can't camp out here until the middle of the week. I'm due at work tomorrow and the children are due at nursery school. I can't just ring in and say we're not turning up.'

'I'll send a car and get someone to escort you in.'

'No.' Because it wasn't really the press that was the problem. Maybe he'd understand if she dropped a hint about what really worried her. 'What if Michael's associates see the papers and crawl out of the woodwork?'

'They won't,' he reassured her. 'If they do try anything, I'll have the police onto them straight away—both in here and in Italy.'

Oh, but they had already. And the police wouldn't be able to help, Rosie was sure. Michael's associates were right in that she had no proof. 'You have a security team in Italy,' she said tentatively. 'Maybe you'd better make sure they take extra care with your mother.'

'Why?' His voice sharpened. 'Rosie, are you trying to tell me they've been in touch with you?'

Oh, help. She'd forgotten how quick his mind was. Of course he'd work it out for himself that she wasn't just being overprotective—that something had happened to worry her. 'No,' she lied. 'I just think you should take extra precautions—with yourself as well as with your mother. And you need to get your PR people to make a statement to the press, saying that we're nothing more to each other than colleagues.' Even though Leo could've been the centre of her life. She had to give him up. To keep him safe.

'But, Rosie—'

'No,' she cut in. Why did he have to make this so hard? Why couldn't he just walk away, the way he normally walked away from his girlfriends? 'I've thought about it and thought about it, and this is the only way. It has to end.' It was the last thing she wanted. But there was no other way. 'It has to end *now*. I'm sorry. Goodbye, Leo.'

She switched off her mobile phone after she cut the connection, and she ignored her landline when it shrilled.

How stupid she'd been, thinking she could escape Michael's shadow. It would always be there, and would always darken anything she did. And it wasn't fair to Leo or his family to expect them to deal with it, too.

The only way out of this was to end it between them.

Even though her heart felt as if someone had ripped it into tiny shreds and stomped on it and ground it into the floor. Because she'd fallen in love with Leo. Not the Duke—yes, the glitziness of the ball had been fun, but it wasn't who Leo was. She'd fallen for the man. The man who'd been so good with the twins. The man with the huge, huge heart. The man who really cared and wanted to make a difference to the world.

She wanted to be with him. But there just wasn't a way she could do that and keep everyone safe, and it wasn't fair to make everyone spend the rest of their days looking over their shoulders, worrying that her past was going to catch up with them. All that worry and mistrust would eat into their love like woodworm, little tiny bites at a time, and eventually what they felt for each other would simply crumble and fall apart, undermined by all the worry.

So she'd tell the children that Leo had had to go back to Italy, and she'd distract them every time they asked if they could go back to the *palazzo* to see him. And she'd hope that Leo could find the happiness he deserved with someone else—someone whose past wouldn't be a problem.

And even though she wanted to sob her heart out for what she'd lost, she didn't. Because some things hurt too much to cry.

Her last call was to the police. They sent someone to interview her, but it turned out that her fears were spot on: she didn't have anywhere near enough information to identify Michael's associates.

'We can check your phone records,' the policeman said, 'but we still might not be able to trace them. They might have used an unregistered mobile to call you.'

'Unregistered?' Rosie queried.

'Pay-as-you-go, bought with cash and with no ID to link to the phone. But if they do call you again, ring us straight away.'

'I will,' Rosie said, though it just made her feel hopeless.

And, when she went to bed that night, she couldn't sleep. She was haunted by that gravelly voice and the threat to her children and Leo's mother—three people who were too vulnerable to protect themselves. Then there was Leo himself. He was strong: but Michael's associates were capable of anything. She couldn't bear to think that they'd arrange an accident for him, the way she was sure they had for Michael. And how could you fight a nameless opponent, someone who stayed so deeply hidden in the shadows?

Hopefully Leo's PR team would get the word out that they weren't an item. Then Michael's associates would realise that he wasn't going to pay them, and they'd give up—just as they had when Michael had died.

And, although it broke her heart to do it, the alternative was worse. At least this way, Leo had the chance of finding happiness in the future. This way, Leo would be safe.

CHAPTER ELEVEN

THE PAPARAZZI WERE still outside Rosie's house the next morning, albeit not quite so many of them as there had been the previous evening. Rosie was much less worried about them than about the possible repercussions from Michael's former associates, but she took a taxi to the hospital instead of using the Tube, and she had a quiet word with the head of the nursery school about the situation and to ask for an extra layer of security for the twins.

And then it was time to face the ward.

'I saw you in the news this morning,' Kathleen said cheerfully. 'Loved the dress. So when did you and Leo get together?'

'We're not together,' Rosie said firmly. 'You know what the press is like. They add two and two and make a hundred.'

'But you went to Italy with him.'

'Yes,' Rosie admitted.

'Florence is really romantic.'

'I was looking at the Italian healthcare system and what we could learn from it,' Rosie fibbed. 'We went to a ball, yes, because it was to raise funds for a paediatric clinic that the Duke of Calvanera supports.'

Given that she so rarely went out on hospital eve-

nings out, she really hoped that Kathleen would accept
the story. Especially as most of it was true. To Rosie's
relief, the other nurse simply smiled. 'Well, it was still
a lovely dress.'

'Thank you,' Rosie said.

'So did you really save someone's life?'

Rosie grimaced. 'It wasn't just me. I was part of a
team. And you would've done the same if someone had
collapsed in front of you, wheezing and having trouble
breathing, with a massive swelling on his hand where a
wasp had stung him.'

'So you did save someone's life,' Kathleen said. 'Because that sounds like the beginning of anaphylaxis to
me.'

'It was. Luckily he's fine now. And I'd better get my
skates on.'

'You're on the allergy clinic this morning,' Kathleen
said. 'With Leo.'

Rosie's heart sank. She'd known that she'd have to face
Leo this week and they'd have to work together at some
point, but she'd hoped for a little more time to prepare
herself. To remind herself that no matter how attractive
she found him, she had to put the safety of her children
and his mother first.

'Nurse Hobbes,' Leo said, and gave her a cool little
nod, when she rapped on the door and walked into the
consulting room.

Formal was good. She could cope with that. 'Dr Marchetti.' Though she couldn't look him in the eye. Or the
face, for that matter—because then she'd remember how
his mouth had felt against her skin, and it would undermine her attempts to stay cool and calm in front of him.
She looked down at the notes in her hand. 'I believe our

first patient is Madison Turner, for the next session in her anti-venom treatment.'

How ironic. An allergy to wasps: just what had drawn the press's attention to her at the ball.

If Alessandro hadn't been stung, would she and Leo have got away with it? Or would the press still have tried to make up a story about them and Michael's associates would've crawled out of the woodwork anyway?

'If you'd like to bring Madison through, please,' Leo said, his voice cool.

When she sneaked a glance at him, Rosie realised that he was trying just as hard not to look at her. Guilt flooded through her as she realised she'd hurt him. But she hadn't dumped him because she didn't like him. Quite the opposite. She'd ended things with him solely to keep him, his family and the twins *safe*.

Not that she intended to discuss it with him. Talking about it wouldn't make things better—if he knew the full story, it might lead him to do something brave and reckless, and her sacrifice would've been for nothing. She couldn't bear to think of him being badly hurt. Or worse.

'I'll just go and get Madison,' she said.

She really hoped the tension between them didn't show, for the sake of their young patients and their parents. She did her best to be her usual professional self, and concentrated hard on getting the observations right and recording everything thoroughly. Leo barely spoke to her, except when he wanted some information from notes that she was using.

The rest of the morning's clinic was just as awkward. Rosie was glad to escape at lunchtime, and even more relieved that she had a cast-iron excuse to avoid Leo, because Monday was one of her days for reading to Penny.

'I saw your picture in the paper,' Julia said.

'It was a lot of fuss about nothing,' Rosie said with a smile. 'Any nurse would've done the same, in my shoes.'

'I didn't mean about the poor man who was stung. You were at that fancy ball with Leo Marchetti, weren't you?'

'As a colleague,' Rosie fibbed. In a desperate bid to divert Julia from the subject, she said, 'The sun's shining for once—you really should make the most of it. And I'm dying to find out what happens next in that ballet story, Penny.'

'Me, too!' the little girl said with a smile.

Thankfully Leo wasn't in the staff canteen when Rosie grabbed a sandwich and a cold drink from the kiosk before going back to the ward. But the afternoon allergy clinic was just as awkward as the morning's. She simply didn't know how to behave towards him. Friendly felt wrong, given that she'd just ended their relationship; but coolness felt wrong, too, as if she were adding insult to injury.

She was really glad when clinic ended and she was able to go down to the nursery school to pick up the twins.

'Was everything all right today?' she asked Nina, trying to damp down the anxiety in her voice. 'Nobody tried to...' *Take the twins.* She could barely get the words out.

'No. Everything was fine,' Nina reassured her. 'Is the press still hounding you?'

'I didn't go outside at lunchtime; it's my day to read to Penny,' Rosie said. Though even if it hadn't been, she wouldn't have gone outside. She planned to use a taxi to and from the hospital for the foreseeable future rather than taking the Tube, too, even though it was going to make a hole in her budget. The most important thing was that the children would be safe.

'I'm sure Leo can do something. Maybe his press team—'

'It'll be fine,' Rosie said with a smile. 'I'd better get the twins home. Thanks for everything, Nina.'

Leo was thoroughly miserable.

He missed Rosie.

And he missed the twins.

The weekend in Tuscany had been wonderful. Hearing children's laughter flood through the *palazzo*, watching the twins run around the gardens, seeing their delight in being allowed to touch the tiny suit of armour…

He'd actually felt like a father.

And, for the first time in his life, he'd actually wanted to be a father. Wanted to share his ancestral home with the next generation down. He'd loved showing Lexi and Freddie around.

Even more, he'd loved being with Rosie. Her quiet calmness. Her sweetness. The way she'd been unflappable at the ball, ignoring the fact that she was wearing haute couture and real diamonds and focusing instead on saving someone's life.

The sweetest bit for him had been dancing with her on the grass in the moonlight, just the two of them and the roses. And then making love with her. Losing himself in her. Falling asleep with her curled in his arms.

Yet ironically his home country had been the cause of their problems. If he hadn't taken Rosie to the ball, she wouldn't have caught the attention of the press.

She'd been pretty clear that it was over between them.

That it had to be over, for the sake of her children. Although she'd put the blame on the press, she was obviously terrified that Michael's associates were going to crawl out of the woodwork and threaten the twins. And, for the second time in his life, Leo felt utterly powerless. The first time had been when his father had driven Emilia away, and Leo hadn't been able to convince her that he could keep her safe—that their love would be enough.

How ironic that he was in exactly the same position now. Except his family wasn't the problem: his mother had welcomed Rosie and the twins warmly, and he was pretty sure that Rosie had liked his mother, too. The problem was that Rosie was scared, and she couldn't get past the fear for long enough to let him solve the problem. Leo was pretty sure he could sort it out: a good lawyer would be able to get her an injunction. Even if she didn't know who they were, he'd be able to find out. Or his security team would.

This was crazy. He was supposed to be a doctor, a man who fixed things. Right now, he didn't have a clue how to fix this. How to make Rosie see that he *could* keep her safe. That everything would be just fine, if she'd give them a chance.

He'd just have to think harder. Work out what would be the one thing to make her trust him. But in the meantime he did what she'd asked and instructed his PR team to make it very clear that he and Rosie were absolutely not an item. And he had a quiet word with his legal and security team to see what they could find out about Michael and his associates, and to keep an eye on Rosie and the children. If the thugs really were watching her, his team would know very quickly—and he'd be able to keep Rosie and the children protected. And then maybe, once she realised that he could keep her safe, she'd learn to trust him.

Tuesday was just as difficult, Rosie found. Ward rounds, when she was rostered on with Leo; a staff meeting that spilled over into lunch and they all agreed to order in some sandwiches, so Rosie had to spend her lunch hour with Leo whether she liked it or not. She knew she had to speak to him, otherwise someone would notice the tension between them and start asking questions she didn't want to answer; but oh, it was hard. How did you make small talk with someone when you'd shared such a deep intimacy with them and remembered the feel of their skin against yours?

The worst thing was, she missed Leo. Like crazy. The children asked after him, too, wanting to know if he was coming to the park or if they were having pizza with him. Rosie was rapidly running out of excuses. And every lie ripped another little hole in her heart. If only she could be with him. If only she'd never met Michael—or if only Michael hadn't mixed with the wrong people because of his gambling problem…

But Wednesday morning brought her a different set of worries. The paparazzi and her fears about Michael's associates were forgotten when she went to wake up the twins and Freddie refused to get up.

Her son was often quiet, but he wasn't the grizzly sort.

'My tummy hurts,' he said.

And his face and hair were damp, she noticed. She sat down on the bed next to him and gently placed the back of her hand against his forehead.

It was definitely too hot.

'Does anywhere else hurt, Freddie?'

'Here.'

He pointed to his neck, and she went cold.

Had he just lain awkwardly during the night—or was it something more serious?

The first thing she needed to deal with was that temperature. And then she'd better call work to say that she couldn't come in, and the nursery school to say that the twins wouldn't be in today.

She grabbed the in-ear thermometer from the bathroom cabinet, along with the bottle of infant paracetamol. A quick check told her that her instincts were right: Freddie had a fever. 'I've got some special medicine to help you feel better,' she told Freddie, and measured out the dose. 'And I think you need to stay in bed this morning. If you're feeling a little bit better this afternoon, we'll all cuddle up on the sofa with a blanket and we'll watch *Toy Story*.' It was Freddie's favourite, guaranteed to cheer him up.

'I'm hot, Mummy,' he said.

'I know, baby.' She kissed his forehead. 'I'm going to get Lexi dressed, and then I'm going to bring you some juice.' It would be gentler on his stomach than milk. 'Do you want some toast? Or some yoghurt?'

He sniffed. 'No.'

'All right. I'll be back in a minute. Love you.'

'Love you, Mummy.' His lower lip wobbled, and a tear trickled down his cheek.

Once she'd got Lexi dressed, Rosie made her daughter some breakfast and grabbed the phone. Work was able to get agency cover for her, and the nursery school confirmed that a couple of children had gone down with some sort of tummy bug. Probably tomorrow both of them would be down with it, she thought wryly.

She'd just gone up to Freddie when he suddenly stiffened, twitched, and his eyes began to roll.

Oh, no.

'Freddie? Freddie?'

He didn't respond, and then the seizure began in earnest.

Pretend he's not yours. Pretend he's a patient, she reminded herself, and let her nursing training kick in. She glanced at her watch as she put him in the recovery position. OK. This was the first time he'd ever had a seizure—and he had a high temperature. Given his age, this was a perfectly normal thing.

As long as it lasted for less than five minutes.

She kept half an eye on him and half an eye on her watch. When the timing of the seizure reached seven minutes, she knew he needed better medical attention than she could give him at home. Given the time of day, it would be quicker for her to drive him to Paddington Children's Hospital herself rather than call an ambulance.

'Lexi, Freddie's not very well and we're going to take him in the car,' she said.

Somehow she managed to get both twins out to the car.

There were a couple of paparazzi loitering outside. 'Rosie!' one of them called. 'What's wrong?'

'My little boy's ill,' she said, pushing past them. 'Can't you find something better to do with your time than hassle me? I need to get him to hospital. Now!'

'Can we help?' the other one asked.

'Just go away. *Please*,' she said. She strapped the children into their car seats and hooked her phone up to her

car's stereo system so she could make her phone calls
safely. As soon as they were on the way to the hospital,
she called the ward. 'Kathleen? It's Rosie. I'm bringing
Freddie in with a febrile seizure.'

'Right. We'll be ready,' Kathleen said. 'Take care and
we'll see you in a few minutes.'

'Thanks.' She cut the call and called her mother; to
her relief, her mother answered on the fourth ring, and
agreed to meet her at the hospital and take Lexi back
home with her.

Just please, please let Freddie be all right, she thought
grimly, and headed for the hospital.

'Was that Rosie?' Leo asked.

'Yes,' Kathleen confirmed.

'And she said that Freddie's ill?'

'Febrile convulsions.'

'I'll take the case,' he said.

'But—'

'I'm a doctor,' he said softly. 'And that comes before
anything else. I'll look after Freddie.'

Though when Rosie appeared in the department, a
couple of minutes later, carrying Freddie and with Lexi
trotting along beside her, she didn't look particularly
pleased to see him.

'I'm on duty. Treating children is my job,' he reminded
her, taking Freddie from her and carrying the little boy
over to one of the side rooms.

'Will you make Freddie better, Leo?' Lexi asked as
he laid the little boy on the bed.

'I'll try my best,' he promised. Obviously Rosie hadn't
had anyone who could look after her daughter at extremely
short notice; at the same time, he needed to distract the

little girl so he could find out exactly what symptoms Freddie had. 'Lexi, can you draw a picture of a dog for Freddie while I talk to your mummy, please?'

She nodded solemnly, and he gave her some paper and a pen.

'My mum's going to pick her up from here. She's on the way,' Rosie said.

'Not a problem,' Leo said gently. 'Kathleen said Freddie's had febrile convulsions. Can you give me a full history?'

'I'm probably overreacting,' she said, but he could hear the underlying panic in her voice. 'Freddie had a high temperature this morning, and he said his tummy and his neck hurt.'

A sore neck and a high temperature: that combination could mean something seriously nasty.

Clearly she was thinking the same thing, because she said, 'I checked and there's no rash.'

Though they both knew it was possible to have meningitis without a rash.

'I've given him a normal dose of infant paracetamol,' she said. 'It hasn't brought his temperature down. And then he started fitting.' She swallowed hard. 'Neither of the twins has ever had any kind of fit before. I know he's of the age when he's most likely to have a febrile seizure, but it went on for more than ten minutes.'

'And you did exactly the right thing bringing him in. You're a paediatric nurse, so you know it's really common and most of the time everything's fine.'

But he could see in her expression that she was thinking of the rare cases when everything wasn't fine.

'It could be a bacterial infection causing the temperature and the fit,' he said. 'Not necessarily meningitis: it could be a urinary tract infection, an upper respiratory tract infection or tonsillitis, an ear infection or gastro-enteritis.'

She dragged in a breath. 'But it could be meningitis—you know a rash isn't the only sign.'

He nodded. 'Did Freddie have a vaccination for meningitis C?'

'Yes, at twelve weeks and again at a year,' Rosie confirmed.

'Again, that's a good sign,' he said gently. Small children didn't always get the classic triad of meningitis, but it was worth asking. 'Apart from saying his neck's sore, has he shown any signs of confusion, or a dislike of bright lights?' When Rosie shook her head he continued, 'Has he had any pains in his legs? Are his hands and feet cold, or has he said they feel cold?'

'No.'

'Again, that's a really good sign.' He checked Freddie's temperature, heart rate and capillary refill, and looked in his ears. 'Did he show any signs of pallor before the fit, or has there been any change in the colour of his lips?'

'No.'

'That's good.' But Leo also noted that Freddie wasn't smiling, and he was very quiet. Was that because the little boy had gone back into his shell or simply because he wasn't feeling well?

'I'm going to take a urine sample for culture,' he said. 'Given what you've told me, I'm not going to take any risks and I'll treat him for suspected meningitis until I can find out what the problem is. I'll need to do a lumbar puncture.'

Rosie went white.

How Leo wanted to hold her. Tightly.

But right now it wasn't appropriate. He needed to be a doctor first. 'You know the drill,' he said, 'and you also know it takes a couple of days to get the test results back, so I'll need to admit him to the ward. I'll start him on antibiotics and I might put him on a drip if I'm not happy with his hydration. I'll give him antipyretics as well, so I need you to tell me exactly when you gave the last dose, and I'll need you to sign the consent form.'

'All right,' Rosie said.

There was a knock on the door and an older woman stood in the doorway. 'Rosie?'

'Thanks for coming, Mum.'

Even if Rosie hadn't spoken, Leo would've known exactly who the older woman was; she had the same bright blue eyes as Rosie and her hair would've been the same colour years ago. Rosie was clearly trying her best to keep it together in front of the twins, but Leo could see the strain in her eyes.

'Mrs Hobbes. I'm Dr Marchetti—Leo,' he said.

He could see the moment that the penny dropped. Yes, he was *that* Leo. 'Take care of our Freddie,' Mrs Hobbes said quietly.

'I will,' he promised.

'Lexi, are you ready to go with Nanna?' Rosie asked.

The little girl nodded. 'Freddie, I drawed you a doggie to make you better.' She handed the picture to her twin and gave the pen back to Leo.

'Mum—before you go.' Rosie lowered her voice, as did Mrs Hobbes, but Leo caught every word they said. 'Just be careful. Michael—those men...'

Mrs Hobbes looked grim. 'Have you told the police?'

'They said to call them if I got another call. But just…
Be careful, Mum.'

'She'll be safe with me,' Mrs Hobbes promised. She
turned to Lexi. 'Come on, sweetie. We'll go back to my
house now, and Mummy can text us to let us know how
Freddie is.'

Lexi took her hand and left the room beside her grandmother.

Leo really wanted to talk to Rosie about Michael's
associates, but it would have to wait; he needed to treat
Freddie first. But then he'd deal with the situation. Because now he knew exactly why Rosie had ended things
between them and he had a pretty good idea why she
hadn't told him the full story.

'Freddie, I'm going to take a little bit of fluid from
your back so I can do some tests,' Leo said. 'I've got
some special cream, so it won't hurt.'

'Promise?' Freddie asked.

'Promise,' Leo said solemnly.

'Will you sing me a song?'

If it would distract the boy, it was a great idea. 'Sure I
will, while Mummy holds your hand,' he said, and sang
Freddie all the nursery songs he knew in Italian and English while he performed the lumbar puncture.

'All done,' he said, and then he saw that Rosie was crying. Silently, but the tears were running down her face.

Ah, hell.

He couldn't just ignore it.

He wrapped his arms round her.

She pulled away. 'This isn't appropriate.'

'Yes, it is,' he said softly. 'You're my colleague, you're

on your own and you're upset. I'm not an unfeeling monster who can walk away from that, regardless of whatever else might have happened.'

She leaned her head against his shoulder for just a moment, as if wishing that she really could rely on him, then pulled away. 'I have to be strong, for Freddie's sake.'

'But you don't have to be alone,' he reminded her. 'I'm here. Any time you need me.' And he wanted her and the twins in his life. For good.

He wasn't going to put pressure on her now, but once Freddie was on the mend they could discuss it. In the meantime he would just be there for her. No strings, no talking. Just there.

'Rosie—I heard what you said to your mum.'

She looked away. 'It's not your problem.'

'I can help. Right now you've got more than enough on your plate. Let me take some of the burden.'

'I can't.'

He sighed. 'There aren't any strings, if that's what you're worried about. Look, it's my fault that they've been in touch with you. If you hadn't come to Italy with me, the press wouldn't have heard about you, and Michael's associates wouldn't have contacted you. So, actually, it *is* my problem.'

She looked utterly miserable. 'I need to concentrate on Freddie.'

'Exactly. Let me deal with this so you can concentrate on him instead of worrying.'

She looked torn, but finally she said, 'All right. And thank you.'

He hated the way she sounded so broken and defeated. But, once Freddie was on the mend, she'd have that layer of worry removed. In the meantime he'd do his best to support her. And he'd solve her problem with Michael's associates.

The following two days were the worst forty-eight hours of Rosie's life. It was hard to keep Freddie's temperature down, and even though he was on antibiotics she worried that it really might be meningitis. If she lost him...

Leo kept a close eye on Freddie, and he also brought in sandwiches and coffee for Rosie.

'I can't eat,' she said.

'You have to, if you want to be strong for Freddie.'

But she couldn't face eating anything, not when she was so worried. And she didn't want to leave her little boy that night, so Leo made sure she had blankets and fresh water.

'I'll stay with you,' he said.

And how tempting it was. The idea of being able to lean on him, having someone there to support her. But she'd ended it between them. She couldn't be that selfish.

'No. You're on duty. You need a proper sleep.'

'I've done my time as a junior doctor. I can sleep in a chair.'

How she wanted to say yes. 'Thank you, but we'll be fine.'

'OK. Call me if you need me.'

At three in the morning, she thought about what he'd said. She was bone-deep tired, but how could she possibly sleep when her little boy was so sick? And it wouldn't be fair to call Leo, just because she felt alone and helpless. He'd offered, and she knew he'd be there within minutes if she called him. But it just wouldn't be fair of her.

Her eyes felt gritty from lack of sleep the next morning. And then Leo walked in with a paper cup of coffee from Tony's, fresh pastries and a pot of prepared strawberries, raspberries and blueberries.

She stared at him, unable to pull any coherent words together.

'Eat,' he said. 'I'm pulling rank as your senior colleague. You need to eat.' He glanced down at the sleeping child. 'I'm not leaving until you've eaten at least half the food and drunk that coffee.'

She knew he meant it. And although he didn't make her talk to him—he spent his time looking through Freddie's chart—having him there did make her feel better. Less alone.

'Better?' he asked when she'd managed to force down the fruit and one of the pastries.

'Better.'

'Good. Go and have a shower.' He produced a toothbrush and toothpaste. 'Hospital shop, before you ask. It'll make you feel a bit more human. I won't be going anywhere until you're back.'

'If he wakes—'

'—then I'll tell him where you are. Stop worrying.'

Gratefully, she took a shower and cleaned her teeth. Although she didn't have fresh clothes, just the shower and cleaning her teeth made her feel better. And the fact that Leo cared enough to do that for her, even though she'd dumped him...

She scrubbed the tears away. Not now. She had to stay strong.

'Thank you,' she said when she got back to Freddie's bedside to discover that he was still asleep.

'Any time. Hopefully the antibiotics will start to make a difference today. I'll drop by later,' Leo said.

And he was as good as his word. He called in twice to see how Freddie was doing. He also made her go out for a walk at lunchtime while he sat with Freddie.

'But—'

'But nothing,' he cut in gently. 'This is what you do for Julia. Let me do the same for you.'

'What about the press?'

'What about them? I'm a doctor first and a duke second. I couldn't care less about what the press thinks. You, Freddie and Lexi are the important ones here,' he told her. 'And Freddie knows me. He knows I'll do my best for him.'

She couldn't fault Leo as a doctor. He'd been meticulous with all the children they'd treated together, and he'd kept a really close eye on Freddie.

'But, just so you know,' he added, 'I've spoken to my PR team. They're dealing with the press and you don't have to worry any more.'

Maybe not about the press. But medicine was another matter: small children could become very sick, very quickly. And there was still the issue of Michael's associates.

As if he guessed at the fear she'd left unspoken, he said, 'I've also spoken to my security team and my lawyers. They've talked to the police here and they've been doing some investigations of their own. We know who they are. There's an injunction in place now, and my security team is keeping an eye on you, so nobody can get anywhere near you, Lexi or Freddie. You're *safe*.'

She couldn't take it in. Any of it. Everything felt like a blur. He knew who they were? But how? How had his team managed to find out who Michael's associates were, when the police hadn't been able to help her?

'Right. Out,' he said, gesturing to the door. 'Go and get some fresh air.'

Rosie did as she was told, her feet practically on auto-pilot. She wandered aimlessly round the streets outside the hospital, but all she could think of was Freddie. Her little boy. Was he going to be all right?

Unable to bear being away from him any longer, she went back in to the ward, only to find Freddie holding Leo's hand and Leo telling him some story about castles and magic suits of armour.

'Mummy.' Freddie gave her a half-smile and relief washed through Rosie. Was he really getting better? Or was this a slight recovery before he got worse?

There was a knock on the door, and Julia leaned round the doorframe. 'Hi. I won't stop—but Penny heard that Nurse Rosie's little boy wasn't very well, so she's done a drawing for him.' She smiled. 'She wanted to come herself, but...'

'The risk of infection's too great. I understand,' Rosie said, and took the drawing. 'Please say thank you to her. Look, Freddie—Penny's done you a special drawing of a doggie.'

'I like doggies,' he said. 'Thank you.'

She had to hold back the tears.

Leo squeezed her shoulder and murmured, 'It's going to be all right, Rosie, I promise you.'

He brought in a selection of savouries from one of the local cafés to tempt her that evening; and again he made her go out for some fresh air when Freddie fell asleep.

'You haven't slept for a day and a half,' he said when she came back all of ten minutes later. 'Take a nap now.'

'But—'

'I'm here. I'm not going anywhere. Freddie's safe with me. Sleep,' he said.

'I…' She shook her head. 'I can't.'

'Then let's try it this way.' He scooped her up in his arms and sat down in the chair next to Freddie's bed, then settled her on his lap and held her close.

'Leo, we can't—'

'Yes, we can,' he said, completely implacable. 'Go to sleep.'

Rosie didn't think it was possible; but whether it was the warmth of Leo's body, the regularity of his breathing or just the fact that she felt safe, curled in his arms like this, she actually fell asleep.

For four hours.

'I'm so sorry,' she said when she woke and realised how late it was.

'Don't apologise. You needed that.'

'But you should've gone home hours ago.'

'To an empty flat.' His eyes were very dark. 'I'm right where I want to be. By your side.'

'But we…' She swallowed hard. 'We're not together.'

'We could be,' he said.

She dragged in a breath, 'It's too complicated.'

'Then let me make it simple for you,' he said. 'I grew up in a world where I didn't know who I was supposed to be—my father changed the goalposts constantly, and nothing I did was ever right. I thought it was me, and that I was unlovable. Emilia made me think that maybe the problem wasn't me after all, and love might actually exist—but it was so easy for my father to push her out of my life. So I decided that a family wasn't for me. I didn't want to bring children into the mean-spirited world I'd grown up in. And I didn't want to make some kind of dynastic marriage with someone I didn't love and then start making the same mistakes my father did.' He stroked her face. 'And then I met you. And the twins. And suddenly everything was possible. Love and a family... Everything I'd told myself I didn't want, but actually I did. And when you came to Tuscany, it was the first time I could remember feeling really happy at the *palazzo*. Having the place full of the twins' laughter, sharing the garden with you.' He looked her straight in the eye. 'Making love with you and falling asleep with you in my arms. It was perfect.'

It had been like that for her, too.

'And, at the charity ball, I was so proud of you. You saved someone's life—you didn't fuss about your dress or anything, you were just cool and calm and sorted everything out, even though you didn't speak the language. I love you, Rosie. You're everything I want—you and the twins. We can give them a fabulous life together—and you're the one who can help me make the world a better place. Marry me, Rosie.'

Words she'd never thought to hear again.

And she knew Leo wouldn't change. He'd be there right by her side. He'd stick to his vows to love, honour and cherish her.

How she wanted to say yes.

But there was her past. Michael. The press had dredged it up once, and they'd do it again and again. She'd end up dragging Leo down. She remembered him saying that he'd fixed the problem with Michael's associates—but supposing it was only temporary? Supposing they came back? Supposing they regrouped and wanted more and more? Supposing they got past Leo's security and hurt the children, his mother or him?

'I can't,' she whispered.

She tried to wriggle off his lap, but he wouldn't let her. 'Why not?'

Did he really need her to spell it out? 'I can't fit into your world. I'd drag you down.'

He kissed her. 'No, you wouldn't. You've changed my world, Rosie. You've shown me what love and family really means. My mother adores you—so does everyone at the *palazzo*.'

Could it possibly be true? She'd really made a difference to his world? He really, really wanted her there?

'Through you, I've realised that I can give our children a life like the one I didn't have when I was growing up—one where their parents love and respect each other. One where we'll be firm when we have to, but fair, and our children will always know we love them and want to have fun with them.' He paused. 'I love you, Rosie.'

He loved her.

She could see the sincerity in his dark eyes. He felt the same way about her that she did about him. Something that went deeper than the fear that numbed her every time she thought about what Michael's associates could do.

Didn't they say that love could conquer all?

Looking at Leo, she saw strength and compassion and deep, deep love.

And that gave her the courage to admit to her feelings. 'I love you, too, Leo,' she whispered. He was everything she wanted—a man who'd be there in the tough times as well as the good times, reliable and kind and having time for the children. A man who really loved her instead of just expecting her to be some kind of trophy wife.

'Then marry me, Rosie. Forget the dukedom. It's not important. At the end of the day, I'm a doctor and you're a nurse. We're a team at work and we'll be a great team at home, too. And I don't care whether we live in London or Italy: as long as I'm with you, I'll be happy. And I can make you and the twins happy, too. Keep you safe. Make you feel loved and respected, the way you deserve to be.'

Even though she was sleep-deprived and had spent the last couple of days worried sick, she was mentally together just enough to realise that he meant it.

They really could have it all.

Be a real family.

But there was still that one last fear. The one thing that stopped her being able to step forward and take what he was offering her. 'Michael's associates... How could you fix it, when the police couldn't? How could you find out who they were?'

He stroked her face. 'I don't like the man my father was, but maybe he's done us a good turn, in the end.'

'How?' She didn't understand.

'His reputation apparently still has a ripple or two,' Leo said dryly. 'His name is definitely remembered in certain circles. And let's just say that my team have, um, avenues open to them that might not be available elsewhere. So I believe them when they tell me that nobody will ever threaten you or the children, ever again. You're safe with me. Always. Marry me, Rosie.'

You're safe with me.

She believed him. 'Yes,' she whispered.

He stroked her face. 'You're sure?'

'I'm sure.' She dragged in a breath. 'I'll be honest— I'm still scared that somehow Michael's associates will find a way round your security team. That they'll hurt you. But if you're prepared to take that risk, then I can be brave, too.'

'The alternative's being without you. Missing you every single second of every single day. And I don't want to do that,' he said simply. 'And they won't find a way round my security team. As I said, my father was, um, good at warning people off. I'm not my father, but people will remember him. And maybe we can turn his legacy into love. Together.'

'Together,' she echoed, and reached up to kiss him.

Leo stayed with Rosie that night, curled together in a chair.

And in the morning, they got the news they'd both been hoping for.

'It isn't meningitis,' Leo said, and lifted her up and whirled her round. 'We're still not sure what the virus is, but provided his temperature stays down and he keeps responding the way he has, you can take him home at lunchtime.'

'The perfect day,' she said. 'Freddie's all right. And we have a wedding to plan.'

He kissed her lingeringly. 'The perfect day.'

EPILOGUE

One year later

'YOU'RE QUITE SURE you don't mind looking after the children tonight?' Rosie asked her mother-in-law.

'Very sure. You know I love spending time with my grandchildren,' Beatrice said.

'And we like being with Nonna,' Freddie and Lexi added.

Since they'd moved to Florence, where Leo had taken over as the head of the clinic that the Marchetti family supported and Rosie worked there as a nurse, the children had really blossomed. They were almost as fluent in Italian as they were in English. And Rosie rather thought that Beatrice had blossomed, too; she seemed much less frail. Confident enough to come and stay in Leo and Rosie's townhouse in Florence for the night, while they attended the clinic's annual charity ball. And, best of all, her past was staying exactly where she wanted it to stay: in the past. True to Leo's promise, Michael's associates had left her alone.

'Now, off to the ball with you,' Beatrice said. 'And hopefully there will be no wasps, tonight.'

'Hopefully,' Leo said with a smile. 'Though Rosie can

ask for adrenaline herself now in Italian, thanks to your teaching, Mamma.'

'Ah, now I leave the medical terminology to you, Leo,' Beatrice said with a smile. 'You look lovely in that dress, Rosie. I'm so proud of my new daughter.'

'And thank you for lending me your diamonds again, Mamma,' Rosie said, hugging her warmly.

'It's good to see them being worn. Just as they should be, by the Duchessa di Calvanera,' Beatrice said.

'Send us some pictures from the ball,' Lexi begged, 'so we can see all the other pretty dresses, too.'

'We'll try. Be good for Nonna,' Leo said.

'*Sì*, Babbo,' the twins chorused.

Rosie was still smiling when Leo drove them across town to the hotel. 'Funny to think it's a year since my first trip to Florence. And what a year it's been. Our wedding, moving here to work in the clinic…'

'It's been a good year,' Leo agreed, parking the car.

'Just before we go in,' she said, 'I have a little news for you.'

'Oh?'

'You might need to brush up on your nappy-changing skills.'

He stared at her. 'Nappy-changing?'

She spread her hands. 'This is the twenty-first century. Duke or not, I'm expecting you to be a fully hands-on dad.'

'Hands-on…?' The penny finally dropped, and he punched his fist in the air. 'We're going to have another baby!'

Which was when Rosie realised that Leo really *did* think of the twins as his own. He'd always been careful to treat them as if they were his own children; and now she knew he loved them as much as she did.

'You,' he said, 'have just made me happier than I ever thought possible. I know we're not supposed to breathe a word until twelve weeks, but right now I want to climb to the top of the hotel and yell out to the whole of Florence that I'm going to be a dad again. And that I love my wife very, very much. And...'

There was only one way to stop her over-talkative Duke.

She smiled, and kissed him.

* * * * *

Welcome to the
PADDINGTON CHILDREN'S HOSPITAL
six-book series

Available now:

THEIR ONE NIGHT BABY
by Carol Marinelli
FORBIDDEN TO THE PLAYBOY SURGEON
by Fiona Lowe
MUMMY, NURSE... DUCHESS?
by Kate Hardy
FALLING FOR THE FOSTER MUM
by Karin Baine

Coming soon:

HEALING THE SHEIKH'S HEART
by Annie O'Neil
A LIFE-SAVING REUNION
by Alison Roberts

FALLING FOR
THE FOSTER MUM

BY
KARIN BAINE

First Published in Great Britain 2017
By Mills & Boon, an imprint of HarperCollins*Publishers*
1 London Bridge Street, London, SE1 9GF

© 2017 Harlequin Books S.A.

Special thanks and acknowledgement are given to Karin Baine
for her contribution to the Paddington Children's Hospital series.

ISBN: 978-0-263-92644-6

Printed and bound in Spain
by CPI, Barcelona

Dear Reader,

This book has been such a rollercoaster to write—
I really hope you enjoy reading my slice of life at
Paddington Children's Hospital.

As excited as I was about taking part in my first
continuity series, the prospect of writing along with
such fabulous established authors was daunting for
a newbie, to say the least! I shouldn't have worried.
These ladies had such fabulous ideas for the series,
and are so much better organised than I am, it made
the process easier.

A book set in London was also a great excuse for a
research trip—and it just so happened to coincide
with my twentieth wedding anniversary! I had a
lovely day at the zoo with my hubby, following in
Quinn, Matt and little Simon's footsteps. Albeit in the
rain…

Maybe for our silver anniversary I'll plan a research
trip somewhere a bit more exotic. Surely they have
doctors on Mediterranean cruises too…

Happy reading!

Karin xx

This one's for Jennie, Stephen and Samantha, my London travelling companions/supervisors, because we all know I can't be trusted out on my own!

Along with John. You've always been so supportive of my writing and it's much appreciated. xx

Thanks to Catherine, Abbi and Chellie, who've helped me so much with my research.

Karin Baine lives in Northern Ireland with her husband, two sons, and her out-of-control notebook collection. Her mother's and her grandmother's vast collections of books inspired her love of reading and her dream of becoming a Mills & Boon author. Now she can tell people she has a *proper* job! You can follow Karin on Twitter, @karinbaine1, or visit her website for the latest news—karinbaine.com.

Books by Karin Baine

Mills & Boon Medical Romance

French Fling to Forever
A Kiss to Change Her Life
The Doctor's Forbidden Fling
The Courage to Love Her Army Doc

Visit the Author Profile page at millsandboon.co.uk for more titles.

Praise for
Karin Baine

'The moment I picked up Karin Baine's debut medical romance I knew I would not be disappointed with her work. Poetic and descriptive writing, engaging dialogue, thoroughly created characters and a tightly woven plot propels *French Fling to Forever* into the must-read, highly recommended level.'
—*Contemporary Romance Reviews*

PROLOGUE

QUINN GRADY WAS officially the worst mother in the world. Barely a week into the job and her charge was already lying in the hospital.

Simon mightn't be her *real* son but that made her role as his foster mum even more important. As someone who'd been passed from pillar to post in the care system herself, it meant everything to her to provide a safe home for him. Yet here she was, sitting on her own in the bright corridors of the Paddington Children's Hospital, nerves shredded, waiting for news on his condition.

She'd done everything by the parenting handbook, even when life had thrown her that 'I'm not ready to be a dad' curveball from Darryl right before Simon had come into her life. Her focus had remained on his welfare regardless of her own heartbreak that her partner had gone back on his word that he was going into this with her. The sleepless nights she'd spent with her mind running through every possible scenario she might encounter as someone's guardian hadn't prepared her for this.

A fire at the school.

As she'd waved a tearful goodbye this morning and watched Simon walk away in his smart, new uniform she'd half expected a phone call. He'd looked so small, so lost, she'd almost been waiting for the school to call and ask her to pick him up, to come and hug him and tell him everything was going to be all right.

Not this. A fire was totally beyond her control. She couldn't have prevented it and she couldn't fix it. Apparently all she could do was fill in endless forms and she hadn't even been able to do that until she'd contacted the local fostering authority to notify them about what had happened. Watching the frantic staff deal with the influx of injured schoolchildren, she'd never felt so helpless.

She knew Simon was badly hurt but she hadn't been able to see him yet until they stabilised him. He could have life-changing injuries. Or worse. What if he didn't make it? Her stomach lurched, terror gripping her insides at the thought of his suffering. This was supposed to have been a new start for both of them, to wipe out the past and build a better future. Now all she wanted was to see him and know he was okay.

She fidgeted in the hard plastic chair doing her best not to accost any of the nurses running from department to department. Perhaps if she was a *proper* mum she'd feel more entitled to demand constant information on his condition.

'Are you Simon's mother?'

A vision in green scrubs appeared beside her. His lovely Irish lilt was the comfort blanket she needed at this moment in time.

'No. Yes.' She didn't know the appropriate response for this kind of situation.

As a pair of intense, sea-green eyes stared at her, waiting for an answer, she realised her temporary status didn't matter. 'I'm his foster mother.'

It was enough to soften the doctor's features and he hunched down beside her chair.

'I'm Matthew McGrory, a burns specialist. I've been brought over to assess Simon's condition.'

Quinn held her breath. *Good news or bad?*

She searched his face for a sign but apart from noting how handsome he was up close she discovered nothing.

'How is he?'

Good?

Bad?

'Would you like to come through and see for yourself?' The doctor's mouth tilted into a smile.

That had to be positive, right?

'Yes. Thank you.' She got to her feet though her legs weren't as steady as she needed them to be. Nonetheless she hurried down the corridor, powering hard to keep up with the great strides of a man who had to be at least six foot.

He stopped just outside the door of the Paediatric Intensive Care Unit, the last barrier between her and Simon, but an ominous one. Only the most poorly children would be on the other side and he was one of them. Not for the first time she wished she had someone to go through this with her.

'Before we go in, I want you to be prepared. Simon has suffered severe burns along with some smoke inhalation. It's not a pretty sight but everything we're doing is to minimise long-term damage. Okay? Ready?'

She nodded, feigning bravery and nowhere near ready. Whatever the injuries, they would affect her and Simon for a long time but they were in this together.

'He needs me,' she said, her voice a mere whisper as she tried to pull herself together. She wondered if clinging to the hunky doctor's arm for support was an option but he was already opening the door and stepping into the ward before she could make a grab for him.

They passed several cubicles but she couldn't make out any of the faces as the small bodies were dwarfed by monster machinery aiding their recovery.

'Oh, Simon!' Her hand flew to her mouth to cover the gasp as she was led to the last bed on the row. She wouldn't have recognised him if not for the glimpse of curly hair against the pillow.

The face of the little boy she'd left at the school gates only hours ago was now virtually obscured by the tubes and wires going in and out of his tiny form keeping him alive. His pale torso was a contrast to the mottled black and red angry skin of his right arm stretched out at his side. Lying there, helpless, he looked even younger than his meagre five years.

Quinn's knees began to buckle at the enormity of the situation and the tears she'd been desperately trying to keep at bay finally burst through the dam.

Strong hands seemed to come from nowhere to catch her before she fell to the floor in a crumpled heap of guilt and manoeuvred her into a chair.

'I know it's a lot to take in but he's honestly in the best place. Simon has severe burns to the face and arm and we have him intubated to help him breathe after the smoke inhalation. Once the swelling has gone down and we're happy there's no damage to his eyes, we'll move him to the burns unit for further treatment.'

She blinked through her tears to focus on the man kneeling before her.

'Is he going to be okay?' That was all she needed to know.

'The next forty-eight hours will be crucial in assessing the full extent of his burns. He'll need surgery to keep the wounds clean and prevent any infection and there's a good chance he'll need skin grafts in the future. I won't deny it'll be a long process, but that's why I'm here. I'm a reconstructive surgeon too and I will do my very best to limit and repair any permanent scarring. The road to recovery is going to be tough but we're in this together.' This virtual stranger reached out and gave her hand a squeeze to reassure her but the electric touch jolted her back into reality.

She was a mum now and following in the footsteps of her own amazing adoptive mum, who'd moved heaven and earth to do what was best for her. It was time for her to step up to the plate now too.

'I'll do whatever it takes. Simon deserves the best.' And something told her that the best was surgeon Matthew McGrory.

CHAPTER ONE

Two months later

QUINN WISHED THEY did an easy-to-read, step-by-step guide for anxious foster mums going through these operations too. It was difficult to know what to do for the best when Simon resisted all attempts to comfort him pre-op.

He turned his face away when she produced the well-worn kids' book the hospital had provided to explain the surgical process.

She sighed and closed the book.

'I suppose you know this off by heart now.' Not that it made this any easier. After the countless hours he'd spent on the operating table they both knew what they were in for—pain, tears and a huge dollop of guilt on her part.

She hadn't caused the fire or his injuries but neither had she been able to save him from this suffering. Given the choice she'd have swapped places with the mite and offered herself up for this seemingly endless torture rather than watch him go through it.

'Can I get you anything?' she asked the back of his head, wishing there was something she could do other than stand here feeling inadequate.

The pillow rustled as he shook his head and she had

to suppress the urge to try and swamp him into a big hug the way her mother always had when she'd been having a hard time. Simon didn't like to be hugged. In fact, he resisted any attempt to comfort him. That should've been his *real* mother's job but then apparently she'd never shown affection for anything other than her next fix. His too-young, too-addicted parents were out of the picture, their neglect so severe the courts had stripped them of any rights.

Quinn and Simon had barely got to know each other before the fire had happened so she couldn't tell if his withdrawal was a symptom of his recent trauma or the usual reaction of a foster child afraid to get attached to his latest care giver. She wasn't his parent, nor one of the efficient medical staff, confident in what they were doing. For all she knew he'd already figured out she was out of her depth and simply didn't want to endure her feeble overtures. Maybe he just didn't like her. Whatever was causing the chasm between them it was vital she closed it, and fast.

As if on cue, their favourite surgeon stepped into the room. 'Back again? I'm sure you two are sick of the sight of me.'

That velvety Irish accent immediately caught her attention. She frowned as goose bumps popped up across her skin. At the age of thirty-two she should really have better self-control over an ill-conceived crush on her foster son's doctor.

'Hi, Matt.' An also enchanted Simon sat upright in bed.

It was amazing how much they both seemed to look forward to these appointments and hate them at the same time. Although the skin grafts were a vital part of recovery, they were traumatic and led to more night terrors once they returned home as Simon relived the events of the fire in his sleep. He'd been one of the most seriously burned children, having been trapped in his classroom by falling debris. Although the emergency services had thankfully rescued him, no one had been able to save him from the memories or the residual pain.

Matt, as he'd insisted they call him, was the one constant during this whole nightmare. The one person Simon seemed to believe when he said things would work out. Probably because he had more confidence in himself and his abilities than she did in herself, when every dressing change made her feel like a failure.

The poor child's face was still scarred, even after the so-called revolutionary treatment, and his arm was a patchwork quilt of pieced together skin. Technically his injuries had occurred in school but that didn't stop her beating herself up that it had happened on her watch. Especially when the fragile bond they'd had in those early days had disintegrated in the aftermath of the fire. Unlike the one he'd forged with the handsome surgeon.

Matt moved to the opposite side of the bed from Quinn and pulled out some sort of plastic slide from his pocket. 'I've got a new one for you, Simon. The disappearing coin trick!' he said with flare, plucking a ten pence piece from the air.

'Cool!'

Of course it was. Magic was a long way away from the realities of life with second- and third-degree burns. Fun time with Matt before surgery offered an escape whilst she was always going to be the authority figure telling him not to scratch and slathering cream over him when he just wanted to be left alone.

Somehow Simon was able to separate his friend who performed magic tricks from the surgeon who performed these painful procedures, whereas she was the one he associated with his pain. It was frustrating, especially seeing him so engaged when she'd spent all day trying to coax a few words from him.

'I need you to place the coin in here.' He gave Simon the coin and pulled out a tray with a hole cut out of the centre from the plastic slide.

Concentration was etched on his face as he followed instructions and once Quinn set aside her petty jealousy she appreciated the distraction from the impending surgery. After all, that's what she wanted for him—to be the same as any other inquisitive five-year-old, fascinated by the world around him. Not hiding away, fearful of the unknown, the way he was at home.

'Okay, so we push it back in here—' he slid the tray back inside the case '—and this is the important bit. We need a magic word.'

'Smelly pants!' Simon had the mischievous twinkle of a child who knew he could get away with being naughty on this occasion.

'I was thinking along the more traditional abracadabra line but I guess that works too.' Matt exchanged a grin across the bed with her. It was a brief moment which made her forget the whole parent/doctor divide and react as any other woman who'd had a good-looking man smile at her.

That jittery, girlish excitement took her by surprise as he made eye contact with her and sent her heart rate sky high. Since Darryl left her she hadn't given any thought to the opposite sex. At least not in any 'You're hot and I want you' way. More of a 'You're a man and I can't trust you' association. She wasn't prepared to give away any more of herself—of her time or her heart—to anyone who wouldn't appreciate the gift. All of her time and energy these days was directed into the fostering process, trying to make up for the lack of two parents in Simon's life. Harbouring any form of romantic ideas was self-indulgent and, most likely, self-destructive.

She put this sudden attraction down to the lack of adult interaction. Since leaving her teaching post to tutor from home and raise Simon, apart from the drive-by parents of her students, and her elderly neighbour, Mrs Johns, the medical staff were the only grown-ups she got to talk to. Very few of them were men, and even fewer had cheekbones hand-carved by the gods. It was no wonder she'd overreacted to a little male attention. The attraction had been there since day one and she'd fought it with good reason when her last romantic interlude had crashed her world around her. Everything she'd believed in her partner had turned out to be a lie, making it difficult for her to trust a word anyone told her any more. She kept everyone at a distance now, but Matt was such a key figure in their days that he was nigh on impossible to ignore. As the weeks had gone on she found herself getting into more arguments with him, forcing him to take the brunt of her fears for Simon and the annoyance she should have directed at herself.

Matt waved his hand over the simple piece of plastic which had transformed Simon's body language in mere seconds.

'Smelly pants!' he shouted, echoed by his tiny assistant.

The magician-cum-surgeon frowned at her. Which apparently was equally as stimulating as a smile.

'It'll only work if we all say the magic words together. Let's try this again.'

Quinn rolled her eyes but she'd go along with anything to take Simon's mind off what was coming next.

'Smelly pants!' they all chorused as Matt pulled out the now empty tray.

'Wow! How did you do that?' Simon inspected the magic chamber, suitably impressed by the trick.

'Magic.' Matt gave her a secret wink and started her tachycardia again.

Didn't he have theatre prep or intensive hand-scrubbing to do rather than showing off here and disturbing people's already delicate equilibrium?

'I wish I could make my scars disappear like that.' Simon's sudden sad eyes and lapse back into melancholy made Quinn's heart ache for him.

'I'm working on it, kiddo. That's why all of these operations are necessary even though they suck big time. It might take a few waves of my magic wand but I'll do my very best to make them disappear.'

Quinn folded her arms, binding her temper inside her chest. He might mean well but he shouldn't be giving the child false hope. Simon's body was a chequered, vivid mess of dead and new flesh. He was never going to have blemish-free skin again, regardless of the super-confident surgeon's skills, and she was the one who'd have to pick up the pieces when the promises came to nothing. Again.

'You said that the last time.' Not even Simon was convinced, lying back on the bed, distraction over.

'I also said it would take time. Good things come to those who wait, right?' It was a mantra he'd used since day one but he clearly wasn't *au fait* with the limited patience of five-year-olds. Unlike Quinn, who'd had a crash course in tantrums and tears while waiting for the miraculous recovery to happen before her very eyes. Her patience had been stretched to the limit too.

'Right,' Simon echoed without any conviction.

'I'll tell you what, once you're back from theatre and wide awake, I'll come back and show you how to do a few tricks of your own. Deal?'

Quinn couldn't tell if it was bravado or ego preventing the doctor from admitting defeat as he stood with his hand held out to make the bargain. Either way, she didn't think it was healthy for him to get close to Simon only to let him down. He'd had enough of that from his birth parents, who'd given up any rights to him in favour of drugs, foster parents, who'd started the adoption process then abandoned him when they'd fallen pregnant themselves, and her, who'd sent him to get burned up in school. It might have failed her once but that protective streak was back with a vengeance.

'We couldn't ask you to do that. I'm sure you have other patients to see and we've already taken up so much of your time.' She knew these extra little visits weren't necessary. They had highly skilled nurses and play specialists to make these transitions easier for the children. These informal chats and games made her feel singled out. As if he was trying to suss out her capability to look after Simon outside of the hospital. The nurses had noticed too, remarking how much extra time he'd devoted to Simon's recovery and she didn't appreciate it as much as they probably thought she should. He wasn't going to sneak his way into her affections the way Darryl had, then use her fostering against her; she'd learned that lesson the hard way. She could do this. Alone.

'Not at all. I'm always willing to pass on my secrets

to a budding apprentice.' He held out his hand again and Simon shook it with his good arm, bypassing her concerns.

'I just mean perhaps you should be concentrating on the surgery rather than performing for us.' The barb was enough to furrow that brow again but he had a knack for getting her back up. Handsome or not, she wouldn't let him cause Simon any more pain than necessary.

The wounded look in his usually sparkling green eyes instantly made her regret being such a cow to him when he'd been nothing but kind to Simon since the accident. His smile was quickly back in place but it no longer reached anywhere past his mouth.

'It's no problem. I can do both. I'll see you soon, kiddo.' He ruffled Simon's hair and turned to leave. 'Can I have a word outside, Ms Grady?'

As he brushed past her, close enough to whisper into her ear, Quinn's whole body shivered with awareness. A combination of nerves and physical attraction. Neither of which she had control over any longer.

'Sure,' she said although she suspected he wasn't giving her a choice; she felt as though she was being called into the headmaster's office for misbehaving. A very hot headmaster who wasn't particularly happy with her. Unsurprising, really, when she'd basically just insulted him on a professional level.

She promised Simon she'd be back soon and took a deep breath before she followed Matt out the door.

'I know you're having a tough time at the moment but I'd really appreciate it if you stopped questioning my dedication to my job in front of my patient.'

It was the first time Quinn had seen him riled in all of these weeks. He was always so calm in the face of her occasional hysteria, so unflappable through every hurdle of Simon's treatment. Although it was unsettling to see the change in him, that intense passion, albeit for his work, sent tingles winding through her body until her toes curled, knowing she was the one who'd brought it to the fore. She found herself wondering how deep his passions lay and how else they might manifest...

He cleared his throat and reminded her she was supposed to speak, to argue back. She questioned what he was doing, he pulled her up on it and claimed rank when it came to Simon's health care—that was the way this went. It kept her from going completely round the bend imagining the worst that could happen when she'd be the one left dealing with the consequences on her own. She was supposed to be the overprotective mother voicing her concerns that everything being done was in her son's best interests, just as he was the one to insist he knew what he was doing. Fantasising about Matt in any other capacity, or his emotions getting the better of him, definitely wasn't in their well-rehearsed script.

'Yeah...well... I'd appreciate it if you didn't give Simon false hope that everything will go back to normal. We've both had enough of people letting us down.' Not that she knew what normal was, but although he deserved a break, they had to be realistic too.

'I'm not in the habit of lying to my patients...'

'No? What about this miracle spray-on skin which was supposed to fast-track his recovery? It's been two months and his burns are still very much visible. I should've known it was too good to be true when you would only use it to treat his facial burns and not the ones on his arm. I mean, if it was such a wonder cure it would make sense to use it everywhere and not make him go through these skin grafts anyway.' She was aware her voice had gone up a few decibels and yet she couldn't seem to stop herself when something good she'd believed was going to happen hadn't. This time it wasn't only *her* hopes that were being dashed.

Matt simply sighed when Quinn would've understood if he'd thrown his hands up and walked away. Deep down she knew he'd done his best, and yet, they were still here going through the same painful process.

'I can only reiterate what I told you at the start. It will take time. Perhaps the progress we have made isn't as noticeable to you because you see him every day, but the scars *are* beginning to fade. It's as much as we can hope for at this stage. As I explained, this is a new treatment, not readily available everywhere in the UK, and funding is hard to come by. The burns on Simon's arm are full thickness, not suitable for the trial, otherwise I'd have fought tooth and nail to make it happen. But he's young— his skin will heal quicker than yours or mine. Besides, I'm good at what I do.' There wasn't any obvious arrogance in his words or stance. It was simply a statement of fact. Which did nothing to pull her mind out of the gutter.

'So you keep telling me,' she muttered under her breath. However, despite his conscientious efforts, Simon no longer resembled the child she'd been charged with minding, either physically or mentally.

'I meant what I said. I'm not in the habit of lying to sick kids, or their beautiful mothers.' His forehead smoothed out as he stopped being cross with her.

The renewed smile combined with the reassuring touch of his hands on her shoulders sent those shivers back Irish dancing over her skin. She was too busy squealing inside at the compliment to correct him again about being Simon's *foster* mother.

Unfortunately, in her experience she couldn't always take people's word as truth. It wasn't that long ago Darryl had sworn he was in this thing with her.

'I hope not,' she said, the cold chill moving to flatten the first fizz of ardour she'd felt since her ex abandoned her and the future they'd planned together.

Simon's fate was entirely in this man's hands. Matt's skills on the operating table would determine his long-term appearance and probably his self-esteem along with it. It was too much to expect her to put her faith entirely in the word of a virtual stranger. Especially when the men closest to her had littered her life with broken promises and dreams.

Quinn Grady was a grade-A pain in the backside. In the most understandable way. Matt had seen his fair share of anxious parents over the years. His line of work brought people to him in their most fragile, vulnerable state and it was only natural that emotions ran high, but she'd spent most of the last couple of months questioning his every decision, seemingly doubting his ability to get Simon through the other side of his injuries. It was exhausting for all of those concerned. Normally he outlined his treatment plan and got on with it but somehow this case had drifted off course.

The spray-on skin was a relatively new treatment. Instead of these painful skin grafts, a small sample of healthy skin was removed from the patient and placed in a processing unit where it reproduced in a special suspension solution which was then sprayed over the damaged area where it continued to grow and multiply. There was no risk of the patient's body rejecting it because it was from the patient's own cells. The regenerative nature of this process meant the wounds healed rapidly in comparison to traditional techniques, such as the one he was performing now. If it wasn't for the extensive burns on Simon's arm, where he'd defended himself from the flames, he wouldn't have to go through the skin grafts or worry about scarring because the spray-on skin would stretch with him as he grew.

He'd expected Quinn to be wary; he'd had to convince her as well as the board that this was worth trialling, but the constant clashing had tested him. Naturally, she wanted instant results, for the burns to fade and heal overnight, but that wasn't how it worked. Almost every day she demanded to know 'Why?' and he couldn't always give her the answer she wanted. *He* knew the results were favourable compared to some he'd seen, and indeed, Simon's facial burns were exceptionally better healed than those on his arm but he was still disfigured. For now. Until the boy resembled his pre-fire self, Matt was going to take the flak, and so far he'd been happy to do so.

He knew he'd probably become too involved with Simon's case, more so than the other children he'd seen at Paddington's as a result of the fire at Westbourne Grove Primary School. Perhaps it was because his burns had been so extensive, or perhaps the reason was closer to home. The single foster mum reminded him a lot of himself and the hand he'd been dealt once upon a time.

Although he assumed she'd voluntarily agreed to take on the responsibility for other people's children. His role as a stand-in father had been thrust upon him when his dad had died and left him in charge of his younger siblings.

Matt recognised the fear in Quinn's brilliant blue eyes, even when she was giving him grief. He'd spent over a decade fretting about getting his sisters through their childhood in one piece with much the same haunted expression staring back at him in the mirror.

It was only now that Bridget, the youngest of the brood, had gone off to university he was able to relax a little. Of course, that didn't mean he wasn't still handling relationship woes or doling out crisis loans, but at least he could do most of his parenting over the phone these days, unless they came to visit him in London.

It meant he had his life back, that he'd been able to leave Dublin and take this temporary contract. When his time was up here he would have no reason to feel guilty about moving on to somewhere shiny and new and far from Ireland.

Quinn wouldn't have that luxury for a long time with Simon being so young. As his foster mother, she was probably under even more pressure to get him through his injuries, and naturally, that had extended to his surgeon. If fostering authorities were anything like social services to deal with, she'd have to jump through hoops to prove her suitability as a parent.

Life was tough enough as a substitute parent without the added trauma of the fire for her and Simon. Especially when she appeared to be doing this on her own. He hadn't spotted a wedding ring, and to his knowledge there hadn't been any other visitors during Simon's hospitalisation. When the cancer had claimed his father, Matt had been in much the same boat and being a sounding board for Quinn's frustrations was the least he could do to help. Unless her comments were in danger of unnecessarily upsetting Simon.

A boy needed a strong mother as much as a father. Matt's had been absent since shortly after Bridget's birth, when she'd suddenly decided family life wasn't for her. With his father passing away only a few years later, there had been no one left for them to turn to. For him to turn to. He'd had to manage the budget, the bills, the parent/teacher meetings and the numerous trips to A&E which were part and parcel of life with a brood of rambunctious kids, all on his own. Most of the time it had felt as though the world was against him having a life of his own.

He knew the struggle, the loneliness and the all-encompassing fear of screwing up and he would've gone out of his way to help anyone in a similar situation. At least, that's how he justified his interest. It wasn't entirely down to the fact he enjoyed seeing her, or the sparks created every time they had one of their 'discussions.' Attraction to single mothers wasn't something he intended to act upon and certainly not with the parent of one of his patients.

He'd only just gained his freedom from one young family and he wasn't ready, willing or able to do it again. As it was, he would be in young Simon's life for a long time to come. Perhaps even longer than Quinn. There were always going to be more surgeries as the child grew and his skin stretched. Treatments for scar tissue often took months to be effective and new scar contractures, where the skin tightened and restricted movement, could appear a long way down the line in young patients who were still growing.

'He's out.' The anaesthetist gave the go-ahead for the team to begin.

Time was of the essence. Generally they didn't keep children under the anaesthetic for more than a few hours at a time in case it proved too much for their small bodies to cope with. Hence why the skin grafts were still ongoing months later. Before they could even attempt the graft they had to clean the wound and harvest new skin from a separate donor site.

And Quinn wondered why recovery was taking so long.

'Saline, please. Let's get this done as quickly and accurately as we can.' Despite all the support in the operating theatre from the assisting staff, Matt had never borne so much responsibility for a patient as he did now.

Simon was completely at his mercy lying here, lost among the medical equipment surrounding the operating table. The slightest slip and Matt would have to face the wrath of the Mighty Quinn.

He smiled beneath his surgical mask at the thought of her squaring up to him again, her slight frame vibrating with rage as the mama bear emerged to protect her cub. She was a firebrand when she needed to be, not afraid of voicing her opinion if she thought something wasn't right. Matt didn't take offence; he was confident in the decisions he made on his patient's behalf and understood Quinn's interference came from a place of love. That didn't mean he wanted to give her further reason to berate him or challenge his authority.

He was as focused as he could be as they debrided Simon's wounds, cleaning and removing the dead tissue to clear the way for the new graft so it would take. As always, he was grateful for his perfect eyesight and steady hands as he shaved the thin slices of tissue needed for the graft. His precision as he prepared this skin before placing it on the wound could impact on Simon for the rest of his life.

No pressure.

Just two vulnerable and emotional souls relying on him to work his magic.

CHAPTER TWO

IF WAITING WAS an Olympic event, Quinn would never make it through the qualifying rounds.

Although she'd had enough experience to know to come prepared, she hadn't been able to sit still long enough to read her book or make any lesson plans for her tutored students. She'd even added an extra body to the picket line outside to save this hospital from closure in the hope it would take her mind off Simon going under the knife again. It was hard to believe anybody thought it was a good idea to merge this place with another outside the city when so many walked through the doors every day, and she was happy to wave a placard if it meant Simon's treatment continued here without any disruption.

The kids called it the Castle because of the beautiful architecture, and the story-like turrets and spires certainly gave it more character than any modern glass building could hope to replicate. Quinn had actually found it quite an imposing place at first but that could have been because of what she'd had to face inside the walls. These days it had almost become their second home and the people within were now all so familiar she didn't want anything to change.

'How's Simon?'

'You poor thing…'

'And you're out here? With us?'

'Have you heard how Ryan Walker is?'

'He's still an inpatient. I don't think there's been any real improvement. Even if he gets to go home I think the family are going to need a lot of help.'

'And they have a toddler to look after too. It's such a burden for them. For you too, Quinn, with Simon.'

The other Westbourne Grove Primary parents on the picket line had been well-meaning but the chit-chat hadn't helped her paranoia. Ryan, who'd suffered a serious head injury during the fire, was still critical and he and Simon were among the last of the children still receiving treatment. The raised eyebrows and exchanged glances at her presence anywhere other than Simon's bedside made her wonder if she had done the right thing in participating in the event and she'd abandoned her post in a hurry. Perhaps a *real* mother would've acted differently when her son was in surgery and she worried people would think she wasn't compassionate when that couldn't have been further from the truth.

That little boy meant everything to her. He might only be with her for a short time but she was as invested in him as if he was her own flesh and blood. All she wanted was for him to feel safe and loved and she'd failed on both accounts, if his continued apathy towards her was anything to go by. Perhaps when these operations became less frequent, and without the constant disruption of hospital appointments, they might actually find the time and space to bond.

She tossed her uneaten, soggy ham sandwich back into the crumpled aluminium foil. Not even the chocolate biscuit nestled in her pre-packed lunchbox could tempt her into eating. She had no appetite for anything other than news on Simon's condition. It might be a standard procedure for the staff but she knew there were risks for any surgery under general anaesthetic—breathing difficulties, adverse reaction to medication, bleeding—she'd done her Internet research on them all. Of course, none of these had occurred thus far but that didn't mean they *couldn't* happen.

In a world so full of danger she wondered how any parent ever let their offspring over the doorstep alone. It was taking all of her courage just to let Simon get the treatment recommended by the experts. At the end of the day, parental responsibility had been handed over to her and it was her job to keep him safe until adoption took place with another family.

That permanent knot in her stomach didn't untangle even when she saw him safely wheeled back onto the ward.

'How did it go?' she asked the first person who walked through the doors towards her. Of course that person had to be Matt.

Deep down she was grateful; the surgeon was the best person to keep her informed. It was just…he was always here, disturbing her peace of mind, reminding her he was doing a better job of taking care of Simon than she was.

Matt saw no reason to prolong Quinn's misery any longer. 'It all went well. No complications or unforeseen problems. Now we just have to wait for this young man to come around again.'

It had been a long day for him with surgery and his outpatient clinic but Quinn had every right to be kept in the loop and he'd wanted to end the day on a high for all of them by coming to speak to her. He wanted to be the one to smooth out the worry lines on her brow. Besides, he'd rather she torture him for information than take out her frustrations on the rest of the staff. He could handle it better because he understood it better. After being thrown in at the deep end and having to learn on the job, he hadn't exactly been a model parent either when he'd fought his siblings' battles.

'Thank goodness.'

The fleeting relief across her face and the glimpse of the pretty, young woman beneath the mask of combative parent was Matt's reward for a job well done.

She followed the bed into the private cubicle with him, never letting go of Simon's hand although he was still drowsy from the anaesthetic.

'Once he comes around and he's ready for home, we'll make sure you have painkillers to take with you. If there's any further problem with itching or infection let us know.'

'I think I've got the number on speed dial,' she said with the first sign of humour of the day.

Matt knew they'd been through this routine countless times but it was part of his duty to make sure the correct treatment was followed up at home. Quinn's co-operation was just as important as his in the recovery.

'As usual, we'll need you to try and keep the dressings dry until you come back to have them changed. You've got an appointment with the child psychologist too, right? It's important that Simon has help to process everything he's going through.' Never mind the fire itself, the surgery alone could be traumatic enough for someone so young to get past. He already seemed so withdrawn and Matt wanted to make sure they were doing all they could as a team to make him better.

'The psychologist, the physiotherapist, the dietitian—

we've got a full house in appointment bingo.' Her voice was taking on that shrill quality which was always an indication of an impending showdown.

'I know it's a lot to take on but it won't be for ever. It's all to ensure Simon recovers as quickly and effectively as possible so you can both go back to your normal routine outside of these hospital walls.' He didn't know what that included since she seemed to spend every waking moment here. Almost as if she was afraid to go home.

These days he had an entirely different outlook on his personal time. There was nothing he loved more than reclaiming the peace and quiet of his apartment and the freedom of doing whatever he felt like without having to fit around other people's schedules.

'Don't.' Her small plea reached in and squeezed his insides, making him wonder how on earth he'd managed to upset her in such a short space of time.

'Don't what?' He didn't understand the sudden change in her body language as she let go of Simon's hand to wrap her arms around her waist in self-comfort.

'Don't make any more promises you have no way of keeping.'

Matt frowned. He was supposed to be the harbinger of good news, not enemy number one. 'Ms Grady, Quinn, I've assured you on many, many occasions we are doing everything in our control—'

'I've heard it all before but there always seems to be one thing after another—infections, fevers, night terrors, haemo-wotsit scars—'

'Hemotrophic.'

'Whatever. Life is never going to be *normal* when every surgery creates further problems.' Her voice, now reaching levels only dogs and small unconscious children could hear, brought a murmur from Simon before he drifted off to sleep again.

This wasn't the time or the place for one of her dressing-downs about how nothing he did was good enough. Venting or not, Simon didn't need to hear this.

He placed a firm hand under Quinn's elbow and, for the umpteenth time since they'd met, he guided her out of the room. Whatever was going on he couldn't continually let her undermine him in front of his patient. If Simon didn't believe he could help him he might lose hope altogether.

Quinn dug her heels in but it only took a pointed glance back at the bed and an extra push to get her moving again.

'I'm not a child,' she insisted, shaking him off.

'Then stop acting like one. This is a conversation that needs to be held away from impressionable young ears.' His own temper was starting to bubble now. Why couldn't she see he would do anything to help them? She seemed determined to make this situation more difficult than it already was. Perhaps it was time he did back off if his presence here was partly to blame for getting her riled. Once he'd said his piece today he'd go back to his official role of reconstructive surgeon and nothing more.

She huffed into the corridor for another round of their battle of wills. He waited until the door was firmly closed behind them and there was no audience to overhear what he was about to say.

'The graft was a success. That's what you should be focusing on here.'

'That's easy for you to say. You're not the one he runs away from crying when it's time to bathe him, or the one who has to rock him back to sleep when he wakes from the nightmares, screaming.' Quinn's eyes were shimmering with tears, the emotions of the day clearly coming to a head.

He kept an eye out for a female member of staff who'd be in a better position to comfort her. For him to hug her was stretching the boundaries of his professionalism a tad too far. Whilst he sympathised, at the end of the day, she wasn't one of his siblings and not his direct responsibility.

'Perhaps it would help to talk to one of the other parents? I know they're bound to be going through the same struggles right now.' He didn't doubt she was having a tough time of it personally but he really wasn't the one to guide her through it.

This was why he should treat all patients exactly the same and not let sentiment, or physical attraction to a parent, cloud his judgement.

'They probably are but I'm not part of the *clique*. I'm the new kid on the block as much as Simon. Most of them have known each other for years through the Parent Teacher Association and I haven't even been around long enough to organise a playdate for Simon, much less myself. Even if I did, I'd probably have to make sure they all had background checks done first. Not the way to start any budding friendship, I'm sure you'll agree. No, we've managed this far on our own without inviting strangers in to witness our misfortune. I think we can persevere a little longer.'

She was insisting she could go it alone but those big blue eyes said otherwise and prevented Matt from walking away when he knew that was the best thing he could do to save himself.

'The staff here will always be available for you and Simon but I do think perhaps our personality clash isn't helping your stress levels. Unless there are any complications I'm sure the nurses can take care of you until the next scheduled surgery. I'll make sure I keep my promise to him today though. I will come back when he's awake and show him that magic trick.'

This time he did manage to move his feet, but as he took a step away, Quinn took one closer.

'Oh, yeah. It's so easy for you to gain his trust. A few stupid magic tricks and he thinks you're the best thing since sliced bread, but me? He hates me. I've given up my job, lost my partner and abandoned any hope of a social life so I could focus on fostering, and for what? I've failed at that too.'

The thing he'd been dreading most finally happened. The dam had burst and Quinn was weeping onto his scrubs. There was no possibility of him leaving her now. She needed a shoulder to cry on and it was simply rotten luck for both of them—he'd been the wrong person at the wrong time.

'He doesn't hate you. You're in a…transition period. That's all. After all of the trauma it's going to take a while for him to settle down.' He heard the chatter of passersby and took it upon himself to reposition Quinn so she was against the wall and his body was shielding her from view. She was so slight in his arms, so fragile, it was a natural instinct to want to protect her.

As if he didn't have enough responsibilities in his life.

She shook against him, her sobs wracking so hard through her petite frame he was afraid she might break.

'I. Wish. I. Was. More. Like. You,' she hiccuped against his chest.

'I've never performed a sex change and I think it might be weird if I started making clones of myself.' He wanted to add that it would be a shame to tamper with the beautiful body she'd been given but it sounded inappropriate even in a joke. He wasn't supposed to be thinking about her soft curves pressed against him right now in anything other than a sympathetic and completely professional manner.

The sobbing stopped and she lifted her head from his chest, either because she'd rediscovered her sense of humour or he'd completely creeped her out. He held his breath until he read her face and exhaled when he saw the wobbly smile start to emerge.

'I mean, you're a natural with Simon, with all the kids. I'm starting to think I'm not cut out for parenthood.' Her bottom lip began to quiver again in earnest and Matt made it his personal mission to retrieve that smile.

He tilted her chin up with his thumb so she stopped staring at the floor to look at him instead. She needed to believe what he was telling her. Believe in herself.

'I've picked up a few child-wrangling tips along the way. Parenting isn't easy and that parent/child bond simply needs a little nurturing. I have a few short cuts I can share with you if you promise never to breathe a word of my secrets. I would hate to dent my reputation as the resident child-whisperer.'

'Heaven forbid. I'm sure that would break the hearts of many around here who worship the ground you walk on.' She blinked away the tears and for a split second it would be easy for Matt to forget where he was and do something stupid.

If they weren't standing in a hospital corridor he

might've imagined they were having 'a moment.' She'd made it clear she wasn't one of his devoted followers and yet her body language at present said entirely the opposite.

Matt's stomach growled, a reminder he hadn't eaten anything substantial since mid-morning, and distracted him from her dilated pupils and those swollen pink lips begging him to offer some comfort. He couldn't go back on his word to help but he did need a timeout to regain his composure and remember who he was. That definitely wasn't supposed to be a man prepared to cancel a hot date in order to spend some unpaid overtime counselling families.

'Listen, there's a pub across the road—the Frog and Peach. Why don't I meet you over there in ten minutes to talk things over? We can grab a drink or a bite to eat and come straight back here the minute Simon wakes up.' There was nearly always a contingent from the hospital propping up the bar at the end of their shift and he was counting on someone else to jump in and come to Quinn's aid before he committed to something else he'd come to regret. The phone call he was going to have to make would end his most recent love interest before it even began.

She gave a wistful glance at the room behind her before she answered. The sign of a true mother thinking of her son before herself, even though she didn't realise it.

'I'll leave word to contact us the second he opens his eyes.' He wasn't going to beg but he did want to fulfil his obligations ASAP so he could finish his working day and head home. Alone.

'Only if you're sure…' Her hesitation was as obvious in her doe-like eyes as it was in her voice.

Matt wasn't any more certain this was a good idea than Quinn but a chat in a pub had to be infinitely safer than another five minutes with her in his arms.

CHAPTER THREE

QUINN SCROLLED THROUGH her phone, paying little attention to the social media updates on the screen. She wasn't in contact with any of these people; they weren't part of her *actual* life. Recent events had proved that to her. Virtual acquaintances could be chock-full of sympathy and crying emoticons on the Internet but a distinct lack of physical support from anyone other than Mrs Johns next door had made her see an online presence was a waste of her valuable time. This sudden interest in what people were having for dinner, or who had the cutest kitten meme, was simply to occupy her hands and give the impression she was at ease on her own.

Matt had directed her towards the pub across the road and assured her he'd be with her as soon as he could get away. The Frog and Peach, as nice as it was, was a busy hub in Paddington and she was self-conscious sitting outside, occupying one of the much sought after tables.

She envied the carefree patrons meeting their friends to toast the end of their working day. It reminded her of the camaraderie she'd once had with her fellow teachers inside and outside of the school. A friend was the one thing she was desperately missing right now—someone she could share a laugh with, or pour her heart out to without judgement. Mrs Johns was the closest thing to that, volunteering to babysit if she ever needed a hand, but it wasn't the kind of relationship where she could really confide everything that was getting her down at the minute. She only really had her mum to talk to on the end of the phone for that, but even then she was almost ashamed to be totally honest about her situation and admit she wasn't coping when her mother had been her fostering inspiration. When she did return home to her Yorkshire roots, she wanted it to be a journey of triumph with Simon as happy as she'd been as a child who'd finally settled.

Quinn drained the water from her glass. After the day she'd had fretting over the surgery and making a fool of herself crying on Matt's shoulder, she could probably do with something stronger but she wouldn't touch alcohol while Simon was under her care. She took her responsibilities seriously and she couldn't sit here getting pie-eyed when she still had to get them both home across the city.

'Are you finished?' A male member of staff was at her side before she managed to set the empty glass down.

She nodded but felt the need to explain her continued occupation of valuable drinking space. 'I'm just waiting for someone.'

There was a brief flicker of something replacing the irritability in the young man's eyes and Quinn's cheeks burned as she realised it was sympathy. He thought she'd been stood up. It was the natural assumption, she supposed, as opposed to her waiting for her foster son's surgeon, who she'd emotionally tortured until he'd agreed to meet her here.

'I'm sure he'll be here any minute.' She began to defend her party-of-one residency but the busy waiter had already moved on to clean the next table, uncaring about her social life, or lack of one.

Unfortunately, the jitterbugs under her skin weren't entirely down to her anticipation of an evening in a hot doctor's company. The excitement of a singleton let loose in the city didn't last for ever and these days the skippety-hop of her heart tended to come from fear of what was going to happen to Simon next.

Still, as Matt finally came into view across the street there was a surge of girlish glee she'd imagined had vanished out the door with her ex. There was something about seeing him in his casual clothes that felt forbidden, naughty even. She was so used to him in his formal shirt and trousers combo, or his scrubs, that a pair of jeans and tight T shirt seemed more...intimate.

There was something voyeuristic watching him negotiate the traffic, oblivious to her ogling. It was amazing how one scrap of plain material became so interesting when stretched across the right body, marking out the planes of a solid chest and rounding over impressive biceps. As he jogged across the road, with his jacket slung over his arm, Matt had no clue how good he looked.

Long-dormant butterflies woke from their slumber, mistaking the handsome man coming towards Quinn as a potential date, and fluttered in her stomach as she followed his progress. They quickly settled when she turned to check her reflection in the window and was reminded this was more of a pity party than a hook-up.

She knew the second he spotted her in the crowd on the pavement as a smile spread across his lips and he lifted a hand to wave. He'd been incredibly understanding considering her sometimes erratic behaviour and this was above and beyond the call of duty. It also did nothing to diminish her crush.

'Hey,' he said as he pushed his way through to reach her table, the last of the evening sun shining behind him and lighting his short blond hair into a halo. It made him almost angelic, if it wasn't for that glint in his ever shifting blue-green eyes which said there was potential for mischief there. It made her curious to find out if there was a wicked side to Saint Matt when he was off duty.

'Hi, Matt.' She pulled out a chair for him and couldn't resist a smug grin as the surly waiter passed by and did a double take.

'Do you want to go inside to order? The smokers tend to congregate out here…unless you'd prefer that?'

'It's okay, I'm not a smoker.' It earned him more Brownie points too—as if he needed them—he obviously didn't approve of the habit.

She popped her phone back in her bag and got up to follow him. It was easy to see him when he was head and shoulders above most of the crowd, but soon the mass of bodies was too thick for her to fight through to reach him.

'Excuse me…sorry…can I just get past?'

On the verge of giving up and heading back out for some fresh air, she felt a large hand clamp around her wrist and pull her through the people forest. Somehow she ended up taking the lead with Matt creating a force field around her with his body alone. She revelled in that brief moment of nurturing where someone put her welfare first. It had been a long time since anyone had been protective of her feelings and she missed that kind of support.

Since moving away from home it had been in rare supply at all. Even Darryl, who she'd thought she'd spend the rest of her days with raising children, had put his selfish needs before her or any potential foster kids.

'There's a table over here.' Matt cleared away the dirty dishes left behind by the previous occupants so they could take the comfy leather sofas by the fire. He obviously wasn't the sort of man who only thought of himself. It showed in his every action. Even if her jealousy had prevented her from appreciating the extra care he'd given to Simon, Matt's generous nature would make some lucky woman very happy indeed. A woman who wouldn't second-guess his every gesture, waiting to find out what ulterior motive lay behind it.

'I'm sorry I've been such a nuisance.' She leaned forward in the chair, taking a sudden interest in the patina of the wooden table, unable to meet Matt's eyes. It would be fair to say she'd been an absolute horror to him these past weeks. Now the hysteria had subsided and the voice of reason had restored calm, her bad behaviour became very apparent. Based on her past experience with men, her paranoia had led her to question his judgement, his professionalism and his methods when the man had simply been trying to do his job. It was a wonder he hadn't called security to remove her from the premises at any point. His patience clearly stretched further than hers.

'Don't worry. You're an anxious mum. I get it.' He reached across the table and squeezed her hand, pumping the blood in her veins that bit faster.

She flashed her eyes up at him, surprised at the soft warmth of his touch and the very public display of support. Matt met her gaze and there was a connection of solidarity and something…forbidden, which both comforted and confused the hell out of her.

'Are you ready to order?'

At the sound of an intruder, they sprang apart, the moment over, but the adrenaline continued surging through Quinn's body as though they'd been caught doing something they shouldn't. She began to wonder if the gum-chewing waiter was stalking her, or was more interested in her date.

Doctor. Friend. Not date.

'I...er... I'll have the burger and fries.' Matt snatched up the menu and barely glanced at it before ordering. She could read into that by saying he was as thrown by his actions as she was, or he simply ate here a lot.

'The chicken salad wrap, please.' Her appetite had yet to fully re-emerge since the fire but it would be nice to sit and enjoy a meal in company. In Matt's company. Except he was on his feet and following the waiter back towards the bar.

'I should've ordered drinks. I'll go and get some. Wine? Beer? Soft drink?' He called from an increasing distance away from her, walking backwards, bumping into furniture and generally acting as though he couldn't wait to get away from her.

Second-thoughts syndrome. He'd probably only suggested doing this to prevent another scene at his place of work.

'Just water, please.' She sighed, and slouched back in her chair, whatever spark she'd imagined well and truly extinguished.

A romantic interest from any quarter was nothing more than a fantasy these days anyway. She was going through enough emotional turmoil without leaving herself open to any more heartache. No, she should be grateful for what this was—a meal in adult company and a short respite from her responsibilities. Simon would be awake soon enough and the next round of anxious parenting would begin.

As she took in her new surroundings from her place of safety in the corner, she supposed it was a nice enough place. It had old-fashioned charm—Victorian, she guessed from the dark wood interior—and not the sort of establishment which immediately sprang to mind for a well-heeled surgeon. Matt was young, fashionable and, from what she could see, totally unencumbered by the ties she was bound by. Not that she regretted any of her choices, but if their roles were reversed she'd probably be living it up in some trendy wine bar hoping for a Matt clone to walk through the door and make her night. By weeping her way to a dinner invitation she'd no doubt spoiled the night for many single ladies across the city waiting for him to show.

'The food shouldn't be too long.' Matt took a seat opposite and placed a jug of iced water and two glasses on the table between them.

At least his agitation seemed to have passed as he poured the water with a steady hand. He was probably saving the heavy drinking for whenever he got rid of her and he could cut loose without having to babysit her.

'So…you were going to give me a tutorial in basic child-rearing…'

They may as well get this over with when they knew they both had other places to be. Ten minutes of him telling her where she was going wrong and they could all get back to their real lives, which, for her, generally didn't include pub dinners with handsome men. It was the highlight of an otherwise fraught day, it had to be said.

'Hey, I never claimed to be an expert. All I can do

is pass on the benefit of my experience in dealing with young children in very trying circumstances.'

'All suggestions for helping gain a five-year-old's trust will be gratefully received.' As was the arrival of her dinner. Although she hadn't been hungry up until now, it was infinitely more appetising than the sandwich she'd binned earlier, and it was a nice change from potato smiley faces and alphabet spaghetti which were the only things Simon would eat at present.

'A cheap magic set,' Matt managed to get out before he took a huge bite out of his loaded burger. He attacked it with such a hunger it gave Quinn chills. There was more than a hint of a wild thing lurking beneath that gentlemanly exterior and a glimpse of it was enough to increase her appetite for more than the bland safe option she'd chosen.

'Pardon?'

She had to wait until he'd swallowed for an answer.

'I use bribery as a way in. I keep a box of child-friendly toys in my office for emergencies. Toy cars, colouring books, bubbles… I've even got a couple of hand puppets I break out when they're too shy to speak directly to me. I find being a friend makes the whole experience less traumatic for them.' He snagged a couple of fries from the plate and tossed them into his mouth, making short work of them too before she'd even taken her first bite.

'Tried that. He's got a room full of new toys at my place but apparently you can't buy your way into a child's heart. I think you've just got a knack with kids that apparently I don't.' It was something she'd assumed would happen naturally since she'd been in the system herself and could relate to the circumstances which would bring foster children to her.

Unfortunately, she was finding it took more than enthusiasm and a will for things to work out to make an impression on Simon. Not every child would fit seamlessly into family life the way she had. Not that it had been easy for her either when her adoptive father had decided he couldn't hack it, but she'd had a special bond with her mother from the first time they'd met and they'd faced all the unexpected obstacles together. At least until she became an adult and decided she should venture out into the big wide world on her own. She wanted that same show of strength they'd had for her to enable her and Simon to work through the aftermath of the school fire but it wasn't going to happen when he kept shutting her out.

Matt shrugged. 'I don't know about that but I've had a lot of practice.'

Quinn nearly choked on her tortilla wrap. 'You have kids of your own?'

It would certainly explain how comfortable he was in that parenting role if there were a load of mini-Matts running around. The lack of wedding ring had blinded her to that possibility. Then again, marriage wasn't always a precursor to fatherhood. He could also be an absentee father but he didn't seem the type to have abandoned little Irish babies around the countryside either.

He spluttered into his glass. 'Hell, no!'

The emphatic denial should've pleased her to know he wasn't a feckless father but it was a stark reminder that the life she'd chosen wasn't for everyone. At least he was upfront about it, unlike Darryl, who'd pretended to be on board with family life and bailed at the last minute.

'You're not going to tell me you actually hate kids or

something, are you?' Her heart sank in anticipation of more disappointment. She couldn't bear to find out this affable surgeon had been nothing more than an act. If so, he deserved an Oscar for well and truly duping everyone who knew him from the Castle.

The sound of his deep chuckle buoyed her spirits back up again.

'Not at all. They're grand. As long as I'm not in charge of them outside work.'

'Ah, you're not the settling down type, then?' It was blatant nosiness but he seemed such perfect husband and father material she couldn't let it pass without comment. Not that she was actively looking for either when it hadn't worked out so well the first time around. She'd clearly been out of the dating scene too long since she was sitting here thinking about playing happy families with the first man to show her any attention.

'I've only just been released into the wild again. My dad died a while back, when I was in medical school. Cancer. I was left to raise my three sisters on my own. Bridget, the youngest, enrolled in college last year and moved away so I feel as though I'm finally starting my adult life. Child free.' He took a short break from devouring his dinner, the subject interfering with his appetite too.

Both she and Matt's siblings had been lucky they'd had someone special who'd been willing to sacrifice everything to provide for them. She wanted to do the same for Simon if he'd only let her.

'That must've been tough.' She was barely coping with one small boy and a part-time job. It was almost incomprehensible to imagine a young Matt raising and supporting a family while studying at the same time. Just when she thought this man couldn't be any more perfect his halo shone that bit brighter.

It was a shame that no-kids rule put him firmly off-limits. Along with the whole medical ethics thing and the fact she'd chosen celibacy over trusting a man in her life again. As if she'd ever stand a chance anyway after he'd witnessed her puffy panda eyes and been drenched in her tears of self-pity. He'd probably endured a lot more as a single parent and cried a lot less.

'Do you want some of my chips? Help yourself.' He shoved his plate towards her and it took a second to figure out why he was trying to feed her.

'Er…thanks.' She helped herself to a couple to detract from the fact she'd probably been staring at him longingly.

Better for him to think she was greedy than love struck. She wasn't too happy about the nature her thoughts had taken recently either.

'It wasn't easy but we survived and you will too. You figure this stuff out as you go along.'

It was good of him to share some of his personal details with her—he didn't have to and she knew he'd only done it to make her feel better. It did. He was no longer an anonymous authority figure; he was human and he was opening up to her. A little knowledge of his private life made it easier to trust another kindred spirit. She supposed it was only fair she gave something of herself too, although he'd probably already heard more than enough about her for one day.

'I thought with my background this would all be familiar territory. I was a foster kid myself. My birth parents were too young to handle parenthood and I bumped around the system until I was finally adopted. My mum never seemed to struggle the way I have, even when her husband walked out. I'm afraid history repeated itself. My ex left me too when I decided I wanted to foster.' It was difficult not to take it personally that any important male figures in her life had abandoned her. From the emotional outbursts and irrational behaviour Matt had probably already figured out why no man wanted to face a future with her.

'We're all full of good intentions, but it's not long before a cold dose of reality soon hits home, eh?' He was smiling at her but Quinn was convinced there was a barbed comment in there. Perhaps he'd meant well by asking her to meet here but he'd found it tougher going than he'd imagined listening to her whining.

'I'm sorry. I shouldn't be lumbering you with all my problems. It's not part of your job description and I'm putting you off your food.'

'Not at all.' He wedged the last bit of his burger into his mouth to prove her wrong.

'I tutor from home so it's been a while since I've had any adult company to vent with. Lucky you, you get to hear me offload first.'

'It's a hazard of the job. I'm a surgeon-cum-counsellor.' His grin said he didn't mind at all.

It was a relief to get off her chest how much these past two months had impacted on her and not be judged on it. She was doing enough of that herself by constantly comparing herself to her mother when the circumstances were so different. She'd been a young girl in the country, desperate for a family, and Simon, well, he wasn't more than a baby and had already been through so much. He'd been passed around like an unwanted guest and now he was burned and traumatised by the fire, with no real idea of what was going to come of him.

Her mother had had an advantage simply by living in her rural surroundings. Fresh air and wide open spaces were more conducive to recovery and peace of mind than the smog and noise of the city. However, this was the best place for him to be for his treatment and there was no choice but to soldier on, regardless of location.

'Do you have a couch in your office we can share?' It wasn't until he raised his eyebrow in response she realised how inappropriate that sounded. Today, it was becoming a habit.

An image of more inappropriateness on the furniture behind closed doors with Matt filled her head and made her hot under her black tank top and slouchy grey cardigan. If she'd had any intention of flirting she definitely would've picked something more attractive than her slummy mummy attire. Comfy leggings and baggy tops were her security blanket inside the hospital and hadn't been meant for public display.

'I mean... I feel as though I should be lying on your couch...you taking notes. As a counsellor, obviously. Not some sort of sofa fetishist who gets off on that sort of thing. I'll shut up now before you do actually use your authority to call the men in white coats to lock me up.' Quinn clapped her hands over her face as if they provided some sort of invisibility shield for her mortification. Unfortunately, they weren't a sound barrier either as she heard Matt cough away his embarrassment.

Very smooth. Not.

Far from building the beginnings of a support system with Matt as a friend, she'd created an even bigger chasm between them with her weirdness. She'd made it crystal clear to herself, and Matt, through her awkward small talk and vivid imagination that she fancied the pants off him. Why else would she be stumbling over her words and blushing like a schoolgirl trying to make conversation with him.

Great. On top of everything else she was actually picturing him with his pants fancied all the way off! The poor man had no clue about the monster he'd created by being so nice to her.

A sweaty, red-faced monster who'd apparently woken up from hibernation looking for a mate.

CHAPTER FOUR

For a second Matt thought he was going to need someone to perform the Heimlich manoeuvre on him to dislodge the French fry in his throat. The shock of Quinn's imagery had made him swallow it whole.

He gulped down a mouthful of water, relief flooding through him as it cleared his blocked airway.

She hadn't tried to choke him to death on purpose. There'd been absolutely no malice or deliberate attempt on his life as far as he could tell, when Quinn emanated nothing but innocence and the scarlet tint of embarrassment. Neither, he suspected, had she meant to flirt with him but his body had responded all the same to the idea of them rolling around in his office. Around this woman he lost all control of himself, body and mind. Not to mention his common sense.

His first mistake had been to come here outside of work, only to be compounded by swapping details of their personal lives. Then there was the touching. Offering a reassuring hand, or shoulder to cry on, was part and parcel of his job, but probably not when they were lost in each other's eyes in a crowded pub.

She drew that protective nature of his to the fore when he'd spent this past year trying to keep it at bay. He'd only intended to show her she wasn't alone because he knew how it was not to have anyone to turn to when you were weighed down with family stresses. She didn't have to apologise for the feisty spirit she'd shown as they clashed over Simon's treatment; she'd need it to get her through. He simply hadn't expected that spark of attraction to flare to life between them as if someone had flicked a switch.

It had thrown him, sent him scurrying to the bar to wait until it passed. Quinn was the mother of one of his patients.

A mother. His patient.

Two very good reasons to bypass that particular circuit, but no, he kept on supplying power.

Telling her about his family was an eejit move. That was personal and this wasn't supposed to be about him. He listened, he diagnosed and he operated but he never, ever got personally involved. Not only had he given something of himself by revealing his family circumstances, now he knew her background too. The fact she'd been through the foster system only made her strength all the more remarkable to him.

She was a true survivor and yet she was still willing to give so much of herself to others. He needed to direct her somewhere those qualities weren't a personal threat to his equilibrium.

'You know, if you're at a loss for company, I can introduce you to members of the hospital committee. I'm sure you've heard the board is trying to close the place down and we'd be only too glad to have someone else fighting in our corner.' It would give her something to focus on other than Simon's treatment and, in turn, might create a bit of distance between them too. She might make a few more friends into the bargain. Friends who weren't afraid to get too close to her in case it compromised their position or freedom.

'I did do a spot of picketing today. It would be such a shame to see the place close. Especially after everything you've done for Simon there. What happens to you if they do close? What happens to us?'

He could see the absolute terror in her eyes, that brilliant blue darkening to the colour of storm-filled skies, at the thought of more disruption in their lives. It was also an indication that she was relying on him being present in her life for the foreseeable future and that wasn't an expectation he could live up to.

'I'd hate to see the place get phased out. Hopefully the campaigning and fundraising will make a difference. As for me, I'm on a temporary contract. I'll move on soon enough anyway. Like I said, I prefer to be footloose and fancy free these days.'

'Simon will miss you terribly.' She broke eye contact and diligently tidied the empty plates into a pile for the server to collect.

A dagger jabbed Matt in the heart at the idea that he'd be the one to cause either of them any further distress.

'Don't worry, I'll be around for a while yet and if I stay local there's always a chance he'd get referred to me anyway.' At least by then he would've had a cooling off period from this particular case.

Quinn nodded, although the lip-chewing continued.

This was the first time his casual new lifestyle had given him cause to rethink his idea of moving from one place to another whenever the mood took him. Whilst the notion of experiencing new people and places was more attractive than remaining stagnant in Dublin, he hadn't given any thought to patients who might get too attached, or vice versa.

It would be tough to leave his patients here when the time came, but better for him. He'd spent a huge chunk of his life on hold, waiting until others were ready to let go of him. This was supposed to be *his* time to spread his wings and not get dragged back into any more family dramas.

Despite the hustle and bustle of the pub around them, he and Quinn fell into an uneasy silence. His attraction to her was in direct competition with his longing for a quiet, uncomplicated life. The two weren't compatible, and whichever won through, it would undoubtedly leave the bitter taste of loss behind.

The vibration in his pocket shocked him back into the present, his pager becoming a cattle prod to make sure he was back on the right path. Although the message informing him Simon was awake had come too late to save him from himself or from straying onto forbidden territory.

'Simon's awake. We should head back.' And put a stop to whatever this is right now.

Quinn's face lit up at the news, which really wasn't helping with the whole neutral, platonic, not-thinking-of-her-as-anything-other-than-a-parent stance he was going to have to take.

'Oh, good! What are we waiting for?'

There was genuine joy moving in to chase the clouds of despair away in those eyes again. Whether Quinn knew it, or wanted it, Matt could see Simon was the most important thing in her life. He knew fostering was only supposed to be a temporary arrangement until a permanent home for the child was secured and if she wasn't careful with her heart she'd end up getting hurt. If he'd had to, Matt would've fought to the death with the authorities to gain custody over his siblings and he knew he'd have been heartbroken to see them shipped out to strangers after everything he'd done for them.

He didn't know what Quinn's long-term plans were, but it was important she didn't lose sight of her own needs or identity in the midst of it all. At least he'd had his career to focus on when his family had flown the nest and stripped him of his parent role.

Quinn was the sort of woman who needed to be cared for as well as being the nurturer of others.

He didn't know why he felt the need to be part of that.

The good news that Simon was awake was a welcome interruption for Quinn. She wasn't proud of the display she'd put on today and it would be best if she and Simon could just disappear back to the house and take her shame with her. At least she could unleash her emotions there without sucking innocent bystanders into the eye of the storm along with her.

Poor Matt, whose only job was to operate on Simon and send them on their way, had run the gauntlet with her today. Irrational jealousy, fear, rage, self-pity and physical attraction—she'd failed to hide any of them in his presence. That last one in particular gave her the shame shudders. He'd been antsy with her ever since that sofa comment.

That sudden urge to crumple into a melting puddle of embarrassment hit again and she wrapped her cardigan around her body, wishing it had a hood to hide her altogether.

She wasn't stupid. That suggestion she should join the hospital committee was his subtle way of getting her to back off and go bother someone else. He'd made his position very clear—he was done with other people's kids unless it was in the operating theatre.

'Are you cold?' Matt broke through her woolly invisibility shield with another blast of concern. He was such a nice guy, it was easy to misinterpret his good manners for romantic interest and that's exactly what she'd done.

If she asked around she'd probably find a long line of lonely, frightened women who were holding a candle for him because of his bedside manner. One thing was sure, when he did move on he'd leave a trail of broken hearts behind him.

'Yeah.' She shivered more at the thought of Matt leaving than the sudden dip in temperature as they ventured outside. He'd become a very big part of their lives here and she couldn't imagine going through all of this without him.

Warmth returned to her chilled bones in a flash as perfect gentleman Matt draped his jacket around her shoulders. In another world this would have been a romantic end to their evening and not a doctor's instinct to prevent her from adding hypothermia to her list of problems. She should have declined the gesture, insisted it wasn't necessary when they'd soon be back indoors, to prevent her from appearing any more pathetic than she already did. Except the enveloping cocoon of his sports coat was a comfort she needed right now. It held that spicy scent she associated with his usually calming presence in its very fabric.

She supposed it would be weird if she accidentally on purpose forgot to return it and started wearing it as a second skin, like some sort of obsessed fan.

When they reached the hospital lobby she had no option but to extricate herself from the pseudo-Matt-hug. If she didn't make the break now there was every likelihood she'd end up curled up in bed tonight using it as a security blanket.

'Thanks. That'll teach me for leaving home without a coat. Mum would not be happy after all those years of lecturing me about catching my death without one.' Although she'd be tempted to do it again for a quick Matt fix if she thought she could achieve it without the cringeworthy crying it had taken to get one.

He helped her out of his jacket and shrugged it on over his broad shoulders.

Yeah, it looked better on him anyway.

Given their difference in height and build she'd probably looked even more of a waif trailing along behind him. So not the image any woman wanted to give a man she was attracted to. If she was to imagine Matt's idea of a perfect partner it would be one of those oh-so-glamorous female managers who seemed to run the departments here, with their perfect hair and make-up looking terribly efficient. Nothing akin to a messy ponytail, and a quick swipe of lipgloss on a bag lady who didn't know if she was coming or going most of the time. Any romantic notion she held about Matt needed to be left outside the doors of this elevator.

'You don't have to go up with me. I know this place like the back of my hand. Thanks for your help today but I can take it from here. We'll see you again at our next appointment.' She jabbed the button to take her back to Simon, trying not to think about who, or what, Matt had planned for the rest of the night without her.

'I'm sure you can but I promised Simon I'd come and

see him. Remember? I wouldn't want to renege on our deal.' Matt stepped into the lift behind her.

It wasn't unexpected given his inherent chivalry but as the steel doors closed, trapping them in the small space together, Quinn almost wished he had gone back on his word so she could breathe again. In here there were no other distractions, no escape from the gravitational pull of Matt McGrory.

She tried not to make eye contact, and instead hummed tunelessly rather than attempt small talk, meaning that the crackling tension remained until another couple joined them on the next floor. Extra bodies should've diffused her urge to throw herself at him and give in to the temptation of one tiny kiss to test her theory about his hidden passion, but the influx only pushed them closer together until they were touching. There was no actual skin-to-skin contact through the layers of their clothes but the static hairs on the back of her neck said they might as well be naked.

Another heavyset man shoulder-barged his way in, knocking Matt off balance next to her.

'Sorry,' he said, his hand sliding around her waist as he steadied himself.

Quinn hoped her cardi wasn't flammable because she was about to go up like a bonfire.

His solid frame surrounded her, shielding her from any bumps or knocks from the growing crowd. He had a firm grip on her, protecting her, claiming her. She thought it was wishful thinking on her part until they arrived at their floor and he escorted her out, refusing to relinquish his hold until they were far from the crowd. His lingering touch even now in the empty corridor was blowing her he's-only-being-polite theory out of the water. Surely his patience would've run out by now if all of this had simply been him humouring her?

It was a shame he hadn't come into her life before it had become so complicated, or later, when things were a bit more stable. Pre-Darryl, when she hadn't been afraid to let someone get close, or post-Simon, when she might have some more control over what happened in her life.

He'd made it clear he wasn't interested in a long-term relationship with anyone but she didn't want to close the door on the idea altogether. Men like Matt didn't come around very often and someday she knew she'd come to regret not acting on this moment. Perhaps if one of them actually acknowledged there was more going on between them other than Simon's welfare she might stand a chance of something happening.

'Matt, I think we should talk—'

Before she could plant the seed for a future romantic interlude, Matt sprang away from her *à la* scalded cat. She barely had time to mourn the loss of his warmth around her when she spotted the reason for the abrupt separation.

'Hey, Rebecca.'

Another member of staff headed towards them. A woman whose curves were apparent even in her shapeless scrubs. The rising colour in Matt's cheeks would've been endearing if it wasn't for the fact Quinn was clearly the source of his sudden embarrassment.

'Hi, Matt. What on earth are you still doing here? Weren't you supposed to be going somewhere tonight?' A pair of curious brown eyes lit on Quinn and she immediately realised how selfish she'd been for monopolising his time. It hadn't entered her head that he would've given up a glamorous night out to sit listening to her tales of woe in a dingy pub.

Matt slid his green-eyed gaze at her too, and Quinn hovered between the couple, very much an outsider in the conversation. There was clearly something unsaid flying across the top of her head. Metaphorically speaking, of course. She had the advantage of a couple of inches in height on the raven-haired doctor. But it was the only one she had here, as she didn't know what they were talking about, or indeed, what relationship they might have beyond being work colleagues. It wasn't any of her business, yet she had to refrain from rugby-tackling the pretty doctor to the ground and demanding to know what interest she had in Matt.

Okay, so she was a little more invested in Matt than she'd intended.

'I…er…changed my mind. I wanted to check in on one of my patients, Simon, one of the kids from the school fire. This is his mum, Quinn. Quinn, this is Rebecca Scott, a transplant surgeon here at the Castle.'

Finally, she was introduced into the conversation before she started a catfight over a man who wasn't even hers.

'I'm so sorry you were caught up in that. I know it's been horrendous for all involved but I hear Simon's treatment's going well?' Rebecca reached out in sympathy and dampened down any wicked thoughts Quinn might've harboured towards her.

'It is. In fact, I'm just going to see him now after his surgery.'

'Well, he's definitely in the best hands.' There was admiration there but Quinn didn't detect anything other than professional courtesy.

'Yes, he is. Listen, Matt, I'm going to go and see how he is. I'll catch up with you later. Nice to meet you, Rebecca.' She didn't hang around for Matt's inevitable insistence he accompany her, nor did she look back to overanalyse the couple's body language once she'd left. They had separate lives, different roles in Simon's future, which didn't necessarily equate to a relationship or a debt to each other. She was confusing her needs with his and a clear head was vital in facing the months ahead. It was down to her to prepare Simon for his future family and she couldn't do that whilst pining for one of her own. Until then, she'd do well to remember it was just the two of them.

'What are you doing?' Rebecca moved in front of Matt, blocking his view of Quinn walking away.

'Hmm?' He was itching to follow her so they could see Simon together but the manner in which she'd left said she didn't want an audience for the reunion. She could be emotional at the best of times and seeing her five-year-old post-surgery would certainly give her cause for more tears. He'd give her a few minutes' privacy before he joined them, and as soon as he'd fulfilled his promise to the boy, he'd do what he should've done in the first place and go home.

Quinn rounded the corner and vanished from sight. It had been a long day for all of them and he didn't want to abandon her when she was so fragile. Instead, he turned his attention back to Rebecca to find her with her arms folded, eyebrows raised and her lips tilted into a half-smile.

'I told Simon I'd show him how to do a few magic tricks before he went home. I thought cheering him up was more important than a few drinks with someone I hardly know.'

'I believe you,' she said, her voice dripping with enough sarcasm to force Matt to defend his presence here post-shift.

'What? You think there's something going on with me and Quinn? She's having a nightmare of a time with Simon and he seems to respond better when I'm around. That's all.' He shut down any gossip fodder without the utterance of a lie. Anything remotely salacious resided entirely in his head. For now.

'Uh-huh? It's not like you to turn down a hot date for a charity case.' Rebecca wasn't about to let this drop and he knew why when he'd been enthusing about the date he'd lined up all week, only to have blown it off at the last minute. It was no wonder he'd developed something of a reputation due to his reluctance to settle down with one woman.

It was true; there'd been a few female interests over the course of his time in London but that didn't mean he jumped into bed with a different partner every week. Sometimes he simply enjoyed a little company. However, the slight against his character was nothing to the umbrage he took to Quinn being denigrated to a pity date. After two months of sparring and making up, he'd go as far as to say that they'd bonded as friends.

He pursed his lips together so he wouldn't defend her honour and give Rebecca any more ammunition to tease, or admonish, him.

'You know me, I'm never short of female company.' Generally he wasn't big-headed about such matters but it was better to shrug it off as a non-event than turn it into a big deal. The girl he was supposed to be seeing tonight, Kelly—or was it Kerry?—was just someone he'd met the other day. It was nothing special and neither of them had been particularly put out when he'd phoned to call it off so he could meet with Quinn instead. He wasn't a player and it wasn't as if he was trying to keep his options open. There was a good chance he'd never see or speak to Kelly/Kerry again.

'No, but it is quite uncharacteristic of you to be so… hands on, at work.'

So she'd seen him with his arm around Quinn. He couldn't even defend his actions there. There'd been no excuse for him to maintain that close contact after they'd exited the packed lift except for his own pleasure. He'd enjoyed the warmth of her pressed into him, her petite frame so delicate against his bulk and the scent of her freshly washed hair filling his nostrils until he didn't want anything else to fill his lungs.

'Simon's a special boy. He's in foster care and I guess I do have a soft spot for him. He's one of the first patients I've been able to treat with spray-on skin, so I'm particularly interested in his progress for use in other cases.' He didn't delve into any other personal aspects of his affinity for the pair. Rebecca knew he had younger sisters, but as this was his new start, he hadn't seen the need to divulge his personal struggles to reach this point. As far as anyone needed to know, he was simply escorting an anxious mother back to her son post-surgery.

'It's easy to get attached. I guess I was hoping for some juicy gossip to take my mind off things.'

'Well, I'm not the one everyone's talking about around here. The rumour mill's gone into overdrive now Thomas is back.'

Rebecca's sigh echoed along the corridor at the mention of her ex-husband. It might have come across as a dirty trick to shift focus from one taboo subject to another but he was genuinely concerned for his friend too. By all accounts the end of her marriage had been traumatic. The car crash which had claimed the life of her young daughter had also proved too much for the marriage to survive. Now her ex, a cardiologist, was here on loan, it was bound to be awkward for both of them.

Matt had seen grief rip apart many families in his line of work and in that respect he was lucky to have kept his own together. The alternative didn't bear thinking about.

'Me and Thomas? There's no story to tell, I assure you. In fact, we haven't exchanged a word since he got here. You'd never believe we knew each other, never mind that we were married once upon a time.' Her smile faltered as she was forced to confront what were obviously unresolved issues with her ex.

'How long has it been since you saw him last?'

'Five years, but in some ways it feels like only yesterday.' The hiccup in her voice exposed the raw grief still lingering beneath the surface.

'I'm sure it's not easy. For either of you.' They'd both lost a child and it was important to remember they'd both been affected. He didn't know Thomas but he knew Rebecca and she wouldn't have given her heart away to someone who wasn't worthy of her.

'It's brought a lot of memories back, good and bad. At some point I think we do need to have an honest conversation about what happened to clear the air, something we never managed when we were still together. Perhaps then we might both get some closure.'

Given that they were going to be working together, they'd need it. According to the staff who'd seen them together, the tension was palpable, and it wasn't like Rebecca not to speak her mind. As she'd just proved with this ambush. Thank goodness she hadn't spotted them getting cosy in the pub or he'd really have had a job trying to explain himself.

'I hope you sort things out. Life's too short to stay mad.'

'We'll see. When all is said and done this isn't about us. We're only here to do our jobs.' On cue, her pager went off and put an end to their impromptu heart-to-heart. She shrugged an apology as she pushed the call button for the elevator.

'I'm sure it'll all work out in the end.'

Rebecca was a professional, the best in her field, and there was no way she'd let personal matters interfere with her patients' welfare. That was one of the golden rules here and one he'd do well to remember himself.

'We've all got to face our demons at some time, I guess. Right, duty calls. Stay out of trouble.'

If he was going to do that, he wouldn't be heading to Simon's room, straight towards it.

CHAPTER FIVE

ALTHOUGH SEEING SIMON had come through the surgery successfully was always a relief, his aftercare never got any easier. Each stage of the treatment was often punctuated with a decline in his behaviour once they left the hospital grounds. From the moment he opened his eyes it was as if they'd taken two steps backwards instead of forward.

She'd stroked his hair, told him what a brave boy he was, promised him treats—all without the normal enthusiastic response of a child his age in return. Of course, they'd see the psychologists, who would do their best to get him to open up and help him work through the trauma, but the onus was still on her to get him past this. With a degree in child psychology herself, she really thought she'd make more progress with him. At least get him to look at her. She'd aced her written exams but the practical was killing her. Most kids would only be too glad to get out of here and go home—she knew she would be—but no amount of coaxing could get him to even acknowledge her.

When Matt strolled into the room and instantly commanded his attention she had to move away from any items which could suddenly become airborne. Although, after their dinner chat, she was able to watch their inter-action through new eyes.

He'd had more experience in parenthood than her, his ease very apparent as he engaged Simon in his magic know-how. Perhaps that's what made the difference. He was comfortable around children, whereas she'd had vir-tually no experience other than once being a child her-self. Even then, she hadn't socialised a great deal. Her mother had worked hard to keep a roof over their heads and often that meant missing out on playdates and birth-day parties to help her at her cleaning jobs.

It could be that Simon's unease was in direct correla-tion to hers and he was picking up on the what-the-hell-am-I-doing? vibes. In which case his lack of confidence in her was understandable. Unfortunately, the fostering classes she'd attended hadn't fully equipped her to do the job. Unlike star pupil Matt, who was deep in conversa-tion sitting on the end of Simon's bed.

'What's with all of the whispering going on over there?' She dared break up the cosy scene in an attempt to wedge herself in the middle of it.

There was more whispering, followed by a childish giggle. A sound she thought she'd never hear coming from Simon and one which threatened to start her blub-bing again. She was tempted to throw a blanket over Matt's head and snatch him home with her to keep Simon entertained.

'Can't tell you. It's a secret.' Simon giggled again, his eyes bright in the midst of the dressings covering his face.

'Magician's code, I'm afraid. We can't divulge our se-crets to civilians outside our secret circle.' Matt tapped the side of his nose and Simon slapped his hand over his mouth, clearly enjoying the game.

Quinn didn't care as long as he was talking again and having fun.

'Hmm. As long as we're not suddenly overrun with rabbits pulled out of hats, then I'll just have to put up with it. Tell me, what do you have to do to be part of this prestigious group anyway?' She perched on the bed beside Matt, getting a boost from sitting so close to him as much as from the easy-going atmosphere which had been lacking between her and Simon.

'We're a pretty new club so we'll have to look into the rules and regulations. What do you say, Simon? What would it cost Quinn to join?' Matt's teasing was light relief now her green-eyed, monstrous alter ego had left the building. This wasn't about one-upmanship; he was gaining Simon's confidence and trust and gradually easing her in with him.

'Chocolate ice cream!' he shouted without hesitation.

'We can do that.' She was partial to it herself and something they could easily pick up on the way home. A small price to pay for a quiet night.

'That should cover her joining fee…anything else?' Matt wasn't going to let her off so easily.

'Umm…' Simon took his time, milking her sympathy for all it was worth with Matt's encouragement.

He eventually came back with 'The zoo!' knowing he had her over a barrel.

There was no way she could say no when they were making solid progress. Not that she was against the idea; it simply hadn't crossed her mind that he would want to go.

'Nice one.' Matt high-fived his mini-conspirator and Quinn got the impression she'd walked straight into a trap.

'A day at the zoo? I've never been myself, but if that's the price I have to pay to join your club I'm in.' It was worth it. He hadn't expressed a desire to leave the house since the fire, unwilling to leave the shadows and venture out into the public domain, so this was a major breakthrough.

It could also turn out to be an unmitigated disaster, depending on how he interacted with other visitors. He'd already endured much staring and pointing from the general public who didn't understand how lucky he was just to survive the injuries, but it was a risk worth taking. If things went well it could bring them closer as well as give him a confidence boost.

'You've never been to the zoo?' Matt was still staring at her over that particular revelation.

'We never got around to it. Mum was always working weekends and holidays to pay the bills and I tagged along with her.' It wasn't anyone's fault; spending time together had simply been more important than expensive days out.

'You don't know what you're missing. Lions, penguins, gorillas...they're all amazing up close.'

She couldn't tell who was more excited, both big kids bouncing at the idea. Although she was loath to admit it, there was a fizz in her veins about sharing the experience with Simon for the first time too. As if somehow she could recapture her childhood and help him reconnect with his at the same time.

'Matt has to come too!' Simon tried to wedge it into the terms and conditions of the deal but he was pushing his luck now.

'I've been before. This is something for you and your mum to do together.' Matt turned and mouthed an apology to her and the penny dropped that he'd been trying to broker this deal for her benefit alone.

'Matt has lots of other patients to treat and he'd never get any work done if he had to keep taking them all to the zoo whenever they demanded it. We'll go, just the two of us, and make a day of it.' Quinn could already sense him shrinking back into his shell. Negotiating with an infant was a bit like trying to juggle jelly—impossible and very messy.

'You can take loads of photos and show me the next time you're here.'

Bless him, Matt was doing his best to keep his spirits up but the spark in Simon had definitely gone out now he knew his favourite surgeon wasn't involved. She knew the feeling.

'Right, mister, it's getting late. We need to get you dressed and take you home.' Any further arguments or tantrums could continue there, out of Matt's earshot. She wouldn't be surprised to find out he'd taken extended leave the next time they were due back to see him.

'I don't have a home!' Simon yelled, and single-handedly pulled the sheet up over his head, his body shaking under the covers as he sobbed.

Quinn genuinely didn't know what to do; her own heart shattered into a million pieces at his outburst. He didn't count her as his mum, didn't even think of her house as a place of safety, despite everything she'd tried to do for him.

She was too numb to cry and stood open-mouthed, staring at Matt, willing him to tell her what to do next. It wasn't as if she could leave him here until he calmed down; he was her foster child, her responsibility, and it was down to her to provide a home he'd rather be in instead of here.

The foster authorities would certainly form that opinion and it was soul-crushing to learn he'd take a hospital bed on a noisy ward over the boy-friendly bedroom she'd painstakingly decorated in anticipation of his arrival.

She'd been happy to have one parent—why couldn't he?

'You're being daft now. I know for a fact you and Quinn live in the same house. I bet you've even got a football-themed room.' As usual Matt was the one to coax him back out of his cotton cocoon.

'I've got space stuff.' Simon sniffed.

'Wow! You're one lucky wee man. I had to share a room with my sisters so it was all flowers and pink mushy stuff when I was growing up.'

'Yuck!'

'Yuck indeed.' Matt gave an exaggerated shudder at the memory but it gave Quinn a snapshot of his early life, outnumbered by girls.

'Do you wanna come see?' He peeked his head above the cover to witness the fallout of his latest demand.

This time Matt turned to her for answers.

They were stuffed.

If she said no, she hadn't a hope of getting Simon home without a struggle and she was too exhausted to face it. A 'yes' meant inviting Matt further into their personal lives and they couldn't keep relying on him to solve their problems. He'd made it clear he didn't want to be part of any family apart from the one he'd already raised. In her head she knew it was asking for trouble but her heart said, 'Yes, yes, yes!' So far, he'd been the one blazing ember of hope in the dark ashes of the fire.

She gave a noncommittal shrug, leaving the final decision with him. It was a cop out on her behalf, but if he wanted out, now was the time to do it. She was putting her faith in him but his hesitation was more comforting than it should've been. At least she wasn't the only one being put on the spot and it proved some things were beyond even his control. His mind wasn't made up one way or the other about getting further entangled in this mess and that had to be more promising than a firm no.

'My apartment isn't too far away… I suppose I could get my car, drop you two home and take a quick peek at your room…' The confidence had definitely left his voice.

A five-year-old had got the better of both of them.

'I really couldn't ask you to—'

'Cool!' Simon cut off the polite refusal she was trying to make so Matt didn't feel obligated, even though she didn't mean it. Inside, she was happy-dancing with her foster son.

'Well, it would save us a taxi fare.' She folded easily. A ride home would be so much less stressful than the Tube or a black cab. As efficient as the London transport system was, it wasn't traumatised-child-friendly. The fewer strangers Simon had to encounter straight after his surgery, the better.

'I'll go get the car and meet you out front in about thirty minutes. That should give you plenty of time to get ready.' He bolted from the room as soon as she gave the green light. It was impossible to tell whether he wanted to put some distance between them as soon as possible, or whether he intended to get the job done before he changed his mind. Whatever his motives, she was eternally grateful.

For the first night in weeks, she wasn't dreading going home.

* * *

Matt stopped swearing at himself the moment he clocked the two figures huddled at the hospital entrance waiting for him. He'd been beating himself up about getting roped into this, but seeing them clutching each other's hands like two lost bodies in the fog, he knew he'd done the right thing. He wouldn't have slept if he'd gone home and left Quinn wrestling a clearly agitated child into the back of a taxi. For some reason his presence was enough to diffuse the tension between the two and, as Simon's healthcare provider, it was his duty to ease him back to normality after his surgery. Besides, it was only a lift, something he would do for any of his friends in need.

The only reason he'd hesitated was because he didn't want people like Rebecca, or Quinn, reading too much into it. He really hadn't been able to refuse when he'd had two sets of puppy dog eyes pleading with him to help.

'Nice car.' Quinn eyed his silver convertible with a smile as he pulled up.

'A treat to myself. Although I don't get out in it as often as I'd hoped. Much easier to walk around central London.' It had been his one great extravagance and what might appear to some as a cliché, to him it had been a symbol of his long-awaited independence.

Yet here he was, strapping a small child into the back seat...

'Yeah. This is made for long drives in the country with the top down.' She ran her hand over the car's smooth curves, more impressed than a lot of his friends who thought it was tragic attention-seeking on his part.

'That's the idea.' Except now he had the image of Quinn in the passenger seat, her ash brown hair blowing in the wind, without a care in the world, he wondered if it was time he traded it in for something more practical, more sedate.

Quinn's modest house was far enough from the hospital to make travel awkward but it had the bonus of peace and quiet. It was the perfect suburban semi for a happy family and the complete opposite of his modern bachelor pad in the heart of the city. He at least had the option of walking to PCH and did most days. Since moving to London he'd fully immersed himself in the chaos around him. Probably because he'd spent most of his years at the beck and call of his siblings, his surroundings dictated by the needs of his dependents. This kind of white picket fence existence represented a prison of sorts to him and he couldn't wait to get back to his alternative, watch-TV-in-my-pants-if-I-want-to lifestyle.

'You can't get much better than a taxi straight to your door.' He pulled the handbrake on with the confidence of a man who knew he'd be leaving again soon. This was the final destination for any feelings or responsibility he felt for Quinn and Simon today. Tomorrow was another day and brought another list of vulnerable patients who would need him.

'I really can't thank you enough, Matt. I wasn't up to another burst of tantrum before we left.' Quinn's slow, deliberate movements as she unbuckled her seat belt showed her weariness and reluctance to go inside.

The stress she was under was relentless—juggling Simon's injuries with the fostering process and her job. All on her own. The two of them could probably do with a break away from it all.

He glanced back at Simon. 'Someone's out for the count now. He shouldn't give you any more trouble.'

'If I can get him up to bed without disturbing him I might actually get a few hours to get some work done. Then I'll be on standby for the rest of the night with pain relief when he needs it.' She was yawning already at the mere mention of the night ahead.

'Make sure you get a couple of hours' sleep too.'

'That's about as much as we're both getting at the moment.' She gave a hollow laugh. The lack of sleep would definitely account for the short tempers and general crankiness, not to mention the emotional outbursts.

'Why don't you open the door and I'll carry Sleeping Beauty inside for you?'

She was strong and stubborn enough to manage on her own, he was sure—after all, she'd been coping this far on her own—but it didn't seem very gentlemanly to leave her to carry the dead weight of a sleeping child upstairs. If he delivered Simon directly to his bed there was more chance of him getting out of here within the next few minutes. That was his excuse and he was sticking to it.

Quinn opened her mouth as if to argue the point, then thought better of it, going to open the door for them and leaving him to scoop Simon out of the back seat. It was an indication of how weary she was when she gave in so easily.

As Matt carried Simon up the steep staircase to bed, careful not to jar his arm in the process, he knew he'd made the right call. Leaving a tired, petite Quinn to manage this on her own would have been an accident waiting to happen. He'd had enough experience of doing this with baby sisters who'd sat up long past their bedtimes to negotiate the obstacle with ease.

'Which way?' he mouthed to Quinn, who was waiting for them on the landing.

'In here.' She opened one of the doors and switched on
the rocket-shaped night light at the side of the small bed.

Matt eased him down onto the covers and let Quinn
tuck him in. She was so tenderly brushing his hair from
his face and making sure he was comfortable that in that
moment an outsider wouldn't have known they were anything other than biological mother and son.

They tried to tiptoe out of the room together but Simon
unfurled his foetal position and rolled over.

'Do you like my room, Matt?' he mumbled, half asleep
and hardly able to keep his eyes open.

'Yeah, mate. You're one lucky boy.' He could see how
much effort Quinn had gone to in order to create the perfect little boy's room. From the glow-in-the-dark stars on
the ceiling, to the planet-themed wallpaper, it had been
co-ordinated down to the very last detail. The sort of
bedroom a young boy sharing a council flat with three
sisters could only have dreamed about.

'Now Matt's seen your room he has to go and you
need to get some sleep.' Quinn tucked the loosened covers back around him.

'What-about-the-zoo?' he said in one breath as his
eyes fluttered shut again.

'We'll do that another day,' she assured him, and tried
to back out of the room again.

'Can-Matt-come-too?' He wasn't giving in without
a fight.

Quinn's features flickered with renewed panic. This
wasn't in the plan but they knew all hell would break
loose again if he left and denied this request. Their si-

lence forced Simon's eyes open and Matt had to act fast or get stuck here all night trying to pacify him.

'Sure.' He glanced back at her and shrugged. What choice did he have? With any luck Simon would forget the entire conversation altogether. Especially since the required answer sent him back to sleep with a smile on his face.

This time they made it out of the room undetected and Quinn released a whoosh of breath from her lungs as she eased the door behind them.

'I thought we'd never get out of there alive.' She rested her head against the back of the door, all signs of tension leaving her body as her frown lines finally disappeared and a smile played upon her lips. It was a good look on her and one Matt wished he saw more often.

'We're not off the hook yet but hopefully we've stalled the drama for another day.' Preferably when he was far from the crime scene.

'I appreciate you only agreed to the zoo thing to get him to go to sleep. Don't worry, I won't hold you to it.' She was granting him immunity but he remembered something she'd said about people letting her down and he didn't want to be another one to add to her list.

'It's no problem at all. I told you, I love the zoo.' It just wasn't somewhere he'd visited since his sisters had entered their teenage years. An afternoon escorting the pair around the sights wasn't a big deal; he'd been the chaperone on a few organised hospital trips in his time and this wouldn't be too dissimilar. It would be worth a couple of hours of his free time to see them happy again.

'Thanks for the idea, by the way. I kind of fell apart when he said he didn't have a home to go to.' The crack in her voice was evidence of how much the comment had hurt.

'He's frightened and it's been another tough day for both of you. It's easy to hit out at the ones closest to us. I've lost count of the amount of times my sisters told me they hated me and they couldn't wait to move out. They didn't mean it, and nor does Simon. It's all part of the extras package that comes with parenthood, I'm afraid.'

There'd been plenty of rows over the years as teenagers rebelled and he'd been the authority figure who'd had to rein them in. However, they were still a close family and he was the first person they'd call if they needed help.

'I'd hate to think I was making things worse for him. He seems so unhappy.' The head was down as the burden of guilt took up residence again on her shoulders.

He crouched down before her so she had to look at him. 'Hey, I don't know Simon's background but I do know he's a lucky boy to have you as a foster mother. You're a wonderful woman, Quinn, and don't you forget that.'

She fluttered her eyelashes as she tried to bat away the compliment but he meant every word. The burden she'd taken on with Simon's injuries and her determination to make a loving home for the duration of his time with her took tremendous courage. A strong, fiery soul wrapped up in one pretty package was difficult not to admire.

Now free from the responsibilities of work and away from the stares of co-workers and impressionable youngsters, Matt no longer had anyone to stop him from doing what he'd wanted to do for a long time.

He leaned in and pressed his mouth to hers, stealing the kiss they'd been dodging since their time in the pub. It wasn't his ego make-believing she wanted this too when her lips were parted and waiting for him.

Away from the hospital they were more than an over-attentive doctor and an anxious parent. In another time, in different circumstances, he wouldn't have waited a full day before taking her in his arms the way he did now.

He bunched her silky hair in his hands and thought only of driving away the shadows of doubt already trying to creep in and rob him of this moment. The instant passion which flared between them was a culmination of weeks of building tension, fighting the attraction and each other. Every fibre of his being, with the exception of several erogenous zones, said this was a bad idea. She was a single mother and this went against all of his self-imposed rules. This new carefree lifestyle was supposed to mean he went with the flow, free to do whatever he wanted. And in the here and now, Quinn was exactly what he wanted, so he ignored the voice that told him to leave and never look back, and carried on kissing her.

Either Quinn had died and gone to heaven or her exhaustion had conjured up this mega-erotic fantasy because it couldn't possibly be happening. It was beyond comprehension that she was actually making out with her foster son's surgeon in her own house.

The tug at her scalp reminded her it was very real.

Matt took her gasp as an invitation to plunge his tongue deeper into her mouth, stealing what was left of her breath. He was so thorough in his exploration, yet so tender, he confused her senses until she couldn't think beyond his next touch.

His fingers wrapped around her hair, his mouth locked onto hers, his hard body pressed tightly against her—it was too much for her long-neglected libido to process at once. It was as though every one of her forgotten desires had come to life at once, erasing the loneliness of these past man-free months.

Her ex's betrayal had devastated her so much she'd convinced herself romance in her life didn't matter but Matt McGrory had obliterated that theory with one kiss. It most certainly *did* matter when it reminded her she was a hot-blooded woman beneath the layers of foster mum guilt. She'd forgotten how it was to have someone kiss the sensitive skin at her neck and send shock waves of pleasure spiralling through her belly and beyond. In fact, she didn't remember ever swooning the way she was right now.

Today, Matt had successfully operated on Simon, talked sense into her when she'd been virtually hysterical, held her when she'd cried, supported her when she'd fallen apart and carried a sleeping child to his bed. He was perfect. It was a crying shame the timing was abominable.

He slid a hand under her shirt and her nipples immediately tightened in anticipation of his touch. If he ventured any further than her back she doubted she'd be able to think clearly enough to put a stop to this. As enjoyable as the feel of his lips on her fevered skin was, this wasn't about her getting her groove back on. Simon was her priority and she wouldn't do anything to jeopardise that.

Matt was his surgeon and this could lead to all sorts of complications regarding his treatment and the fostering authorities. That wasn't a risk she was willing to take. She wanted to break the cycle of selfish behaviour which had plagued her and Simon to date, and if it kept her heart protected a while longer, all the better.

'I think we should probably call it a day.' She dug deep to find the strength to end the best night she'd had for a long time.

With her hands creating a barrier between their warm bodies, she gave him a feeble push. Her heart wasn't in the rejection but it did stop him in his tracks before he kissed his way to her earlobe and discovered her kill switch. His acquiescence did nothing to ease her conscience or the throbbing need pulsating in her veins.

'You're probably right.' He took a step back, giving them some space to think about the disaster they'd narrowly averted. Then he was gone.

One nod of the head, a meek half-smile and it was Goodnight, Josephine.

Quinn exhaled a shaky breath as the front door clicked shut.

It had been a close call and, now she knew the number, it was going to be a test of endurance not to put him on speed dial.

CHAPTER SIX

IT HAD BEEN several days since the infamous kiss but Quinn hadn't laid eyes on Matt at all. Quite a feat when she'd spent every waking moment back at the hospital. She thought he'd be there when Simon had his dressings changed, an ordeal in itself. Although it was the nurses who routinely did that job, he usually called in to see how they were. He was definitely avoiding her.

Whilst his noticeable absence had prevented any awkwardness between them after locking lips together, a sense of loss seemed to have engulfed her and Simon as a result. They'd become much too invested in his company and now she had very fond, intimate memories to make her pine for him too.

It had been her decision to stop things before they'd gone any further. Hot kisses and steamy intervals didn't bring any comfort when there was no commitment behind them. Passion didn't mean much to her these days when she'd found out the hard way men used it to hide their true intentions. She'd thought Darryl had loved her because he was so attentive in that department but when it came down to putting a child's needs before his he'd shown how shallow he really was. She wouldn't be duped for a second time into believing a man's interest in her body was anything more than just that. Darryl had nearly broken her spirit altogether with his betrayal, to the point she'd questioned her own judgement about foster care. What was the point if the whole ideal of a happy family was a sham concocted so the male species could satisfy their own selfish needs?

It was meeting Simon which had convinced her she'd taken the right path and she wouldn't be so easily diverted from it again. A handsome face and a kissable mouth weren't enough for her to risk her or Simon's future if she was dumped again and sent spiralling back down into despair. Things were difficult at the moment but she was still soldiering on, wasn't ready to give up the fight. One more knock to her confidence might well change that. No, she'd made the right call and she'd just have to learn to live with it. Regardless of how much she wanted Matt to be the man she'd always thought would be the head of her perfect little family.

Today, to distract herself from the events of that evening, she'd joined the committee fighting to save the Castle. Whilst Simon was busy with his physiotherapist, who was working with him to make sure he maintained the movement in his right arm, she had some time to herself. She chose to spend it putting the world to rights with other committee members over a latte in the canteen. Her position also allowed her to keep watch on the door in case of a glimpse of the elusive Mr McGrory.

'I'm so glad you've joined us, Quinn. It'll really help our cause to have parents of our patients on board, as well as the staff. This is about the children, and showing the board the Castle is an important part of the community, and is more than just a lucrative piece of land.' Victoria Christie sat forward in her chair, fixing Quinn with her intense hazel eyes. She was a paramedic, the head of the committee and apparently very passionate about the cause.

With her buoyant enthusiasm she was the perfect choice for a front woman and Quinn got the impression she would attach herself to the wrecking ball should the dreaded demolition come to fruition.

'I'm only too happy to help. I'll sign a petition, wave a placard, write a personal impact statement…whatever it takes to make a difference. Matt…er… Mr McGrory suggested I join since I spend most of my days here any-way.' Mostly, she suspected, to get her out of his lovely blond hair, but at least it was a more productive way of filling her time than fretting and crying on shoulders of very busy surgeons.

'Matt's very passionate about his work and his pa-tients. He's one of the good guys.' The tall blonde she'd been introduced to at the start of this meeting was Robyn Kelly, head of surgery at the hospital and the commit-tee's PR person.

Quinn shifted her gaze towards the pile of papers on the table outlining their press coverage so far in case her blush gave away her thoughts about that very per-sonal, private moment she'd spent with her colleague at her house.

'He's been very patient with Simon, and me, but we're well on the way to recovery. I hope future patients are as lucky to have him on their side.' She smiled as brightly as her pained cheeks would allow. In truth, she didn't want anyone to get as close as she had been to him but that didn't mean she'd deny another family his expertise.

'That's a really good idea!' Victoria slammed her

cup back down on the table, sloshing the contents into the saucer.

'What is?' With one hand Robyn quickly moved the newspaper cuttings out of the path of the tea puddle slowly spreading across the table, and used the other to soak up the mess with a napkin.

She exuded a self-confidence Quinn had once had, before a runaway boyfriend and being catapulted into life as a single foster parent had robbed her of it. With a little time and more experience she hoped she'd soon be able to clear up her own messes as swiftly and efficiently.

Although she'd never regret her decision to leave her full-time teaching position to raise Simon, she did envy both women to a certain degree. They were still career women, free to gossip over coffee without feeling guilty about taking some 'me' time. It was just as well they'd been so welcoming, arranging this meet as soon as she'd expressed an interest in the committee. Otherwise her jealousy might have got the better of her again.

'Personal impact stories, of course. Perhaps we could collate short statements from patients and their families, past and present. They could give an account of what the hospital has done for them and what it would mean to lose its support.

'That could add a really heartfelt element to the cause...'

'I could make a start with the families of the other children who were treated after the school fire.' Quinn knew most of them by sight now, if not personally, and they were certainly aware of Simon. Their kids had been discharged from the hospital long ago whilst he and Ryan, who'd suffered the most serious injuries, were still receiving treatment.

This new mission would give her an introduction into a conversation which didn't have to solely revolve around Simon's trauma. She wasn't the one who bore the physical scars but even she was sick of the sympathetic murmuring every time they walked past.

'Fantastic. That would be better coming from you, a concerned parent, rather than a soon-to-be-out-of-work member of staff.' Victoria's smile softened her features and her praise endeared her to Quinn even more.

'We might even get the papers to run a series of them to really hammer home how much a part of the children's recovery the Castle has become. Honest raw emotion versus cold hard cash... I think my contacts at the paper would be only too glad to wage war on some corporate fat cats.' Robyn was furiously scribbling in a reporter's notebook she'd plucked from her handbag.

'Quinn, I'll pass your name on to a few of the patients who want to help. You could be the co-ordinator for this leg of the campaign, if that's not too much trouble?' After draining her cup, Victoria got to her feet and effectively ended the meeting.

'Not at all. I could even make up some questionnaires to hand out if it would make things easier?' Admin she could do, and while paperwork had been the bane of her teaching career it was something positive here. It gave her an identity which wasn't merely that of Quinn, the single mother. She still had one useful function.

'I'll leave the details to you and try to organise a collection point for the completed papers. I'm really glad you've joined us, Quinn.' Another smile of acceptance and a firm handshake to solidify her role on the team.

Robyn, too, was packing up to leave. 'All excellent suggestions. I'll be sure to put your name forward for a medal or something at the next board meeting if we pull this off. In the meantime, I'm going to go make some more phone calls.'

She gave a sharp nod of her head as though to assure Quinn she'd just passed some sort of initiation test before she vanished out the door after Victoria. It seemed she was the only one not in a hurry to get anywhere.

She took her time finishing her latte and the caffeine seemed to have kicked in as she went to collect Simon with a renewed bounce to her step. Her well-received ideas today gave her hope that somewhere down the line she might come up with another brainwave to aid Simon as well as the hospital.

She rounded the corner and stopped dead, the rubber soles of her shoes squealing in protest on the tiled floor as she pulled on the emergency handbrake.

Unless her eyes were deceiving her, Simon and Matt were walking towards her. Panic slammed into her chest that something was wrong; there was also a fluttering in her pulse, followed by irrational fear again…then relief because they were both smiling. And finally, a surge of gratefulness she'd chosen a dress today instead of her jeans and cardi.

So, her wardrobe choices had become decidedly more feminine this week. It was an ego boost; she felt better inside when she knew she looked good on the outside. It held no significance where Matt was concerned. She definitely hadn't been paying more attention to her make-up and clothes in case she ran into him again so she looked her best. That would mean she regretted telling him to leave the other night which wasn't possible. Her primary focus would always be Simon and any other future foster children over men with wanderlust in their bewitching green eyes.

'Hey. Is everything all right?' She managed to keep her voice steady and un-chipmunk-like regardless of her heart pounding a dizzying beat.

All of the thoughts she'd had about him since that night hit her at once as the sight of him reminded her she hadn't exaggerated the effect he had on her. Her lips tingled with the memory of him there, her skin rippled with goose bumps as though his hand still rested upon her and the hairs stood on the back of her neck where he'd kissed her so tenderly.

She supposed it would be really out of order to grab the fire extinguisher off the wall and hose herself down before she forgot where she was and tried to jump Matt's bones.

'I thought I'd call in and see how things were going.' He ruffled Simon's hair, not meeting her eyes.

Did he mean that in a purely professional capacity? Was he checking in to see how she was after their moment of madness, or just Simon? Why was she overanalysing his every word like a neurotic teenager when she was the one who'd called it a night? She'd forfeited her right to be on his watch-list when she'd directed him towards her front door rather than her bedroom door.

And now her imagination was really going into overdrive, along with her heart rate. Any minute now her tachycardia was going to require a hospital stay of her own if she couldn't stop thinking about Matt without his scrubs.

She cleared her throat and refocused. He was wearing clothes. They were in public. He had Simon by the hand. Anything remotely erotic beyond that was in her disturbed mind.

'We're chugging along as usual.' The only disruption to their carefully organised schedule were the distractions she was seeking to stop her obsessing over a certain medic. 'Oh, and I've volunteered my services to the hospital committee.'

'Good. Good. We can use all the help we can get.' Matt rocked forward and back on his toes, displaying the same unease about seeing each other after their last meet.

Yet, he'd come to seek her out. Albeit using Simon as some sort of barrier between them.

'How did you get on today, sweetheart?' It was never fun waiting on the sidelines no matter what the purpose of the visit because there was no telling how his mood would be at the end of these appointments. No child enjoyed sitting still for too long or being poked and prodded by doctors and nurses. Although there was no dragging of heels when he was with Matt. She should really capitalise on that and get him home while there were some happy endorphins going on.

'Okay.' It was probably as good an answer as she could hope for.

'I took the liberty of checking on Simon while I was here. Everything seems to be healing nicely.'

'Yes. Thanks to you and the rest of the staff.' Praise where it was due, Matt was very skilled at what he did and everyone here was working to ensure Simon's scarring would be as minimal as possible.

'And you. Aftercare at home is equally as important.'

Quinn didn't know how to respond to his kind acknowledgement that she'd contributed to his recovery in some small way. So far, she'd only seen the areas in which she'd failed him.

As they ran out of things to say to each other, memories of that kiss hovered unattended between them, the air crackling with unresolved sexual tension.

'Matt says we can go to the zoo tomorrow.' Leave it to Simon to throw her even more off guard with extra last-minute drama.

'I don't think so.' They'd had this conversation so she could prepare him for the disappointment when they ended up going alone, impressing upon him the importance of Matt's job and how he couldn't take time off when small boys demanded it.

She wouldn't expect Matt to keep his word given the circumstances, when he'd either be nursing a bruised ego or breathing a sigh of relief after she'd rebuffed him. Although, strictly speaking, she hadn't rejected his advances; she'd simply declined a further sample of his wares before she became addicted.

Simon's bottom lip dropped, indicating the moment of calm was about to come to an abrupt end.

'If you have other plans I totally understand. I really should have got in touch sooner.' Matt raked his hand over his scalp, mussing his usually neat locks.

Quinn found it oddly comforting to find she wasn't the only one trying to keep her cool.

'No plans.' Certainly none which included spending another day in adult male company because she apparently had trouble containing herself when left alone with one.

'Good. It's a date, then.' Matt's very words, no matter how innocently intended, shattered her fragile composure.

Whatever deal these two had struck this time, there

was no going back on it; otherwise Simon would never forgive her for it. She couldn't afford to be the bad guy here.

'Great,' she said, smiling sweetly while glaring daggers at Matt. She didn't understand why he'd insisted on making this happen when it had been made very clear socialising between them wasn't a good idea at all.

Matt strolled towards the designated meeting point for his day out with Quinn and Simon. He never imagined he'd be back playing the stand-in father figure so soon but he couldn't go back on his word to Simon.

Okay, he wasn't being *totally* altruistic; he hadn't been able to stop thinking about Quinn, or that kiss they'd shared, no matter how hard he'd tried to avoid her. In the end he'd resigned himself to see this through, spurred on in part by the glimpses he'd caught of her flitting in and out of the department like a ghost until he hadn't been entirely sure if she was anything but a figment of his overactive imagination.

It was difficult to convince yourself you weren't interested in someone when they were at your place of work every day and driving you to distraction when you knew how it was to hold them, taste them, be with them.

In the cold light of day he should've been relieved when she'd sent him home for a cold shower. After all, he'd had more than enough family duty stuff to last him a lifetime. Instead, he and his dented male pride had brooded, mourned the loss of something which could've been special.

It was seeing Quinn carry on taking care of Simon regardless of her own wants and feelings which had made him see sense in the end. Forget the playboy car and bachelor pad in the city; he was a thirty-five-year-old man, an adult, and Simon was the child who had to come first.

Now he was committed to this he was going to make it a day to remember. One which wouldn't be dictated by hospitals and authorities for Quinn and Simon. If Matt had learned anything about raising younger sisters, it was how to have fun and keep their young minds occupied away from the harsh realities of life.

Quinn had declined his offer of a lift but he hadn't minded since it reduced his responsibilities for the afternoon. It gave the impression he was more of a tour guide today rather than a date, or part of the family, and that suited him fine. As soon as they were back on the train home he was off the clock with a clear conscience and his promise kept.

Little Venice, with its pretty barges and canals, was only a short distance from his apartment and the Tube station. The perfect place to pick up a couple of tourists already waiting on the bridge for him. They were watching the boats below, oblivious to his arrival, and Matt took a moment to drink in the sight.

Quinn, dressed in a daisy-covered strappy yellow sundress and showing off her toned, tanned limbs, was the embodiment of the beautiful sunny morning. Simply stunning. Simon, too, was in his summer wear, every bit as colourful in his red shirt and green shorts. Quinn knelt to slather on sun cream to Simon's exposed skin and plonked a legionnaire-style cap on his head. As per instructions, she wasn't taking any chances of the sun aggravating his already tender skin.

'Look, Quinn. It's Matt!' Simon spotted him over the top of his foster mother's head and was suddenly running at him full pelt.

'Oof!' A five-year-old hug missile knocked out what was left of his breath after seeing Quinn.

'Hi,' she said, brushing her hair from her eyes as he walked towards her.

Matt held out his hand to help her back to her feet, with Simon still attached one-handed to his waist. 'It's nice to see you too.'

'Sorry, he's very excited.' With a warning to calm down before Matt changed his mind, Quinn untangled the little person from him. The threat wasn't the least bit likely but it did the job.

'Me too.' Matt's grin reflected that of his co-chaperone for the day and sealed a non-verbal agreement that they'd put their indiscretion behind them and start over.

'Where are the animals?' Simon piped up, understandably anxious when he'd been promised monkeys, giraffes and all kinds of exotic new friends, only to find water and barges as far as the eye could see.

It was all part of Matt's plan to build the excitement a while longer and capture Simon's attention for the main event.

'They're at the zoo, which we're going to, but a tourist trip around London isn't complete without taking in a show.' He could see Quinn frowning at him out of the corner of his eye but the surprise was just as much for her.

Simon skipped between the two adults as they walked down towards the red-and-yellow barge covered with a huge stripy canvas top. They must've looked like any other young family from a distance and he was surprisingly comfortable with that thought…as long as it was short-lived. Today all Matt wanted was for Simon to feel comfortable and the beaming faces beside him said the lie was worth telling.

'A puppet show?' Quinn's eyes were wider than those of the other children trooping past them on the gangplank into the quirky theatre barge.

'I've heard the kids love it and it'll get Simon used to being on board before we take a water taxi on up to the zoo.' Apart from being the perfect excuse for him to see it for himself, the dimly lit area would also serve as a gentle icebreaker into the general public. He didn't want Simon to become too overwhelmed by the hordes of people who'd undoubtedly be at the zoo on a day such as this.

'You really do think of everything.'

It was a compliment, not a criticism, but it was truer than Quinn would ever know. He hadn't left anything to chance, having planned every tiny detail of this trip in those moments he'd lain awake since agreeing to it.

Matt escorted them to their tiered seats looking down on the small stage, away from prying eyes. The one concern he'd had was that Simon might find the small space too claustrophobic. On his initial admission his notes had mentioned he'd been trapped in one of the classrooms and Quinn had mentioned his nightmares regarding his entrapment and not being able to find his way out. He needn't have worried. Simon was as enthralled with the old-fashioned marionettes adorning the walls as any of the other children. Matt was the only one experiencing difficulties with the low ceiling and small walkways and that was purely down to his height.

'I've never seen a real puppet show before.' Quinn leaned in to whisper in the darkness, her thighs touching his on the small bench where they sat, her excitement inadvertently increasing his.

'Well, they say it's recommended for small kids from five to ninety-five and I think we fall right in the middle of that age bracket.' He reached across to whisper back, the soft waves of her hair brushing his cheek, and it was all he could do not to nuzzle closer and breathe in her sweet scent. This was supposed to be a PG-rated show and he didn't want to run the risk of being asked to walk the gangplank of shame because he couldn't control himself around her.

'In that case, we're the perfect audience.' Her eyes glittered in the darkness as she hugged Simon close.

'Perfect.' Matt ignored the rising curtain, mesmerised by Quinn's childlike wonder instead.

Quinn was in her very own fairy tale. So far she and Simon had been enchanted by their favourite childhood tales brought to life by puppets and had a good old singalong to some very familiar nursery rhymes. Simon had really thrown himself into the audience participation, as had Matt.

Perhaps it was the relative safety of dimmed lighting which brought her boy out of his shell, or maybe he was simply following the exuberance of Matt's tuneless singing, but in that hour no one could tell he was different from any other boisterous child.

Matt had whisked them straight onto another barge when the show ended and they'd trundled along the tranquil waterways towards the zoo. It was the best route they could've taken, so peaceful, and a world away from the crowded streets beyond the green banks.

She'd been on boats before but never the barges. The hand-painted green-and-red beauty they were travelling on transported them to another era, a parallel universe where everything was well in her world.

How was it Matt could take such a simple idea and turn it into something special?

That was the talent which charmed adults as much as the children.

He was sitting with Simon now, spending the journey time pointing out the sights through the tiny side windows. He had a love and knowledge of the world around him that he was keen to share. Then there was that fun side to him as he encouraged his sidekick to wave at passers-by and make silly noises every time they went under a bridge. A distraction, she guessed, from the odd curious stare and a fear of the dark.

It was probably the first time in his young life he had two adults working together to put his needs above their own. She hoped one day he would have this for real even if she wouldn't. There would be a family for Simon someday but she doubted she'd ever find another Matt who'd take her and her planned foster brood on for anything other than an afternoon. She wasn't lucky that way.

Their gentle journey came to an end in a leafy area which still seemed miles from civilisation. As if sensing her confusion, Matt reached his arm across the seat and rested his hand on her shoulder.

'The waterbus tours have their own entrance into the zoo so there's no need for us to join the queues at the main entrance.'

A warmth started in the pit of Quinn's stomach and gradually spread its way through her system and it wasn't purely because they couldn't seem to help themselves from making body contact when and where they could. On this occasion it was Matt's thoughtfulness which had really captured her heart. Something which had been sadly lacking from the people in her and Simon's lives to date. Without making a big deal about it, he'd carefully constructed a tailor-made route into the busy zoo to suit all of a traumatised child's needs.

From the magical puppet theatre, to the tranquil method of transport, and now this, the trouble he'd gone to just so they could arrive at their destination relaxed brought a lump to her throat.

If only she and Simon had had male role models who took such care of others, they mightn't have had the past heartaches they were both still trying to overcome.

They waited until all the other passengers had disembarked before they left their seats, with Quinn hesitant to leave the sweet memories of their journey here to rejoin the masses on the other side of the hill.

'Your sisters are very lucky to have you,' she said as Matt helped her ashore. If he treated his siblings as well as he did his patients and families they would never have been in doubt about being loved, and that was the most important aspect of growing up in any family.

His brow knitted together trying to fathom what to make of her compliment. She had no doubt he'd experienced the same general struggles as she'd had as a single parent, yet the very fact he didn't expect thanks for getting through them spoke volumes. A person didn't become a parent for awards and accolades but to create the best possible start in life for their children. Be it younger siblings or foster children. Simply by doing her best for Simon, Quinn was beginning to see she was already the best mother he'd ever had.

Simon squeezed her hand as they moved through to the main part of the zoo with people as far as the eye could see. She squeezed back, reassuring him she was here whenever he needed her. That was all she could do for as long as he was with her—love him and protect him as well as she could. Someday that might be enough for him.

As more children, and adults who should've known better, turned to stare at the little boy with the scars and burned skin, she held him closer. Matt took up residence on the other side so they created a protective barrier around him. Somehow they'd get through this together.

CHAPTER SEVEN

'Is it still the done thing to go to the zoo? Should I feel guilty about walking freely around here peering in at caged animals?' As excited as she was to be here, she did have a social conscience and the child-versus-adult argument about it in her head was in danger of tainting the experience.

'There are two very different schools of thought but the zoo today is much more than the sideshow attraction it used to be. It's educational and provides a natural environment for the animals. Then there are the conservation projects which are funded through the admission fees...'

'Okay. Okay. I'm sold. I can enjoy the view safe in the knowledge I'm not contributing to any ill treatment.' She trusted Matt's judgement. He'd done his homework and he wasn't the sort of man to throw his weight behind a cause unless it was for the greater good. He was principled and not the type to bend the facts to suit his own agenda. Unlike her ex, who'd pretended he wanted a family so he could move in with her.

Quinn shooed away the negative thoughts from her past to replace them with the positive. Such as Matt, positively yummy in his casual clothes again this morning. As he turned to study the map, she was free to ogle his backside encased in black denim and the perfect V of his torso wrapped in dark grey cotton.

'What are you smiling at, Quinn?' Simon quizzed, drawing Matt's attention back from the map.

Caught in the act of perving at Matt's physical attributes, lies didn't come easy to her. 'I, er... I was just thinking nice thoughts.'

She spun on her heel and started walking again, ignoring the smirk on Matt's face and the heat of her own.

'What ones?' Simon tugged her hand with the unfiltered curiosity only a child could get away with.

The puppets. The boat. Matt's butt.

She could've said any of those things and they would've been true.

In the end she went with, 'About how much fun I'm having with you both today.'

Curiosity satisfied, Simon moved on to his new topic of interest, staring at the pictures of ice creams depicted on an advertising board.

'Can I have one?'

'It's a bit early for ice cream but we can get one later. All good boys and girls deserve a treat now and then, don't you think, Quinn?' Matt was so close his breath tickled the inside of her ear and did something to her that made her a very bad girl.

She so wanted him to be talking about more than a child or an ice cream.

Up until now she'd been the very model of restraint but she was wondering if she deserved a treat too? They did say a little of what you fancy was good for you and there was no denying what it was she fancied more than anything.

'Absolutely. Life can get very dull if you don't give in to temptation once in a while.' She locked eyes with

Matt so that all pretence they were still talking about dairy products vanished without trace.

Eye contact definitely constituted flirting when the heat flaring between them was hotter than the morning sun. They'd proved they could be adults, and whatever did or didn't happen between them personally wouldn't become an issue where Simon was concerned. There was no fostering law against her seeing someone either, except the one she'd created herself. By trying to protect her heart she might actually be denying herself the best thing that had walked into her life since Simon.

Despite the unexpected trials and tribulations which had made their journey more difficult than it should've been, she couldn't imagine her existence without Simon in it. Or Matt, for that matter, and therein lay the danger. The damage had already been done, because she knew when the time came for these two to leave, all she'd have left would be a broken heart and some wonderful memories.

Today was all about making those memorable moments and as long as they avoided any empty promises they might actually get to make a few. Matt was a boost to her confidence when he did his best to convince her she could handle whatever fate threw at her. That was every bit as enticing as the soft lips which had caressed hers and the warm hands she could still imagine on her skin. He was right. She did deserve a treat.

Away from impressionable young eyes who might read more into an adult relationship than was true, she wanted one more taste of her dishy doc.

They made their way around the exhibits, each animal becoming Simon's new favourite as he was introduced to their habitats, and eventually circled back to the area where they'd started. Their route had been dictated according to which animals Simon wanted to see rather than the logical, more traditional route everyone else was following. It had probably added a few extra miles to their journey but that could be to their advantage later when exhaustion caught up with him.

Quinn had to admit a pang of self-pity for her inner child when she was only getting to experience this herself at the age of thirty-two. Watching Simon's face light up every time a penguin swam close or a monkey swung by, she ached for the little girl who'd been denied this joy with her own parents.

Every child should experience the fun and wonder to be had in the world beyond school and the foster system and she vowed to do it for whoever entered her care. It didn't have to be the zoo, or with Matt, but she wanted her future foster children to have at least one day of simply being a kid.

'You wish you could get in there, don't you?'

'Sorry?' Quinn panicked that Matt had caught her ogling his backside again.

'The meerkat tunnels. I can see you're busting to get in those with him.' He nodded over towards Simon, who'd popped his head up in the plastic capsule overlooking the enclosure.

'Yeah. This place is great, so interactive for the kids, but us adults might want to find out what it's like to be a meerkat for the afternoon too.' She covered herself quickly, happy to acknowledge her play envy before her relationship daydreams. After all, she didn't know if Matt saw her as anything other than an acquaintance now.

He'd certainly been in control of any more urges to kiss her. More's the pity.

Despite the flirting and the unnecessary touching, which she could have misconstrued entirely, he hadn't made another move on her.

'Poor Quinn. I hear they do some adult-only tours of the zoo at night. Perhaps we should sign up for one?' He was teasing her but he painted an enticing picture of an intimate party of two having some fun together at night.

'It seems to me that we both missed out on the whole childhood fun thing. It mightn't be a bad idea for us to have some quality time in the dark.' Her temperature rose with the bold proposal, as did Matt's eyebrows.

'Hold that thought,' he growled into her ear as Simon came running back to greet them.

'When are we getting something to eat?'

'Soon.' She was glad he was getting his appetite back and she would simply have to set aside her hunger for anything other than lunch until she and Matt were alone again.

Matt thought he'd imagined the heat shimmering between them, a manifestation of his own frustration that he and Quinn hadn't progressed to anything beyond that one sizzling kiss. He'd wanted more but when she'd given him his marching orders he'd done his best to ignore the temptation. That was until he'd seen the darkening of her eyes, the sapphire fire matching the one burning inside him.

He wasn't a man to disappoint anyone if he could help it but there was a time and place for everything and at this very moment they had a hungry boy to feed.

He'd arranged a special child-sized lunch for them. Although the restaurant was crowded with most tables and chairs occupied, they were able to slip into a quiet side room where they served a more civilised afternoon tea.

'This is amazing! You're really spoiling us today.' Quinn clapped her hands together as the arrangement of mini-rolls, sandwiches and bite-sized cakes and scones arrived, presented on a small picnic bench.

'You're worth it,' he said, hoping he sounded more complimentary than cheesy.

He meant it. She should have someone treating her every day and making her feel special. The delight on her face and her grateful smile puffed Matt's chest out that he'd been the one to put it there and he didn't want anyone else to have the privilege.

When he'd planned this day he'd convinced himself he'd be glad when it was over, his responsibility to the pair outside the hospital over for good. Now that they were coming to the last stages, he was beginning to have second thoughts. He could honestly say this was one of the best days he'd had since moving to London and that was entirely down to the company. It would be stupid to end things here and now simply because there was a child involved. There'd always been children in his life. Children who weren't his. If Quinn was willing to be brave about it, then so was he. A relationship didn't have to mean a family and he was sure he could keep the two separate. Especially when the arrangements were all so fluid.

When they'd eaten their fill they headed to the indoor exhibits they'd bypassed in favour of some of the more exotic creatures.

'We are now entering the Rainforest Life,' he said in the style of a nature documentary voiceover artist.

Simon ran ahead into the tropical wilderness, hopped up on mini-desserts and fruit juice.

'He's going to have one hell of a crash when that sugar rush wears off.' Quinn attempted to scold him but he knew she'd savoured every mouthful of that lunch. Each heavenly groan and lick of her lips attested to her pleasure as well as increasing his discomfort. He'd heard those sounds before and intended for her to make them again soon, somewhere more private.

'Look at him!' Simon was off again, following the path of a bright blue bird flitting through the plants and vines.

'He's pretty.' Quinn was observing the exotic display from the balcony beside him, unaware she was adding to the beauty of it all.

Never mind the rare birds flying overhead or the small monkeys swinging freely through the vines, this was all about Quinn for him. The pure delight she took in her surroundings was refreshing and contagious. He'd been so caught up in material possessions and showing he could cut it as a single man in the city, he'd forgotten what it was to just enjoy life. The barrier he'd erected to protect himself had become as much of a prison as that council flat in Dublin.

Given the chance he'd swap his fancy car to travel on a barge anywhere if she was part of the deal. It was as if he was recapturing that lost childhood of his too, by being with her.

He'd been forced to grow up too quickly. From his mother walking out on her family, through his father's illness, and ultimately his death, Matt had never had time for the mischief and fun other kids had experienced. With Quinn he didn't have to be embarrassed in his joy at a puppet show when she was here spinning around, letting the mist fall on her face and telling the sloth how sleepy he looked. Matt had had enough of being the adult and there was plenty of room for his inner child, not to mention the randy teenager.

They stepped out of the light and moved into the nocturnal area. Faced with the creatures of the night, including giant rats and flitting bats, it wasn't long before he found Quinn cuddled up next to him.

'I don't know how Simon is enjoying this.'

'He's a boy. We like gross stuff.'

'I don't want to stay in here,' she whispered, fear pitching her voice until only the bats could probably hear.

Matt felt her hand graze by his knuckles as she fumbled for his reassurance in the dark. He took hold of her and turned so she could make him out in the dimmed light.

'I'll keep you safe.'

In that moment they were locked into their own world, staring into each other's eyes and holding hands like lovers who'd just sworn their lives to one another. The rest of the group had moved on, leaving them alone so the only sounds he could hear now were scurrying animals and the frantic beat of his heart for Quinn.

He cupped her face in his hands and found her mouth easily with his, honing in as if she was a beacon of light guiding him home. This time, instead of pushing him away, she wound her arm around his neck and pulled him closer. He dropped his hands to her waist as she sought him with her tongue and leaned her soft curves against him.

'Have you seen this? He's got really big eyes.' The sound of Simon's voice from across the room somewhere broke through the darkness, alerting them to his presence and throwing a bucket of cold water over them.

'I think that's a bush baby.' Matt's breath was ragged as he fought to regain control so Simon wouldn't think anything was amiss.

'We should probably follow the rest on to the next exhibit.' Quinn was already backing away from him.

'We'll talk about this later,' he whispered, low enough so only she would hear.

'I'm a mum. I have mum things to do.' That uncertainty was back in her wavering voice and Matt fumbled for her hand again in the blackness. He didn't want the guilt to start eating away at her for enjoying a moment of her own.

'Don't forget, the adult fun starts after the *real* dark.' This wasn't over and although she couldn't see him wink, he was sure he sensed her smile.

Somehow they'd find a way to be together without compromising their roles in Simon's life.

His peace of mind depended on it.

Quinn stumbled back out towards Simon and the rest of the visitors tripping out of the exhibit. Her unsteadiness on her feet was more to do with Matt's epic bone-melting prowess than the unfamiliar territory. He had a way of completely knocking her off balance when she was least expecting it.

Yes, she'd encouraged him with a few flirtatious gestures, but phew, that had taken hot to a whole new level. Wrapped in his embrace she'd forgotten who she was, where she was or what day of the week it was, and let the chemistry consume her.

Dangerous. Irresponsible. Intoxicating.

It only made her crave more.

If Simon hadn't reminded them that they weren't here alone, they could've created quite a scene. They were lucky he hadn't seen anything of their passionate embrace or they would've had some explaining to do. Unfortunately, now as she made her way back into the light, the interruption had left her throbbing with unfulfilled need which only Matt could help relieve.

As he'd pointed out, they had things to say, things to do, but they'd have to wait until Simon was safely tucked up in bed and her parental duties were over for the day. The anticipation of where and when they might get to explore this exciting new development uninterrupted was an aphrodisiac in itself. As if she needed it! Quinn was finally starting to believe there could be room in her life for more than foster children. If she dared risk her heart again.

Simon's pace began to slow up and it struck her for the first time about how much energy this day had taken out of him. Not that his enthusiasm had waned once.

'Can we go to the shop now?' His eyes were wide and it was no wonder. A building stuffed to the rafters with soft toys and souvenirs was probably one of the highlights for most of the children. For her, there'd been many others. With one in particular still lingering on her lips, and she wasn't talking about the cakes.

'Sure. What do you say about taking in the rest of the way from a giraffe's point of view?' Matt, obviously picking up on his sudden weariness too, stooped down and gently hoisted Simon up onto his shoulders. It was a balancing act to avoid jarring Simon's right side but he managed it, holding on to make sure his passenger was comfortable and secure.

Rather than make a fuss, he'd found a way to turn

a potential meltdown into something fun. A tired and cranky tot was just as difficult to reason with as a frightened, injured one.

Crisis averted, Simon perched happily on Matt's broad shoulders for the remainder of their walk around the grounds with a hand resting on his head. If either of them were in any discomfort they made no mention of it. The smiling twosome blended into the crowd of other fathers and sons and Quinn had to remind herself it was an illusion. It wasn't real. Matt wasn't always going to be around, but for now, it was good for Simon to have someone other than her who actually wanted the best for him.

'I wanna get down.' He only became restless once they reached the shop entrance, so Quinn helped Matt lift him off his shoulders so they could let him loose.

Matt cricked his neck from side to side and massaged his neck. 'I'm getting too old for that.'

'Never.' She got the impression he'd done this sort of thing a lot for his kid sisters. It seemed a shame he was so set on making sure he never committed to fatherhood again. He'd have made a great dad for some lucky child.

'My thirty-five-year-old aching muscles beg to differ. You, on the other hand, strike me as someone who's young at heart and never too old to appreciate these.' He lifted a cuddly bush baby, its big eyes begging Quinn to take him home.

'It's so cute.' She hugged it close, unable to resist the aww factor.

'And a souvenir from our time in the night life exhibit.' His devilish arched eyebrow and wicked smirk immediately flicked her swoon switch.

She'd never been a bad girl, always on her best behaviour, trying to please people so they wouldn't have cause to reject her. Matt drew out that reckless side she'd suppressed for so long and she kind of liked it.

She knew the score. Unlike Darryl, Matt had never said he'd stick around and raise foster kids with her. He was going to leave no matter what. She didn't have to be a good girl where he was concerned, and based on previous experience he had a hell of a naughty side she wouldn't mind getting to know better. Arousal rushed through her like a warm summer breeze, bringing promises of hot sweaty nights to follow.

It would've been futile to try and stop him from taking the poignant reminder of their day together over to the cash register when he hadn't let her pay for anything so far. She went to look for Simon, who'd disappeared behind the shelving at the front of the shop, probably lining up a selection of animal friends he'd talk Matt into buying for him.

When she walked around the corner she was horrified to find him in tears, surrounded by a group of older boys.

'What's going on?' She went straight into mama bear mode, defending her young and putting a barrier between Simon and whatever was upsetting him.

The three backed off, still laughing, and tossed a plastic monkey face mask at her feet. 'The freak might look better with one of those.'

At that point Matt came striding over, a formidable figure with a thunderous look on his face which sent Simon's tormentors scurrying out of the shop. 'Are you two okay?'

Quinn was winded from the cruelty she'd witnessed directed at Simon but she hugged him close, letting his tears soak through her dress.

'He's only a baby,' she gasped to Matt, her own tears bubbling to the surface.

They'd had a lovely day and now the actions of some stupid kids had set them back at square one, undoing all the progress they'd made by bringing him here.

Matt crouched down so he was level with Simon's bowed head. 'Hey, wee man. Don't you listen to them.'

Every jerky sob broke her heart a little bit more as Simon clung to her with his one good arm. If she had her way she'd wrap him up in cotton wool so this kind of thing would never happen again. A child this young shouldn't have had to go through so much in his short life.

'No one's ever going to want to be my mummy and daddy because of my stupid face.'

The emotional punch of Simon's words knocked them both into silence.

That belief was at the very heart of the child's fears and why he wouldn't let anyone get too close. He genuinely thought his injuries made him unlovable and that few minutes of taunting had given credence to his worries.

This time Quinn was forced to swipe away a rogue tear but she steeled herself against any more. For her to become an emotional wreck now wasn't going to do Simon any favours.

'Well, I know people who think the world of you. Why else would they have bought you your very own spider monkey?' Matt opened the long arms of the cuddly primate and attached them around Simon's neck. 'I've got some zoo mugs for us too. Why don't we go back to my house to test them out?'

Simon glanced up at her with puffy, red, irresistible eyes. 'Can we?'

'Sure,' she said as brightly as she could muster, thankful that the master of distraction had found a quick and simple way to ease his immediate pain. It was going to have to be down to her to find the long-term solution and show him how loved he was.

Matt stood up and spoke quietly for her ears only. 'I know this wasn't in the plan but my place is closer. We can get a taxi there, get him calmed down again before we get you home.'

She nodded, afraid to verbalise her thanks in case she burst into grateful tears.

Just as he'd reassured Simon, he took her hand and squeezed it. 'Everything's going to be grand.'

She didn't know why but even in the most trying circumstances she believed him.

'Take us home, Matt.' She sighed, content to let the pretence go on a while longer.

CHAPTER EIGHT

THE BACK OF a taxi was a luxury compared to the packed trains or buses at rush hour. The busy streets somehow seemed further away from the sanctity of their private black carriage. It was a shame Quinn's mind couldn't defend against the outside stresses as well as the thick glass windows.

The tears had dried on Simon's face now as he played with the stuffed animals on his lap. Finally sharing what had been troubling him seemed to have taken a weight off his mind, but it hadn't eased hers any. She'd been digging for so long to find out the cause of his inner turmoil she'd imagined it would bring relief. That they would deal with it and move on, naively thinking it would make her better equipped to help him. Far from it. She knew all too well that fear of never belonging, never being loved, and how it never really left, not completely. Despite the efforts of those who'd eventually taken her in. She was always waiting for that moment of final rejection which repeated itself over and over. It had to be the same for Simon, even before his injuries were added to fears which weren't completely unfounded.

Adoption was a long and complicated process and the odds of finding a family for him could well have been worsened with his serious medical, and probable future psychological, problems which not everyone would be willing to take on. Her heart ached for him, and between her and Matt, they had to work together to help him transition into the next phase of the process and find his for ever family.

Matt's home was everything she'd expected it to be on arrival—modern, expensive and in the busy hub of the city—everything hers wasn't. His apartment spoke volumes about their contrasting lifestyles and future plans. He was very much enjoying his freedom as a man about town, whilst her Victorian terraced house had been built with family predominantly in mind.

The floor-to-ceiling windows were impressive, as was the view of the river, but for her it lacked the personal touch, the evidence of family, to make it a home.

However, Matt did his best to make them comfortable for the short time they'd be here. She was certain he'd never intended for them to cross his threshold and this had been nothing more than an emergency stop to prevent her going home with the company of a distressed child to look forward to. Yet, here he was washing up after home-made omelettes and freshly squeezed orange juice as though he'd expected them for dinner all along.

'Were you a Boy Scout? You're always prepared, no matter what catastrophe I bring to your door.' Literally, in this case.

Matt laughed as he stacked the dishwasher. 'I'm no Boy Scout. I still do a big weekly shop, a leftover habit from having a houseful of ravenous teenagers, I suppose.'

'Well, I appreciate it and apparently Simon does too.' She passed him an empty plate. At least Simon's appetite was improving despite the new drama.

'It's not a problem. Actually, it's been a while since I cooked for anyone. I forgot how much I enjoy doing it.' He leaned against the kitchen worktops and for the first time looked almost unhappy about living on his own.

'Are you seriously telling me you haven't brought women back to show all of this off? Most men would have photos of this as their profile picture all over social media.' Not that he would need to use his money to draw interest. A man who could cook and clean, on top of everything else, was designed for seducing women, her included. No matter how much he tried to hide it, domesticity was very much a part of him.

'I didn't say that. I've just never cooked for any of them. That's what expensive restaurants are for.' The wink he gave her made her sick in the stomach thinking of the women who'd been here before her under entirely different circumstances.

'I guess I'm more one for home-cooked meals than whatever's fashionable.' She sniffed, despising those who'd put more store in the material things Matt could give them instead of appreciating the qualities which made him who he was— a kind-hearted, generous man, with the patience of a saint. A man she was falling much too hard for and yet she was powerless to stop herself. She was unable to resist when there was still so much to discover about him, and herself.

He'd been generous with his time where Simon was concerned but his support had also boosted her confidence that she wasn't the only stand-in parent in history who'd struggled. As everything in her life had been, this was a rough patch she simply had to fight her way through and that was something she was well practiced in.

'Hey, I only break out the chef's apron for very special guests.' Matt held her chin between his thumb and forefinger and parted her lips.

Her eyelids were already fluttering shut before he settled his mouth on hers, much too briefly. She peered over his shoulder to see how much of this little moment Simon had witnessed. It wouldn't do to have two of them confused about what was happening between her and Matt.

'I think the excitement's all got too much for him.' Matt followed her gaze to the small figure hunched up on the end of the leather sofa.

'How on earth am I going to get him home now?' Although it was a blessed relief to see him so soundly asleep, she didn't relish the thought of having to wake him to get him home and run the risk of him not getting back to sleep again.

'You know what they say, let sleeping five-year-olds lie.' Matt didn't appear to be in a hurry for her to leave, unmoving from his position in the open-plan living room between her and her sleeping babe.

'I think you'll find that's dogs,' she said, gently nudging him aside so she could go and check on Simon.

'It won't do him any harm to sleep there for a while. I swear I'll take you both home as soon as he's awake.' He crossed his heart. 'Scout's promise.'

She narrowed her eyes at him but he did make her laugh. 'He can't be comfortable in that position though.'

He was curled into the foetal position, his head bent awkwardly over the arm of the chair. It was cramp waiting to happen. Worse, it could aggravate his injuries if he lay like that too long.

'I can move him into the spare bedroom. There's plenty of space for him to stretch out there and sleep undisturbed.'

'You'll have to be careful not to wake him.' She hovered as Matt scooped him up into his big strong arms as though he weighed nothing.

'Don't worry, he's sound asleep.'

Simon didn't so much as flinch as they transferred him down the hall, his arms and legs hanging limply from Matt's hold. The fresh air had obviously done him the world of good.

Matt elbowed the door open and Quinn couldn't have been more surprised about what lay behind it if she'd found an S&M dungeon rigged up. The room was decorated in pretty pinks and purples, flowers and fairies, and everything he'd said he'd despised in home décor growing up. At the far side of the room next to a mountain of children's toys and teddy bears was a child-sized bed and a white wooden cot. The perfect little girl's room and nursery.

'Is there something you want to tell me?' He'd made such a big production about not wanting family responsibilities, she hoped she wasn't about to discover he was, in fact, a divorced dad of two little girls. She didn't think she could handle it if he'd lied to her about who he was when that was the very man she'd fallen for.

He carefully laid Simon on top of the bed covers and pulled a comforter over him before he attempted to explain himself.

'I told you I have sisters. Anne, the eldest, is married with two daughters, Jaime and Lucy. Sometimes they come visit.' He fussed around, closing the curtains and making sure the floor was clear of any debris Simon could trip over.

It was a far cry from the self-centred bachelor he'd portrayed and she wondered why he'd withheld this snippet of information. Perhaps his family situation would have put off a different type of woman, one who'd have been horrified at the thought of being required to babysit or change dirty nappies someday. Not her.

She backed out of the room with a snigger. 'So, basically, you're a granddad?'

Matt rolled his eyes and closed the door softly behind him. 'See? This is why I don't generally share the details of my personal life. It changes the way people see me. I have two sides. To the outside world I'm a young, single, successful surgeon. To my family, I'm an agony aunt and a doting uncle. I don't tend to let the two worlds collide.'

'And which side am I seeing?' They were standing toe to toe in the hallway and Quinn was sure he could hear her heart thumping against her ribcage. The more she got to know the *real* Matt, the more she wanted to believe they stood a chance of making this work.

'Well, Quinn, you are an anomaly.' He reached out and tucked a strand of her hair behind her ear. 'Somehow you've managed to set a foot in both camps and I'm not sure how I feel about that.'

It was the kind of honesty she appreciated. He wasn't promising her the world to get what he wanted, only telling her that she'd made him think about what they were getting into and that was enough for now.

'Me either.' She didn't know what each step further into his life meant for her down the line except more heartache but for now the one thing she was sure of was that she wanted him.

She leaned closer but Matt was already there to meet her, meshing his lips with hers as though they'd always meant to fit together.

Her conscience drifted between taking him by the hand and leading him to the bedroom, or setting up camp outside Simon's door in case he needed her. 'What about Simon? What if he wakes up and doesn't know where he is?'

She couldn't blame Matt for wanting to avoid ready-made families when they were such a passion killer at the most inopportune moments. Every time their make-out sessions got steamy it seemed to trigger the baby alarm.

No hanky-panky! You have a child to think about!

Not what any hot-blooded man wanted interrupting his love life and Matt wouldn't have any trouble finding a willing partner elsewhere if he kept getting sex-blocked by a five-year-old and his panicky mum.

She was already preparing herself for the 'This isn't going to work' speech as Matt took off towards the living room. She trudged behind him and wondered how they were going to put the time in during Simon's unexpected nap now. A game of chess perhaps? Or maybe he had a photo album of all of his glamorous, readily available exes she could flick through while they waited. If she'd had a coat she would've fetched it.

'I have one of these.' Instead of his sex life in pictures, he produced a baby monitor and set it on the coffee table with a proud flourish as if he'd solved the world's hardest equation. For her, he had.

No matter what obstacles crept up he always found a way over them. He didn't quit at the first sign of trouble and that was new to her as far as men were concerned. It was difficult not to get too attached to someone who, so far, had done everything possible to show her she could trust him. Rely on him.

'Of course you do,' she said with a great big grin.

All the signs were pointing to a brother and uncle who took his family duties very seriously even if he didn't want people to know. He was a loving family man whether he liked it or not. It was the idea of taking on someone else's which was the sticking point for him, and prevented any notion of a relationship between them.

'I'll just nip in and turn on the one in the bedroom so we can hear if he gets up. I'll be two seconds.'

Quinn took a seat on the sofa to wait for him coming back, fidgeting with the hem of her dress and unable to sit still, thinking about what was going to happen next as if she was waiting for her first kiss.

Things with Matt had gone far beyond that. This would be the only quality time they'd spent together alone and she was afraid it mightn't live up to the hype of that fevered embrace in the dark corner of the zoo.

He wanted her to stick around. He'd told her there was more to come. Surely the next step they were about to take wasn't all in her head?

'Would you like a drink?' Matt was back, padding into the kitchen.

'A glass of water would be nice, thanks.' Suddenly, her tongue was sticking to the roof of her mouth and her hands were clammy. Just what every guy was looking for in a hot date. Not.

She thought of all those other women he'd had here who'd never seen the kitchen. They were probably too busy ripping his clothes off in a frenzy to get to the bedroom to care. She must seem so dull in comparison but she no longer saw herself as sexy, spending her days watching cartoons and washing dirty clothes, lucky if she'd had a chance to brush her hair that morning, so why should she expect a man to?

At least with advance warning she'd be spending the day with Matt, she'd been able to put an effort into her clothes and make-up today. It couldn't hurt to try and reconnect with her inner sex siren, who'd disappeared under a mountain of paperwork and rejection.

The sofa dipped as Matt sat down next to her and handed her a glass of water. She took a sip and flicked her tongue out to wet her parched lips, fully aware he was watching her every move. He reached up to rub the back of his neck and Quinn seized the opportunity to get physical.

'Turn around and I'll give you a quick massage. You've earned one after all the carrying you've done today.' She set her glass on the floor and kicked off her shoes so she could kneel on the couch beside him.

'I probably should have stretched before I started bench pressing dead weights.' He turned around so she was faced with the solid wall of his back. She bit back the comment about bench pressing her anytime in case that bordered more on the side of desperate and crass rather than sexy and irresistible. This too-long abstinence had really brought out the worst in her.

With trembling hands she kneaded his shoulders, the thick muscle resisting her attempts to manipulate the tissue.

'Perhaps you should…er…take your shirt off. You're really knotted up in there.' Not very subtle and as bold as she dared but he complied nonetheless, shrugging the shirt off over his head.

'Wow,' she mouthed as she got to see the impressive

physique beneath for the first time in the flesh, albeit from the back. If only she could find the excuse to start massaging the pecs she knew would be on the other side of that muscular frame.

She worked her fingers over his warm skin, smoothing her hand down the length of his spine until she reached the waistband of his jeans. With a sudden burst of bravado, or lust, she slid her hand beneath and reached around until she felt that smooth V of taut skin leading down to…

Matt sucked in a sharp breath and clapped his hand over hers, stopping her pathetic seduction attempt dead in its tracks.

'I'm sorry… I…' What? How the hell was she going to pass this off as anything other than a blatant grope?

She rocked back on her heels, contemplating a commando-style roll onto the floor so she could crawl away without having to look him in the eye again, but he had too firm a grip on her wrist.

He spun around so she had no option but to face him. Okay, it wasn't all bad; she'd got a sneak peek at the goods, but she would need something good to remember anytime she replayed this humiliation in her head. For the record, she was pretty sure they'd used a mould of his chest and abs for those superhero costumes with the fake muscles.

'You don't have to try so hard, Quinn.' He was smiling, not recoiling in disgust, which she took as a good omen.

'Wh-what do you mean?' She tossed her hair back, aiming for the nonchalance of a woman who stuck her hand down a man's pants whenever she felt like it.

'You don't have to force this. Let it happen naturally.'

In slow motion he moved closer until his breath whispered on her lips, turning her to a rag doll liable to slip off the furniture in a cascade of molten limbs. She closed her eyes and let nature take its course.

He captured her in a soft kiss, leaned her back against the cushions as he took possession of her. It was true—there was no need for planning or acting out a part she thought she needed to play when chemistry did all the work.

Quinn was lying flat out beneath him, clinging to him, although there was no chance of going anywhere with his weight pinning her down. They were both where they needed to be.

She'd surprised him by taking the lead when, to date, she'd been the one reluctant to let this go further than snatched kisses. It wasn't unwelcome, parts of him were throbbing with delight, but he'd needed to take back some control. Not of her, or the situation, but of himself.

He was getting too caught up in her and Simon. Although bringing them back here had been more of an intervention than an invitation into his personal life, the result had been the same. They were invading his personal space, and his heart.

He'd raged inside today after Simon had been bullied by those kids, ached for him, and Quinn, who'd had to deal with the fallout. All he'd wanted to do was take some of that pain away, regardless that it meant compromising himself in the process.

If he took his own advice and simply let this thing take its natural course he could find himself saddled with more parental duties he hadn't asked for. That's why he needed a clear head, to focus on something other than his own pleasure—Quinn's.

These big blue eyes peered up at him with such trust and longing it was a test of strength not to take the easy route to instant gratification and sod the consequences. Even though it was killing him, this self-punishment would serve as a reminder to him not to start something he couldn't finish. Like getting involved with a single mother.

Quinn didn't have any such reservations as she pulled him ever closer until his chest was crushing hers, her soft mounds rubbing against him and undoing his restraint bit by bit. Eager to feast his eyes on her naked flesh, he slipped the shoestring straps of her dress down her arms and peeled away her strapless bra. Her cherry-peaked breast fit easily into the palm of his hand, so ripe and ready he couldn't resist a taste. He took her in his mouth and suckled her sweetness.

He shifted his position slightly so the evidence of his arousal wasn't so uncomfortable for either of them but Quinn tilted her hips so it nestled between her thighs instead. He released her sensitive nub with a groan as his resolve eroded by the second, clearly underestimating the effect she'd have on him even with his trousers firmly buttoned up. A fact which hadn't gone unnoticed by a partner who was doing her best to address that problem, popping his buttons open one by one.

This woman was driving him crazy and if he wasn't careful his good intentions would soon give way to lust, a short-term solution to his current predicament but undoubtedly with long-term consequences. He needed to bring this to some sort of conclusion which made her feel good without giving too much of himself in the process.

He inched his hand up her thigh and, with a quick tug, divested her of her undies. Her giggle as he tossed them onto the floor only spurred him on in his devilment. With a trail of kisses, over her clothes this time, he made his way down the centre of her body and ducked his head under the skirt of her dress.

'Matt—' she gasped, her hands immediately lighting atop his head, but she didn't ask him to stop.

He took his time savouring that first taste of her, teasing his tongue along her folds before parting her to thrust inside her core. She bucked against him, drawing him deeper between her thighs. He cupped her buttocks, holding her in place so he could direct his attention straight to that sweet spot.

He circled that little nub of flesh, sucking and licking his way to heaven until her breathy pants almost brought him to climax too. She tightened around him and he could sense that impending release. Her fingers were digging into his shoulders, her body rising and falling with the clench and release of her inner muscles.

She was slick with arousal, inviting him to join with her on the climb to that final peak but he couldn't take the chance he'd never want to come back down to earth. He withdrew, only to plunge back inside her again, and again, until she came apart beneath him. It was a shame he couldn't hear her cries of ecstasy as she slapped a hand over her mouth to muffle the sound. There was nothing he wanted more than to hear and see her completely undone, not holding anything back and without a trace of self-consciousness, but he understood why she couldn't turn off that mothering instinct. When he was long gone, she still had Simon to think about.

He sat back, giving Quinn space to recover as she fought to catch her breath, and a chance to regain his own composure. Not an easy task when her face was flushed, her pupils dilated and she was still half naked.

The lights on the baby monitor flashed, accompanied by the sound of rustling sheets, saving Matt from himself. Simon was stirring and he'd made a vow to get them home the minute that happened. It was his get-out clause before he did something even more stupid than falling for this beautiful woman he'd just ravished on his sofa.

'I'll go check on him,' he told her, keen to get a minute alone to gather his thoughts now both of their worlds had been rocked.

'Thanks.' Quinn sat up and adjusted her clothes to cover her nakedness, suddenly bashful. She'd no need to be embarrassed. He was the one who'd screwed up.

Whether he'd given in to temptation or not he'd still fallen for the one woman he couldn't have. Quinn came as part of a package deal, and although he was fond of Simon, there was every chance her foster brood could expand later on and he wasn't signing up for that. He hadn't left his family to move out to London only to have his longed-for independence curtailed by someone else's children.

He and Quinn were on completely different paths but they couldn't seem to stop intersecting and complicating things. Something had to give and it sure as hell wasn't going to be his freedom. Whilst he was treating Simon, cutting off all contact was out of the question, even if he thought he could.

The whole day had been an eye-opener for him but his resistance had been stretched to breaking point for now. If he didn't get his house guests back to their own home soon, he'd find this slipping into a long-term arrangement and this was supposed to be his time, a new start. He wasn't going to fall into the same old trap.

Matt McGrory was young, free and single, and that was the way it would stay. He just had to keep chanting that mantra to himself so he'd start believing it, or find someone else to take his place in Quinn and Simon's affections.

CHAPTER NINE

THE LAST FEW days had passed Quinn by in an out-of-body, did-that-actually-happen? daze.

There had to be a catch somewhere in a man who'd spent the day piggybacking a five-year-old around the zoo, and at night had made her pleasure his sole purpose. At this moment in time she didn't care what that flaw might be when her body was still glowing from the after-effects of his attentions.

Even now, another delicious shudder rippled through her at the memory of his lips on her. The only problem was, she hadn't seen the man of the moment since. She'd convinced herself it was because he was so busy at work, too invested to believe what they'd shared could be ignored so easily.

She turned her face away from the patients and staff walking towards her in the hospital corridor in case they read her X-rated thoughts. Her infatuation with the surgeon was probably there on her smiling face for the world to see and she could do without lectures from do-gooders who might take it upon themselves to warn her off a man committed to bachelorhood. They couldn't tell her anything she hadn't already told herself.

You're going to get hurt. He won't commit.

She didn't want to hear it when it was all too late anyway. She was in love with Matt and for once she didn't want to think about the consequences. That day had shown her how important it was for her to take some time for herself and that didn't always have to include getting naked with Matt, as enjoyable as that had been. The smallest thing such as a chat, a meal or a walk without stressing about Simon's issues had made her feel lighter than she had in months. A state of mind which would benefit them both.

Simon had been much more content the next morning than usual. The day's exertions had meant he'd slept through the night, even after Matt had driven them home, and the rarity of his uninterrupted sleep had improved the atmosphere between them.

To date, she hadn't availed of any outside help to care for her boy. She'd wanted to prove she could manage on her own and turned down any offers of respite care in case it disrupted Simon any further. There was also the fear that it would highlight her inadequacies even more. Now she was beginning to rethink those ideas of extra support.

That was how she'd come to be at the hospital now without her little bundle of curls in tow. He'd been excited when she'd suggested he could spend some time with Mrs Johns, as had her widowed neighbour when she'd broached the subject of babysitting. She was on the list of approved contacts with the authorities as she'd volunteered to help from day one when she found out there'd be a little one in the street. Quinn had only given her name in case she needed someone at a moment's notice in an emergency but perhaps she and Simon needed to venture beyond the bubble they'd created for themselves since the fire.

No doubt he'd be spoiled and filled to the brim with home-baked goods by the time she returned, but a young boy should have doting elders, playdates and adventures. A grown woman should have coffee mornings, gossip and a love life where possible. It was time to bring some normality back into their lives.

Of course, she'd seen to her other responsibilities before she'd gone in search of the man who'd convinced her she didn't need to remain celibate in order to be a good mother.

She'd added her voice to the ongoing protest out front for the first shift of the day and she'd had a ball this time with the knowledge that Simon was safe and happy. There was a rush of feel-good endorphins from volunteering her services to a good cause and they didn't come any greater than trying to save this iconic building from decimation. Perhaps she could make this a regular thing and when Simon went back to school permanently she might think about volunteering somewhere else that might need her help. They were already in the process of rebuilding the school and she would need something to distract her when it was time for him to go back there.

For now, she was collecting personal statements from some of the parents she'd seen coming and going on a regular basis.

'That's fantastic. I really appreciate your help,' she said, adding another paper bullet to the committee's arsenal of weapons against the board's decision.

'Anything I can do to help. We'd be lost without this place and we've made so many friends here I can't imagine starting over somewhere new.' Mrs Craig's daughter,

Penny, was a regular feature around the Castle's corridors, an outpatient but still dependent on oxygen at all times. Quinn had heard on the grapevine she was waiting for a life-saving heart transplant.

'Neither can I.' She'd spent those first days after the fire praying Simon would pull through, not eating or sleeping until she knew for sure he was going to survive. What Mrs Craig and Penny had been through, still had to go through, didn't bear thinking about. For her treatment to be transferred elsewhere away from the staff, who'd probably become like family, would be a wrench. Quinn knew how it was to rely on these people, get closer than she should, and how devastating it would be when they were no longer part of her life.

This was exactly the kind of emotional impact the money men didn't stop to consider when they were cost-cutting and paper shuffling.

'Are you Simon's mum?' The little girl in question wheeled her way in between the two adults, demanding attention, though she was difficult to ignore dressed in her pink tutu anyway.

'Yes. I'm his foster mum, Quinn. Pleased to meet you.' She held out her hand to shake on their introduction.

'I'm Penny and I know everyone here,' she said matter-of-factly.

'And quite the celebrity, I believe.' Quinn gave the mother a knowing smile. All of the kids had their own way of coping with life on the wards but Penny's integration into the hospital community and her self-confidence was something she envied on Simon's behalf.

'Nosy, more like,' Mrs Craig muttered under her breath.

'You're seeing Matt, aren't you?' Penny tilted her head to one side to study her.

Quinn's cheeks were on fire. She hadn't been able to keep her feelings hidden for long. Goodness knew how he'd react when he saw her again if it was plain enough for a child to see she was mad about him. He probably wouldn't be renewing any local contracts again soon, that was for sure.

'Er—'

'He's not here today. I wanted to show him my new tiara but Rebecca says he's off today.' She patted the pretty plastic band perched on her head as if it was a perfectly good reason for Matt to make time to see her—though knowing him, he probably would.

'Penny, I'm sure you're supposed to be doing something other than gossiping in the corridor. Come on and let Quinn get on with her job.'

'Okay, okay.' She spun her chair around towards the elevator.

Quinn gave her thanks again and waved goodbye. The news about Matt's sudden absence had unsettled her all over again.

He hadn't said anything that night about taking time off. In hindsight, he hadn't said much after Simon had woken up. She'd been too caught up in her own orgasmic euphoria and subsequent worry about getting Simon home without disturbing him too much to contemplate Matt's state of mind. He'd given so much without taking anything for himself. Whilst she'd taken so much pleasure in his unselfishness in the moment, now she was scrutinising his motives. Very few men would've been happy to be left unattended to and it wasn't because he'd been immune to the heat of the moment. She'd seen and felt the hard evidence of his arousal against her.

They could've found a way to be together. If Matt had

suggested she and Simon stayed the night she would've jumped at the chance. His readiness to get rid of all traces of them from his apartment didn't marry with her idea of carrying on where they'd left off.

Okay, he was never going to declare his undying love and set up house with them but it didn't bode well if he needed time off to recover after only a few hours in their company.

It wasn't as if he lived a million miles away. Her brain flashed through all the possibilities his actions could mean. She wanted to make it clear she wasn't expecting anything from him other than what they already had together.

All she wanted was a little more time together to explore what was happening between them and the effect it was having on her. Emotional significance aside, if they focused on the physical progression of their relationship they could have a good time together before his contract ended and he disappeared for good. If nothing else, she needed to return the favour he'd done her. She didn't like to be in anyone's debt.

She started off at a brisk pace towards the shiny, modern apartment block with her sights set on ripping Matt's clothes off and seducing him. Unfortunately, the doubt crows soon caught up with her, flapping their wings in her face to slow her down.

Did she really have the right to turn up, unannounced, on his doorstep? He could be sick, or perhaps this wasn't about her at all. There were a multitude of reasons he might not want to see her right now.

She could stand outside staring through the glass of the lobby like a child at a toy shop window on Christmas Eve, or she could stop wasting her precious time and find out the answer.

With her finger poised to buzz him, she braced herself to start overanalysing the tone of his voice over the intercom. The door suddenly swung open and one of the residents held it open for her. Clearly she wasn't a threat to anyone's security—except, perhaps, her own.

'Thanks,' she said as Mr Suit rushed on to whatever meeting he was going to, paying no mind to who he'd let into his building.

Every crisp step along the marble hallway towards Matt's apartment made her stomach roll more violently. If anyone from the hospital was aware she was here they'd probably advise him to get a restraining order. He was Simon's surgeon. Then again, what they'd shared that night broke whatever rules and boundaries long before she'd walked in off the street.

She took a deep breath before she knocked on the door, not knowing what to expect from this encounter. He mightn't even be home. After all, he had family and doctor commitments she wasn't party to. It wasn't likely he'd take time off at short notice to sit at home in the shadows to avoid running into a one-night stand, or whatever she was to him. If he wasn't in she could pretend this had never happened and let him make the next move.

Suddenly, the door whooshed open and her breath was sucked into a vacuum.

'Quinn! The very person I need to speak to.'

Not the welcome she'd expected, particularly as he was slamming his front door shut behind him and jangling his car keys.

'I...er...you haven't been around much—'

'I know. I know. Wait, where's Simon?'

'He's staying with a neighbour. I thought we could both do with a playdate this morning.' With one obviously going better than the other.

'Good idea,' he said, but he was still walking away from his apartment rather than dragging her back inside.

'I can see you're busy. Maybe we'll catch up another time.' She could salvage some dignity if she walked away now without forcing a conversation about what significance she held in his life. She had her answer right here with a closed door in her face.

Matt slowed his brisk pace as if it had only occurred to him how odd her visit was. 'You didn't make the journey all the way here just to see me, did you?'

It sounded such a desperate act when he put it that way that she immediately had to deny it. 'No. I was at the hospital anyway helping the committee. Young Penny said she'd heard you'd taken some leave. I thought I'd call in and see if you were sick or something.' If she'd stopped to buy grapes on the way here she might've made that more plausible.

He laughed. 'Ah, yes. Penny. There are no secrets where she's concerned.'

'I was collecting statements from the parents.' That was right up there with 'I carried a watermelon' in lame excuses but she didn't want him to think she'd been stalking the corridors seeking him out.

'They're definitely one of the most familiar families at Paddington's and Penny is such a live wire despite her condition.' He was clearly fond of the little girl even though she wasn't one of his own patients. Another indication that his devotion went far beyond the parameters of his job description.

'She is and I can report back and tell her you're fine

and there's no need for her to worry.' Quinn scooted outside into the sunlight first, taking the path back to the
hospital so she didn't trip on her lies. It was her who'd
wanted to know why he wasn't at work and her who'd
stumble back home with her tail tucked between her legs
for thinking she could simply turn up here and take what
she wanted from Matt, ignoring his wishes, which clearly
included being left alone.

That heavy weight was back on her shoulders, almost
doubling her over with the effort of having to carry it
again.

'Aren't you coming with me?'

It took a strong hand wrapped around her waist for
the words to register.

'Do you want me to? I mean, you were on your way
out before I got here.' *Without me.*

'It will make this easier. I would've had to contact
you anyway to make the final decision.' He practically
bounced into the front seat of his car, pumped up by
whatever he had planned.

'That sounds ominous. Where are we going?'

'It's a surprise. Relax. It's nothing bad. Just sit back
and enjoy the ride.'

The car purred to life at his touch, much the way she
had.

They stopped and started their way out of the city until
eventually they made their way onto the quieter roads.
She had no clue how long they were going to be in the
car or how far they'd be driving but she didn't care. For
now, she was content to sit back and relax in his company as he'd suggested. It wasn't what she'd planned but
it was preferable to the scenario where he told her he
didn't want to see her again.

She trusted him to give her a good time. He hadn't let her down yet.

Matt was in the dark about what had brought Quinn to his door but her visit was providential. He'd been contemplating a major commitment for her and Simon so it was only polite he should seek her opinion on the matter.

Since that day he'd spent with them, and most of the evening, he'd been trying to concoct a plan to keep them in his life without stepping into the role of surrogate dad again. It would be easy to get carried away, especially when a different part of his body other than his brain was trying to make decisions for him.

If he'd given in to what it was he'd really wanted he'd be in an ever bigger mess where Quinn was concerned. That first-hand experience of bringing up a family was the only thing which had prevented him from taking her to his bed, letting Simon sleep the night in his spare room and waking up to a new domesticity he hadn't asked for. His fear of that had somehow won out over his libido. He couldn't promise that would always be the case so he'd hit on the idea of a third wheel in their relationship, or a fourth if he included Simon.

'A dog pound?' Quinn's raised eyebrows drew into a frown as they pulled up outside the animal rescue centre in a blend of undisguised curiosity and disappointment. Exactly what he'd been trying to avoid.

He'd delayed getting back in touch when he knew nothing he said or did could possibly match up to any expectations she might have had after that night. Now, he was counting on the tried and tested distraction technique of canine cuteness.

'It's an idea I've been toying with. Pet companions are known to be very therapeutic, loving unconditionally without judging people's appearances or background. You saw what a great time Simon had at the zoo. He loves animals and this could really help build his confidence.' It would also give them the sort of close companionship that they were both craving on a long-term basis.

Quinn was silent as they entered the reception and he hoped it was because she was mulling over the idea of adopting a dog, not that she was filled with quiet rage at him.

'It's a nice idea, in theory, but it's not very practical. I have enough to deal with without adding house-training a puppy to the list.'

'This one's a year old, fully trained. No extra work.' A puppy would've secured the deal because who wouldn't fall in love with a bundle of fur but she wouldn't have thanked him for the puddles around the house or using her furniture for oversized chew sticks. He'd been there when Siobhan, his middle sister, had suckered him into housing one of a litter of unwanted pups. Thankfully, she'd taken the little poop machine with her when she'd moved out soon after.

'This one?' She raised an eyebrow, seemingly unimpressed as he showed her the computer printout of his research subject.

'Frankie. She's a collie cross. I saw her online and made this appointment to come and see her before I spoke to you. You know, to make sure she's suitable for you and Simon.' He gave his details to the receptionist and waited for them to bring out the dog he thought could be the answer to everyone's prayers.

'How very thoughtful of you.' The sarcasm wasn't lost on him. It had been very presumptuous of him to make these arrangements, supposedly on her behalf, without giving her the heads-up. He preferred to think of it as being proactive.

'She's supposed to be a lovely wee thing.' He'd made sure this was a dog they could be satisfied was comfortable around children, and from everyone he'd spoken to, she was very good-natured.

'Wee?' Quinn was nearly knocked off her feet by the black-and-tan slobber monster which accosted her.

'Well, those handbag dogs aren't for boys. She's a good sturdy size for cuddling.'

It was his turn to pet the reason they were here and he was rewarded with a rough doggie tongue licking his face.

'What's wrong with her neck?' Quinn hunkered down to inspect the patch of shaved fur and jagged scars zigzagging around her throat.

'They found her wandering the streets. Someone had let the skin grow over her puppy collar and the vet had to operate to remove it. Hence the name "Frankie," after Frankenstein's monster.' He'd seen the pictures and read the case file so she'd already claimed a place in his affections. Quinn's too, by all accounts, as she stroked and cuddled the pooch.

'Poor girl. You deserve a pretty name. If you were mine I'd call you Maisie.'

'Maisie?' He tried to suppress a grin and failed. The scarred, scrawny mutt looked as girlie as he did.

'Every girl should be treated like a princess. Calling her after a monster will do nothing for her self-esteem. If I'd ever had a daughter, Maisie's the name I would've chosen.' For such a young woman, she sounded as though she'd given up on the idea of ever having kids of her own. Fostering probably seemed enough of a challenge without bringing up her own children minus a partner. Still, if Maisie filled that particular void too, then Matt's job here was done.

'We'll have to bring Simon up for a visit but I can register our interest now in case someone else wants her in the meantime.'

'I'm sure he'll love her, Matt, but would it really be fair to give him a dog only to take it off him when he moves on? I couldn't break his heart again.' She was already distancing herself from the mongrel, who just wanted to be loved too.

Matt hadn't considered the long-term consequences. It was so unlike him to go for the temporary solution, but she was right—he couldn't use the dog as a sticking plaster. The moment Simon had to leave her behind would devastate him all over again and who was to say Quinn would want to be tied down to a pet once Simon had gone.

There was no other option but for him to take her on if he wanted this adoption to go ahead. It was a commitment he'd never anticipated making but a dog had to be less trouble than raising kids, surely?

'What if I adopt her? You and Simon could help with her when I'm at work. He can still bond with her but technically she'll be my dog.' A single man was still a single man with a pet. It would be company for him instead of coming home to that empty apartment at the end of every shift. He'd hate to let this opportunity pass for Simon and Maisie to find some comfort in each other.

'You mean joint custody?' Naturally, Quinn wanted clarification. She was a woman who didn't like to leave room for misunderstandings.

It was surprising, then, that she'd yet to quiz him on his intentions as far as she was concerned. It was the main reason he'd maintained a little distance because he genuinely didn't know what either of them wanted to come from this relationship. If Quinn in her usual forthright manner told him she expected some sort of commitment to her and Simon, he'd be forced to walk away and he wasn't ready for that yet.

'I guess…' Adopting a stray dog was more than he'd committed to in a long time, stretching the boundaries of his comfort zone and the best promise he could give in regards of a future together.

For the duration of Simon's stay with her, he and Maisie would be a part of their lives and that was the most he could give of himself without compromising his own plans. He'd still be moving on to pastures new someday, except now he'd have a slobbery hound in tow.

'Simon's going to be so excited.' Quinn dropped down to hug the new family friend and Matt didn't know if she or the dog had the biggest smile on their face.

He had to admit he felt good to have been the one to have orchestrated this. Quinn's happiness was his weakness and most likely guaranteed to be his greatest downfall but he reminded himself he was a live-in-the-moment guy and bundled in on the fun. As he joined the group hug, the excitement proved too much for Maisie, who slipped out of their hold for a mad dash around the room.

'Thank you for this.' Quinn dropped a kiss on his mouth as they tumbled to the ground. He wanted to freeze time, keep her there for ever so they didn't have to worry about anything except keeping that simple contact between them.

When she was with him, touching him, happy to be with him, he wanted to give her the world. He'd already broken all the singleton rules and was about to adopt a stray dog just so this feeling would last. He was afraid of what he would do next in the name of love.

There was no doubt about it. Given the lengths he'd gone to and his wish to lie here with her for ever, he was totally head over heels for Quinn Grady. It should've made him want to bolt from the room, pack his bags and catch the first flight back to Dublin but that wouldn't solve the problem. Wherever he went he knew he'd be thinking of her. The only way to get this out of his system was to let it run its course until they reached some sort of crisis point where having him in her life was no longer tenable. She was going to have to be the one to make that decision because, for once, Matt wasn't the one in charge. His heart was.

CHAPTER TEN

'WE HAVE A small communal garden she can use, and of course there's the nearby park.' Matt's application for Maisie-homing hadn't been as easy as simply signing a form, and rightly so. The animal shelter had insisted on doing a home visit to see for themselves that the ground-floor apartment was a suitable environment for her, and Quinn had agreed to be here for it.

She was still in shock he'd come up with the idea in the first place, never mind taken on primary responsibility of a dog to aid Simon's recovery. An act which certainly wouldn't have been part of his Hippocratic oath. This level of kindness couldn't be taught; it was pure Matt.

She didn't want to get her hopes up, much like she didn't want Simon to get too attached to him, or Maisie. At least by getting Matt to adopt the dog she'd managed to put some sort of safety prevention in place. When their dalliance inevitably came to its unsatisfactory conclusion they could go their separate ways without any ill will or duty to the other. The dog would be his responsibility, and Simon was hers.

'And where will doggie sleep?' The lady with the clipboard peered in the various rooms sussing out what preparations Matt had made for his new house companion.

'This is her bed here and Quinn's going to let her in and out while I'm at work.' Matt proudly showed off the comfy new dog bed full of new toys and treats he and Simon had picked out at the pet store.

It was all Simon could talk about since Matt had told him the news. He'd been clear to point out Maisie would be his but Simon could help out.

'Yes, we'll take her for walks and make sure she gets plenty of exercise when Matt's not here.' It was something she was looking forward to too. It would get them both outdoors more and be a step towards his recovery if the dog had his attention rather than the people around him. All thanks to Matt.

'I'll take a quick look at the garden to make sure it's safe and secure for Maisie but I don't think we'll have any problems giving the adoption the green light.' The lady who held Maisie's future in the palm of her hand gave a thumbs up before she ventured outside.

Quinn breathed a sigh of relief and left Matt to deal with any last-minute details with the inspector. If the process for adopting children was as straightforward it would have made life a lot easier for Simon. He might have found a family and settled down a long time ago if he hadn't been caught up in the bureaucracy for so long. Although that would've meant she'd never have got to meet him, and no matter what hardships they'd endured so far, she couldn't imagine being without him. Evidently she wasn't able to keep her emotions out of any relationship.

For someone who'd only ever meant to provide a safe and loving home for children until they'd found their adoptive families, she'd managed to fall for Simon and Matt along the way. They'd saved her at a time when she'd been at her loneliest. Now she knew how it was to be part of a family, however accidental, however dysfunctional, her life was never going to be the same without either of them. Regardless of what the future held, this was the most content she'd ever been and she'd learned never to take that for granted.

Happiness had come late in her childhood, infrequently in her adulthood, and was something she intended to make the most of for however long she was able to give and receive it.

'I don't think that could've gone any better. It won't be long before we hear that pitter-patter of little feet around here.' Matt was every inch the proud new adoptive dad when he returned.

Quinn would be lying if she said she didn't experience a pang of longing for a man who'd feel that way about children. In an ideal world Matt would be as joyful about the prospect of adding foster children to his family as he was about the dog. Maybe if she had a partner like that to support her she might've found the strength to adopt Simon herself, confident she could give him a more stable life than the one his neglectful parents had provided.

'I should go back. It's not fair on Simon, or Mrs Johns, to make a habit of this.'

'Twice isn't a habit. It's simply making the most of a good thing.' He advanced towards her with a hunger in his eyes that made her pulse quicken as fever took hold of her body.

This was the first time they'd been truly alone with no outside distraction from the simmering sexual attraction and no reason to stop it bubbling over.

'So, it's okay to do something naughty twice without having to worry it's the wrong thing?' She took a step forward to meet him, resting her hands on his chest, desperate to make body contact again.

'Definitely. Especially if you didn't technically *do it* first time around.' He teased her lips with the breath of innuendo, leaving her trembling with anticipation.

'If you say so—' She plucked the top button of his shirt open, ready to get the party started once and for all. They mightn't ever get the chance to do this again and then she really would have regrets. She'd had a sample of how good they could be together and not following it up seemed more idiotic than taking the risk.

If Simon wasn't in the picture she wouldn't hesitate to give herself to Matt and when this was over the only consolation she'd have was that she'd been true to herself.

'I do.' His mouth was suddenly crushing hers, the force of his passion hard and fast enough to make her head spin.

She trembled from the sheer intensity of the embrace as he pulled her close. Her knees went completely from under her as Matt swept her up into his arms, her squeal of surprise quietened by his primitive growl. She clung tightly to him, her hands around his neck, her mouth still meshed to his, afraid to break contact in case she started overthinking this again. When he was touching her it was all that mattered.

He strode down the hallway and she heard the heavy thud as he kicked the bedroom door open to carry her inside. She'd never gone for macho displays but, somehow, knowing the usually unflappable Matt was so impatient to get her to bed was the greatest turn-on ever.

He booted the door shut behind them again, ensuring they were completely cut off from the rest of the world. There was just her, Matt and a bed built for two.

They fell onto the mattress together, each pulling at the other's clothes until they were naked with no barriers left between them. They'd had weeks of foreplay, months if she counted all of those arguments at the hospital, and she didn't want to wait any longer.

She was slick with desire as they rolled across the bed in a tangle of limbs and kisses. Once Matt had sheathed himself in a condom he grabbed from his night stand, he thrust inside her. His hardness found her centre so confidently and securely she knew she'd found her peace.

Matt had finally lost his control, yet joining with Quinn brought him more relief than fear. He'd been strong for too long, trying to do the right thing by everyone when his body had been crying out for this. For Quinn.

He moved slowly inside her at first, testing what little there was left of his restraint, luxuriating in her tight, wet heat. She was a prize he knew he didn't deserve and one he'd only have possession of for a very short time. Quinn was her own woman who wouldn't be so easily swayed by great sex. It would soon become clear he didn't have anything else to bring to the party. If she expected anything more he'd only leave her with extra scars to deal with.

Quinn tightened her grip around his shaft to remind him this wasn't a time for inner reflection and stole the remnants of his control. As much as he wanted to pour inside her he also wanted this to be something she wouldn't regret. This should be a positive experience they could both look back on fondly, not a lapse of judgement they'd come to resent.

They'd gone into this fully aware this wasn't the beginning of some epic love story. No matter how he felt about her this couldn't be about anything more than sex.

He could never say he loved her out loud; that would place too much pressure on him to act on it when it wasn't a possibility. He wasn't about to turn his life upside down again for the sake of three little words.

She ground her hips against him, demanding he show her instead. Carnal instinct soon took over from logical thinking as he sought some resolution for them both.

His strokes became quicker with Quinn's mews of pleasure soon matching the new tempo. He captured her moans with a kiss, driving his tongue into her mouth so he had her completely anchored to him. She didn't shy away from his lustful invasion but welcomed it, wrapping her legs around his back to hold him in place.

Matt's breath became increasingly unsteady as he fought off the wave of final ecstasy threatening to break. Only when Quinn found her release would he submit to his own.

He gripped her hips and slammed deep inside her. Once, twice, three times—he withdrew and repeated the rhythm. The white noise was building in his head, his muscles beginning to tremble as his climax drew ever nearer.

Quinn lifted her head from the pillows, her panting breath giving way to her cries of ultimate pleasure and he answered her call with one of his own. His body shook with all-encompassing relief as he gave himself completely to her. For that brief moment he experienced pure joy and imagined how it would be to have this feeling last. Making love to someone he was actually in love with was a game changer. He couldn't picture sharing his bed with anyone else again and that scared him half to death. The other half was willing to repeat the same mistake all over again.

He disposed of the condom and rolled onto the bed beside her, face first into the mattress, content to die here of exhaustion instead of having to get up again and face reality.

'What do we do now?' Quinn turned onto her side so he had a very nice view of her pert breasts.

'Try and breathe,' he said, unable to resist reaching out to cup her in his hand even through his exhaustion.

'I mean after that.'

He knew exactly what she meant but he didn't have the answer. At least, probably not the one she wanted to hear. She wanted to know what happened now they'd finally succumbed to the chemistry, to their feelings, but for him he couldn't let it change anything.

To enter into a full-blown relationship with Quinn entailed having one with Simon too. One which went beyond professional or friendship. He couldn't do that in good conscience when he could never be the father Simon needed. He wouldn't give him any more false hope.

He was done with the school runs, the birthday parties and the angsty teenage rebellion stage. Whilst he didn't regret being the sole provider for his sisters, he was too jaded and tired to go through it all again.

Yet, he was advancing ever further towards the vacancy.

'You're fostering Simon, right? Someday he'll be adopted and you'll start the process over with someone new?'

'Well...yes. The children are only placed temporarily in my care until a family can be found for them.' Quinn frowned at him and he could tell the idea of not having the boy around was already becoming a touchy subject. They'd both got in over their heads but Matt was determined he, at least, was going to keep swimming against the tide.

'What if we apply the same restriction to our relationship?' It was the only logical way this could continue without any one of them coming to serious harm.

'You want me to foster you too?' Quinn danced the flat of her hand down his back, over the curve of his backside and across his thigh until he was back to full fighting strength and falling for her blatant attempt to leave this discussion for another time.

'More of a co-dependency until you've found your for ever family too.' In his heart he couldn't let it go on once Simon left her. There could never be a future for them as a couple because there would always be a child in need and Quinn's heart was too open to deny anyone the love they craved.

It wouldn't be fair to stop her simply because his heart was closed for business.

She sighed next to him, the heavy resignation of the situation coming from deep within a soul still searching for its mate. It was too bad it couldn't be him, then his own wouldn't be howling at the injustice he was doing to it.

'I'm beginning to think that's an impossible dream.'

'You're a great foster mother, a beautiful woman and an incredible lover.' He traced his thumb across her lips, hating they were talking about the next man who'd get to kiss them.

'Yeah?' She coquettishly accepted his compliment and he was in danger of digging a hole in the mattress as his libido decided they should make the most of their time together in bed.

'Yeah, and I think we should make a few more memories so I never forget.' Not that it was likely.

Quinn was the one woman, other than his sisters, who'd ever truly touched his heart and gave his life more meaning simply by being in it. The same probably couldn't be said about him when he'd only be able to give her fun and sex at a time when she needed stability. When she looked back she'd see they'd muddled personal feelings with the intensity of Simon's treatment. What he didn't want was for her to end up hating him for taking advantage of her. If they kept it light, kept it fun, kept it physical, there'd be no need to get into the heavy emotional stuff he had no room for any more.

He threw an arm across Quinn and rolled onto his back, bringing her with him so she straddled his thighs. With her sex pressed against his, the logical side of his brain finally shut up.

Quinn wasn't stupid. Sex was Matt's way of avoiding deep and meaningful conversation. She didn't blame him. Nothing good was going to come of them in their case. When Simon left, so would he, if not sooner. At some point in the near future they'd both be gone, leaving nothing but memories and a void in her heart. It was much easier to take pleasure where she could find it in the here and now than face the prospect of that pain. She'd rather have this kind of procrastination than ugly crying over bridal magazines for a relationship that would never happen.

For every fake idyll that popped into her head of her and Matt and their foster brood, she ground her hips against him to block it out. The rush of arousal instantly channelled her thoughts to those of self-pleasure instead of an impossible dream.

With her hands braced on Matt's sturdy chest, she rocked back and forth. His arousal strengthened as she slid along his length so she took him in hand and guided him into her slick entrance, giving them both what they craved for now. They fit perfectly, snug, as if they'd both found their other halves.

Matt was watching her, his eyes hooded with desire, but this time he was letting her make all the moves. Only thinking of herself for once, taking what she wanted, was kind of liberating. With a firm hand she teased the tip of his shaft along her folds until she was aching to have him inside her again. She anchored herself to him and that blessed relief soon gave way to a new need. Every circular motion of her hips brought another gasp of self-pleasure and a step closer to blinding bliss.

She doubled over, riding out the first shudders of impending climax. Matt sat up to capture one of her nipples with his mouth and sucked hard until it blurred the pleasure and pain barriers. Her orgasm came quickly and consumed her from the inside out, leaving her body weak from the strength of it.

Matt held her in place as he thrust upwards, finally taking his own satisfaction. Each time his hungry mouth found her breast or his deft fingers sought to please her again, another aftershock rippled through her. Only when she felt him tense beneath her, his grip on her tighten and the roar of his triumph ring in her ears did she finally let exhaustion claim her.

'That was…unexpected. Great, just…unexpected.'

As much for her as it was for him. She didn't recall ever being that confident in the bedroom before.

'I'm full of surprises, me.' She gave him a sly smile and hoped now he saw her as much more than a fragile foster mum he didn't want to be lumbered with for the rest of his days. There was still a sexy, independent-thinking, fun-loving woman inside her. She just hoped he assumed it was *her* husky voice he was hearing and not the raw-throated mutterings of a girl brought to the edge of tears by great sex.

He slung his arm around her shoulders and pulled her close. She didn't know how long they'd been locked away in this room, in their own world of fire and passion where time didn't matter. There was that residual parental guilt that perhaps she'd spent too long indulging her own needs while neglecting her son's but the warmth of Matt's skin against hers and the steady rhythm of his heart beating beneath her ear soon convinced her to stay here for a while longer. Simon was safe, and in Matt's arms, so was she.

'We'll pick Simon up once we've had a rest,' he mumbled into her hair.

Without prompting, Matt had raised the matter, something she'd been hesitant to do in case she ruined the moment. Her last thought as she drifted off to sleep was a happy one.

CHAPTER ELEVEN

'CAN I WALK HER? Please?' Simon hovered between Quinn and Matt, eyeing the dog's lead as if it was the hottest toy of the year.

Quinn glanced at Maisie's *official* owner for confirmation it was okay even though she and Simon walked her in the park practically every day.

'Sure.' Matt handed over control without a second thought. It was that kind of trust between him and Simon which was helping to build up the boy's confidence. That, and a hyperactive dog which kept them all too busy to dwell on any unpleasantness.

They'd fallen into a new routine, one which included exercising the dog and therefore getting Simon out and about in between hospital visits. Dare she say it, things had begun to settle down and they had so much going on now Simon's scars no longer seemed to be their main focus. Especially when those on his face were slowly beginning to fade.

As well as their dog-sitting duties, Quinn had the hospital committee meetings to attend and Simon was working towards his return to school. There'd been a phased return to classes held in the nearby hall, and although he'd been nervous, it had helped that some of his classmates were still being treated for minor injuries, including some burns. They understood what had happened to alter his appearance better than most but it didn't stop Quinn worrying.

'Hold on tight to Maisie's lead and don't go too far ahead,' she shouted after the enthusiastic duo haring through the park, although the sound of happy barking and childish laughter was music to her ears.

'They'll be grand. With any luck they'll tire each other out.' Matt cemented his place as the laid-back half of the partnership content to hang back and let the duo explore the wide open space, whist she remained the resident worrywart.

'Getting that dog was the best decision we could have made.' She knew pets were sometimes used as therapy for patients but she hadn't expected such impressive results so quickly. Simon was finally coming out of the shadows back into the light.

'Not *the* best decision.'

Quinn gave a yelp as he yanked her by the arm behind a nearby tree. He quietened her protest with his mouth. The kiss, full of want and demanding at first, soon softened, making her a slave to his touch. Okay, taking that long-awaited step into the bedroom had been one of the highlights of her year, perhaps even her lifetime. That in itself caused her more problems, as once would never be enough.

'We should really make sure those two aren't getting up to any mischief.'

'Like us?' He arched that devil eyebrow again, daring her to do something more wicked than snatching a few kisses out of sight.

She swallowed hard and tried to centre herself so she didn't get carried off into the clouds too easily.

'I hope not,' she muttered under her breath. If Simon was in a fraction of the trouble she was in right now she'd completely lose the plot.

'I want you.' Matt's growl in her ear spoke directly to her hormones, sending them into a frenzy and making her thankful she had a two-hundred-year-old oak tree to keep her upright.

These illicit encounters were all very exciting, but for someone as sexually charged as Matt, her inability to follow it through to the bedroom again would get old real quick.

Now that she'd discovered how fiercely hot their passion could burn, left unchecked there was nothing she'd enjoy more than falling into bed with him, but it was difficult to find enough Simon-free time to revel in each other the way they wanted to.

It was wrong to keep asking Mrs Johns to babysit and she was afraid if she started sleeping over at Matt's she would have to inform the foster authorities of his involvement in her life. That meant forcing him into a commitment he'd been very clear he didn't want and could signal the end of the good thing they had going. No matter how frustrated she was waiting for some more alone time it had to be better than never seeing him again.

Matt grazed his teeth along her neck, gave her a playful nip, and she began to float away from common sense all over again.

A snuffling sound at her feet and a wet tongue across her bare toes soon grounded her. She should have known open-toed sandals were a bad move for a dog walk.

'Maisie?'

The dog apparently had a shoe fetish, having already chewed one of Matt's expensive work shoes and buried the other. It was just as well she was cute or she might have found herself back in doggie prison. Thankfully, Matt's soft spot for waifs and strays was greater than his affinity for Italian leather. Although it must have been a close call.

'Yay! She found you.' Simon came into view still attached to the other end of the lead and Quinn was quick to push Matt aside.

'She's a good tracker.' She bent down to rub Maisie's ears. It wasn't their canine companion's fault she didn't understand the necessity for discretion.

'Whatcha doin' here?' Simon tilted his head to one side as he assessed the scene.

'We...er—' She struggled for a cover story.

'Were playing hide and seek. You won.' Matt stepped in with a little white lie to save her skin. He could very well have told Simon the truth that they were together and stopped all of this pretence but that would entail following up with an *actual* relationship which involved sleepovers and paperwork. Perhaps Matt's eyes were open to all the baggage that she'd bring and he'd decided it wasn't worth the effort after all.

She had a horrible feeling their fragile relationship was already on the countdown to self-destruction.

'Is it our turn to hide?' Simon's eyes were wide with excitement, the biggest smile on his face at the prospect of the game. It was going to be tough when it went back to being just the two of them.

She forced down the lump in her throat. 'Yup. We'll count to twenty and come and find you.'

Surely none of them could get into too much trouble in that short space of time?

She was rewarded with another beaming smile and a lick. Neither of which came from Matt.

'I'm as fond of a quickie as the next guy but twenty seconds? You wound me.' He clutched his chest in mock horror at the slight against his stamina.

That pleasure might seem like an age ago now but she could attest that it definitely wasn't a problem. She evaded eye contact and ignored the renewed rush of arousal as her body recalled the memory in graphic detail or they'd be in danger of losing Simon in the woods altogether.

'One…two…three…'

'You're killing me, you know.' He shook his head and from the corner of her eye Quinn saw him adjust the crotch of his trousers. A sight which was becoming more common with the increased rate of these passionate clinches. It wasn't fair on either of them.

'I don't mean to be a tease.' She gestured towards his groin area.

'I know but we really need to find a way to make this work.'

'Your penis?' She wanted to make him laugh, to steer the conversation away from that area of conflict they'd never be able to resolve satisfactorily.

It almost worked. He laughed at least.

'No, I'm fine in that department as you very well know. I mean us. We can't go on indefinitely hiding as though we're doing something wrong.'

'It's not as simple as clearing a space in my bathroom cabinet for your hair care products.' Her levity was waning as he made her face the reality of their situation.

'Of course. I'll require considerable wardrobe space too.'

'For an overnighter?'

'I do like a selection so I can dress according to my mood.'

Why couldn't life be as easy as their banter? Then perhaps her stomach wouldn't be tied up in knots waiting for the asteroid to hit and annihilate her world.

'All joking aside, we both know having you stay at my place, or us at yours, will only confuse Simon more than we already have. If we become an official couple I'll have to let the foster people know. I probably should've done that already but I didn't want to jinx this by putting it down on paper.'

The warmth of Matt's hands took the chill from her shoulders as he reassured her. 'As long as we're not signing a contract of intent I don't see why that should change things between us. It's understandable they'll want to protect Simon with background checks on anyone in his life but it's none of their business what our arrangement is. We can remain discreet where he's concerned. I'm the last person who wants him thinking I'm his replacement father. I can come over when he's asleep, leave before he's awake and make that time in between ours.'

She shivered, although there was no breeze in the air. It was a tempting offer, better than she expected in the circumstances. Yet there was something cold about the proposition. It snuffed out the last embers of hope that he'd ever want more than a physical relationship with her. Somewhere in her romantic heart she'd still imagined he could've been nudged further towards a more permanent role in their family. This was exactly the reason she'd wanted to keep Simon protected, because it was too late for her.

'That could work,' she said, not convinced it was the answer but the best one available for the moment.

At some point she was either going to have to push for more or sever all ties. Neither of which she was brave enough to do without prompting. The one consolation was that he was willing to stick around in some capacity and hadn't used this as an excuse to walk away. These days she took all the positives where she could find them and that new attitude had propelled her and Simon further forward than she could have hoped for.

Not that she was ready to admit it to anyone until she was one hundred percent sure it was the right thing to do, but she was thinking of making her and Simon's relationship more permanent. He was finally settling into her home, relaxing in her company and opening up to her. It wouldn't be fair to ask him to start all over again in a new town, with a new family and go to a school where they knew nothing of what he'd been through. Above everything else, she loved him as though he was her own son. He mightn't be of her flesh and blood, but she hurt when he hurt, cried when he cried, and seeing him happy again made her happy. They needed each other.

Adoption wasn't going to be straightforward, not even for a foster parent. She needed a bit more time to be certain it was right for both of them before she committed to the decision. There was no way she'd promise Simon a future if she thought she couldn't deliver. It would also be the end game for her and Matt.

His whole take on their relationship was based on the temporary nature of hers with Simon too. There was no way he'd stay involved once he found out she had ideas of becoming a permanent mum and all of the baggage that entailed. She wasn't ready to say goodbye to Matt either. For the meantime, it was better if the status quo remained the same.

'We'll talk it over later. When Simon's in bed.'

She would've mistaken his words for another wicked hint of what he wanted to do to her except he was taking her hand and leading her back towards Simon and the dog. It was his way of telling her he understood her concerns and was happy to comply. She swore her heart gave a happy sigh.

'Nineteen…twenty. Here we come, ready or not.'

Simon wasn't difficult to spot, his red jacket flashing in the trees and Maisie rolling in the grass beside him.

Quinn motioned for Matt to flank him from the far side whilst she approached from the other.

'Gotcha!' she said as she tagged him. It was only then she noticed his poor face streaked with tears.

'What's wrong, wee man?' Matt crouched down to comfort him too, as Quinn fought the urge to panic or beat herself up. She'd only left him for a few minutes.

'Are you hurt? Did you fall?' She rolled up his trousers searching for signs he'd cut himself or had some sort of accident.

He sniffed and shook his head. 'I thought you weren't coming for me.'

She was numb for the few seconds it took for the enormity of his fears to hit home. Simon longed for stability, had to be confident there'd be at least one person constant in his life taking care of his interests, or he'd never feel truly safe. Ready or not, it was her time to commit.

She hugged Simon tight and kissed the top of his head. 'I'm always going to be here for you. I love you very, very much and don't you ever forget it.'

Another sniff and a big pair of watery green eyes stared up at her.

'Thanks… Mum,' he said softly, as if testing the name on his lips. It almost had her sobbing along with him.

There was zero chance of her letting him go back into the system again without a fight. Whatever happened now, Simon was going to be the biggest part of her future and his happiness was her greatest reward.

She pulled him close again, channelling her love and hope for him in the embrace, and caught a glimpse of Matt's face over the top of his head as he joined in on the group hug. He was including himself in this moment of family unity when he could easily have stepped back and played no part in it. It was impossible not to let that flutter of hope take flight again when everything finally seemed to be coming together. She'd been brave enough to make that leap for Simon's sake and now it was Matt's turn to decide who, and what, he wanted.

It was a three-letter word—not the three little words Matt couldn't bring himself to say—which spelled the beginning of the end.

Mum.

He was happy for Quinn. It had been a beautiful moment watching them create a bond that nothing in this world could break. Including him. Not that he intended to come between them but he simply wasn't compatible with the new set-up. It was early days so it wasn't clear what role they expected him to play as the dynamics changed, but he was already becoming antsy about it.

Now they were back at Quinn's. She was putting Simon to bed, the dog was snoring by his feet and the scene would've been enough to content any family man.

Except he wasn't a family man. Not with Quinn and Simon at least.

He enjoyed the lifestyle he had now. The one before they'd gatecrashed his apartment. He'd worked hard to gain his freedom and he wasn't about to trade it in for another unplanned, unwanted fatherhood. Some part of him had hoped that might change, that he might step forward and be the man they all needed him to be. Yet the overriding emotion he'd felt as they'd hugged wasn't happiness. That generally didn't bring on heart palpitations and an urge to run.

He was as fond of Simon as he was his own sisters and nieces and he was in love with Quinn, but it wasn't enough to persuade him to stay for ever. What if it didn't last anyway? He knew from experience his conscience wouldn't let him walk away from a child who counted on him for support and he didn't want to become emotionally tied to two families. It would be a step back and he wasn't afraid to admit he wasn't up to the job this time around if it meant saving everyone unnecessary pain later on.

Quinn tiptoed back downstairs from Simon's bedroom and curled up beside him on the settee. She rested her head on his chest the way she did most nights when they had five minutes together and yet tonight it seemed to hold more significance than he was comfortable with.

This wasn't about sex; it was about unwinding with each other at the end of the day, sharing the details of their struggles and triumphs. The companionship was becoming as important as the physical stuff, as were the emotions. Stay or go, it was going to hurt the same.

Her contented sigh as she cuddled into him reached in and twisted his gut. If only he was as settled there wouldn't be an issue but he was dancing over hot coals, afraid to linger too long and get burned.

'That was some day,' he said as he stroked the soft curtain of her hair fanned across his chest.

'Uh-huh. I never saw it coming. I mean, I was having a hard time thinking about him moving on but to hear him call me Mum—' Her voice cracked at the sentiment and Matt's insides constricted a little tighter.

'It's a big deal.'

'We'll have to get the ball rolling and make our intent known regarding the adoption. The sooner he knows this is his real home, the better.' She was full of plans, more invigorated by the breakthrough than Matt was prepared for.

'We?' Matt's fingers tangled in her hair, his whole body tense. This was exactly how he hadn't wanted this to play out.

'It's a figure of speech.' She sat bolt upright, eyes wide and watching his reaction. He wasn't that good an actor and neither was she. Slip of the tongue or not, Quinn didn't say things she didn't mean. She was already including him in the plans for Simon's future.

He leaned back, creating a healthy space between them so he could think clearly without the distraction of her softness pressed against him.

'Quinn—'

'Would it really be so bad though? I know we've danced around the subject but we *are* in a relationship, Matt. I need to know if you're behind me in this before we go any further.'

Nausea clawed its way through his system, his breathing shallow as the walls of his world moved in around him. He may as well be back living in that tiny council flat in Dublin where he'd barely enough room to breathe.

'Of course I'm behind you. I think adopting Simon will be good for you both.'

Quinn took a deep breath. 'I need to know if you're going to be part of it. I can't go through this again unless I know you're going to be with me one hundred percent. He's been through so much—neglected by his parents…abandoned by a foster family who'd promised him for ever—Simon needs, deserves, people willing to sacrifice everything for him. So do I.' She was braver than he, putting everything on the line and facing facts where he wasn't able to. It sucked that she was giving him a choice because then he had to make it.

'I just…can't.'

'But you already are. Don't you see? You're already part of our lives. All I'm asking is that you'll commit to us. I love you, Matt.'

The words she thought would fix everything only strengthened his case against this. It didn't matter who loved who because in the end they'd come to resent each other for it anyway. Love tied people together when the best thing could be for them to go their separate ways and find their own paths to happiness. Quinn and Simon would be better off without someone who'd learned to be selfish enough to want a life of his own.

'And what? Do you honestly think telling me that will erase my memory? I told you from the very start I didn't want anything serious. Adopting Simon sounds pretty damn serious to me. I told you I don't make promises I can't keep—that's why I was very sure not to make any.' Even as the words came out of his mouth he wanted to take them back, tell her he was sorry for being so harsh and take her in his arms again. He couldn't. Not when he was trying to make her see what a lost cause he was and how she'd be better off without him. He wanted her to hate him as much as he hated himself right now. It would be easier in the long run for her to move on by thinking he was capable of such cruelty when, actually, his own heart was breaking that this was over.

Quinn's blood ran cold enough to freeze her heart, Matt's words splintering it into tiny shards of ice.

It was happening all over again.

Just as she thought things were slotting into place, a man had to ruin everything.

Matt mightn't have verbally promised anything but the rejection hurt the same as any other. More so since she'd seen how he was around children, with Simon. They could've been great together if he'd only chosen them over his bachelorhood.

It didn't feel like it at the moment, but it was best she find out now he wasn't the man she thought he was than when Simon started calling him Dad.

Her son was her priority more than ever and she wasn't going to subject him to a string of fake relatives who'd dump them when they got tired of playing house. She couldn't be as logical in her thinking as Mr McGrory; her emotions would always get the better of her common sense.

'Yes, you were. How silly of me to forget you had a get-out clause.'

'Don't be like that, Quinn. We had a good time together but we both want different things.' He reached out to take her hand but she snatched it away. He didn't have the right to touch her any more and she couldn't bear it now she knew this was over. It hurt too much.

'We want you. You don't want us. Plain and simple. There's probably no point in drawing this out.' She unfurled her legs from beneath her to stand, faking a strength she didn't possess right now.

Matt took his time getting up. Contrary to every other night he'd been here, Quinn wanted him gone as soon as possible. She wanted to do her ugly crying and wailing in private. A break up was still painful whether you saw it coming or not and she needed a period of mourning before she picked herself up and started her new life over. One without Matt.

'I'll look into transferring Simon's care to another consultant.'

'No. I never wanted him to suffer as a result of our relationship. He deserves the very best and that's you. I think we can be grown-up enough to manage that. If not, I'll stay out of your way and let you get on with it.'

Appointments at the Castle were never going to be the same. The fairy tale was well and truly over but she hoped there was still some sort of happy-ever-after in sight even without her Prince Charming. She would miss his supporting role at the hospital as much as out of it. He'd got her through some of those darkest days but she couldn't force him to want to be around.

He nodded, his professional pride probably making the final decision on this one. 'Of course. There's no point in causing him any more disruption than necessary. We should probably make alternative arrangements for the dog too.'

She was the worst mother in the world, before she'd even officially been handed the title. Simon was going to lose his two best friends because she couldn't keep her emotions in check.

'Maybe you could email me your schedule and we'll work something out.'

She knew Matt didn't have the time, not really. The dog had been another pie in the sky idea that they hadn't fully thought through. Maisie was going to end up as another casualty of their doomed affair if they didn't take responsibility for their actions.

'You should take her. We got her for Simon's benefit after all, and it would prevent any…awkwardness.' He clearly wanted a clean break with no ties that weren't strictly professional.

The quick turnaround from an afternoon where he couldn't keep his hands off her was hard to stomach.

'I suppose if Simon's going to be here permanently there's no reason why we can't take her on.' Yet deep down she was still hoping for one just so there'd still be some sort of tenuous link between them.

Matt didn't appear to have any such sentimental leanings.

'I should go.' He turned towards the door, then back again, as if he wanted to say something more but didn't. Only an uneasy silence remained, giving her time to think about the days they'd had together, and those they wouldn't.

'Yes.' She'd always been too much for any man to consider taking on and there was no reason this time should've been any different. Now the last hope she'd had for a *normal* family had been pounded into dust, she had to make the most of the one she had. From here on in it was just her, Simon and Maisie.

She watched him walk away, telling herself she'd started this journey on her own and she was strong enough to continue without him.

The first tears fell before Matt was even out of sight.

He daren't look back. It had taken every ounce of his willpower to walk out of that door in the first place, knowing he was leaving her behind for good. Another glimpse of Quinn in warrior mode, those spiky defences he'd spent weeks breaking down firmly back in place, and he might just run back and beg for forgiveness. That wasn't going to solve anything even if it would ease his conscience for now.

She was a strong woman who'd be stronger without him, without putting her hopes in someone who could never be what she needed—a husband and a father for Simon. If he was out of the picture, at least in a personal capacity, they stood a better chance of a stable life and he, well, he could return to the spontaneity of his.

He pushed the button on the key fob to unlock the car door long before he reached it so he wouldn't start fumbling with it at the last minute and betray his lack of confidence in his decision-making. Once inside the vehicle he let out a slow, shaky breath. This was the hardest thing he'd ever done in his life because he'd *chosen* to walk away; it wasn't a decision forced upon him.

She'd told him she loved him. He loved her. It would have been easy to get carried away in the romance of the situation and believe they could all live happily ever after but real life wasn't as simple as that. Unfortunately, loving someone always meant sacrificing his independence, something he'd fought too hard for to let it slip away again so soon.

He started the car and sneaked a peek back at the house, hoping for one last glimpse of Quinn before he left. The door was already firmly shut, closing him out of her home for ever. He would still see her from time to time at the hospital but he was no longer part of her life. From now on Quinn, Simon and Maisie were no longer his responsibility. Exactly what he'd wanted. So why did he feel as if he'd thrown away the best thing that had ever happened to him?

CHAPTER TWELVE

'How ARE YOU, Simon?' It had been a couple of weeks since Matt's world had imploded. He'd taken a back seat, letting the nurses change the boy's dressings to give him time to get used to the idea he wasn't always going to be around.

It had been harder for Matt than he'd expected. Of course, he'd kept up to date on the boy's progress, interrogating the staff who'd treated him and scanning his notes for information. None of that made up for seeing him, or Quinn, in person.

He could operate and perform magic tricks for hundreds of other patients and their families but it wasn't the same. Apparently that connection they'd had was one of a kind and couldn't be replicated.

'Okay.' Simon eyed him warily as he'd done way back during the early stages of treatment as though trying to figure out if he could trust him or not. A punch to Matt's gut after all the time they'd spent together, and it was nobody's fault but his own.

He'd had a sleepless night with the prospect of this one-on-one today. Although Quinn had kept to her word and stayed out of sight whilst he did his rounds it didn't stop his hands sweating or his pulse racing at the thought she was in the building.

'How's Maisie?' he asked as he inspected the skin already healing well on Simon's face.

'Okay.'

He definitely wasn't giving anything away. Perhaps he thought sharing too much information was betraying Quinn in some way. It wasn't fair that he'd been stuck in the middle of all of this. Matt hadn't hung around for the nature of the break-up conversation between mother and son. It must've been difficult to explain his disappearance when they'd tried so hard to keep their relationship secret from him.

Simon's reluctance to talk could also be because he saw him as another father figure who'd abandoned him, in which case he'd every right to be mad at him. It was still important he trusted Matt when it came to his surgery.

'I miss her around the place, even though my shoes are safer without her.' He never would've imagined his place would be so lonely without the chaos, and he wasn't just talking about the dog.

'Is that why you don't want to see us any more? Did we do something wrong? I promise I won't let her eat any more of your stuff.'

The cold chill of guilt blasted through Matt's body and froze him to the spot. He couldn't let Simon think any of this mess was his fault when he'd been nothing but an innocent bystander dragged into his issues. They were his alone.

It was the earnest pools of green looking at him with pure bewilderment which eventually thawed his limbs so he could sit on the end of the hospital bed.

'What happened between me and Quinn…it wasn't because of anything you, or Maisie, did. We've just decided it's better if we don't see each other.' This might've been easier if they'd co-ordinated their story at some point over these past weeks in case he contradicted anything he might've already been told.

At least Quinn mustn't have painted him as the bad guy if Simon thought he should somehow shoulder the blame. It was more than Matt deserved given his behaviour.

'Don't you like each other no more?'

If the situation had been as simple as Simon's point of view they would've still been together. He liked— loved—Quinn and she'd been fond of him enough to want him to be a part of their family. On paper it should've been a match made in heaven but he'd learned a long time ago that reality never matched up to rose-tinted daydreams.

'That's not really the problem.' As much as he'd tried, he couldn't switch off his feelings for Quinn. Not seeing her, talking to her or touching her hadn't kept her from his thoughts, or his heart. In trying to protect himself he'd actually done more damage.

How could he explain to a five-year-old he'd lost the best thing that had ever happened to him because he was afraid of being part of a family again, or worse, enjoy it too much? The one thing he was trying to avoid was the ultimate goal for a foster kid.

'She misses you. Sometimes she's real sad when she thinks I'm not looking but she says she's going to be my new mummy and we'll have lots of fun together.'

It didn't come across as a ploy concocted to get Matt to

break down and beg to be a part of it all again but he was close to breaking when Quinn was only a corridor away.

'I tell you what, after this surgery I'll have a chat with her and see if we can all go out for ice cream again some time.' They'd done the hardest part by making the break; meeting up for Simon's sake surely couldn't hurt any more than it already did. She still had Simon, and the dog, but the knowledge he'd saved himself from playing happy families didn't keep him warm at night.

The bribe did the trick of getting Simon back onside again and prevented any further speculation about what had happened. If Quinn had a problem, well, she'd simply have to come and talk to him about it.

He was just glad he and Simon were back on speaking terms again. He was such a different character from the withdrawn child he'd first encountered and Quinn was to thank for that. A part of him wanted to believe he'd helped in some small way too, aside from the cosmetic aspects. Despite all of his misgivings about becoming too involved, it was good to know it wasn't only his heart which had been touched by their friendship.

He hadn't realised quite how much until they were back in theatre, Simon asleep and completely at his mercy. For the first time in his career, Matt hesitated with the scalpel in his hand.

He would never operate on any of his sisters, or his nieces, because he was too close, too emotionally involved, and that could mess with his head. The consequences of something happening to someone he loved because he wasn't thinking clearly was a burden he could never live with.

Yet, here he was, hovering over a boy who'd come to mean so much to him, with a blade in his hand.

Simon *was* family, as was Quinn, and he'd abandoned them for the sake of his own pride. He'd always wondered how his life would've panned out if he'd shunned the responsibility thrust upon him to concentrate on his own survival. Now he knew. It was lonely, full of regret and unfulfilling without someone he loved to share it with.

His skin was clammy with the layer of cold realisation beneath his scrubs.

'Is everything all right?' One of the theatre assistants was quick to notice his uncharacteristic lapse in concentration.

'Yes.' He was confident in his response. He had to be. When he was in theatre he couldn't let his personal issues contaminate the sterile atmosphere.

He took a deep breath and let his professional demeanour sweep the remnants of his emotions to the side so he could do what was expected of him. It would be the last time he'd operate on Simon and he wasn't looking forward to breaking the news.

Quinn would never get used to the waiting. For some reason today seemed worse than all the other times Simon had been in surgery. The can't-sit-still fidgets were part parental worry and part running-into-an-ex anxiety.

With Matt still treating Simon it made an already stressful situation unbearable. There was no clean break like she'd had with Darryl. She hadn't seen him for dust once she'd insisted on going ahead with the fostering plan. This time she faced the prospect of seeing the man who'd broken her heart at every hospital appointment. She never knew which day might be the one she'd catch a glimpse of him to drive her over the edge.

Sure, things were going well with Simon in his recovery, and the adoption, but that didn't mean she could simply forget what she and Matt had had together. Could've had. She'd loved him and she was pretty sure he'd loved her, though he'd never said it and he hadn't been willing to trade in the single life for her. That was going to come back and haunt her every time she laid eyes on his handsome face. Out of Simon's sight, she'd cried, listened to sad songs and eaten gallons of ice cream straight from the tub but she hadn't reached the stage where she was ready to move on. She wasn't sure she ever really would.

No one got her like Matt; he seemed to know what she needed, and gave it to her, before she did. Except for what she'd wanted the most. Him. That's why it hurt so damn much. He'd known exactly what it would do to her by walking away; he'd told her long before she'd figured it out for herself. She could do the parenting alone, she just didn't want to.

For her, Matt had been the final piece of that family puzzle, slotting into place to complete the picture when there had been a void between her and Simon. Without him, she feared there'd always be a sense of that missing part of them and who knew where, or if, they'd ever be truly complete again. All she could do was her best to give Simon a loving home and pray it could make up for everything else.

Missing boyfriend and father figure aside, Simon had been making great progress in terms of his recovery and schooling. Those days of being a *normal* mother and son no longer seemed so far out of reach. It was only on days such as this which brought home the memories of the fire and the extra worry she'd always shoulder for Simon's welfare.

The thumbs up from the nurses was always the cue

she was awaiting so she could relax until he came around from the anaesthetic. This time her relief was short-lived as Matt came into view to add more stress to her daily quota.

'Did everything go to schedule?' It was the first time she'd spoken directly to him since they'd confronted the painful truth of their non-relationship so there was a flutter which made its way from her pulse to her voice. Worse, he was frowning, lines of worry etched deeply enough on his brow to put her on alert. Matt wasn't one to cause unnecessary drama on the wards and if he was worried about something it was definitely time to panic.

'Yeah. Fine… I need to talk to you.' He dropped his voice so other people couldn't hear and thereby induced a full-on panic attack.

It was never good news when doctors did that. Not when they were grabbing your arm and dragging you into a cubicle for a private word. Her heart was pounding so hard with fear, and being this close to him after such a long absence, she was starting to feel faint.

'What's happened? Is there an infection? I've tried to keep the dressings clean but you know what boys are like—' Her breathing was becoming rapid as she rattled through the possible disasters going on in her head.

Matt steered her towards the bed, forcing her to sit when the backs of her legs hit the mattress.

'He's fine. There were no problems or complication. I just can't treat him any more. I'm sorry but—'

The blood drained from her head to her toes and her limp body sank deeper into the bed. The moment things seemed to be going well for Simon, she'd messed it up. She couldn't let him do this because of her. Simon needed him.

'Is it me? Next time I'll stay out of the way altogether. You don't even have to come onto the ward. I'll talk to the nurses or I can get Mrs Johns to bring him to his appointments. I'll do whatever it takes. I don't want to be the one to mess this up.'

Any further resolutions he had for the problem were silenced as Matt sealed her lips with his. The stealth kiss completely derailed her train of thought, leaving her dazed and wanting more. She touched her fingers to her moist lips, afraid it had been a dream conjured up by falling asleep in the corridor.

'What was that for?' she asked, almost afraid of the answer.

'It was the only way to shut you up so I could finish what I was saying. Well, probably not the only way, but the best one I could think of.' He was grinning at her, that mischievous twinkle in his eye sending tremors of anticipation wracking through her body, but she still didn't know what there was to smile about.

'But why? Why would you feel the need to kiss me after dumping me and then telling me you're dumping Simon too? It doesn't make any sense. Unless this is your idea of a sick joke. In which case I'm really not amused.' Her head was spinning from his bombshell, from the kiss and from the way she still wanted him even after everything he'd done.

'Do I need to do it again to get you to listen?' He was cupping her face in his hands, making direct eye contact so she couldn't lie.

'Yes,' she said without hesitation, and closed her eyes for one last touch of him against her lips.

Whatever the motive, she'd missed this. She hated herself for being so weak as she sagged against him and let him take control of her mouth, her emotions and her dignity when she should be railing against him for putting her through hell.

Although she kissed him back, she remained guarded, wary of getting her hopes up that this was anything more than a spontaneous lapse of his better judgement. Once the pressure eased from the initial flare of rekindled passion, she broke away.

'What's this about, Matt?'

He raked his hand through his hair before crouching down so they were at eye level.

'I've missed you so much.'

Her stomach did a backflip and high-fived her heart but she kept her mouth shut this time. Words and kisses didn't change anything unless they were accompanied by a bit of honesty. She wasn't going to fall into that same trap of hoping she could change a man and make him want to be a permanent fixture in her life. In fact, she might draft that into a contract for future suitors so she could weed out potential heartbreakers. Although a Matt-replacement seemed a long way off when the real one was still capable of upsetting her equilibrium to this extent.

'I can't do Simon's surgery any more because I'm too close, too emotionally involved. It's a conflict of interests and one which means I have to choose between my personal and professional roles.'

'I don't understand. You're *choosing* not to treat him. Why is this supposed to be good news?' As far as she could see he was simply kicking them when they were down.

'I'm choosing you. If you'll still have me? Seeing Simon today in that theatre…it was like watching my own son go under the knife. It made me realise I'm already part of this family. I love you, Quinn. Both of you.'

She was too scared to believe he was saying what she thought he was saying. There'd been weeks of no communication from him and heartache for her and somehow now all of her dreams were coming true? She wasn't so easily fooled by a great smile and hot kisses any more. Maybe.

'What's changed, Matt? The last time we saw each other you were telling me the very opposite. Are you missing the dog or something? I'm sure we can make arrangements for a visit without forcing you into another relationship.' Okay, she was a little spiky but she'd every right to be after he'd ripped her heart out and she'd spent an age trying to patch it back up. If she meant anything to him he'd put up with a few scratches as he brushed against her new and improved defences.

The frown was back; she might have pushed him a tad too far.

'That's what I'm trying to tell you. I miss you all. This time apart has showed me what I'm missing. I don't want to end up a lonely old man with nothing but expensive furniture and fittings to keep me company. I've seen a glimpse of what life is like without you and Simon and it's not for me. I love you. I want to be with you, raising Simon, or a whole house full of Simons if that's what you want.'

'There's nothing I want more but only if that's truly what you want this time. How can I be sure you won't change your mind when the adoption comes through or there's another troubled kid on the doorstep? There can't be any room for doubt, Matt.' She pushed back at the flutter of hope beating hard against her chest trying to escape and send her tumbling back into Matt's arms.

He stood up, paced the room with his hands on his hips, and she knew she'd called his bluff.

'That's what I thought,' she said as she got to her feet, her voice cracking at the joyless victory.

'Wait. Where are you going?'

'To see Simon.' He was the only reason she hadn't completely fallen apart. She had to be the strong one in that relationship and he'd need her when he woke up and heard the latest bad news.

Matt stepped quickly into the path between her and the door to prolong her agony a while longer.

'What if I move in with you? Would that convince you I'm serious? I'll quit my lease, sell everything. I'll take a cleaning job at the hospital if it means I can stay on. I don't care about any of it. I just want to be with you.'

That made her smile.

'I think the hospital would give anything to keep you here given the chance.'

'And you?' He had that same worried look Simon had when he thought she didn't want him and in that moment she knew he meant every word. He was laying himself open here and this level of honesty was simply irresistible.

'Well, you know I'm a sucker for a stray so I guess I'll keep you too.' It was easier to joke when she was secure in his feelings for her.

'Tell me you love me.' He gathered her into his arms, a smile playing across his lips now too.

'You're so needy.'

'Tell me,' he said again, his mouth moving against hers.

'I love you.' She'd tried to convince herself otherwise

since he'd left but it was a relief to finally admit it aloud without fearing the consequences.

'I love you too. And Simon. And Maisie. And this mad, dysfunctional family we've created.'

'I think there's someone else who's going to be very happy to hear the news.'

'Let's go get our boy.' Matt took her hand and led her towards Simon's room to complete the group love-in.

Quinn's heart was so full she didn't think she'd ever stop smiling.

Now her family was finally complete.

* * * * *

MILLS & BOON®

MEDICAL ROMANCE™

THE ULTIMATE IN ROMANTIC MEDICAL DRAMA

A sneak peek at next month's titles...

In stores from 1st June 2017:

- **Healing the Sheikh's Heart** – Annie O'Neil
  and **A Life-Saving Reunion** – Alison Roberts

- **The Surgeon's Cinderella** – Susan Carlisle
  and **Saved by Doctor Dreamy** – Dianne Drake

- **Pregnant with the Boss's Baby** – Sue MacKay
  and **Reunited with His Runaway Doc** – Lucy Clark

Just can't wait?
Buy our books online before they hit the shops!
www.millsandboon.co.uk

Also available as eBooks.

MILLS & BOON®

EXCLUSIVE EXTRACT

Can a miracle surgery prove to cardiologist
Thomas Wolfe and his ex-wife Rebecca Scott that
it's never too late to give love a second chance?

Read on for a sneak preview of
A LIFE-SAVING REUNION

DON'T MISS THIS FINAL STORY IN THE
PADDINGTON CHILDREN'S HOSPITAL SERIES

The silence that fell between them was like a solid wall.

Impenetrable.

It stretched out for long enough to take a slow breath.
And then another.

They weren't even looking at each other. They could
have been on separate planets.

And then Rebecca spoke.

'I should never have said that. I'm sorry. It was
completely unprofessional. And…and it was cruel.'

'I couldn't agree more.'

'It's not what I believe,' she said softly. '*You* know that,
Tom.'

It was the first time she'd called him Tom, since he'd
come back and it touched a place that had been very safely
walled off.

Or maybe it was that assumption that he knew her well
enough to know that she would never think like that.

And, deep down, he had known that, hadn't he? It had
just been so much easier to think otherwise. To be angry.

'So, why did you say it, then?'

'You've been so distant ever since you came back. So
cut off. I don't even recognise you anymore.' There was a

hitch in Rebecca's voice that went straight to that place that calling him Tom had accessed. 'I guess I wanted to know if the man I married still exists.'

His words were a little less of a snap this time.

'I haven't changed.'

'Yes, you have.' He could feel Rebecca looking at him but he didn't turn his head. 'Something like what we went through changes everyone. But you...you disappeared. You just...ran away.'

There was that accusation again. That he was a coward.

The reminder of how little she understood came with a wave of weariness. Thomas wanted this over with. He wanted to put this all behind them effectively enough to be able to work together.

He wanted...peace.

So he took another deep breath and he turned his head to meet Rebecca's gaze.

Don't miss
A LIFE-SAVING REUNION
by Alison Roberts

Available June 2017
www.millsandboon.co.uk

AND IF YOU'D LIKE TO CATCH UP WITH ANY OF THE OTHER BOOKS IN THE PADDINGTON CHILDREN'S HOSPITAL SERIES THEY ARE ALL AVAILABLE NOW:

THEIR ONE NIGHT BABY by Carol Marinelli
FORBIDDEN TO THE PLAYBOY SURGEON by Fiona Lowe
MUMMY, NURSE...DUCHESS? by Kate Hardy
FALLING FOR THE FOSTER MUM by Karin Baine
HEALING THE SHEIKH'S HEART by Annie O'Neil